Minnissippi

Minnissippi

J Shulman

Disclaimer:

None of the characters or settings in this book is inspired by real people or places. Any resemblance of the characters and settings to real people and places is pure coincidence. Do not be surprised, however, if you feel you know the people and places.

"In the end, we will remember not the words of our enemies, but the silence of our friends."

- Martin Luther King, Jr.

Chapter 1

Isaiah slipped in mud mixed with snow. He struggled up the hill, but the mud and snow were slick, like Vaseline. And it was cold! As fast as he moved his feet, he could not get ahead of the mud and snow. Freezing rain slapped his face. The icy rain blended with his tears so no one knew he was crying.

"Boy!" a voice boomed. "You think you can get away from me?"

Isaiah tried to move faster, to get away. He glanced back. He was fifteen years old. He was not ready for this. All he wanted was to get away from the man chasing him. The man's face looked angry, like a crazy person. Isaiah tried not to look at the man's face. He glanced again, then he slipped. This time he fell flat on his stomach. His fingers clawed at the mud. He pushed his knees forward. A strong hand grasped his shirt. Isaiah tried to cry out for help, but mud and snow filled his mouth.

"You're mine, boy!" the voice commanded. "Now you pay the price."

Isaiah crumpled into the mud and snow, wishing he could escape. He didn't know what would happen next—only that it would be bad. A hand grabbed his leg. He heard the clink of metal. He tried to pull his leg away, but the grip on his leg was too strong. The metal closed around his leg. Then a hand grasped his other leg. Another heavy clink of metal chain and a metal clasp closed.

Isaiah wiped his eyes and looked down at his legs. He was in shackles. There would be no escape. At least the icy rain hid his tears.

Like a Buddhist monk, Eileen was having an out of body experience. It was one of those situations you could not take seriously or you would lose your mind, especially when you dealt with these situations every day. Twenty-five years in a big city school system taught a lot of hard lessons.

Eileen inhaled, calming herself and regaining mindfulness. In the conference room, the principal, Mr. Hardwell, was impassive. The mother was indignant. The boy...he looked bored.

"I have been through all your processes!" the heavy African-American mother screamed, her brown chin jiggling, her braids flailing. "You can't tell me I don't care. I do care!"

The boy's eyes twinkled as his mother berated the principal.

Eileen looked at Mr. Hardwell. Despite the mother's screaming, he gazed at the wall. Eileen followed Hardwell's eyes. He appeared to be fixated on a smudge. Eileen looked above the smudge at the inspirational slogans painted in Rasta red, black, green and yellow on the wall:

"I am somebody!"

"Si se puede!"

"Respect."

Eileen looked again at the woman. Her face heaved. Her large flat nose perspired. Was she really out of control, Eileen wondered, or was the ranting a put-on? Was she giving a performance for her son? Was she truly angry with Hardwell? More likely, she was displacing anger from the rest of her out-of-control life onto the hapless principal. Perhaps he represented all the men who had abused her. Now she had an irresistible chance to hit back, with Eileen as her witness-protector.

Eileen had seen the pattern so many times before—a boy skipping school, a dead-end job, a series of shiftless, abusive boyfriends. By the look of the woman's frayed, out-of-date clothing, money was a problem. Diet was too. The woman was at least sixty pounds overweight.

"You gonna do something?" the woman screamed again. "Or you just goin' sit there like you stupid?

It took a moment before Eileen realized the woman was screaming at her, not the principal. Feigned or not, the intensity felt different now, unpleasant. Eileen smiled, trying to reassure the large woman. "Why don't we talk this through."

"You supposed to take care of this," the mother snorted. "I don't know why I waste my time with you. You all the same."

"I think we should calm down," Eileen suggested. "Yelling is counterproductive."

The large woman glared at Eileen, evidently unsure what Eileen meant. The word "counterproductive" had found a treasured place in Eileen's vocabulary for that very reason. It was like injecting morphine into the uneducated.

Eileen was irritated that Hardwell refused to do his part. She knew his perspective—that caving in only encouraged more tantrums—but she had no intention of caving in, not to this behavior. She tried to remember the woman's name. The boy's last name was Jefferson, same as his grandfather, the local civil rights leader. Why had the mother changed her name, and to this name, for heaven's sake?

"Ms..." Eileen paused. It was one of *those* names. She tried not to butcher it... "Onyekachukwu," she stuttered. "Can't we talk about this as adults? Let's at least be a good example for your son."

The woman continued glaring, but refrained from screaming. She listened, waiting.

Eileen needed a caucus with Hardwell. He had been in the district less than two years. She needed to educate him about certain facts of life. "Mr. Hardwell," Eileen said in a firm voice. "Why don't you and I step outside for a moment."

Hardwell took a long time to raise his sleepy eyes from the smudge on the wall. Was this deliberate? Was he trying to undermine her? Eileen hoped he was smarter than that, hoped he would not cross that line. She decided to let him know she would escalate, if necessary. She kept her tone pleasant, as always, even as she stood up. "Mr. Hardwell, let's step outside." Her movement was hard, uncompromising. With Eileen standing, Hardwell now had to follow her...or lose his job. Not instantly, but soon. It might take days or weeks, but not months or years. It was *when*, not if.

Hardwell sat long enough that Eileen was unsure what he would do. She could sense anticipation building in Onyekachukwu and the boy. They knew the principal was on the spot. They luxuriated in his humiliation. Eileen knew she had created an enemy in the large black man. It came with the territory. She just hoped Hardwell would not underestimate her. That would only cause more pain, for him.

Eileen held the door open and waited for Hardwell to follow her out of the conference room. She kept her face still, her breathing steady. She wore heavy-duty deodorant, as always. She was ready for conflict if the principal needed to test his manhood. Eileen had done this meeting more times than Hardwell could imagine. She did not relish conflict, but it came with the job. As Special Assistant to the Superintendent of a large urban school district, Eileen did the district's dirty work. She cleaned up other people's messes. And Hardwell was creating a mess.

Hardwell finally rose.

Eileen exhaled, relieved. The principal's face revealed nothing. He followed Eileen into the hallway and stopped, frozen, waiting for an explanation. "Let's go to your office," Eileen suggested.

Hardwell followed Eileen. When they got to his office, the principal sank into the large chair at his desk, sullen. Eileen sat in a small chair on the other side of the desk. The seat Eileen took was significantly lower than the principal's chair. Eileen was not fazed by that.

The low chair for "guests" in the principal's office was Minnepious district policy. A consultant who worked with big city districts all over the country had recommended this change, among others, to instill within the district's stakeholders the requisite respect for authority. Given the immense power she wielded over Hardwell, Eileen found it ironic that the low chair she sat in was supposed to remind her how powerful the principal was.

"Look," she began. "I know you don't like that I'm here. But I'm here to help, not step on your toes." She paused, waiting for a reaction. There was none.

"Bunny asked me to sit in," she continued, then paused again. "It's not because of anything you've done, or not done. You have to understand, this Onyekachukwu is trouble. Her kid's on his third middle school. He gets kicked out everywhere he goes." She paused again. "Her father knows a lot of people. Got her a show on cable access. *Black Power Positions*. Bunny doesn't want trouble."

Hardwell did not respond.

Eileen frowned. She smelled a rat. If the principal thought he could lay this on her, he was mistaken. She was too experienced for that. She had been in the district a long time. She knew how to handle herself. And more important, Superintendent Bunny Washington had her back. "What do you want to do?" Eileen pressed.

"You tell me," the principal parried.

Eileen stared at the large black man. The low chair did not help. He was already a foot taller than she. And even if the size difference didn't matter, it felt like it mattered. She reminded herself that she held all the cards. She had to smoke him out. Angry and out-of-control, she could handle. A large, angry, *impassive* black man was something new. She decided she liked the challenge. Eileen smiled, trying a different approach. "I'm just here to help. It has to be your decision."

"How can it be my decision if Bunny sent you?"

"That's a fair question," Eileen agreed. "Let me explain where we are." She paused. "You're from Mississippi, right?"

Hardwell did not respond.

"Things work a little different up here. There are certain…facts of life. Certain people we cannot afford to offend. Certain people we have to work with. I'm not saying it's the best way to do things. It's just the way we do it." She paused again. "Bunny wants you to succeed in this school…It's just…" Again, Eileen paused. "We can't have a problem with Onyekachukwu."

"So tell me what you're going to do," Hardwell said.

Eileen could not allow the principal to lay this on her. It *had* to be his decision. "Unless you object," she suggested. "We could live with a one day suspension."

Hardwell leaned back in his chair, staring at Eileen. "That boy wore gang colors. When I told him to go home and change, he said he'd be waiting for me *with his boys* after school."

Eileen looked away. She felt a twinge of sympathy for the principal. But she knew what had to be done. Onyekachukwu had too many relationships, and her cable access show had a small but vocal following. By contrast, Hardwell had no constituency. He had been the principal at this school less than a year. If he tried to play hardball, the district would leak the school's dismal student achievement data to a sympathetic reporter and have angry black parents spontaneously denounce the carpetbagging principal. Eileen's job was to see that it did not come to that.

—⚏—

Charity fought her nerves as she entered the "Welcome Center." She never felt welcome at school. She had dropped out in tenth grade. That was because of Isaiah. He rescued her from school when he was born. Even as a baby, he was a good boy. Nobody just did understand him.

Now Lakeesha, she could be trouble, but that's just the way of girls. And she did good in school! All her teachers in Chicago said so.

Then there was little Isaac. Well, maybe he wasn't so little any more. He was only nine, but he was already taller than his mama and he weighed almost 150 pounds. He was a handful. Charity didn't know what she should tell these school people here in Minnepious about Isaac.

"May I help you?" a white woman asked. She smiled, but it looked fake.

Charity was not used to talking to white people. She had come to Minnepious because she heard about decent Section 8 housing, jobs that paid more than minimum wage, and schools that didn't send Black boys to prison. Plus, Isaiah's probation officer in Chicago had a uncle here. Got Isaiah right into Afrocentric Success Academy in Minnepious. Just this morning, Charity found a small apartment too. The area was supposed to be bad, but it looked plenty good to Charity. And Isaiah was doing good at school, as far as she could tell.

Charity realized she had to say something to the white woman with the big teeth. Aware that her two youngest children were watching her, she said, "I'm lookin' for schools for my kids."

"Did you just arrive from Chicago?"

How did she know? "That a problem?"

"Oh no," Theresa reassured the scraggly woman with scraggly children. "Not a problem at all."

"My kids need schools. Their brother's goin' to Afrocentric Success Academy..." Charity trailed off. She wasn't sure what else to say.

Theresa nodded. She had a deep aversion to charter schools, especially those that purported to emphasize certain cultures over others. They siphoned students from the district at a time when budgets were already tight. Theresa knelt down to the level of the girl. She addressed the girl directly, ignoring the mother. "What's your name?"

"I'm Lakeesha," the girl boasted. She liked the nice white lady.

"What grade are you in, Lakeesha?

"I'm in fifth grade."

"We'll find a nice school for you, Lakeesha," Theresa promised. Then she rose and turned to the large boy, who studied her. "What is your name, young man?"

Isaac did not answer.

Theresa waited. "It's okay," she said when it was clear the boy would not speak. "You can tell me later." Then she turned to the mother.

"Isaac," the boy mumbled.

Theresa glanced at the boy and smiled.

"He got a learning disability," Lakeesha volunteered. "And he hyperactive too. He should be in the third grade, but they holdin' him back."

"Lakeesha!" Charity reprimanded her daughter.

Isaac looked away.

Theresa nodded. Judging by the children's appearance, and the mother's lack of formal education, the kids would need to be screened for disabilities. Then each child would require an Individual Education Plan, or IEP, according to state and federal law. Unfunded mandates that disproportionately drained urban districts of resources with so many students suffering from behavioral disabilities. Theresa reflected on the tragic fact that mild mental retardation and poverty were so closely linked.

In her rotation through the district's Welcome Center, Theresa had come to accept the cruel reality of poverty-related deprivation. Lead paint, poor nutrition, excessive television, drug use, fetal alcohol syndrome, absentee parents...A cycle of despair that sometimes made Theresa ponder the futility of trying to make a difference.

Before this rotation through the Welcome Center, when Theresa was teaching elementary school, she had felt she could make a difference. Now, in the Welcome Center, the sheer numbers overwhelmed her. In the classroom, if you could reach just one child, it made the sacrifice worthwhile. Just to see one first grader learn her colors, one third grader master the concepts of subtraction and addition...what a difference you could make in a child's life. As a teacher, you got to know the children. Sometimes you could see possibilities, you could hope for a better future. Theresa had learned the hard way, though, that in an inner city school district, hope was the cruelest emotion.

Here, at the Welcome Center, hope was impossible. The poverty numbed you. Ignorance and despair overwhelmed you. Single mothers and their raggedy broods broke you down until you just wanted out. Theresa was already looking for a job outside the district. "It's the last week of November, almost December," Theresa told the woman from Chicago. "Most of the schools are full."

"I didn't get you," Charity responded.

"It would be best if you wait till next year to register the children."

"But my kids gotta go to school now," Charity objected, confused.

"The first semester is almost over," Theresa explained. "It would be disruptive for them to go to a new school now. It would be better to give them a fresh start next year."

This did not sound right to Charity. "Will their grades and credit from Chicago transfer over?"

Theresa ignored the question. There was no point putting these kids into a new school right now. It would be disruptive for the school and for the children. Most likely, the woman would return to Chicago with her children after the holidays anyway.

"Their brother just started school here," Charity persisted. "He's doin' good, too."

Theresa nodded.

"And Lakeesha and Isaac did good at their school in Chicago."

"I'm sure they did."

Charity realized the white woman was playing her. She raised her voice. "They was in honors programs!"

"Okay, ma'am," Theresa tried to pacify the woman. She did not understand this tactic of adults throwing tantrums when they couldn't get what they wanted. It broke Theresa's heart to think that the woman's impressionable daughter would fall into this same trap. It was a learned behavior. Only conscious intervention could break the cycle. "I'll see what I can do," Theresa offered, retreating to the computer terminal at her desk.

Charity waited.

Lakeesha and Isaac tried not to fidget too much. This place was like church. Lakeesha stuck her tongue out at Isaac, and he punched her. Their mother grabbed them and held them apart.

Theresa searched the enrollment records for the district's schools. She located two vacancies, then returned to Charity and the kids. "I've found some possibilities. There's a Hornets program for Lakeesha at Afrocentric Pride Academy. Isaac can start in Afrocentric Alternatives Academy. They're both feeder programs for Afrocentric Success Academy, where you say their brother is doing so well."

—ᴍ—

Bunny breathed easier as she entered the house. She could relax. She was home.

"Mama, you gotta slow down," her daughter Bea whispered so the grandchildren wouldn't hear. "It's cold out, Mama. This ain't Mississippi. You can't be runnin' around without a proper coat."

Bunny smiled at her daughter. It was an easy smile. She glanced at her grandchildren playing in the living room, a fire blazing in the hearth. It felt right, felt comfortable. Comfort was something in short supply these days. But wasn't that the lot of Black folk, she reflected. No matter how far you came, you were never there. "How was school today?" she asked Bea.

Bea knew her mother was changing the subject, but she also knew her mother needed to find her groove and wind down. It was this way every evening when her mother dropped by on the way home from work. Lately, the evening drop-ins were getting later. Her mother looked more and more tired. Haggard was not the right word, but Bea noticed the difference. Raspy breathing, not wearing a proper coat on a cold Minnesoule winter night, the dimming of those eyes that had always gleamed. She worried about her mother. "It was good, Mama. School was good. Those kids are little devils, though. You know I love those kids, Mama."

"I know you do, baby."

A shriek from the living room pierced the comfort of the hallway.

"Sounds like your own need a little lookin' after, too." Bunny's smile softened the words.

"They were staying up to see their Grandma."

"Have you read to them tonight?"

"Mama, don't be like that."

Bunny leaned forward and hugged her daughter. "You're a wonderful mother, baby."

The two women, separated by a generation, walked arm-in-arm into the living room.

"Grandma!" eight-year-old Brent shrieked. He was quicker than his five-year-old sister Melissa. He clutched his grandma's knees and pressed his face into her thighs. "I saw you on TV!"

Bunny stooped to pick up her grandson and glanced at her daughter.

Bea sighed. Kids never let you get away with anything. She had only left them for a few minutes of the six o'clock news while she cooked their dinner. They had been screaming, out of control. Bea's husband was still at work…at least that's where he said he was. Bea had just needed a few moments of peace, just enough to finish dinner. It was the *news*, for God's sake. Would that kill them? She knew she had not heard the last of it.

Brent soaked up his grandma's undivided attention. He was lost in her bosom, shielded from the world. His mama never held him like this. She said he was too big. But grandma always reached for him.

"Gramma!" Melissa shrieked and tugged on Brent's leg to dislodge him. Brent tried to free his leg from his little sister, but he was already on his way down. Melissa hugged her Gramma. Even though Brent beat her to Gramma, Melissa knew Gramma loved her more. Her Mama told her so. Melissa hugged her Gramma tight. A funny buzz tickled her chest. "Phone!" she shouted, thrilled to be the first to announce the ring of her Gramma's cell phone.

Before Bunny could put Melissa down, Bea was at her side, slipping the phone from her mother's jacket pocket. "Hello?" Bea answered. "Oh…" her tone betrayed disapproval. "Just a minute."

Bea held the phone as if the caller might infect them.

"Who is it?" Bunny asked.

Bea shook her head, covering the phone. "The Evil Elf."

Bunny reached for the phone.

Bea pulled it away. "You gonna let that prune into *my* house?"

Bunny put Melissa down and reached for the phone.

Bea handed it to her. She would never understand why her mother kept that nasty shriveled up white bitch around. There were plenty of people who could do that job, plenty who knew what the school district was about. Her mother needed someone who could help a Black superintendent steer clear of trouble. Someone who could be trusted.

It wasn't that the Evil Elf was white. Well that was part of it. Why should her mother have a white chaperone when all the white superintendents before her had picked their own senior staff? It sent the wrong message to the community. And it sure as hell sent the wrong message to the district's Black employees. That's why her mother needed to replace the Evil Elf—to send a message. She needed to let people know who was in charge. She needed to reassure Black folk that their time had come for real. That shriveled white bitch hovering around her mama sent the opposite message.

Bunny observed her daughter. There was a generation gap between them. It went to their cores. It defined their sense of self, infused all their experiences and guided their conscious thoughts. And it was a uniquely Black thing. Unlike the white generation gap, which was dissected *ad nauseum* in the mainstream media, the Black generation gap never made the news. As far as the white media was concerned, today's rapper was yesterday's Black militant. Yesterday's Black rapist was today's Black rapist.

The Black generation gap was defined by the divide between those who had experienced Jim Crow, and those who hadn't. It was the difference between being bitten by police dogs and keeping dogs in your home. *MTV radicals*, Bunny mused of her daughter's generation. Either you had experienced Jim Crow—and understood what it was to be Black—or you had not, and did not. For the younger generation, being Black meant buying kente cloth from a Black-owned shop, dining out at a soul food restaurant, watching BET, spending four years at Howard or Morehouse or Spellman, and celebrating Kwanzaa.

"This had better be good, 'Leen," Bunny said into the phone.

"Bunny, you're not going to believe this."

Bunny had never heard Eileen so excited. She tried to stay calm, but her heart began to race and her face flushed. "What is it?"

Eileen paused to savor this. It was not just a sensational conclusion to a hard day. Heck, *every* day was a hard day. But this was different. Eileen had been working her whole career for this. She had sacrificed for this. Her closest friends wondered why she stayed in the school district as it collapsed around her. Her friends called her a saint to her face and a fool behind her back, and sometimes the reverse. Her social standing plummeted as the district's chronic incompetence, cronyism and corruption played out daily on the front page of the newspaper. Sometimes Eileen herself could not believe she had stayed in the city schools all these years.

Her friends and family pointed out in their circumspect, politically correct way that Eileen's boss was a hack, a political appointee rising like a turd in the proverbial punch bowl, lifted by a sea of blacks. This always struck Eileen as rich given how those same friends bemoaned the shortcomings of their own bosses in the vaunted private sector. To be sure, white flight enabled Bunny's ascent. But Eileen knew there was more to the story.

The consummate insider, Eileen had a more nuanced view. Eileen could admit that her boss was a mediocre administrator. And it was of course true that, unlike Eileen, Bunny had not truly earned her stripes. The same flood of blacks that carried Bunny to the top had impeded Eileen's career. Despite her skills, Eileen had hit a glass ceiling, where skin color trumped all else. In the rapidly darkening Minnepious schools, Eileen's complexion became a liability.

But even as her friends and family "commiserated" over Eileen's subservience to an under-qualified, overwhelmed black, Eileen knew the district needed true professionals like herself now more than ever. She had seen firsthand what happened when those with the skills to make a difference abandoned the city's public schools. It only exacerbated and accelerated the collapse. Without Eileen's support, Bunny could never do her job. And what kind of society would that leave? One didn't have to imagine the outcome. There were plenty of examples: Detroit, Cleveland, New Orleans, Chicago, Oakland, Philadelphia. It was like a deadly virus spreading across the country.

Sure, Eileen could have run off like the rest of her friends and family to the suburbs or to a private school. But that would be taking the easy way out, and Eileen had never taken the easy route. She had even committed her own kids to city schools. According to family and friends, that was a sacrifice of Abraham-like proportions. The whispers died down when her eldest son Jake got into Brown—God staying Abraham's hand before he slayed Isaac. And though her youngest Ethan was still in high school and still a challenge, Audray's admission to Vassar last year had further vindicated Eileen's choice to keep her children in the district.

It seemed good things happened to good people, after all. *And now this!*

Today, after twenty-five years of toil, twenty-five years of watching her peers abandon the city school system, Eileen's hard work was being rewarded at the highest levels in the nation. *"Bunny, we did it!"* Eileen whispered into her phone.

"C'mon, 'Leen, I don't have time for this."

"How long have we been working together, Bunny?"

"I'm gonna hang up if you don't tell me what's up."

"Okay, okay. Bunny, I just got the call from Washington."

Bunny felt dizzy. She eased herself onto her daughter's couch. She could not believe this was happening. It was a life's work, a life's dreams. "Eileen, you better not be playing with me."

"Munson called from the Presidential transition team. He says we've got to keep it secret…"

Bunny savored the words. She inhaled slowly and smiled. She wanted to enjoy this moment. She *needed* to enjoy it. But she sensed something hard and unpleasant, like a pebble in her shoe. As a survivor of Jim Crow, Bunny knew there could only be bad with the good.

—✦—

The house music pounded Carmen. She lost herself in the beat. She didn't know why she had agreed to go out with her friends. Actually, they weren't really her friends. They were the closest she had to friends in Minnepious, though.

It was that time of the month again: "BMT"—the Big Monday Throw-down hosted by MAAAL, the Minnesoule Association of African-American Lawyers. Carmen still could not believe what a trifling bunch this tiny fraternity of Black lawyers in the cultural backwaters of the upper Midwest had turned out to be. As usual, their BMT was a throw-down in name alone. Carmen glanced at the young, and not-so-young, Black lawyers drinking, dancing, chatting around her. In every way, their party, if you could call it that, was lame.

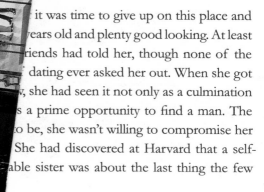

it was time to give up on this place and ⟨y⟩ears old and plenty good looking. At least ⟨f⟩riends had told her, though none of the ⟨⟩ dating ever asked her out. When she got ⟨⟩, she had seen it not only as a culmination ⟨a⟩s a prime opportunity to find a man. The ⟨t⟩o be, she wasn't willing to compromise her ⟨⟩ She had discovered at Harvard that a self-⟨⟩able sister was about the last thing the few

So here sh⟨e⟩ ⟨⟩ng out with a bunch of 'Bamas. They might be lawyers by day, but at night this group was a bunch of hicks in suits. After a few drinks chased away their inhibitions from daytime shuckin' and jivin' for the white partners in their law firms, *these Negroes could sure get down!* Carmen shook her head. It was time to return to New York. She just needed to get a job there first.

Carmen suddenly realized that some white boy was standing nearby saying something. She couldn't hear what he was saying. She pointed to her ears to indicate she couldn't hear him. The white boy started shouting, but she still couldn't hear him over the house music. Carmen wondered what he wanted. She shook her head to discourage him. The white boy leaned in closer, trying to be heard over the din.

The DJ softened the mix.

"Hi!" the white boy shouted a moment too late.

Oh shit, Carmen panicked, *everyone's looking.* "Hi," she replied.

The white boy extended his hand. "I'm Bob."

She shook his hand. "Carmen."

He smiled. It was a nice smile. Unselfconscious, natural.

"Want to dance?"

Hells no! Not with a white boy. Carmen pointed to her drink and shrugged.

"I'll wait," said Bob.

Carmen nodded. She sipped her rum and Coke, peering at Bob through the glass as she drank. He wasn't half bad looking, at least through the caramel liquid. If white boys were your thing, that is.

MINNISSIPPI

Carmen stopped herself. It was a bad habit she'd picked up in law school. Before law school, white people had been irrelevant to her. Growing up in Brooklyn, and going to college at Fordham, she never came across them. But at Harvard, and here in Minnepious, they were everywhere. Carmen finished her drink. She could see through the empty glass that Bob was still there. Time to give everyone something to talk about, she decided.

Chapter 2

Bunny awoke with a start. It took her a moment to realize her phone was ringing. She felt like a slave to the phone. She pondered the irony of her existence being controlled by a Black man's invention that had been stolen by a white man. The phone rang again. "Yes?"

It was Eileen. "Bunny, sorry to call so early. We just got a call about the basketball player."

"You mean Abu-Rahim?"

Eileen wrinkled her nose. It was another of *those* names. "Right," she said. "Apparently the NCAA is naming him a candidate for National Player of the Year today."

"Isn't it still early in the season?"

Eileen had no idea about the college basketball season. She hated sports. "I don't know how it works, Bunny, but UNLV scheduled a press conference for this afternoon. I thought we could do something with the local press. It could be a nice opportunity. I was thinking we could talk to Fred about it."

Bunny was tired. She did not want to see Fred. She did not need coaching from a white man on what to say about Abu-Rahim. The boy was already a legend in the community. Captain of North High's three time state championship basketball team, Abu-Rahim was worshipped on the north side.

Unlike those other boys on North's championship team—those Chicago boys and Gary boys and St. Louis boys, who showed up in Minnepious, got in trouble and never graduated—Abu-Rahim had grown up in the neighborhood, stayed out of trouble, and graduated on time. He was more than the proverbial local boy made good. He was a source of pride and joy, a real life hero to the beaten down people of north Minnepious. Playing point, Abu-Rahim had led those out-of-town ghetto boys to the state title.

And even though Abu-Rahim did not qualify academically to play his freshman year in college, he was so good UNLV gave him a scholarship anyway. After he sat out his freshman year, and got academically eligible, did that boy ever show his stuff! As a sophomore, he put Minnepious on the national hoops map, dominating ghetto boys from around the country. He was now in his third year of college and was apparently on the shortlist for National Player of the Year. Bunny sure as hell did not need Fred to tell her what to say about Abu-Rahim. "Eileen, do you really think we need Fred on this one?"

Eileen had anticipated the objection. There was another angle, one she was sure Bunny hadn't considered. Eileen had already run it by Fred, and he was fired up. "I just thought there were some other pieces we might consider."

"'Leen, you gotta do better than that. What's up?"

"Humor me, Bunny. Just a half hour with Fred. The press conference is at 10:30. We can see Fred at 9:45. I already put it on your calendar."

"Sounds like a conspiracy."

—⚶—

Carmen pulled the comforter over her head to keep out the cold. No matter how high she turned up the heat, cold air slipped in through the windows and under the doors. She should have rented a newer apartment, but she was a sucker for hardwood floors. And of course there was the rent. Student loans didn't leave much wiggle room, even on an associate's salary.

Carmen glimpsed light coming through the blinds. She had overslept. *Shit!* She had a meeting at nine with some woman referred to her by the NAACP. She poked her head back out from under the comforter, regretting that she had put her name on the NAACP attorney referral list. Not one of the NAACP referrals had turned out to be anything other than a headache. Apparently, only desperate people with no other options went to the NAACP for a lawyer.

Carmen glanced at the alarm clock by her bed. It was only 7:30. She relaxed. Then she remembered she was in the Midwest, where if you weren't in the office by eight, they considered you a lazy grifter. In a place where no one was supposed to stand out, you definitely did not want to stand out as a lazy grifter. Especially if you were from Harvard Law School and you were your firm's first and only Black lawyer.

Carmen forced herself out of bed. She showered and put on the Anne Klein knit suit that tastefully concealed her curves but hinted at possibilities if one gave her a second glance. She grabbed her brown leather briefcase. Her small apartment was chaotic. She needed to straighten it up soon. Maybe tomorrow. She opened the fridge, then glanced at her watch. No time for breakfast. The next bus would arrive in three minutes.

Carmen hurried out of her apartment and ran to the bus stop at the end of the block. An old lady stood there, waiting for the bus. Carmen relaxed. She had not missed the bus. Her stomach growled. She could grab a bagel on her way into the office. The bus arrived and Carmen got on. It was empty, the post-rush hour bus. The driver said good morning and Carmen returned his greeting. It had taken her a while to get accustomed to this Midwestern ritual of greeting strangers, though she had seen the driver before, so he wasn't a complete stranger. She knew what her mother would say.

Carmen sank into her seat as the bus pulled away from the curb. She let her mind wander back to the previous night. She could feel the stares as she followed Bob to the dance floor. She could hear the whispers. *Look! Carmen's dancing with that white boy!*

To her surprise, that white boy could dance. Don't know where he got it, but he had it. Carmen loved dancing. All she needed was someone passable, someone who would not embarrass her. But he had stayed right with her. By the third song, she knew it was no fluke. Bob could dance. And when the DJ played a slow song, Carmen slipped into Bob's arms. She no longer cared what anyone thought or said behind her back.

She had waited a long time for the right brother to sweep her off her feet. It hadn't happened. Now a white boy had fallen out of the sky and into her arms. She wondered what life would bring next.

—⁓—

Bunny waited for the television people to set up their cameras and for the radio people to attach their microphones to the stand the news outlets shared at press conferences. All the TV stations, both major newspapers and four radio reporters were there. As anticipated, there was strong interest in this story. It cut across the newsroom: local boy makes good, city schools' surprising success, local jock as national hero. There was something for everyone.

Bunny did not know all the reporters, particularly the sports types. She took the hand of Lynn White, whom she had known for years and whose son, incongruously named Abu-Rahim Rahim, had made this possible. "You alright Lynn?" Bunny whispered, away from the microphones.

"You just do your thing," Lynn assured the superintendent. "I'm fine, Bunny. You do *your* thing."

Bunny smiled. She had known she could count on Lynn. Lynn understood the sacrifices Bunny had made to reach this point. Bunny carried the expectations of their community every day. Bunny never forgot that. She never let her community down.

Bunny spotted Eileen whispering to *The Strib* newspaper reporter, Sue Wolfen. Wolfen had been on the Minnepious schools beat for over a year now. Bunny waited until Eileen was finished. Eileen's consultation with Wolfen was the key to their press conference strategy.

The district and Wolfen had found a groove, though it had not always been that way. Wolfen's first stories had been a disaster. Licentious tales of dissatisfied white parents. Quotes from "highly placed" officials disparaging Bunny. Comparisons of the district's test scores with suburban scores without clarifying the special challenges faced by urban schools. Bunny shuddered at the memory.

But they had straightened out Wolfen. Eileen and Fred had done the heavy lifting. They moved in ways Bunny could not. Calls to Wolfen's editor. Scoops strategically gifted to *The Strib*'s key competitors, *The St.*

Powell Pony Press and Minnesoule Public Radio. After a month of hard lessons, Wolfen and her editor had requested a meeting with Bunny to "clear the air."

The meeting had started out tense, almost accusatory. Each side pleaded its case. *The Strib* cited "journalistic integrity." The district claimed "hardship." As each side grasped the other's constraints, a wary mistrust yielded to understanding. There was no overt agreement, of course, just an unspoken truce.

Like estranged family members, both sides found that if they made an effort to get along, they could prevent disruptive conflict. Eileen and Fred began to feed Wolfen choice scoops as the tone of her stories changed to reflect her deepening understanding of the district. Wolfen's stories grew more nuanced and skeptical of disgruntled district employees and parents. Bunny took more than a little pleasure in having transformed the district's adversarial relationship with Wolfen into a trusting, mutually beneficial relationship. It was now a true win-win partnership.

No one could build partnerships like Bunny. That was her strength: her ability to connect and build win-win partnerships. Bunny built partnerships with the business community, the state, the teachers union, the school board, community-based organizations, the non-profit community, churches, white parents, and the few *involved* parents of color, like Lynn White.

Bunny glanced at Lynn. Unlike Bunny, Lynn stood on the dais only because of her son's accomplishments. Bunny could not imagine what it felt like to live through your child.

Eileen slipped away from Wolfen and signaled Bunny to start the press conference. Bunny cleared her throat. The press fell silent. Everyone knew the drill. All understood that background noise impaired recording. No one wanted to have to do this again. They all had multiple stories to cover, deadlines to meet.

"This is an important day for Minnepious Public Schools," Bunny began as the cameras rolled. She had memorized the short speech, copies of which Fred and Eileen distributed to the press. "We celebrate success today. We celebrate the success of one of North Minnepious' own," Bunny added, veering from the prepared text.

Eileen gave Bunny a sharp look, but the superintendent ignored it. Bunny knew that line would get play on the news and would be appreciated in the community. She scratched the community's back, and they protected hers. "At this time," Bunny continued. "I would like to acknowledge and thank Lynn White, Abu-Rahim's mother, for all she has given her son, and for all her son has given *us*." Bunny stepped back from the microphones, gestured to Lynn, and applauded. Eileen, Fred and a few of the jock types in the press corps also applauded.

Bunny mouthed, *"Thank you,"* to Lynn, who covered her heart with one hand and brushed away tears with the other.

"Thank *you*, Bunny," Lynn sobbed.

Bunny waited for the last jock reporter to stop clapping.

"Abu-Rahim Rahim is a role model for our youth," she continued. As she spoke, Bunny noticed that the TV reporters ignored her. A couple of them rubbed their hands together to stay warm on this wintry morning. Another read Bunny's written statement. One stared into space. Bunny rolled through the rest of her prepared speech. When she got to the end, she said, "Now I'll take your questions."

As usual, the hostile public radio guy, Leif Reiberson, beat the others to the punch. "Bunny, while he may be a good basketball player, do you really think Abu-Rahim Rahim is a good role model for Minnepious Public School students?"

Bunny was ready for this white liberal pseudo-criticism. She had no doubt that Leif and his kids—if he had any—were glued to the television every time the hometown boy played on national TV. They were probably still steamed that Abu-Rahim had chosen UNLV and snubbed the local U of M. "Leif, as your esteemed listeners on MPR well know, we celebrate the success of our graduates in so many ways: from accomplished professionals, to college basketball stars…to concert cellists."

"Concert cellists?" Reiberson pressed.

Perhaps Bunny should not have made that one up. But she figured Reiberson's listeners on MPR would love it.

"Concert cellists?" Reiberson repeated.

Fuck you, Leif.

Bunny called on the jock reporter from Channel 4, who had his hand raised.

"Do you think the streets of north Minnepious prepared Abu-Rahim for Division I competition?"

Bunny saw Eileen stiffen. Sure, the question was offensive. But so was a lot in life. The question played to Channel 4's white suburban audience. "We are very proud of Abu-Rahim and all he has accomplished," Bunny responded.

Sue Wolfen raised her hand.

Bunny nodded, but called on another TV reporter. "Yes?"

"What does Abu-Rahim's success tell us about your commitment to basketball in Minnepious?"

"Well," Bunny considered. *What a stupid question!* "It tells us to expect excellence from all our students. It reminds us they have many gifts we must nurture."

Bunny turned to Wolfen. "Sue, you've had your hand up for a while."

"Bunny," Wolfen said. "I know this press conference was called to recognize the accomplishments of one of your former students, but I have to ask you about something else."

Bunny frowned. "Can it keep till later?" She gestured toward the other reporters, who were there to cover the Abu-Rahim story.

"I must insist," Wolfen insisted. "With apologies to my esteemed colleagues, I have information that must be revealed."

Bunny drew back from the microphones. She shook her head, as if troubled by this breach of protocol.

Undeterred, Wolfen blurted, "Bunny, are you on the President-elect's shortlist for Secretary of Education?"

The entire press corps, even the jocks, jolted to attention.

"I…I cannot comment on that," Bunny stammered.

Leif Reiberson leaped into the breach. "Then you don't deny it!"

Couldn't help but take the bait, could you, asshole!

"I'm not at liberty to discuss this subject."

Fred and Eileen rushed to Bunny's side, brushing past Lynn White, who stumbled backward. The two officials whisked Bunny from the microphones. The TV cameras rolled, catching it all.

Lynn White regained her balance and waved as Bunny disappeared into district headquarters.

There was a momentary calm as the reporters absorbed this new information. Then all hell broke loose. The reporters dashed to their vans or dialed cell phones. They called their newsrooms, advising the assignment editors about a story bigger than Abu-Rahim Rahim. For a town like Minnepious, forever dreaming of its moment in the sun, this was a rare shot at national recognition.

Fred reached out to Bunny. "Your cell phone."

Bunny refused to hand it over. Her phone was her lifeline. "I won't answer it," she offered.

Eileen intervened. "Vinny will be with you all day. You can use his phone if you need to." A thirty year veteran of the Minnepious police force, Vinny had already put in five years as director of security for the district. He had the utmost discretion. Eileen held out her hand for the phone.

Bunny did not want to surrender her phone, and she did not want a white cop shadowing her all day. It was one of those things a Black woman who had grown up under Jim Crow could not abide. Not that Bunny had anything against Vinny personally. He was okay.

But when she was named superintendent, Bunny had tried to replace Vinny with her first choice, a family friend from Detroit. Eileen had pointed out the public relations complexity of a Black cop from Detroit interacting with white parents in Minnepious. Bunny had backed down. She knew from long experience, you had to pick your fights.

She handed her cell phone to Eileen.

"You're not available," Fred instructed. "Under *any* circumstances."

Bunny stifled the urge to slap him.

"We'll set up the war room," Eileen confirmed. "We'll record everything. We'll keep you posted."

"Just do your part," Bunny snapped. "I'll do mine." She did not appreciate Eileen's tone. And she sure as hell would not tolerate being lectured by a white subordinate in the hallway at district headquarters. Bunny turned and stalked to her office, leaving Fred and Eileen bewildered.

Eileen shrugged. She had grown used to Bunny's occasional outbursts.

—⁂—

Lakeesha tried to stay in line. She looked up and down the line to be sure she didn't stick out, but it was hard. Every time another girl moved, Lakeesha had to move too, or she would stick out. Lakeesha concentrated on the Afro on the girl in front of her. She could not remember the girl's name, but she knew the Afro. Lakeesha waited, very still, hoping the other girls did not move.

She watched children leave the building at the far end of the hallway. Those kids laughed and ran. One or two of them were brown, but most had pinky-peachy skin. They didn't look back at Lakeesha and the brown girls standing in line. Lakeesha bit her lip. She stared at the tiles on the floor. She did not want to see those kids at the other end of the hallway. She felt like crying. The other kids would be gone before Lakeesha and the other brown girls in line were allowed to move.

This was Lakeesha's first week in the Hornets program. She was still learning the rules. It was hard to figure out the rules when you weren't allowed to ask questions. That was the first rule: no questions. You had to "take a break" if you asked questions. *"But it's not a punishment,"* the teacher said when she sent you to stand in the corner of the room.

Lakeesha wanted to ask a question, but she did not want to take a break. "Mrs. Beamon?" Lakeesha asked in her politest voice.

The other girls stiffened.

Mrs. Beamon froze, her brown face hard.

"When do we get to go home?"

Mrs. Beamon walked over. "Did you ask me a question, honey?"

Lakeesha nodded.

"Did I say you could talk?"

Lakeesha knew the other brown girls in line were waiting to see what would happen. She bit her lip. Her eyes welled up, but she didn't cry.

"You're new, sweetie," Mrs. Beamon purred. "You don't know the rules yet. That's all right, though. Cause we goin' teach you." Mrs. Beamon looked at the line of brown faces. "Otherwise you might turn out like the rest of these little nigglets."

Lakeesha nodded.

Mrs. Beamon stared hard into Lakeesha's face. "Now you get this straight, girl. You leave when *I* say you leave. You got that?"

Lakeesha nodded. A tear ran down her cheek.

Mrs. Beamon's brown face softened. She followed Lakeesha's gaze toward the white kids leaving at the other end of the hallway. "You wanna go with them?"

Lakeesha nodded.

"Then you listen to me, and you listen good. You in the Hornets program now. You know why? You got a *behavior* problem. You got that? We goin' fix your behavior problem. Else you ain't *never* goin' get out. You got that?"

Lakeesha nodded.

—⚏—

"They locked up my baby," Charity muttered. She burned at the image of her son locked up, screaming for her, nothing she could do. "They call it the *hole*."

Carmen had no idea what to say. They didn't teach you how to handle this in law school. She got up from behind her desk, walked past the woman and closed the door to her office. She knelt next to the woman, empathizing. Maybe it was not a lawyerly thing to do. But it was the human thing to do.

"They called me from the hospital," Charity continued. "Not the principal. A teacher called. He told me Isaac was there. When I got there..." Charity paused. "They had my baby boy strapped to a table.

They given him drugs. He look like someone beat up on him. They was blood all on his clothes."

Carmen winced.

Charity looked at the young lawyer kneeling next to her. "That teacher told me he did it to hisself. They actin' like my boy beatin' on hisself. Didn't nothin' like this never happen in Chicago…"

Carmen's cell phone rang. She tried to locate it in her purse. She had forgotten to put the ringer on buzz. "Sorry," she said, fumbling for her phone.

Charity stared at the floor. She was used to being interrupted.

"Sorry," Carmen mumbled again. Her phone kept ringing.

"No problem." Charity stared at the wall. It wasn't like she had a choice anyway.

Carmen found her phone. She did not recognize the number. "Hello?"

"Did I interrupt something?"

"Who is this?"

Charity stared at the floor.

"It's Bob. You sure have a short memory!"

"Oh, Bob." Carmen stole a glance at Charity.

"If this isn't a good time, I can call you later."

"I'm with a client."

"I'll call you later. Just wanted to see if you're free for dinner."

"Call me later."

Carmen hung up and looked at Charity.

"Your man?" Charity sniffed, returning Carmen's gaze.

"Excuse me?"

"That's all right, honey. You don't need to explain nothin' to me."

Carmen seethed. *Damn right, I don't!*

"He white, ain't he."

Carmen was taken aback. She did not intend to discuss her personal life with this woman. It irritated her that the woman made an assumption about Bob being white. It irritated her even more that the woman felt entitled to comment on it.

"Ain't no thing," Charity shrugged. "White, black, yellow, they all the same."

Carmen suppressed the urge to kick the woman out of her office.

"Hope you gettin' somethin' from that white boy."

"You don't know me," Carmen snapped, betraying her anger and her Brooklyn roots.

Charity grinned. The tight little bitch had something going on, after all.

—⚋—

Bunny felt tired and irritable. She'd had enough of white people for the morning. Eileen in particular was getting on her nerves. Bunny did not appreciate being treated like a child by her subordinates.

When she entered the foyer to her office, Alain Fried, her administrative assistant, grabbed Bunny by the elbow, blocking her from the inner haven of her office.

Alain was Eileen's alter ego. He was as funny and flexible as Eileen was rigid and humorless. Alain had a lower profile and lower pay than Eileen, but he also had the real power. He controlled access to Bunny. That made Alain the most powerful person in the district after Bunny, and it made him the only powerful man.

Alain handed Bunny a typed schedule with appointments for the day. He kept his grip on her elbow. Bunny allowed Alain this indiscretion. Even though Alain was white, he was gay, a different shade of white.

"Bunny, I got a nasty little surprise for you in there," Alain whispered, rolling his eyes toward her office. "It's Reverend Hal, the *Ball*man. And he's cranky."

Bunny grinned. She knew Alain would have baited the gay-bashing clergyman when he arrived at her office.

She entered her office, bracing for blowback. "Reverend Hal," Bunny welcomed the gaunt man, the newest member of the Minnepious school board. "So good to see you."

Reverend Hal Ballman remained seated, despite the superintendent's entrance. His expression was sour. "You need to get rid of that faggot."

Bunny did not react.

Having got that off his chest, Reverend Hal went straight to the point of his visit. "Bunny, I need to tell you something."

The superintendent nodded and sat down at her desk.

"You know when I ran for school board, I committed to folk that I would hold the district accountable for not educating our children."

Bunny nodded. It was not the first time she had heard a Black politician make that promise.

"Well," Reverend Hal continued. "As God is my witness, praise the Lord, I am man of my word..."

Bunny nodded again.

"And you know I won't let our children fail. Not our precious Black boys." Reverend Hal paused. "Bunny, you know our children ain't Samolian."

Bunny had no idea what that statement meant.

"The state publishes statistics on test scores," Reverend Hal elaborated. "And the state breaks the statistics down by race. Am I right?"

Bunny nodded.

"Well, the state breaks it down by white, African-American, Asian, Latino and Native American. But there ain't no Samolian category. Am I right?"

"I believe that's right."

"Those Samolian kids, they not our people, Bunny. Fact, you ask me, they kinda lookin' white, you know, in a Arab sort a way. They don't speak no English, neither. They ain't got no schools back in Africa, is what I heard. And they keep they girls all covered up like they hidin' somethin'. Them girls can't go to school even if they was one, 'less Oafrey set one up for 'em." Reverend Hal paused, reflecting. "Can't remember if it was Samolia or some other place...But Oafrey did set up a school in Africa. Pretty sure of that."

Reverend Hal had touched a nerve. "South Africa," Bunny interjected. "The school's in *South* Africa."

Bunny had donated $250 after Oafrey did a show about the school and sent a letter asking for money. *"If we don't do it ourselves,"* Oafrey's fundraising letter had said. *"Who's going to educate our beautiful African girls?"* The letter—with pictures of beautiful Black girls in school uniforms—had brought tears to Bunny's eyes. She wanted to visit that school one day. If Bunny got the Secretary of Education job, Oafrey would probably fly her to South Africa on a private jet. That would be something. Served by your own private Black flight attendants…

"South Africa, north Africa," Reverend Hal snorted. "Do it really matter? It ain't America."

"No, it isn't," Bunny agreed. The image of beautiful Black flight attendants evaporated.

"And it ain't Samolia, neither."

"Right."

"Uh-huh. Like I was sayin', that means they ain't no schools for them Samolian girls. Fact, what I heard, they don't even got a written language. That's what I been told. Plus, they sendin' money to terrorists. The FBI all up on top of 'em. And where they gettin' all that money anyhow? Like we don't got enough Black folk shootin' each other up right here in the 'hood. Them Samolians comin' here kinda feel like a Mexican comin' up here to sell drugs!"

Reverend Hal was hitting his stride. "I seen Samolians drivin' big cars, and our people still walkin' barefoot, Bunny. Lord knows, we been here 400 years, last I checked, and didn't nobody give us no cars. We was lucky to be alive by the time we got off them slave ships. Now the government flyin' Samolians over here on *airplanes!* Ain't no slave ships for them Samolians, no sir. Nothin' too good for them. And who you think payin' for all them airplane tickets?"

Bunny dared not respond.

"You and me. That's who." Reverend Hal paused. "But here's the thing, Bunny. Why you think the government doin' that, 'specially when them Samolians keep gettin' caught goin' back to Africa to bomb our troops?" Reverend Hal paused again, gauging Bunny. "What, you don't think I'm tellin' the truth?"

He waited for a response.

"Reverend Hal, we've known each other a long time," Bunny demurred. "I know you're a man of the cloth. And I know you tell the truth. Even when it's *hard* truth."

Satisfied, Reverend Hal continued. "Bunny, do you call those Samolians *African-American?*"

Bunny could not tell if the question was rhetorical.

'Do you call Samolians *African-American?*" Reverend Hal repeated.

Bunny frowned.

"I didn't think so. No self-respecting Black person goin' do that. You know who does?"

Bunny raised her eyebrows.

Reverend Hal lowered his voice. "The state of Minnesoule, that's who. They call them Samolians, what just got here, don't speak no English, they women all covered up, never been to no schools, don't have no written language, doin' all that terrorist smack, the state calls 'em *African-American!*" The reverend paused.

Bunny waited.

"So what you think it look like when the state say *African-American* kids can't pass they tests? You think them white folk say, 'Oh, the state lumpin' all them Samolians in with us real Mandingos?'"

Bunny considered Reverend Hal. The light-skinned man in his fifties did not exactly look like the real Mandingo.

"You think that's what them white folk say?" Reverend Hal paused. "Hell no, that's not what they say. Them whites say..." At this point, Reverend Hal changed his natural baritone into a whiny, nasal voice. "See, *those people* just can't learn. Look at the *achievement gap!* It just won't go away no matter what we do."

Reverend Hal stared at the superintendent.

"Bunny, I'm tellin' you, we bein' set up. We can't let 'em get away with it. The state puts out all them statistics to make it look like *our* kids can't read. I'm goin' put a stop to it, Bunny."

Bunny thought about how to handle this new board member. He was a reverend and a respected community leader. He expected her support. And she was willing to work with him. In fact, she needed him. She could not afford to alienate the only Black school board member, especially the replacement for Willie Grier, her most stalwart ally during that tough first year on the job.

When Willie had died of a heart attack during a school board meeting, it was of course a shock to Bunny and the other board members. It had also left an intolerable void—no Black board member in a district with more than half its students African-American, and most of them failing. Reverend Hal now filled that void. Bunny just wished he had better judgment.

From the day he had announced his candidacy, Reverend Hal was cursed with dim political wits. He kept his daughter in private school even while he ran for the school board. He popped off in *The Strib* about racial inequity and other hot button issues. His comments put Bunny in a tough spot, potentially embarrassing her. She had considered dealing with him then, but ultimately decided to leave him be. Maybe that had been a mistake.

Reverend Hal's candidacy for the school board had straddled the Black man's line between fool and threat. When the Democratic Party refused to endorse him before the primary, Reverend Hal ran anyway. Defying conventional wisdom—and a forty-year Democratic streak of school board victories—Reverend Hal showed well enough in the primary to leapfrog the 21-year-old gay white boy endorsed by the Democratic Party. This qualified the reverend for the general election run-off.

Frazzled, party insiders had consulted Bunny about Reverend Hal's staying power. She assured them the eccentric reverend had grassroots support. She also told them she could manage him once he got on the school board. The party then switched horses from the openly gay candidate to the openly Black candidate. With Democratic Party backing, Reverend Hal enjoyed clear sailing in the general election, particularly in an off year with no national election and the usual 30 percent turnout. The only voters—hard core political activists, white liberals, union members and community organizers—all knew the score.

At his victory speech, Reverend Hal jubilantly claimed the mantle of *Pre-eminent Leader of the Black Community.* Surrounded by his congregation, the newly elected school board member declared that his Christ-like rise from the political grave conferred upon him a *mandate* to hold the district accountable for its sorry legacy of failing Black children.

The party leaders now expected Bunny to keep her part of the bargain and keep Reverend Hal on a short leash. She was prepared to do so. The problem was how to handle a man whose lack of common sense immunized him from the laws of political gravity. Reverend Hal failed to grasp the politician's life blood: the distinction between public and private. This created all sorts of unnecessary confusion and controversy.

Bunny understood that Reverend Hal needed to make wild, unsubstantiated accusations in public. She had no problem with that. To retain credibility, the reverend had to play to his alienated, disenfranchised base. That was the essence of being a Black politician.

But Bunny expected more from Reverend Hal in private. Here he was in her office spouting the same nonsense he speechified to the community. Bunny would have to teach Reverend Hal the facts of political life. And the sooner, the better. He needed to understand he was in *her* house now. "Reverend, do we really need to go there?"

"Come again?"

"Well, there are a lot of Somali children in the district…"

"That's my point!"

"What I'm saying is, do we really want to pick a fight with our Somali friends?"

"Samolian *friends?* Bunny, them white folk usin' Samolians against us. My enemy's friend ain't *my* friend, even if I do turn the other cheek, praise the Lord."

Bunny realized Reverend Hal was going to be a tough nut to crack. He would need to learn the hard way. "Let me talk to Dean Loofa," she suggested. "He's the district's head of statistics and testing. Let's see if we can pull together some useful information."

Reverend Hal thought about it for a moment, then nodded. "You get your boy Dane ready. We can't let 'em get away with this, Bunny."

———※———

The knock on her office door made Carmen jump. She had learned long ago to keep her door shut so the partners could not see what she was doing. It wasn't that she was doing anything wrong. She just found it hard to get enough billable hours from the partners to fill her time, and she did not want to look idle. As a junior lawyer, she had to rely on the firm's senior partners to give her work since they had the client relationships. She had been with the firm just over two years. The partners rarely gave her work.

Every day, when she had to fill out a time sheet, it was an exercise in creativity. She came up with all sorts of novel ways to say the same thing: no billable hours. She wondered why the firm had hired her. During her first week on the job, the President of the firm, Elmer Liechtenstein, had taken her to lunch at a fancy restaurant. After lunch, he gave Carmen an office tour, introducing her to every lawyer in the firm. At the end of the tour, Liechtenstein told Carmen to come to him any time she needed anything.

She had never gone to him, and he had never talked to her again.

As the firm's only Harvard grad and its first Black lawyer, Carmen had assumed the senior partners would make an extra effort to support her, to make sure she succeeded. They all knew Carmen had taken an unconventional path to the firm.

Like most of her classmates at Harvard, Carmen faced a mountain of student debt in her third and final year of law school. Unlike her classmates, Carmen had been unable to secure a job offer from any of the big New York firms she interviewed with. She had always planned to go back home after law school. But when the job market tightened, the big New York firms cut their hiring and Carmen was stuck without a seat in the high stakes game of musical chairs.

So Carmen had to look beyond New York. She read *The Wall Street Journal* for the first time in her life, trying to find a healthy job market for lawyers somewhere in the country. The city that kept coming up in her research was Minnepious. Carmen had never heard of the place, but she didn't let that stop her. She signed up for an on-campus interview with Mike Swenson, a partner from Flint, Hardy and Zoellig, one of Minnepious' top tier firms.

She'd never forget her shock when she met Swenson at her interview. He was blonde, with reddish smooth skin like a boiled chicken. Carmen had never met a blonde lawyer before. In her mind, such a person simply did not exist. All the lawyers Carmen had met during her first summer internship in New York were Jews. And if they weren't actually Jews, they acted like they were. They talked fast and exuded an edgy confidence. They had probably been arguing from the day they were born.

It never occurred to Carmen during her job interview with Swenson that she was the first Black person he had ever talked to. A year after she joined the firm, Swenson told Carmen he had grown up on a farm in southwestern Minnesoule. He confided that he had gone to an all-white high school, an all-white engineering program at Iowa State and an all-white law school in North Dakota. Carmen realized Swenson had marched up the social ladder without ever meeting a Black person. The day after her interview, Swenson called to offer Carmen a job at FHZ. She accepted on the spot. She had no other offers.

For two years at the firm, Carmen had tried to make it work. Now she felt herself slipping. What it meant, and where she would end up, she did not know. Despite her upbeat nature, she found herself considering the possibility that she would fail professionally.

She heard the knock at her door again. "Yes?"

The door opened. A man in bow tie and suspenders entered.

Carmen looked at the senior partner standing before her. He had an awkward—one might uncharitably say, *shit-eating*—grin.

He extended his hand. "I'm Jamie Levine."

Carmen shook hands. She had no idea why he was there.

"I'm Bob's dad," the man said, as if that explained everything. "He told me the two of you met last night."

Minnissippi

Carmen put two and two together. "Oh."

"Can I take you downstairs for a coffee?"

Carmen nodded. "Sure."

She followed the man out of her office with a sense of foreboding.

Chapter 3

"How do you like Minnepious?" Mr. Levine asked when he and Carmen were seated at the Starbuck's in the office tower atrium. "It's not exactly the East Coast."

Carmen did not know how to respond, so she stayed silent. Sunlight shimmered through the crystal court and reflected across the atrium. The place felt almost tropical despite the sub-freezing temperatures outside. Winter had arrived a few weeks early this year. Funny how the sunniest days were the coldest.

The senior partner tried again. "Bob told me he enjoyed getting to know you last night."

Carmen froze. It was a little premature for *the talk*.

"That was clumsy," Mr. Levine laughed. "I'm sorry I haven't reached out to you before." He paused. "I went to law school at NYU. I know it's a big adjustment to move here. That's all I meant."

Carmen relaxed. She liked this senior lawyer who seemed eager to connect with her but could not find the right words.

"I was the first Jew in the firm," Mr. Levine blurted.

Carmen nodded. She tried to think of a tactful way to end this bizarre encounter. "Mr. Levine…"

"Call me Jamie."

"Jamie, I have to do some research on a client project. It's pretty urgent."

"Sounds interesting. What kind of project?"

Carmen was not a good liar. "I'm not sure yet…that's what I'm researching, actually. I'm sorry to cut this short…"

"No," Mr. Levine assured the young associate. "Work comes first. Got to keep the client happy."

—⚏—

A press conference sucked up the entire day. It was not the press conference itself, but all the follow up conversations, the clarifications, the backgrounders, the stock footage, the unanticipated questions. Eileen camped out in the war room down the hall from her office. She had a bank of landlines and two cell phones. She ordered in lunch and cancelled her appointments for the day.

Eileen managed every detail in the aftermath of a press conference. She took calls. She distributed talking points. She organized the obligatory show of supportive parents and teachers for follow up quotes and interviews. Eileen did all the little things that let Bunny shine. In a resource-starved urban school district, Eileen could not delegate. She had to do it all on her own.

Eileen always felt isolated, even paranoid, about the details until the news stories ran. Then the district either looked good or bad. When it came to the district's relationship with the press, there was no in-between, no disinterested, objective high ground. Few voters had children in Minnepious Public Schools, so the district's only meaningful relationship with the voting public came through the media. Eileen knew how high the stakes were. Her career in public education spanned a quarter century. Over that time, she had seen it all.

When she got her first job in the late 1980s, bad news dominated press coverage of the district. From calamitous busing to financial mismanagement to plummeting test scores, the district was an easy target for a press corps and voting public far removed from the challenges of inner city education. As white parents fled city schools, the press chronicled the exodus, creating and validating a compelling national narrative: *Fecund, baby mama hordes of uneducated welfare queen/gangster children were flooding urban schools, threatening hard working white middle class people!*

It was disgraceful fear mongering, to be sure. But as with all stereotyping, Eileen knew it contained more than a grain of truth. To this day, Eileen grimaced every time some outrageous inner city crime story hit the news. Each negative story reinforced the world view of Eileen's friends and family. *Only a fool would remain behind with the poor dark violent hordes overwhelming the city!* As the district continued to careen from crisis to crisis through the decade of the nineties and into a new century, Eileen herself began to wonder if it was time to get out.

Bunny's predecessor as Superintendent of Minnepious Public Schools in many ways marked the low point for the district. Her predecessor was not a human being but a public relations *company*, Public School Strategies, Inc. PSSI's CEO Paul Hatchings had worked for two decades as head of investor relations for Dilton's, a locally headquartered, nationally prominent retailer. After taking early retirement from Dilton's, Hatchings set up PSSI. His timing could not have been better.

PSSI scored its first consulting contract with the Minnepious school district after disastrous statewide math and reading test results came out. The district's black students scored nearly 50 points below the statewide average for reading and 65 points below on math. When the district's white male superintendent at the time, Ryan Bliss, announced at a hastily convened press conference that the test results did not reflect the district's "progress," an academic challenge became a public relations catastrophe.

Paul Hatchings knew corporate crisis management from his career at Dilton's. He had handled numerous racial incidents that threatened the retailer's reputation, including the arrest of a black state Supreme Court justice on shoplifting charges by store security guards. Where Minnepious school board members perceived a crisis, Hatchings saw opportunity, and he moved aggressively to exploit it.

First, Hatchings met privately with a Minnepious school board member who happened to be his neighbor. Then, with the blessing of his neighbor, Hatchings circumvented Superintendent Bliss. He convened a private meeting of the school board and urged the board to go on the offensive. He designated the board's sole black member, Willie Grier, to be the district's spokesman. Images matter, Hatchings explained, especially on television. The district could not afford to have a white man talking about failing black students.

The board loved Hatchings' take charge manner. He was the right man in the right place at the right time. He knew all the right people in the media and in the corporate community. The school board needed help, and needed it fast. With the superintendent sidelined, Hatchings consolidated power. He coined the phrase, "Closing the Gap," which the district adopted as its mantra. He had all district letterhead replaced with this catchy new logo. The new letterhead cost over $50,000—money well spent, as it turned out, even in an age of austerity for urban school districts.

Eileen and her professional colleagues were initially skeptical of Hatchings' obsession with slogans and public relations. After all, slogans did not address the district's very real problems. Still, the district needed time to solve its problems, and all the razzamatazz provided a useful distraction. If new letterhead bought some time, who was Eileen to complain? She had long ago learned that in urban public education, the *appearance* of change was generally more important, and more achievable, than real change.

Hatchings did not stop at the letterhead. All MPS materials, including PowerPoint presentations, data reports, and personnel files, were soon tagged with the bold header, *"Closing the Gap."* PSSI's consulting contract doubled, then tripled. After six months, the school board negotiated a severance package with Superintendent Bliss and signed a four year deal with PSSI to run the district. Designating Hatchings "Superintendent" in name alone, the new contract made his *company* accountable for student achievement, as measured on statewide tests. Nowhere else in the country had a public school district entered into such a contract with a private company.

That soon changed. Minnepious became a national model for "accountability," and a darling of education reformers everywhere. Around the country, education consultants formed companies and lobbied urban school boards for contracts similar to PSSI's arrangement with MPS. Career educators could not compete against consulting companies. Eileen's professional colleagues in other districts told her they could not, in good conscience, sign a contract guaranteeing they would close the achievement gap. By contrast, consulting companies happily signed such contracts. Legally unenforceable, the contracts were designed to reassure skeptical taxpayers that school board members were protecting their interests.

"Accountability" became the new buzz word in urban districts across the nation. When consulting companies failed to deliver on their promises of academic improvement, school boards quietly signed *amendments* to the original contracts based on new *assumptions*. A public weary of urban blight and dysfunction shrugged.

Hatchings' corporate feel-good message did indeed take heat off the district for a time. But public relations gimmicks could only go so far. They did nothing to fix the district's underlying problem—a flood of blacks, immigrants, the poor, the needy. Hatchings claimed the district was making progress, even if periodically released test results did not reflect that progress (*yet*). Each reporting period, a few heads rolled, and even more eyes rolled among the district's senior staff.

At the end of his second year as superintendent, Hatchings held a press conference to announce the firing of Gabe Blouther, the district's widely respected Assistant Superintendent for Educational Accountability. Hatchings did this without consulting, or even notifying, the district's senior staff. Eileen watched in disbelief and horror at the press conference as Hatchings, who had no experience or credentials in educational administration, proclaimed that he was holding Gabe personally "accountable" for the persistent achievement gap between white students and students of color. Unbelievably, the media gave Hatchings a complete pass. According to the press, Hatchings could not be expected to "close the gap" on his own. His job was to hold "career educators" like Gabe accountable for accomplishing this objective.

After the Gabe Blouther debacle, staff morale hit a new low and *"Closing the Gap"* disappeared from the district's letterhead, presentations and reports. It was replaced by a new mantra: *"Accountable for Results."* But "accountability" did not bring success to Minnepious schools, either. As scrutiny from the media and community organizations intensified, and PSSI's rich "accountability" contract with the district became a subject of ridicule, Hatchings withdrew from public functions. He delegated to subordinates all interactions with the media and public. He became "unavailable" for comment whenever the district announced dismal test scores or other bad news.

Hatchings told his unsettled senior staff that he was working with national academic experts on a "turnaround" strategy for the district. Longtime district employees like Eileen remained in the dark about the details of this gestating turnaround strategy as teams of consultants streamed into Minnepious for "academic retreats" at exclusive hotels. The bills for these consultants ran into hundreds of thousands of dollars. At Hatchings' personal instruction, the expenditures were categorized in the district's financial books as "professional development" fees. No one was foolish enough to question the expenditures, or the accounting.

On the eve of the next round of statewide tests, Hatchings revealed to senior staff his two pronged turnaround strategy. First, he proposed to convert the district from centralized control to "site-based management." That elicited a collective yawn from senior staff. The second prong of Hatching's strategy was, by contrast, a shocker. He announced the district would end its failed forty year experiment with forced busing and return to neighborhood schools.

Eileen and her colleagues were stunned. They knew it was the right thing to do, but it would be politically treacherous. Assistant Superintendent Huddlestone asked Hatchings how he planned to handle potential backlash from the black community. Hatchings laughed, assuming the question was facetious. "This plan won't change a thing for blacks," he replied when he realized the question was serious. "Willie Grier is way on board with this. He told me I could say it was his idea if we get any heat."

The district's senior staff relaxed. They could see Hatchings had thought things through.

"The purpose of this plan," Hatchings explained. "Is to stop white flight. If we create neighborhood schools in the southwest of the city, we can offer elementary schools there as good as the best suburban elementaries. If we don't stop white flight, we'll become Detroit."

Staff nodded. Despite all the turmoil of the previous two years, they admired Hatchings' foresight and political courage in developing this turnaround plan.

Before Hatchings could implement his plan, however, external events intervened. The state announced the district's test scores, which were bad. Really bad. The district's black high school students scored at the level of suburban fourth graders. Hatchings was forced to shelve his incipient neighborhood schools plan and scramble instead to find an immediate solution to the ever widening learning gap. "Will no one rid me of these meddlesome test scores?" Hatchings queried his inner circle at an emergency meeting.

Eileen could see the same noose that had ensnared his predecessor Bliss begin to tighten around Hatching's reddening neck.

Senior administrators spread the word to principals at black schools that they had to get their test scores up, no matter what. Hatchings transferred principals from school to school, looking for an elixir that could lift blacks out of the academic abyss. When nothing worked, Hatchings fired principals. *"Accountability,"* he explained.

The next round of test results showed minor improvement in some black schools, and slippage in others. Desperate, Hatchings announced a new accountability plan. Underperforming schools would receive a "fresh start." But it was too little, too late. The new accountability plan was superseded by events beyond Hatchings' control. Despite an all-out assault on black schools, the achievement gap between black students and whites continued to grow. Disgruntled administrators slipped juicy tidbits to *The Strib*, which ran a front page investigative exposé trumpeting the persistence of the racial achievement gap in Minnepious.

Formerly reliable community partners, like the African-American Success Project, now publicly criticized the district, targeting Hatchings personally. At a press conference, a dozen black ministers called for Hatchings and PSSI to be sacked. They said no white businessman should be allowed to inflict "educational genocide" on black children. They demanded that the district hire a black superintendent.

It was combustible stuff. The media loved it. *Black leaders blaming whites for the failure of black children to pass basic tests that the poorest white children passed with ease!*

At an emergency school board meeting, Hatchings tendered his resignation. The board bought out the remaining eight months of PSSI's consulting contract and hired an executive search firm to scour the nation for superintendent candidates who could solve the district's problems. Everyone in the district knew the national search was a sham. Within a month, to no one's surprise, the national search process recommended a consensus local black candidate: Bunny Washington.

There was just one catch. With white flight accelerating, the anticipated appointment of a black superintendent posed a public relations nightmare: *How could white parents be reassured that the schools would get better, not worse?*

The solution—proposed by black board member Willie Grier—turned out to be deceptively simple, even elegant, and ingenious: *Have the new superintendent sign off on Hatchings' shelved "Neighborhood Schools" plan.*

It was a stunning win-win. The board got the black superintendent it needed, and white parents got the explicit reassurance they needed that they would be insulated from whatever mess ensued under the new black superintendent. Bunny agreed to the school board's terms without hesitation.

Eileen had enjoyed a front row seat to all these machinations. She had known Bunny for over a decade before her colleague's ascension to the superintendency. They had served together on multiple district task forces.

Unlike many of her peers, Eileen had no problem with the board picking Bunny to be superintendent. She admired Bunny's way with people and respected her core integrity. No fair minded person could deny that Bunny had the requisite academic credentials and experience: a PhD in education from the U, more than fifteen years as a teacher, and another decade as a principal.

But Bunny's most important credential, as Eileen and everyone else in the district knew, was she was black. This was not to suggest Bunny was unqualified. Far from it. It was an acknowledgement that what the district needed more than anything at that moment was a leader with a black face, particularly if the district was going to announce a return to neighborhood schools to entice white parents to keep their children in Minnepious schools.

The moment Bunny became superintendent, Eileen realized she had underestimated her old colleague. Bunny was not just socially adept and academically qualified to lead the district. She was also ruthless and disciplined. She played to win.

At her first press conference, Bunny announced the district's plan to end forced busing and return to neighborhood schools. Backed by a *Who's Who* of black community leaders, Bunny explained to the press that this was what the black community had long craved. She explained that *Brown vs. Board of Education* was commonly misunderstood. The case was not in fact about busing. It originated out of a black parent's desire to send her child to school closer to home.

The press ate it up.

With a laser focus on public relations, Bunny kept the message simple, and it worked. Bunny became the sole authorized face of the district, literally. Her airbrushed head shot accompanied every press statement or news release. Her warm, grandmotherly smile could melt any skeptic's heart. Eileen marveled at the irony of a black woman beating Hatchings at his own public relations game.

Behind the scenes, Bunny ruled with an iron fist. Job titles and seniority were irrelevant. You were either a trusted member of her inner circle. Or you were out, all the way out. Bunny prized loyalty above all else. Whether straightening out errant reporters or disciplining district staff, Bunny ran a tight ship. She retaliated fiercely against any parent, district employee or community member who took a grievance to the media. Bunny never forgot such transgressions. Nor was she inclined to forgive.

Tickled to see a woman finally assume leadership of the district, Eileen outdid her peers in demonstrating loyalty to the new superintendent. As a result, she found herself increasingly singled out for praise. Before she knew it, she was part of Bunny's inner circle, growing as close to the superintendent as anyone could.

It had been a strange and exhilarating ride over the past three years. And now, Eileen and Bunny were on the verge of the pinnacle. An epic career move to Washington was within their grasp.

Eileen snapped back to the task at hand: the aftermath of the Abu-Rahim Rahim press conference. She and Fred had already implemented the district's standard dual press strategy. They would handle the mainstream press. Bunny would deal with the black press. That was the superintendent's private domain.

Bunny religiously monitored the local black radio stations, cable access television shows and two weekly newspapers. She gave exclusive interviews to the black media and wrote articles targeting the black community. Most important, she committed the district to generous advertising outlays for all local black-owned media and socialized regularly with the owners and managers of black radio stations and newspapers, taking them to dinner at least twice a quarter.

Eileen knew the orchestrated "leak" about Bunny making the shortlist for Secretary of Education had to be handled with care. Bunny could not appear to be overtly lobbying for the appointment. Since support from the black press was a given, the district kept Bunny in hiding for now while Eileen and Fred handled the mainstream media.

One of the war room phones rang. Eileen answered it. She parried the reporter's questions with a series of "no comments" *on the record*. Then she confided off the record that inside sources from Washington had in fact identified Bunny as the *front runner* for Secretary of Education.

The news directors from the three local television stations called looking for "model" schools to feature on the six o' clock news. They wanted examples of how Bunny had managed to educate the poor, the weak, the downtrodden, the huddled masses. Eileen had goose bumps as she fielded the enquiries. Though not religious, Eileen began to suspect she was doing God's work.

Fred joined Eileen five minutes before the twelve o'clock news. Though the tax-paying suburban target market did not watch the midday news, Fred and Eileen could preview the story before it played at 5 and 6. The gist of the story would be the same on the midday and evening news, only the adornments would be more dazzling and elaborate by the evening. By late afternoon, reporters would have had a chance to track down sources in Washington to confirm the rumor and supplement the delicious footage of Bunny, reluctant hero, being hustled away from the microphones. Eileen had to admit, she and Fred were pros at giving the television people the compelling images they craved.

Fred turned on three televisions and recorded the news. Bunny demanded a complete record of all publicity the district received, good or bad. "Continuous improvement" had become the latest mantra in the district. Of course, you could not improve without a baseline of accurate data—good or bad. Eileen and Fred hoped for the best as they settled in for the news.

Eileen's phone rang. "Hey Vinny," she answered.

It was Bunny on Vinny's phone.

"We're on it," Eileen reassured the superintendent. "I'll call you back in ten minutes." She knew it would be the top story.

At noon, Eileen and Fred held their breath. Each newscast opened with the story:

"Channel 5 has learned that Minnepious schools superintendent Bunny Washington is under consideration by the President-elect to become the next Secretary of the United States Department of Education…"

"Welcome to Channel 11 news. Our lead story is about a Minnepious resident receiving national attention. And no, we're not talking about Abu-Rahim Rahim. Reliable sources confirm that our own Bunny Washington, Superintendent of Minnepious Public Schools, may soon be appointed Secretary of the national Department of Education…"

"Channel 4 has learned that Minnepious' own Bunny Washington has made the shortlist of candidates for Secretary of Education …"

When Charity got home, the landlord was waiting for her. She didn't see him until it was too late. The fat white slob blocked her path in the entryway to the Section 8 apartment building. "Get out my fuckin' way," Charity spat, hoping to scare the bastard.

It didn't work.

The fat fucker closed in on her, using his body like a barricade. "Where's my rent?"

Charity started to back up, but she had nowhere to go. "I got some money comin' soon."

"How soon?"

"Next week."

The motherfucker just stood there. His yellow hair looked all greasy, like he didn't take a shower for days.

"You using drugs?"

"You got your nerve! I don't use no damn drugs!"

"You know I can check your apartment if I think you're using."

"I ain't got nothin' to hide."

The bastard let Charity squeeze by him to enter the hallway. He followed her to her unit.

Charity stood in front of her apartment door. "You want me to open it? Or you goin' use your key?"

The fat ass just stood there, so Charity unlocked the door. She stood aside and let him go in first. She didn't have nothing to hide.

The fat man walked in like he owned the place, which Charity supposed he did. But still, it wasn't right how he was acting. She always paid her rent, even if it wasn't always on time. And the government paid their part on time anyhow, so it wasn't like the fat bastard was losing money.

The fat man snooped around in her living room, then went to her bedroom. Charity followed him, just to be sure he didn't take nothing. As soon as she got inside the bedroom, he moved behind her and blocked her way out.

"Ah, fuck no!" Charity yelled. "Get your fat ass out of here!"

The landlord grinned and leaned into her. "We can make a deal on the rent."

He reached for her breasts.

"Get off me!" Charity shouted and pushed the man's hands away.

The landlord leaned into her and pushed her backward onto her bed. Charity tried to fight him off, but the fat bastard was on top of her, and he was heavy. She punched at his face, but he blocked her. He grabbed her arms and pressed them down on the bed. When he lifted his body to move over her, she lashed out with her knee and caught him in the balls.

"Bitch!" he screamed and punched her in the face.

Charity saw a flash in her head. The bastard pressed down on her. She tried to scream, but he put his hand over her mouth. She bit his hand and rolled to the side when he pulled back his hand. She knew he would punch her again, so she started talking fast. "How much months you give me if I fuck you nice?"

The landlord did not say anything. She could see his eyes looked real mean. He was gonna hit her again for sure.

"I got a sweet pussy," she said. "Three months, no rent. How 'bout that? And we split the Section 8 money."

The landlord shook his head. "I keep the Section 8 money," he countered. "You don't have to pay your part for three months."

Charity did the math right quick in her head. $150 a month for three months was almost $500. It was either that, or get beat up real bad. Only a fool would get beat up.

—⁂—

Back in her office, Carmen savored her quick witted escape from Jamie Levine. She figured she might as well see what she could learn about Afrocentric Alternatives Academy, where Charity's son had apparently been abused. She went online and found the school's website. It showed smiling Black children in uniforms and serious Black teachers "*committed to a common vision.*" The school was part of a network of charter schools feeding into the largest charter school in the state: Afrocentric Success Academy.

Carmen clicked on a link for Afrocentric Success Academy and saw more of the same smiling Black children in uniforms. She tried the *Our Mission and Values* link and saw a photograph of the charter school network's Founder and CEO, Kweisi Providence. The website touted *"high expectations"* and *"discipline,"* but Carmen did not find much of use on the school's *Our Mission and Values* page.

She left the school website and searched online for news articles about the school. She was surprised at how much she found. There were dozens of glowing articles in *The Minnepious Strib* about the school's success with *"at-risk"* kids, particularly Black boys. The articles, written by Education Reporter Sue Wolfen, invariably included a profile of CEO Kweisi Providence, a former Marine who had lifted himself up by his bootstraps to become a pioneer of Black educational success. Providence explained in one profile that he had learned the value of uniforms and a sense of *"higher purpose"* on his own life's journey from juvenile delinquent to acclaimed educator.

According to the articles, Providence was a modern day miracle worker. He had lifted test scores of Black children beyond those of the highest performing suburban districts in the state, including Eden, a wealthy suburb adjacent to Minnepious.

"It takes a village," Providence explained in an article summarizing the astonishing performance of Afrocentric Success Academy students on statewide tests. *"In Eden, parents have extra resources to give their kids every advantage. We don't have that in north Minnepious. But we do love our beautiful black children. You have to understand, the difference between Eden and north Minnepious is not only about resources. It's also about expectations. At Afrocentric Success Academy, we expect our kids to compete straight up with those kids from Eden for college placements and jobs. We will not let our children make excuses. We will not tolerate failure."*

In another article, Minnepious Public Schools Superintendent Bunny Washington praised Afrocentric Success Academy as a successful model and source of pride for the entire district: *"We are studying*

Afrocentric Success Academy very closely. While our contract with the teachers union may prevent the district from implementing some of ASA's innovations, like extended school hours and a longer school year, we will certainly consider making changes where we face the same challenges Kweisi and his team have solved."

In an article entitled *"Holy Cow!" The Strib* quoted Providence: *"Our corporate partners and benefactors are the real key to our success. Our kids know if they do their part in the classroom, Afrocentric's partners will provide the internships and scholarship opportunities that ensure success later in life. When our kids finish Afrocentric's entrepreneurship curriculum, they're not setting themselves up for a dead end job flipping burgers. They're putting themselves in position to own the whole cow!"*

Local philanthropist and financier Gordy Lindt praised Providence in another *Strib* article: *"To call Kweisi a miracle worker would be an understatement. What he has done is prove that anyone who says inner city schools can't work, or black kids can't learn, is a liar. This man walks the talk."*

The article noted that Lindt's family foundation had donated $10 million to the Afrocentric Success Academy Foundation to support development of a network of *"feeder"* schools, all based on ASA's proven model of success. Bunny Washington praised that deal: *"This is the type of public-private partnership we need to encourage so all our students can succeed."*

Providence had built a national reputation based on the success of Afrocentric Success Academy. He supplemented his substantial salary as CEO of ASA with speaking engagements and consulting contracts. Still, success and a six figure income had apparently not gone to his head. One glowing profile noted that Providence and his wife of twenty-one years still lived with their four children in the same modest north side home where he grew up: *"The wonderful thing about Kweisi is he's so humble,"* Bunny Washington said in the article. *"He has not forgotten his roots."*

Carmen was impressed. It was quite a success story.

But it did not square with Charity's account of what had happened to her son.

This dissonance did not surprise Carmen. Her limited experience with civil rights work had taught her that those claiming discrimination could be notoriously unreliable. This was not the first time a potential client's horror story did not square with the objectively verifiable facts. That was precisely why she had to research the charter school before deciding whether to take Charity as a client. In her previous referrals from the NAACP, Carmen had learned the hard way that potential clients who exaggerated their claims during initial screening interviews invariably turned out to have bad cases, and be bad clients.

The online articles referred to Afrocentric Success Academy's pathbreaking results on statewide tests. Since the articles did not actually show the test results, Carmen went to the state Department of Education website to see the data for herself. The state website displayed test results by school, by district, and for the state as a whole. It took Carmen a while to figure out how to navigate the website and find what she was looking for. Then it took her a while to comprehend what she was seeing. The data did not square with the articles.

Again and again, Carmen read the test score data. She had to be missing something. Or perhaps she was reading it wrong. The test results showed that Afrocentric Success Academy students—all of whom were Black—scored pretty well on the state's standardized reading and math tests. But they scored very poorly on the state science tests. This made no sense. How could students so competent in reading and math fail so miserably at science?

Overall, taking the science results with the reading and math results, the Afrocentric Success Academy students scored marginally better on the state's standardized tests than other Black students in the Minnepious district. The ASA students did not score better than Minnepious white students, however. And they did not score better than Black students in some Minnepious schools. When Carmen compared Afrocentric Success Academy's overall test results with suburban schools, it was not even close. ASA students scored far below students in the Eden school district, including Eden's few Black students.

Carmen smelled a rat, and it wasn't Charity. How could all these stories trumpet miraculous success that just wasn't there? It made no sense. Carmen thought about what she had just seen, trying to puzzle it out into a coherent picture. Providence was making out like a bandit.

His rich benefactors probably had some angle to promote charter schools or private schools, and undermine confidence in public schools. That much made sense to Carmen.

But what about the newspaper reporter, Sue Wolfen? Was Wolfen, whoever she was, a dupe? Or was she in on it, too? Giving Wolfen the benefit of the doubt, Carmen figured the reporter was most likely overworked, stretched thin, with little time or ability to investigate deeply, or challenge her sources.

But it was so easy to refute Providence's claims. All Carmen had done was check the state's website. If Carmen could do it so easily, why hadn't Wolfen?

And what about the praise heaped on Afrocentric Success Academy by Minnepious schools superintendent Bunny Washington? Why would the superintendent want to promote a charter school that was not actually delivering better outcomes for students?

Carmen was confused. She needed help sorting this out. She called Bartolo Fredericks, Education Chair of the Minnepious Branch of the NAACP. She knew Bart from the three branch meetings she had attended before she realized it was a trifling bunch and stopped going. "Bart," Carmen said when he answered. "It's Carmen Braithwaite."

There was a long pause.

"The attorney," Carmen reminded him. "From Brooklyn."

"Oh, Carmen! How you doin,' young lady?"

"I'm okay, Bart. I was hoping you could help me out with something."

"Absolutely! Tell me what you need."

"I'm trying to get some information about Afrocentric Success Academy."

"Right on. They've definitely set the standard."

"That's what I wanted to ask you about," Carmen prodded. "Everyone seems to think they've cracked the code."

"Right on."

"But their test scores don't look so good to me."

There was no *"Right on,"* this time.

"Bart?"

"Yeah?"

"You there?"

There was a long pause. "I don't know too much about that."

"Well, you are the branch's Education Chair, right?"

"They just put me in this year. No one else wanted to do it."

"So you're telling me you don't know anything about Afrocentric Success Academy?"

"I don't really get your point."

"Look," Carmen explained. "A woman came to me. She got my number off the branch's lawyer referral list. She says her son got abused at Afrocentric Alternatives Academy, which is affiliated with Afrocentric *Success* Academy. But when I go online to research these schools, they look like a paradise of Black empowerment.

"So this woman says one thing, and the newspapers say something else. I figure the woman's making it all up. But just to be sure, I go to the state Education Department website to confirm the test results, and it turns out the Afrocentric charter schools aren't all they're cracked up to be. None of this makes any sense to me. What am I missing?"

After another long pause, Bart said, "I don't know really know the deal, Carmen. And I'm pretty busy right now. You know, end of year stuff. You should call Lily Onyekachukwu. She'll know the score. I'll text you her cell number."

"Okay," Carmen agreed. "Thanks."

Bart had already hung up. His text pinged her.

Perplexed, Carmen called Lily Onyekachukwu. She was familiar with Onyekachukwu from the woman's late night cable access show. Whenever Carmen stayed up late, she channel surfed, and often landed on Onyekachukwu's show. The production values were awful and Onyekachukwu was crazy. But when you were up in the middle of the night, Onyekachukwu could entertain you. She was an opinionated nut, who claimed to be the "*Real Deal*," dishing about Minnepious' Black community and railing against unnamed *"white oppressors."* Carmen had no idea what the Real Deal would be like off the air.

When Onyekachukwu answered her phone, Carmen introduced herself. Onyekachukwu instantly grilled Carmen about who she was, how she had got Onyekachukwu's cell number, and where she was from. Carmen was savvy enough to say, "Brooklyn," not Harvard or the Caribbean. That calmed Onyekachukwu down.

Carmen told Onyekachukwu what she had learned on the web about Afrocentric Success Academy and what she had heard from the mother of a student beaten up at one of ASA's feeder schools. When Carmen finished, Onyekachukwu laughed.

"Honey child, I got you covered. Let me tell you like it is. Providence makin' out like a bandit. Don't believe that shit about him livin' in the 'hood with his wife and kids. Homeboy got a whole lot more than that goin' on! And Bunny full a shit too. She done talk out one side her mouth to white folk. Then she be tellin' us a whole other story. But don't you worry. We goin' give Bunny somethin' to think about."

Carmen's head was spinning, and not only because Onyekachukwu spoke fast. Unlike those two-faced, Bama-ass lawyers at MAAAL, it seemed Minnepious' poor Black folk knew the score. Onyekachukwu would not hesitate to bust on those in power, no matter what their color. This was refreshing, if disorienting.

"Girlfriend," Onyekachukwu continued. "You free for lunch at one o'clock? Got to come to the north side, though. It'll be way worth it."

Carmen jumped at the chance to get out of the office and meet Onyekachukwu in person. If she took the afternoon off, no one would miss her anyway. Carmen slipped out of the office and took the bus home to get her car for the drive to lunch on the north side.

—⚉—

Charity cleaned herself up. She had to make it to a job interview by one thirty. She didn't feel like going out after what that fat bastard did to her, but she needed a job. And Isaiah's probation officer's uncle got her the interview, so she had to go even if she didn't feel like it. Plus, to keep her benefits, she had to prove she was looking for work. That was bullshit, too.

Charity tried on her best clothes. They looked old and beat up. She felt old and beat up, too, from what the landlord did to her. She couldn't remember the last time she bought new clothes for herself. The Goodwill store in Minnepious was better than her old one in Chicago. But she still didn't have enough money to buy clothes for herself. She had to get the kids some new clothes when she got some money. It didn't help that those boys just kept on eating and growing, especially Isaac.

Charity looked at her phone to see what time it was. *Fuck! It was almost twelve thirty!* She had to catch three buses with transfers to get to the community center on the south side for the interview. She slumped back into her couch. The couch sank under her even though she was thin. Her stomach growled, reminding her how hungry she was. There was nothing in the fridge. The kids would get breakfast at school, but yet and still they took whatever was in the fridge before they left.

She looked in the cupboards. All she could find was a can of spaghetti. If she ate that, she wouldn't have anything for the kids when they got home from school. She knew how hungry Isaac and Isaiah would be, but her food stamp card was used up for the month. Charity checked her purse. She had $17.48. That wouldn't get much. If she went to the interview, she wouldn't have time to get food for the kids, and she wouldn't be able to eat anything herself. She looked at her phone again. It was twelve forty-five. She probably wouldn't make it in time for the interview anyhow.

Charity called the community center and asked for Valerie. Valerie was not available, so Charity left a message. She said she was feeling sick and couldn't make it to the interview. "Maybe you could call me back and give me a new time," Charity added before she hung up. She knew Valerie would not call back.

—⚏—

Bunny was running fifteen minutes late for her lunch meeting. She felt good about Eileen's update on the TV news coverage. Eileen and Fred had set up interviews with selected teachers, students, parents and community leaders. This lunch meeting, scheduled a week ago, was a nuisance, but could not be canceled.

Bunny pulled up to the Pleasant Village public housing complex in north Minnepious. "Vinny," she told the district's head of security, who was her chaperone for the day. "This is a sensitive meeting. I'd appreciate it if you could wait outside." She had no intention of bringing a white cop to the meeting.

Vinny nodded. He had no desire to enter the housing project. He was more than familiar with it from his previous career with the Minnepious Police Department. The projects were like a microcosm of the school district: rotten to the core, full of antisocial gangster delinquents. It was no surprise to Vinny that so many MPS students came from the projects.

But Vinny didn't say shit. He had 70,000 reasons to keep his views to himself. On top of his current MPS salary, Vinny enjoyed a fat MPD pension. His career of public service had delivered a suburban home, three college graduates, and a cabin on a lake in northern Minnesoule. No, Vinny would not rock the boat. "You want me to interrupt your meeting if anyone calls?" he asked Bunny.

"No. This won't take long."

Bunny opened the car's trunk. She loved her car, a leased Lexus sedan. In contract negotiations, Bunny's lawyer had convinced the school board they could not afford to allow the district's first African-American superintendent to arrive at meetings looking like a homeless person. What would the Black community think if Bunny did not arrive in style?

Bunny hoisted two grocery bags full of box lunches from the trunk of her Lexus. It had been her idea to schedule the meeting at lunchtime on her adversaries' turf. She tiptoed across the icy parking lot with a bag in each hand. The wind bit her face, stinging her eyes and causing them to water. When she got to the metal exterior door, she put down one bag and rang the buzzer. She wiped her watery eyes and waited.

A face peered through the security glass and chicken wire of the small window. The door remained shut.

Bunny rang the buzzer again.

A second face appeared and the door cracked open. *"What you want?"*

Bunny smiled. The security guard looked like her uncle. "I'm here to see Onyekachukwu."

The security guard stepped back, allowing Bunny to slip through the doorway. He did not help with the grocery bags.

"Thank you," Bunny said, and crossed the hallway to another secure door. She put down the grocery bags and knocked. This time the door opened right away. She did not recognize the man who opened the door. He also made no attempt to help her with the grocery bags. Bunny reached down, picked up the bags, and entered the room. The man who had opened the door left the room.

Onyekachukwu was there. Two other Black women Bunny had seen before were also there. That was not a surprise since Onyekachukwu never met Bunny without a posse. And this was a *big* posse; not that Bunny was small, but these women were *big*.

There was one other woman in the room, who was obviously *not* part of Onyekachukwu's posse. Bunny did not know her. She was young and attractive. She wore a professional outfit. It was obvious that the young professional woman was not from Minnepious. You could tell just by looking at her that she thought she was better than the others.

Bunny placed her grocery bags on the table in the middle of the room. Ignoring the other women, she introduced herself to the young woman. "Hi. I'm Bunny Washington. I don't know you."

The young woman shook Bunny's hand. "I'm Carmen Braithwaite."

"Braithwaite?" Bunny mused. "That's a strange name. Where you from?"

"Brooklyn."

"No. I mean, *originally*."

"Brooklyn."

"You heard her," Onyekachukwu snapped. "She from Brooklyn. Brooklyn, USA."

Bunny glared at Onyekachukwu, who reached into one of the grocery bags and pulled out deli box lunches and pop.

Onyekachukwu opened one of the boxes and peered inside. "These sandwiches have pork?"

"It's written on the box," Bunny replied.

"You know I don't eat pork. I'm a Muslim."

This was the first time Bunny had heard Onyekachukwu claim to be a Muslim. Bunny helped herself to a turkey sandwich box and a Diet Coke. Each box was labeled: turkey, tuna, ham and one roast beef. Bunny had not known how big Onyekachukwu's posse would be, so there were extras, except for diet pop. There were only two diet pops. Those were for Bunny. Inside her box, Bunny found gourmet chips and a large chocolate chip cookie. She nudged aside the apple.

Onyekachukwu grabbed the lone roast beef box before the other women could. The other large women boxed out Braithwaite, who was forced to settle for leftovers. Each woman clutched a box and peered inside.

"There ain't no cookie in mine!" one of the big women exclaimed. "Where's my cookie?"

Bunny put down her own sandwich and opened another lunch box. She fished a large cookie out of the box. "Here, take this one."

The woman took the cookie and put it in her box.

Everyone ate in silence.

When she had finished her sandwich, chips, cookie and Diet Coke, Bunny left her apple on the table. She crushed the trash in her box, and tossed it in a trash can in the corner of the room. "I didn't know Onyekachukwu was a Muslim name," Bunny said to no one in particular.

Onyekachukwu was still eating and her mouth was full. She looked up. She could not decide if Bunny was insulting her, so she kept chewing.

"You all know how much I value your advice," Bunny said, calling the meeting to order. "Is there anything new you all think I should know about?"

Onyekachukwu stopped chewing. She stared at Bunny. "We callin' a school boycott, Bunny."

The superintendent stared back at Onyekachukwu. "Excuse me? What you mean *boycott*?"

"We ain't goin' take it no more, Bunny," Onyekachukwu answered. "This sista here is straight outta Brooklyn, and she's a *civil rights* lawyer. She workin' with the NAACP. She say we don't have to let you miseducate another generation of our precious Black babies." Onyekachukwu paused and glared at the superintendent. "We ain't fallin' for the okey doke no more, Bunny."

The two big women with Onyekachukwu also stared at Bunny.

The girl from Brooklyn—*Braithwaite*—the *civil rights* lawyer—just sat there. *NAACP lawyer, my ass!*

Bunny did not need this shit, not now. Bunny knew the NAACP's Minnepious branch better than they knew their own selves. She was a lifetime member. No way Bunny was going to let some carpetbagging hussy from Brooklyn use the branch to make a name for herself by causing trouble. "I understand your frustration, sister," Bunny assured Onyekachukwu.

"You do not know my frustration!" Onyekachukwu interrupted, shaking her head, her braids snapping like little whips. "You couldn't begin to know my frustration! And don't you *sister* me!" Onyekachukwu paused, her indignation building. "How long we known each other, Bunny? My daddy got you this job. And you actin' more white than that white boy they had in there before you! So don't you *sister* me. And don't talk to me 'bout *you know my frustration.*"

Bunny let Onyekachukwu's tirade run its course. She knew Onyekachukwu just had to blow off some steam. As for the young lawyer, Bunny would have to find out more about her. Then she would decide how to deal with her. The name *Braithwaite* irritated Bunny, though. She knew it was foreign, but she could not place it.

When Onyekachukwu calmed down, Bunny said, "I know where you all are coming from. I'm with you all. You think I don't stay up all night wondering what I can do to make things better? I'm doing my best. It may not be good enough, but I'm doing my best." Bunny paused. "We need to work *together*. When we fight among ourselves, that's what *they* want. That's what they countin' on. You with me?"

Onyekachukwu rocked back in appreciation.

Her posse nodded.

Braithwaite remained unfathomable.

"I've learned a lot since I became superintendent," Bunny continued.

"I know that's right," one of the big women snorted.

"All the research shows that the most important success factor—especially for *our* kids—is attendance." Bunny honed in on Braithwaite. "With homelessness and family mobility being what it is, we have a tough enough time keeping our kids in class. When you all say the word *boycott*, it tells me you don't know your history."

"Are you suggesting," Braithwaite replied in a superior tone. "That a socially conscious school boycott is equivalent to run-of-the-mill truancy?"

Bunny now knew all she needed to know about Braithwaite. That girl needed a hard slap. And Bunny would make sure she got it. Bunny saw no point in prolonging the meeting. She had plenty of other things to do. "I'm telling you what the data shows. I'm here because I believe in our community. I believe in our kids. When you talk about keeping our kids out of school, you sound ignorant. You're gonna make the problem worse, not better."

One of the big women asked, "Bunny, why our kids don't wanna be in school? Why the schools treat 'em so bad?"

Before Bunny could respond, Braithwaite pressed, "Are you saying South Africa's children should *not* have boycotted segregated schools, and just accepted the *Bantu education* forced on them by white South Africans?"

Bunny did not need this. She glared at Braithwaite, then stood up to leave. "I'm sorry you don't understand. You need to think about what I said. Put aside your political agenda, whatever it may be, and put our children first."

Braithwaite also stood up, but not to leave.

Bunny *definitely* did not need this. She put up her hand. "You need to sit back down, *Miss I'm from Brooklyn*. You don't know Minnesoule. We don't need outsiders trying to tell us what to do." She paused and stared hard at the young lawyer. "You think you goin' make people choose sides? Well, I'm tellin' you right now, we don't need that. And one more thing. I don't need *you* to tell me about *South Africa*."

Bunny started to leave, then stopped. Her anger welled up. She pointed at Braithwaite. "Don't you *ever*, *ever* try to tell me about segregation. You understand? I *lived* it."

Bunny turned and glared at Onyekachukwu. "I brought you lunch. And you treat me like this?"

She grabbed the remaining Diet Coke for herself and an extra box lunch for Vinny, then headed for the door.

One of the big women grabbed the other unopened extra box, leaving only the one from which the cookie had been removed.

"I got that one," Onyekachukwu called out, pointing to the last box, as she rushed to intercept Bunny at the door. "Bunny," Onyekachukwu murmured, grasping the superintendent's wrist. "We was just playin' with you."

Bunny glared at Onyekachukwu until the braided woman released her arm. "She's playing *you*," Bunny hissed, glancing toward Braithwaite, then stalked out.

When Bunny got to her car, she gave Vinny his box lunch and borrowed his cell phone. She called a new friend. "Nancy," she said. "It's me, Bunny."

"Bunny!" Nancy Grandishar, the county attorney and daughter of a prominent editorial writer for *The Strib*, exclaimed. She owed a lot to Bunny. With Bunny's support, Grandishar had made a name for herself. The county attorney had designed and implemented an innovative initiative to crack down on minor crimes that eroded quality of life in Minnepious. The initiative relied on a strong partnership between the Hennepious County Attorney's office and Minnepious Public Schools, where perpetrators of minor crimes were bred and festered. By keeping kids in school and off the streets, and holding *parents* accountable for truancy, the school district and county attorney's office had collaborated to drive results.

The philanthropic Minnepious Foundation had also joined the initiative, underwriting a public relations campaign to inform parents they would be prosecuted if their children skipped school. Posters adorned bus shelters. Flyers went to parents in their children's backpacks. The two Black newspapers ran a sponsored series written by Bunny's staff about the importance of school attendance. Public service announcements paid for by the Minnepious Foundation ran every hour on Black radio stations.

The initiative was an unqualified success by any measure. Truancy declined by almost 20 percent. The school district referred 168 cases against delinquent parents to the county attorney's office for prosecution in the first six months. Every one of those referrals had a good outcome. Every case was either resolved informally through a guilty plea or resulted in a conviction for neglect. Most important, the juvenile crime rate in Minnepious plummeted. And accountability fell where it belonged—on the juvenile delinquents and their delinquent parents.

In a series of op-ed pieces, *The Strib* editorial board praised the county attorney's initiative as a *"win-win-win-win."* Grandishar could not have been more pleased by this assessment since she had long harbored ambitions of running for higher office.

"Nancy," Bunny said into her phone. "I just want you to be aware of something that might come up."

"What is it?" Grandishar asked, surprised at Bunny's serious tone.

"This is off the radar, but I just heard some talk of a school boycott. You know, people in the community encouraging kids to skip school. Nancy, you know what the data shows about truancy."

"Your number one problem," the county attorney agreed. "What do you need from me, Bunny?"

"I don't know yet. I just want to keep you in the loop."

"I appreciate the heads up. You have my full support, Bunny. Whatever you need."

"Oh, one more thing,' Bunny added. "There's a young lawyer behind this. She's encouraging kids to skip school. Her name's Braithwaite. She's not from here. You may want to keep an eye on her."

Inside the Pleasant Village housing complex, Carmen was pissed. She did not appreciate being set up by Onyekachukwu. That was what it had been—a setup all the way. She did not know what was going on between Onyekachukwu and Bunny Washington, but Onyekachukwu had clearly used her to get under the superintendent's skin.

This talk of a school boycott was news to Carmen. Onyekachukwu had said nothing about it to her before the meeting. Bunny's angry reaction told Carmen this was not the first time the subject had come up. Onyekachukwu knew how to push the superintendent's buttons, that was for sure. The sooner Carmen got out of this crazy town, the better.

"What you think?" Onyekachukwu asked Carmen. "I told you we could fuck with Bunny."

Carmen just wanted to leave.

"You got a problem?" Onyekachukwu pressed.

"Whatever…"

"Don't you *whatever* me! We just sent a message to Bunny."

"*You* just sent her some kind of message," Carmen corrected.

"You got a problem what that?"

Carmen realized it was pointless to try to reason with Onyekachukwu. "I gotta go."

"Whatever…"

Carmen gathered her blank notepad from the table and pulled on her coat. She said goodbye to Onyekachukwu's friends, Brenda and Latifa. On her way out of the building, she nodded to the security guard and braced for the winter chill.

The wind bit Carmen's face, drying her already ashy skin. She rushed to her car, fumbled with the keys, and creaked open the front door to the old Honda Civic. Once inside, she huddled in the driver's seat. Her numb fingers turned on the engine. She waited for the engine to warm so she could crank up the fan on the heater. She hated the Minnesoule winter. Shivering inside her coat, waiting for the car engine to warm, she cursed her decision to move to Minnesoule.

Carmen wondered how she had let her life get to this point. She had gone from eager, bright but under-prepared high school student in Brooklyn to overachiever at Fordham to improbable winner of the Harvard Law School admissions lottery. And now she was stuck in this frozen tundra?

The plunge began at Harvard. Her expectations had not been realistic. First, the social scene confused her. Flattering interest from all those handsome, intelligent, *new* Black men during her first few weeks of law school turned to "friendship," but nothing more, as all the brothers pursued lighter skinned, less educated prey. Then, she hit the wall academically. Patronizing smiles from white professors and classmates when she spoke in class, pressure-packed essay exams that felt unfair, the questions seemingly unrelated to the course syllabus and class discussion. It was so different from her previous school experiences.

The final straw was her inability to land a decent job. All but a handful of her classmates landed primo jobs, even in a down job market. The few who could not find jobs were either Black or older white students. Carmen's law school grades weren't great. But they weren't bad either. And her degree was still from Harvard, for God's sake. But every job interview brought discomfort and alienation.

Carmen would not have landed her summer associate position in a mid-tier Boston firm but for the intervention of one of her professors, who had gone to law school with the firm's managing partner. Professor Higgins made a phone call after Carmen confided her distress at not being able to find a summer job.

Carmen's summer associate experience had been a disaster. The firm's middle-aged white partners would not talk to her. They even avoided eye contact with her. At the end of the summer, the firm did not offer her a full-time associate position for after graduation. This put Carmen in a precarious position. Unlike virtually all her classmates, Carmen entered her third year of law school burdened not only with crushing student loan debt, but also with no realistic prospect for a high paying job upon graduation.

Mike Swenson and FHZ had bailed her out. But what had seemed like a blessing at the time now felt more like a curse. As she huddled in her old Honda Civic, Carmen shuddered at the cold and the memories.

Harvard Law School had punished Carmen for her dreams. It had shaken her, stolen her confidence.

She glanced at herself in the rearview mirror. From an effervescent child of the Caribbean, her Jamaican mother's darling and the apple of her Trinidadian father's eye, she had grown into what she saw now in the mirror—an uncertain 27-year-old shadow of herself.

How could she have let herself be abused by that nasty old witch Bunny Washington? How could she have allowed that fool Onyekachukwu to use her? The old Carmen—the *Brooklyn* Carmen— would never have tolerated it. Carmen blinked back tears. She was alone in the car and felt for the first time in her life alone in the world.

Carmen thought back on her childhood. Trips to Trinidad and Jamaica; the Labor Day Caribbean carnival on Brooklyn's Eastern Parkway; smells of roti and dhalpourie; the sweet taste of soursop and sorrel, ackee and saltfish; brunch at her grandma's; coming home after curfew on prom night with the whole extended family out on the front porch waiting for her. These sweet images now haunted her, mocked her.

What scared Carmen was not that she had shied away from confrontation with the superintendent. Given Onyekachukwu's petty manipulation and games, it was unlikely Carmen could have anticipated the superintendent's bizarre behavior. There was obviously a context, a history, that only an insider would comprehend. And Carmen did not want to be an insider, not here in Hicksville, Minnesoule. What scared her was that she had let herself get caught up in this madness at all.

Carmen had always fancied herself untouched by the oppression that, in her view, enfeebled African-Americans. It was not that she thought she was better than African-Americans. She did not. She was proud of her Black identity. But there was something she had that most African-Americans did not.

Carmen had a West Indian heritage. Her ancestors had thrown out the white colonialists, a prospect unimaginable to African-Americans. In Carmen's mind, it was no accident that Stokely Carmichael had been the one to coin the phrase "Black Power" in the 1960s. Like Carmen, he was a child of the Caribbean. Like Carmen, he was Trinidadian.

Carmen's West Indian heritage had provided a haven from American racism during her childhood in New York. Her culture offered safety and comfort, something she could no longer find as an adult. Maybe that was just the price of growing up. Or maybe it was something else, something uglier. Could it be that the idealistic West Indian girl was becoming an oppressed African-American woman?

As she sat shivering in her old beat up car, Carmen realized she would have to confront this feeling sooner or later. If she did not, it would destroy all that her childhood had promised. She thought again about Bunny Washington. The superintendent had acted as if she had a lot to lose. How else could you explain her behavior at the meeting? If there was one thing Carmen did not like, it was a bully. As a child, she had dreamed of becoming a lawyer to punish bullies.

Carmen could tell the Minnepious superintendent had everything invested in her position and her reputation. She knew the superintendent had a hard inner core and would fight to the end, if threatened. But Carmen was from Brooklyn. Brooklyn, USA. If she were ever going to confront her malaise, what better time than now, while she could still salvage her dreams.

Carmen looked at herself again in the rearview mirror. This time, she saw something she had not seen in a long time. She saw a sparkle in her eyes. She smiled, forgetting the cold. If Bunny Washington wanted a fight, so be it. Carmen knew deep down that the superintendent was a dinosaur, a relic of a bye-gone era. Bunny Washington would be no match for her.

MINNISSIPPI

Chapter 4

Eileen stared at the bank of televisions in the war room. She could not believe what she was seeing. The 5 o'clock news was a disaster beyond reckoning. How could it have gone so wrong between the 12 o' clock news and 5? The day was a parable of urban public education: no good deed went unpunished.

Eileen stared at the solemn anchor on the Channel 4 news:

"…*Former Minnepious North High basketball star Abu-Rahim Rahim was arrested today in Las Vegas for possession of marijuana and disorderly conduct. Rahim, who had just hours before been honored by the NCAA as a candidate for National Player of the Year, was allegedly caught by Las Vegas police in a limousine with notorious rapper Big Daddy DeeDee. The police report cites marijuana use, open liquor and three underage girls…*"

Eileen surfed the other stations. The Abu-Rahim scandal was everywhere, preempting Bunny, her triumph eviscerated by profligate pathologies of the ghetto. Reluctantly, Eileen made the call. "Give me Bunny," she told Vinny.

"Can I call you back in a minute?" Bunny asked.

She was in a meeting with disgruntled principal Chris Hardwell. She had personally hired Hardwell after a request from an old friend in Mississippi. Bunny understood the need to do small favors. Favors were her currency, her life blood. But Hardwell was not doing his part. He could not adapt to "Minnesoule Nice." The idiot was only now beginning to figure out that *Minnesoule Nice* wasn't nice at all.

"Bunny, it can't wait," Eileen sighed. "It's bad news…about Abu-Rahim Rahim."

Bunny did not react in front of Hardwell.

Eileen wondered if the superintendent was still on the line.

"Eileen," Bunny hissed, turning away from Hardwell. "I'm cleaning up one of your messes right now." Bunny paused to let her displeasure sink in. "Now you're calling me with more bad news?"

Eileen did not understand what "mess" Bunny was talking about. She ignored the comment and plowed forward, knowing there was no easy way to do this. "Rahim just got busted for drugs." Eileen paused. "It's the top news story."

Bunny did not say a thing. She squeezed the phone, trying not to let Hardwell see her distress. She felt a wave of anger and revulsion. Nausea swept into her head. She stared at Hardwell until he dissolved into the background. Bunny reflected on where she had been, where she was now, and where a Black woman in America could ever realistically hope to go. Her stoicism protected her, kept her from becoming just another bitter Black victim of white racism.

The revulsion and anger subsided. The nausea persisted. A migraine would soon follow. Bunny swallowed and took a deep breath. She wiped emotion from her voice in front of the ungrateful Black man in her office. "I see," she said, her voice neutral. She had waited so long for this day, had worked so hard to make it happen.

She turned to Hardwell. "Chris, I'm sorry, but I have to take this call. It's urgent." She glanced toward the door.

Hardwell took his time leaving her office. Bunny made a mental note to deal with him later.

When she was alone, Bunny collapsed and exploded. "That little punk! That little shit! After all I did for him, I can't believe he did this to me!"

Eileen absorbed the outburst. There was a long pause.

"I'm sorry," Bunny finally murmured. "It's been a long day." She sighed. "It's been a long year."

It's been a long life.

That she could not say. There were boundaries between Eileen's world and hers that could not, and *should not*, be crossed. Bunny reminded herself that as a survivor of Jim Crow, she would always experience bad with the good.

Eileen took a deep breath. Bunny's bitter outburst receded to a private place in Eileen's mind, where it would not interfere with their day-to-day interactions. Eileen prided herself on this ability to compartmentalize. It was a necessary survival skill in this gritty world. "Sorry, Bunny. I'm really sorry."

—⁊⁊—

Carmen could not remember the last time she had been on a date. Hell, she couldn't even remember the last time she had eaten at a fancy restaurant. The *Pan-Asian Fusionista Bistro* might not have been her first choice, but at least it was a change from the same boring places and the same boring people.

"What do you think of it?"

Carmen was lost in her thoughts. "Huh?"

"The satay," Bob repeated. "What do you think of it?"

"Yeah, it's good."

"Compared to other satay, or compared to something else?"

Carmen was not sure what he meant.

"Are you into Southeast Asian food? We have so many great Vietnamese and Laotian restaurants in Minnepious."

Carmen glanced at the waiters, who were white. *Am I missing something?* "This doesn't seem very Vietnamese to me."

Bob laughed. "The food or the restaurant?"

"Both."

"I thought the menu would impress you."

Carmen took another bite of the satay. "I'm not too into people trying to impress me. You should be comfortable with who you are."

Bob thought for a moment. "I'm into being more than what the world expects of me."

"And what does *the world* expect of you?"

"Depends."

"On?"

"Who we're talking about. The broader world, or my world."

"Does the broader world really care about you?"

"Depends what I do."

Carmen frowned. "Meaning?"

"Take you and me, for example."

"I didn't know there was a *you and me* yet."

"Maybe not yet," Bob grinned. "But let's imagine the possibility."

Carmen was noncommittal.

"Well, anyway," Bob continued. "I don't think the broader world cares about that sort of thing any more."

Carmen was not impressed with the phrase "that sort of thing."

Bob looked around. All the other diners were immersed in food or conversation. "I mean, no one here seems to care."

"What about *your* world?" Carmen asked.

Bob thought about it for a moment. "I don't know what my family would say. I mean, if we started dating seriously."

"It's a little early for that."

"But what I'm getting at is how much should we care about what other people think about us?"

Carmen frowned again. "I don't care about that."

"Why not?"

"Because I can't control it."

"But it affects you."

"Does it?"

"It does." Bob paused. "On some level, you should care about what others think of you."

Carmen wondered whether he really believed this. Or was he just saying it to test himself, and her? "How do you know I'm affected by what other people think of me?"

"I'd like to think you care about what I think."

Carmen shrugged. "Maybe I do, maybe I don't. Maybe I'm here because I have nothing better to do on a Thursday night."

"I don't think so."

"Oh? Why not?"

"Because you look cute."

"Excuse me?"

"You made an effort to look nice."

"No I didn't. This is how I always look."

"Damn," Bob exhaled. "Then I am a lucky guy."

"Yes you are," Carmen smiled.

The waiter brought the main courses. On Bob's recommendation, they had ordered a spicy Malaysian calamari dish and a Thai green curry. The waiter lingered near Carmen as he placed the dishes on the table. She ignored him, intrigued by Bob's infatuation. It felt nice.

—⁓—

Bunny arrived fashionably late to the cocktail party in her honor at the Minnepious Foundation. Kermit Casson, Chief Executive Officer of the Foundation, had arranged the party on short notice. Kermit was always there for Bunny.

The lobby of his Foundation shimmered like a boutique five-star hotel. It exuded wealth, exclusivity, comfort, discretion. Those who served the public needed this refuge from the snooping, prying scrutiny all public institutions received these days, none more so than urban public schools.

It disgusted Bunny that such scrutiny was applied to the meager opportunities African-Americans enjoyed in a white-dominated society. *Niggardly* was a good word to describe the attitude of white politicians, media, business leaders and other opinion leaders toward her urban school district. She shuddered at the word, with its racist implications and its guarantee of shrinking financial support for a school district run by and for Black people.

Bunny plastered a smile on her face and glided into the party. She spied Kermit in a corner with a champagne glass in one hand and a white benefactor in the other. Keen not to interrupt his rap, she steered clear. As she turned toward the middle of the lobby, a firm hand grasped her elbow.

"Bunny!" Rachel Offerman welcomed the guest of honor. Offerman was the wife of the aptly named Victor Offerman, billionaire entrepreneur and kingmaker in the Minnesoule Democratic

Party. She embraced Bunny and kissed her on both cheeks, in the manner of the French.

From an initial exploratory political fundraiser to a victory (but not concession) speech, the presence of Rachel and Victor Offerman was de rigueur, representing the Democratic Party's unofficial imprimatur. The Offermans' presence was a seal of approval, their absence the kiss of death. For Bunny, the Offermans were always there.

Bunny glanced around the room. She saw a *Who's Who* of city politics and the Democratic Party. Every school board member was there, as were the head of the teachers union, the Mayor, all but two members of the city council, the Editor-in-Chief of *The Strib*, CEOs from three of the state's eight Fortune 500 companies, the CEOs of every local philanthropic foundation, and a smattering of opinion leaders, has-beens and hangers-on. All the people you needed to run a major city were there.

Bunny contemplated the irony that she had become one of those people. No mean accomplishment, given her humble upbringing.

"Everyone!" Rachel Offerman called out over the din of conversation, her arm snug around the superintendent. "Look what I found! She thought she could sneak in here unnoticed!"

Laughter drowned out the few remaining conversations.

Rachel Offerman had the floor. She paused, allowing anticipation to build. She raised a champagne glass in her left hand, still holding Bunny with her right. "Of course you have all heard the wonderful news," Offerman beamed. "The timing could not be more propitious. We are a nation in desperate need of good news these days."

Heads nodded. Many in the audience murmured approval.

"I have to say, the rest of the country is about to discover what we have long known about our dear Bunny." Offerman gazed at the superintendent, whom she had known for over thirty years. "Our dear, dear Bunny…Another wonderful Minnepious secret revealed to the world."

Offerman squeezed Bunny as the gathering applauded.

Bunny wiped away tears. She prided herself on her emotional

control. Yet here she was, unable to staunch the flow. The applause did not help, tapping into a deep vein of emotion. Bunny would have preferred to slip into the party unnoticed and field congratulations one-on-one. She was embarrassed by this sort of tearful display. She stared at the marble floor of the Foundation lobby, wiping away tears.

Rachel Offerman saw Bunny's discomfort, and raised her hand in a protective gesture. Her voice so soft the gathering pressed closer, Offerman stage whispered, "It's easy to feel good when one of your own is recognized."

People nodded and again murmured approval.

"But when it's someone as unpretentious, as down-to-earth as Bunny, it just takes your breath away."

The crowd gasped, as if losing its breath.

"It takes your breath away," Offerman continued. "Because you realize how far Bunny has come. And really, how far we all have come. I met Bunny at the University, when she first arrived from Mississippi. I'll never forget how Bunny had the courage to look me in the eye. It reminded me of my own humanity at a time when too many in our country took our privilege for granted, as if it were the natural order of things.

"But when I saw Bunny's struggle, it made me pause. Bunny forced those of us who have never known such struggle to reflect on our own good fortune. For Bunny, college represented an existential challenge, academically and socially. Yet in her struggles, Bunny served as a conscience to us all.

"Any time I felt sorry for myself over the slightest injustice, Bunny showed me what injustice really was. Alone in cold Minnesoule, Bunny overcame odds she had no business even trying to surmount. But Bunny never complained. No, not Bunny...

"When faced with injustice I could never dream of, Bunny simply worked harder. She had no choice. She had no safety net, no family to catch her if she failed.

"When you look at Bunny, you are looking not at a mere woman, but at the eternal triumph of the human spirit." Offerman paused.

Some in the audience, taking Offerman's message to heart, lowered their heads in shame. After an appropriate interval, they surreptitiously made eye contact with others, and the shame dissipated. A renewal of hope circulated, unbidden and unspoken, through the gathering.

"I watched Bunny rise through the school system," Offerman continued, her voice still little more than a whisper, but her spirit rising. "Hoping against hope that she would someday be recognized for what she means to us. I hoped against hope because there are so few Bunnies in this world, and fewer still recognized for what they do, for what they give us, for what they *mean* to us." Offerman paused, on the verge of tears, tears of joy.

"Those of you who know me," she said, aware that everyone in the room knew her. "Know that I think of Bunny as my little sister." She paused again, struggling to maintain decorum. "We may not have been born to the same mother...or even on the same side of the railway tracks..." She smiled. "But don't you ever doubt we're sisters."

Offerman squeezed Bunny again.

A murmur swept across the crowd. Offerman rarely disappointed, and this was turning into a speech for the ages. Those in attendance could envision one day boasting to their friends and admirers that they had been part of this momentous occasion.

Offerman scanned the familiar, eager faces. "What have I learned from my little sister? Duty, humility and sacrifice, for a start. Bunny has taught me the most important lessons of life, day in and day out, through weeks...years...and now decades.

"If truth be told, I cannot hope to understand *myself* without Bunny. It is through her selfless example that my own life gains meaning.

"As you leave this gathering tonight and return to your daily work, your daily lives, think not what Bunny has done for you; think what you can do to honor her. Reflect on how lucky we are, nay, how lucky *you* are, to have Bunny. And reflect on how lucky our children are to have Bunny."

Tears freely cleansed the marble floor of the Foundation lobby.

Bunny no longer cared that she was crying, for they were all crying together. Bunny had never experienced anything like this. She felt the warmth, the intense belonging, of this moment. Bunny beamed at the crowd through her tears. It had not been an easy journey, could never be easy. Without these courageous people, who had put their reputations on the line to support her, Bunny would never have had the opportunity to succeed. That she had been tapped for the top education post in the nation was their achievement as much as her own. This was her village.

Rachel Offerman stood aside and applauded Bunny. She took no small pride in the audience's emotional response to her speech. She envisioned her speech being hailed for years to come: its tone, its modesty, its subtlety, its restraint capturing the spirit of an age of oratorical austerity.

The crowd surged toward Bunny and Offerman, grasping hands in turn, lavishing affection. Bunny worked the room. She flattered some, cajoled others, and grudgingly accepted praise. When she got to Eileen, she paused. Eileen looked terrible, as if she had run into a wall. "You okay?" Bunny whispered.

Eileen nodded and wiped tears from her cheeks.

"Take some time off later this week."

—⁂—

"Hey, what you doin'!" Charity screamed at Isaac. "We eatin' that tonight!" She grabbed the bag of Doritos from her youngest son, who got a last handful of chips into his mouth. She felt bad doing this to him. She knew he was hungry. But they wouldn't have enough for dinner if he ate the whole bag now. Plus, the other kids wouldn't get none. "Sorry, baby," Charity tried to console her youngest son.

Isaac did not react.

"We havin' mac and cheese tonight," she promised. "I got some extra cheese, too. Goin' make it the way you like it."

Isaac looked hungry. Charity was pretty sure he could hold on till dinner, though. She'd slip him her part, too, when the other kids weren't looking. She already had a dollar value meal for lunch at McDonald's instead of going to the job interview. That would hold her till tomorrow. The day after, her food stamp card would be refilled. She just had to hold on till then.

Taking the bag of Doritos with her so it would not tempt Isaac, Charity went to check on Isaiah and Lakeesha. They were in their room, supposed to be doing homework.

"Hey mama," Lakeesha greeted her when Charity opened the door. Lakeesha was lying on the bed.

Isaiah sat on the floor.

It looked like Lakeesha tried to slip something under her covers.

"What you got there?" Charity demanded.

"Nothin'," Lakeesha answered.

Charity walked over to the bed and rummaged through the covers. "Don't you *nothin'* me," she scolded, pulling a magazine from under the covers. "Where you get this?"

It was a fashion magazine with a skinny white girl smiling on the cover.

"I found it."

"You steal it from school?"

Charity threw the magazine at her daughter. It landed next to Lakeesha on the bed.

"No, mama," Lakeesha replied. "They gave it to me."

Charity looked around the messy bedroom. She wondered what other contraband she might find. She had enough trouble as it was. She didn't need her daughter getting into more. Sure enough, Charity spotted a wooden doll with a fancy dress on it and some fancy looking drawings of clothes. She could never buy something like that for her daughter. She could only imagine what her daughter might have done to score it.

Charity would nip this in the bud, that was for damn sure. She placed the bag of Doritos on the floor and scooped up the doll and drawings. Menacing her with the contraband, Charity grabbed her daughter's arm.

"Stop, mama!" Lakeesha cried out. "You're hurting me!"

Isaiah took advantage of the commotion to grab the bag of Doritos. He ate them as quietly as he could while he watched his mother and his sister.

Charity shoved the doll and drawings in her daughter's face. It gave her no joy to do this, but she would not let Lakeesha fall into the Devil's ways, especially so young. It was one thing for a boy to get in trouble. That was expected. But a girl was another thing altogether. Charity had made those same mistakes herself and paid a heavy price. She would not let her daughter fall into that mess.

"Where you get these?" Charity shouted. Her hand shook with fury. The only thing stopping her from destroying the evidence was the possibility the school might suspect Lakeesha took the doll and drawings.

Lakeesha sobbed. "I made them."

This lie further infuriated Charity. After all she did for her children, the idea that they would lie to her face was more than she could stomach. These ungrateful children had no idea what she went through for them. She hoped they would never know.

Charity threw the doll to the ground and stepped on it. The fancy little dress split and tore. She ripped up the drawings. "Don't you ever lie to me again!" Charity stormed out of the bedroom.

Lakeesha sat on the bed, tears rolling down her cheeks. She did not know where she would be able to find more material to make a new dress for her doll. She pushed the fashion magazine off the bed. It fell on the floor next to Isaiah and the empty Doritos bag.

—∞—

The school board meeting was going to be packed. Reverend Hal Ballman had seen to that, which was quite an accomplishment on a Friday evening when folk had plenty of better things to do. The good reverend had summoned his flock and put out the word to other ministers, too. This was Reverend Hal's show. He needed a live audience, the right audience. He might be new to the school board, but he was not new to politics, not as a reverend in the Black community.

Reverend Hal glanced along the dais at Bunny. He knew she wanted to take him down. He was not fooled by her fake ways. Bunny was like every other ambitious Black woman he had ever known. She couldn't get no man to love her. So she was out for herself. He might play along for a while, but he knew the score. The last thing Bunny wanted was for him to expose the truth. Reverend Hal was the real Mandingo, unafraid to tell the truth, even if Bunny and her bosses in the white power structure couldn't handle it.

Last spring, when Reverend Hal announced his intention to run for school board, Bunny whispered all around town that someone else should run for Willie Grier's school board seat. But Reverend Hal knew the Good Lord struck Willie down for a reason, and he intended to fulfill his destiny and do the Lord's bidding.

He glanced over at Bunny again, sitting there like she owned the joint. *Bunny actually thought she could interfere with the Lord's plans?* Talk about stupid!

Reverend Hal had eyes and ears everywhere in the community. He was not doing this for himself. As a man of the cloth, he served a higher purpose. He would show the meddling superintendent that the Good Lord worked in mysterious ways.

Bunny just could not tolerate a proud Black man stepping into her world. That was the real problem. No, Reverend Hal was not like those predictable downtown Negroes the Democratic Party scraped off the bottom of some white man's shoe to "represent" the Black community. No, sir. Reverend Hal was the anti-Tom, every ambitious Black woman's worst nightmare.

Unlike those downtown Negroes, and Bunny herself, Reverend Hal was still rooted in the community. So what if he didn't put his own children in those sorry public schools. That was the whole reason he needed to get on the school board—to make the schools safe again for Black children. Only an idiot would put his kids in those sorry Minnepious schools if he had a choice.

Today, at this school board meeting, Reverend Hal would start the reform process, with or without Bunny's help. Today, he would strip the white man's dirty little secret buck-naked. No wonder Bunny was all uptight. He shivered at the thought of the fat old prune naked, answering to the white man. Not a pretty sight.

Reverend Hal would bust this bad boy wide open. That's what he had been elected to do.

This wasn't about Bunny, though, even if she was a shameless hussy. As the Good Lord taught, pride was the deadliest sin. The good reverend was simply doing the Lord's bidding by taking Bunny down a peg or two. Reverend Hal smiled at the thought of glorifying the Lord by punking Bunny.

These prideful Black women were killing Black men. Like burrowing parasites, they destroyed the community from the inside out. No living being in God's creation looked more hideous, more unholy, more like the Jezebel herself, than a prideful Black woman who wandered from her people and stripped herself buck-naked just because them kinky white men in business suits had what all Black women wanted: power.

Black men were different. After two decades serving his urban flock, Reverend Hal was nothing if not an expert on Black men. Black men wanted more than mere love, especially if that love came from a diminished Black woman. That's what caused the problem between Black women and men. Sistas could not accept that their love would never be enough.

What more did Black men want?

They wanted to be accepted as equals. Not by diminished, desperate Black women. Black men wanted the real deal, to be accepted by whites. But of course, that was the one thing whites wouldn't never allow. That's why brothers were always angry. A Black woman's love can't never take away that anger. Ask any sista: it's hard to love an angry Black man.

Bunny acted different, though. She acted like she thought she was better than Black men. She looked like a Black woman, but she acted like a white man. Far as Reverend Hal was concerned, you couldn't tell if Bunny was a she or a he.

Thinking about Bunny made Reverend Hal's head hurt. He stopped thinking about her and focused instead on the show he was about to put on. He rehearsed his first few statements. That was the key. You had to hit the right notes from the start.

Reverend Hal knew a thing or two about connecting with an audience. Whether in church or on television, it was the same. You had to capture your audience's attention in the first thirty seconds or people would switch to some bootylicious channel.

Reverend Hal rechecked the published school board meeting agenda. The report on African-American student achievement was supposed to be the third item of business. Reverend Hal's audience could not wait that long.

The meeting room filled up fast. Reverend Hal greeted his friends and members of his congregation as they showed up. He nodded at the reporters from both Black community newspapers. He shook hands with the guys from Black radio and cable TV talk shows and reminded them he would be available later for interviews. As he shook hands, Reverend Hal promised fireworks. *Hell-fire and brimstone!* He would light up the white bosses and expose their okey doke Negro lackeys. He felt a surge of adrenaline as the meeting came to order and the cable access television cameras rolled.

Board Chair Julie Harmer struck her gavel on the dais to start the meeting. Like Bunny, Harmer was another fat prune, but at least she was white. Unlike a Black Jezebel, you never let your guard down against a white hag.

"Point of order!" Reverend Hal exclaimed.

"Excuse me?" Director Harmer paused, surprised at the outburst.

"I need to clarify something."

The board chair did not respond. She grimaced. It was a half-smile she used to defend herself against ad hominem attacks. As Minnepious school board chair and a prominent defender of urban public education, Harmer had grown accustomed to unfounded attacks. Between black grandstanders, like Reverend Ballman, and Republican right wing racists, there was not much middle ground left for people of good conscience. The seemingly insurmountable challenges of urban education called for collaboration, not conflict and unseemly spectacle.

Harmer just sat there with a shit-eating grin, so Reverend Hal took the floor. He looked straight into the cable access television camera with the red light indicating it was live. He cleared his voice. "For those of you watching this meeting, you won't be disappointed. Today, we goin' tell the truth about Minnepious schools."

The other board members glanced at each other and at Bunny, who shook her head to indicate she had no idea what Reverend Hal was doing. It was bad enough that Reverend Hal had requested this special Friday night board meeting, which disrupted everyone's social calendars. But it was absolutely taboo for any board member to sandbag the others at a public meeting by going off script.

If school board members disagreed about policy or anything else, there was an unwritten rule that those disagreements had to be hashed out in private, behind closed doors. For years, every major policy move had been debated in private, disagreements ironed out, and a consensus decision presented to the public. Reverend Ballman appeared to be tossing that convention out the window.

Like passengers on a hijacked airplane, the other board members stared at Reverend Ballman, realizing that a malevolent, previously underestimated adversary had taken control. This new board member, elected without grassroots vetting or *legitimate* Democratic Party support, was now in charge of the meeting.

With the television cameras focused on him, Reverend Hal intoned, "For those of you who don't know me, I'm Reverend Ballman. You elected me to the school board so we can straighten some things out. Well, first, we gotta understand the problem that needs straightenin'. Tonight, we goin' show you that problem, and strip it down. All the way down. No lies. No tricky stuff. Just God's truth. So stick around. Don't touch that remote! You won't be disappointed."

The other school board members stared at Reverend Ballman, aghast. They had no idea what he was up to.

Bunny bit her lip. This was going to be fun. She could have spared Reverend Hal the embarrassment. But she was pretty sure the good reverend needed to learn humility the hard way. Arrogance and pride were deadly sins, as a man of God should know. She slipped a note to Board Chair Harmer.

Harmer read the note: *"Let him go."* She grinned.

"Director Ballman," Harmer inquired. "Do you have a proposed modification to our agenda?"

"Miss Board Chair," Reverend Hal responded. "I have a proposed modification *to this school district.*"

"Very well," Harmer grimaced. "You have the floor."

Reverend Hal turned back to the television camera. "People of Minnepious, sit tight. Prepare yourself to learn the truth!" Reverend Hal paused to let the suspense build, then turned to face Bunny. "Madame Superintendent, would you let the people know the results of our investigation into the truth about African-American student achievement?"

Bunny had never before been addressed as *Madame Superintendent.* "I would be pleased to share this information, Director Ballman."

She turned to the front row of the meeting room, where her senior staff sat. "Dean, could you present the summary of the report?"

Dean Loofa, the burly, bearded director of statistics for the district, opened his laptop computer and approached the podium. He had been doing variations of this presentation for nearly three decades. He knew to ignore the histrionics of school board members. Director Ballman was merely the latest incarnation of the earnest, outraged black board member determined to expose the "root cause" of the achievement gap.

No one knew better than Loofa that the black-white achievement gap never narrowed. Loofa's approach to presenting student achievement data was similarly consistent. Loofa liked to think of himself as a kind of educational reverse proctologist, massaging data so when it emerged, it did not make the superintendent look, and smell, like shit.

Loofa turned on the laptop projector and opened his PowerPoint presentation.

"Excuse me," Reverend Hal interrupted. "I want to thank you on behalf of the community for what you are about to show us."

Loofa nodded, smart enough not to say anything. He displayed the first slide. "Madam Chair, Directors, Superintendent, members of the community," the statistician began. "The information I am about to report has been prepared at the request of the board and disaggregates student performance among African-American students by separating native born African-American from African born students…"

"Hold up," Reverend Hal interrupted. "Let me stop you right there."

Loofa folded his hands behind his back and waited. This sort of interruption by a board member was unconventional but not unprecedented.

"Let's get some things straight," Reverend Hal clarified for the television audience. He pointed to himself and looked at the bearded statistician. "First of all, *I* am the one who requested this report. Isn't that right?"

Loofa did not appreciate being cross-examined. "I will accept your representation on that, Director Ballman."

"Darn straight, you will," Reverend Hal snorted. "Now, I need to straighten you out about something else. You need to understand, Luther, there's a whole lotta folk in the community tunin' in tonight. You got that?"

For all his experience, Loofa was beginning to feel like a deer in headlights.

"That means you goin' have to speak plain English. Don't obliterate the truth with fancy words. We need some plain English. You got that?"

Loofa knew better than to say what he really thought. "Absolutely."

Reverend Hal did not like the white man's tone. He was pretty sure the man was fucking with him, but he decided to let it slide, for now. "All right then. I'm goin' translate what you said in plain English. What you goin' show us is how Samolians is pullin' down African-Americans."

Loofa glanced at Bunny for help. This was definitely beyond the scope of his job description.

The superintendent did not react.

Loofa frowned. *Bitch.* "I would prefer to let the data speak for itself."

"Let's do that then," Reverend Hal agreed, feeling magnanimous toward this uncomfortable white man who was about to serve the cause of Black liberation. "Let the data speak, brother Luther. Let it speak truth."

It occurred to Loofa that the district should start drug testing board members.

"Just remember," Reverend Hal reminded the white statistician again. "Keep it real. Folk in the community need some truth, even if it's *hard* truth."

"Amen, brother!" someone shouted from the back of the room.

Reverend Hal tipped his head to acknowledge the support. The people were enjoying the show.

Loofa ignored the commotion and clicked on his next slide, which displayed a pie chart with the total number of students in the district, divided by race. The slide showed 52% African-American students, 21% white students, 14% Latino students, 8% Asian-American students, and 5% American-Indian students.

"This is the racial breakdown of students in our district," Loofa explained slowly, as if speaking to a dimwitted child. *Is that simple enough for you, asshole?*

"Excuse me," Reverend Hal interjected.

Loofa paused, wondering if the man was a mind reader, too.

"Why don't you break down that *so-called* African-American category for our television audience." As an aside to the television audience, the reverend confided, "Now we goin' hear some *real* truth, brothers and sisters."

"That's my next slide," Loofa mumbled under his breath. He wondered how much more of this Bunny expected him to endure. This sort of grandstanding and race-baiting drove longtime employees to look for greener pastures in suburban districts, where they would be appreciated, not harassed, for their competence.

"Well get to it," Reverend Hal demanded.

Bunny knew Loofa was irritated. She considered intervening, but decided instead to let nature take its course. As much as she wanted to protect her senior staff, Bunny could not afford to be seen by a television audience disrespecting the school board's only Black member.

Loofa's next slide showed another pie chart. "When we further break down the ethnic identities of African-Americans, we see that native-born African-Americans are 92% of our African-American students, and foreign-born students account for a mere 8% of African-Americans in the district."

Loofa couldn't help slipping in the word "mere" in case Ballman was too stupid to grasp the significance of this data—that native-born Black students so outnumbered foreign-born Black students as to render the impact of Somali student performance on overall Black student achievement, statistically speaking, *irrelevant.*

Oblivious, Reverend Hal plowed ahead. "Okay," he translated for the television audience. "When you say *foreign-born*, what you really mean is *Samolians*. Am I right?"

Loofa had no clue what the man was talking about.

Bunny jumped in. "Dean, I believe board member Ballman was asking if the foreign-born African-Americans category includes our *Somali* students."

Reverend Hal shot Bunny an evil look. He did not appreciate Jezebel butting in.

"Yes," Loofa responded. "Somali students would be included in the 8% of foreign-born African-American students." The statistician paused. "Unless of course they are of Somali ancestry, but were born here."

Reverend Hal was not sure what the white man meant. He suspected the statistician was trying to make him look bad.

Bunny perceived Reverend Ballman's confusion. "Dean," she intervened again. "Why don't you show us how native-born and foreign-born African-American students do on the state's standardized achievement tests."

"Right," Loofa agreed. He just wanted this abomination to end. Going to the next slide, Loofa showed student achievement—if it could be called that—for African-American students, disaggregated by place of birth, either native or foreign born. "As you can see from these numbers," Loofa interpreted. "38 percent of native-born African-American students passed the state graduation tests last year. By contrast, 62 percent of foreign-born Black students passed…"

"Excuse me!" Reverend Hal interrupted. This slide did not make sense. There was some trickery going on here. No way Samolians could be doing better than African-Americans. Reverend Hal knew he should not have trusted this white man. "You all think I don't know what you're up to? You all mixin' Samolians into the African-American category! Thought you could get away with that? In the old days, they used to be anti-miscegenation laws 'gainst that sort of thing."

Again, Loofa had no idea what Reverend Ballman was talking about. "I'm sorry?"

"How can you say Samolians aren't the ones bringing down African-American test scores since you mixed in Samolians that were born here with *real* African-Americans?"

Loofa began to feel nauseated. He breathed deeply and visualized himself in a suburban district that held its experienced chief statistician in high esteem.

"How many Samolians you snuck into the native-born category?" Reverend Hal sneered. "'Cause you guessin' they mighta been born here?"

Loofa looked at Bunny, desperate for help.

She looked away.

Fuck this! He was sending his résumé to suburban districts on Monday. "Well, technically," Loofa explained. "If Somalis are born in this country, they *are* African-American."

"I knew it!" Reverend Hal shouted, triumphant. He glared at Bunny as if he had caught her naked on top of Luther. Now *that* was a scary thought. The reverend turned to the television cameras. "Stay tuned, y'all. We onto somethin'. We goin' get to the bottom of this mess at our next meeting. Stay tuned!"

Bunny grimaced. She had no intention of turning school board meetings into *The Reverend Ballman Show* with a new episode every two weeks. The reverend was a tough nut. But if there was one thing she was sure of, she would crack him.

Carmen sat quietly at the back of the packed room, observing the circus that passed for a school board meeting. She could not believe the dysfunction. It made her wonder if there was any rational way to deal with these people.

—⟋⟍—

Lakeesha was still hungry after dinner, but at least she found some thread to stitch up Princess' dress. It didn't look nice like before, but there was no use crying over spilt milk. That's what her mama would say for sure.

Lakeesha felt bad about the Doritos. Isaac cried hard when he found out Isaiah ate them all. That was wrong for Isaiah to eat all the Doritos. He knew how much Isaac liked them. Mama got real worked up about that. She said she gonna kick Isaiah out the house. She always say stuff like that, but she don't really mean it.

The mac and cheese was okay, but Lakeesha didn't like cheese too much. The cheese always made her stomach hurt. And it made her fart. Well, that would serve Isaiah right since he would have to smell her farts all night. Lakeesha farted real loud. It was a nice one. Stinky too.

"Damn!" Isaiah shouted, holding his nose. He had to sleep on the floor. There was only space for one bed in the room. "Mama tole you not to eat stuff what got milk in it."

"That's nasty, Princess!" Lakeesha scolded her doll, giggling. "Don't be fartin' no more!"

"That weren't Princess," Isaiah corrected. "Don't blame yo' farts on her."

Lakeesha farted again. "I tole you to stop, Princess!" She giggled.

"It ain't funny!" Isaiah screamed. *"Mama! Lakeesha fartin' again! And she blamin' it on that stupid doll!"*

Lakeesha giggled and held Princess tight.

—⟋⟍—

Bunny and Julie Harmer had dinner together, as they did after every board meeting. It was an informal way to debrief and stay on the same page. Eileen usually attended, as a sort of amanuensis, to keep an unpublished record of their discussions. They always ate at the same place, *The Nordeast Diner*, an institution in northeast Minnepious. The menu never changed, and neither did their orders.

Bunny tucked into her pastrami sandwich. She loved the dill pickles made on site that accompanied this deli favorite. Julie ate a grilled cheese sandwich. The cheese was extra sharp, homemade, from an organic family farm in northwestern Wisconsin. Eileen enjoyed a bowl of acorn squash chowder. It was more a meal than a soup.

The women ate in silence. They savored the food and each other's company, with no need for talk just yet. That would come. For women of their age and power, this was a rare opportunity to decompress away from the public spotlight and the demands of their varying, needy constituents. They always had the same waiter, Susie, who knew after more than a year of this routine when to approach, and when to leave the women in silence.

When they had finished their food and were sipping coffee, Julie started the conversation. As Board Chair, by tradition, Julie spoke first. Eileen spoke only if spoken to. "Can you believe what that buffoon was wearing?" Julie began. "I mean, what did he think?"

Bunny shook her head.

Eileen did not react, taking her cues from her boss.

"And what an idiot!" Julie continued. "*'Samolians?'* I mean, really. Where did he pick that up?"

Again, Bunny shook her head.

Eileen maintained her poker face.

"Bunny," Julie suggested. "You have to find someone to run against that idiot in the next election. Someone we can work with."

"It's a little complicated," Bunny averred, cognizant of Reverend Ballman's network of spies in the community. "Don't get me wrong. He's a pain in my backside…"

"You're telling me!" Julie nodded.

"I can handle him," Bunny assured her board chair. "Just give me some time, Julie. We'll figure something out."

Julie looked at Eileen, who nodded to confirm her agreement with Bunny's assessment.

—ᨆ—

Chris Hardwell had planned to leave the Minnepious school district's annual Black Administrators Holiday Ball right after dinner, but he needed to talk to Bunny, and she still hadn't arrived. The superintendent was supposed to have come straight to this event from the school board meeting. It had only taken Hardwell twenty minutes to get from the school board meeting to the Hilton ballroom. He didn't understand what was holding up Bunny.

More than a hundred administrators and guests filled the ballroom. Everyone was decked out for the black tie ball. Some brought spouses or dates. Most did not. A local band was setting up. The district had sprung for the band and an open bar. So much for austerity. Drinks flowed freely. Taxis were on the house.

Hardwell didn't drink. He looked at his watch. It was already nine. There was no telling when Bunny might show up. He did not want to leave before she arrived. That would look bad. More important, he still needed to talk to her about the situation at his school. But he didn't know how much more of this he could take.

Lisa Brown, Assistant Principal at King Elementary, sat on his left side, demanding his attention. She was extremely attractive. And she wasn't the kind of attractive you could ignore. She wore fishnet stockings and a tight dress with a long slit on the side that kept riding up her thigh.

Hardwell looked away fast after Lisa crossed her legs and the long slit rode up high enough to expose a garter belt. Even though he looked away, Hardwell could not get that image out of his mind. Without being impolite, he tried to ignore Lisa, conversing instead with Amy Cartwright on his other side. Amy was boring, safe. He kept his gaze fixed on Amy, but his mind kept creeping back to Lisa's garter. Rumor had it, Lisa had just broken up with Kweisi Providence.

Amy excused herself and left the table. Hardwell kept his eyes away from Lisa. He scanned the room, looking for any diversion. He spotted Providence, who was at another table, across the room.

Lisa sipped her wine. It had to be her third or fourth glass. No one was counting. She followed Hardwell's gaze. "This is the last time he'll be here," Lisa said.

"I'm sorry?" Hardwell replied. He did not look at her.

"Kweisi. He thinks he's too big for us, now."

Curiosity got the better of Hardwell. Keeping his gaze above her legs, he looked at Lisa. "Is he?"

"Depends what you mean by big," Lisa whispered.

"I meant *professionally*. Is he as big a deal as everyone says?"

Lisa smiled. "Professionally, he's on his way. But don't kid yourself. He's a fake."

Hardwell met Lisa's gaze. "Really?"

Lisa winked. "I would know." She sized up Hardwell. "*Un*professionally, Kweisi's definitely not big."

Hardwell ignored the comment.

"You came alone tonight, Chris."

"Alecia's with the kids. Couldn't get a sitter."

Lisa gave a mock frown. She leaned close. Her breath smelled of wine. Her breast rubbed against Hardwell's arm.

Hardwell shifted subtly away. He did not want to embarrass Lisa.

Lisa smiled again and ran her tongue over her upper lip.

Hardwell could swear something was crawling up his leg. He reached down to see what it was. He felt something soft, wiggling.

Lisa giggled.

It was her stockinged foot. Hardwell caught her foot just before it reached his crotch. He didn't know if he should release the foot or hold it. The toes kept wiggling and nestled in his hand.

Lisa leaned close. "I'm so glad you came alone," she whispered.

As gently and gracefully as he could, Hardwell disentangled himself from the drunk assistant principal. He pushed back from the table and excused himself. The conversation with Bunny would have to wait.

—ɯɯ—

Carmen walked into the small, dimly lit nightclub and allowed her eyes to adjust to the dark. The music was awesome. It was seventies disco, and it was pumping. Carmen looked around for Bob. She had agreed to meet him at the club at midnight, which seemed late for a date, even on a Friday night, but he had insisted he couldn't meet earlier. As her eyes adjusted to the lighting, Carmen saw a scene she had no interest in joining. The dance floor was packed with white people. There were a few Asians, and what appeared to be a couple light skinned African-Americans, probably biracial. The music was Black, the dancers white.

Carmen had no idea how she would spot Bob. Better to let him find her in this crowd. She stood where she was, waiting. After a couple minutes, Bob still had not appeared. Carmen grew annoyed. It was bad enough to meet him at midnight. But what really pissed her off was that Bob had chosen this party. She had no interest in being the token Black person in Bob's white world.

Gloria Gaynor's *"I Will Survive"* faded, and Carmen caught the beat from the next song, Kurtis Blow's *"White Lines."* At least the DJ was good. She glanced over to where the DJ was mixing and did a double take. There he was, grinning at her like a fool.

Carmen crossed the dance floor, dodging the white dancers until she made it to Bob. "You're a DJ?"

Grinning, he put his arm around Carmen and gave her a peck on the cheek. He was bobbing to the beat.

Carmen shook her head. This white boy was full of surprises.

—ɯɯ—

Eileen got home late. Dinner with Bunny and Julie Harmer had gone longer than usual. Afterward, she had stopped for a drink at Danny's Pub. She was in no hurry to get home. She knew Ethan would be out late. And Joel would be home. Eileen glanced at the clock. It was almost one in the morning. Ethan was still out. *Where was he?*

Even though he was a senior, his curfew was supposed to be midnight. He was probably out with one of those cheerleaders. It seemed like a different cheerleader each week, most of them sophomores or freshmen. Eileen could look the other way as long as Ethan used protection, but she did not trust him. He was young and foolish.

Eileen felt less like a mother to Ethan than a chaperone. Once her son outgrew these adolescent hormones, she hoped he would make better decisions. Eileen had to protect these girls from her son before he did something really stupid, like getting one of them pregnant. She was counting down the days until August, when Ethan would leave her custody for Dartmouth. Then, her job would be done. He would be out of her hands. At least at Dartmouth, the girls her son attracted would be more mature and sophisticated than these high school cheerleaders.

Eileen glanced at the clock again. It was one thirty. *Where the hell was he?* She knew better than to try his cell phone. That would only make her look pathetic. She decided to wait up until he got home.

—w—

Carmen invited Bob up to her apartment. It was two thirty in the morning, but she wasn't tired. She felt invigorated. She just hoped Bob wouldn't get the wrong idea. She put on Alecia Keys and poured rum and Cokes. Bob sat on the couch.

"Jamaican or Trinidadian rum?" Bob asked when Carmen handed him the drink.

"Barbadian. *Mount Gay.*"

"The best," Bob complimented.

Carmen sat beside Bob on the couch. Close enough to talk, but not close enough to give the wrong impression.

Bob slid closer.

Carmen tipped her glass against his. "Cheers."

"Cheers."

"How did you decide to be a DJ?" Carmen asked after a sip of her drink.

"You mean because my dad's a lawyer?"

"I just never thought of you as a DJ…"

"Because I'm white?"

Carmen smiled. "Maybe."

"I've always loved music. But I'm not good enough to make a living creating it…so I spin it."

"Very clever."

Bob again shifted closer to Carmen.

She leaned against him. His body felt warm.

"Why'd you go to the school board meeting tonight?" Bob asked.

Carmen shook her head. "It was crazy. I've never seen anything like it."

"Oh?" Bob murmured and put his arm around Carmen.

Carmen gently removed Bob's arm and slid back an inch, so she could face him. "I don't want you to get the wrong idea."

Bob looked hurt.

"I like you, Bob," Carmen explained. "But I need time."

"We're cool."

Carmen relaxed.

"Tell me about the school board meeting."

Carmen rolled her eyes. "Oh my goodness. You've never seen such crazy people."

—⚹—

Isaac groaned. Blood dripped from his mouth onto the floor. He had been in this room before. He snorted to clear his nose. More blood sprayed the floor.

"Let him alone," a voice said.

Isaac knew that voice. He snorted again. His eyes followed the stream of snot and blood.

"That's enough."

Isaac felt dizzy. His face pressed against the cool, hard floor. His mind floated away.

Minnissippi

Chapter 5

Carmen stared at the photograph. The boy's face was bruised and cut. It was hard to look at, impossible to ignore. The longer she looked at the photo, the angrier she became.

Charity watched Carmen. She knew the lawyer would have to do something.

Carmen considered the situation. Why had she gone to law school if not to help those who could not help themselves? But the timing was bad. Carmen already had a lot on her mind. Could she really afford for her conscience to pull her deeper into Charity's world? Would there ever really be a good time?

It was not that Carmen thought she was *better* than Charity. She did not. She was not a better person, a more moral person. But as much discrimination as Carmen might have experienced in her young legal career, she still enjoyed access to wealth, power and prestige that Charity could never dream of. Carmen was painfully aware that Charity and her three children were stuck in a hell created for them by those with power and privilege. As a beneficiary of that same system of power and privilege, Carmen felt an obligation to do something. Unlike a white lawyer, she could not pretend that her own relative power and privilege were unrelated to Charity's distress.

Carmen looked at the photo of the boy again. She was disgusted that anyone in the education system would do such a thing. She now had something tangible with which to go after the superintendent of Minnepious schools. She knew the fight would be difficult. It would get ugly. And she had other things to sort out, like when to move back to New York and what to do about Bob. But first, she would deal with this.

Charity stared at the purple rug on the floor. There were little stains and marks on it if you looked close. But from far away, it looked real nice. She hoped this lawyer would do the right thing. But she knew better than to trust her. Then again, she had nowhere else to turn.

Carmen looked at Charity. She knew what she had to do. If she abandoned Charity and this boy now, she would be abandoning herself. If she did not follow her conscience, if she did not go all the way now, wherever that might lead, she would be lost forever. The rest of her life would be a series of rationalizations about what was "realistic," about the limits of her power as a Black woman in a white-dominated society.

Carmen would not go there. She refused to descend into what she had always perceived to be the hell of the Black bourgeoisie— an emotional, cultural and intellectual oblivion—knowingly and unknowingly validating the cultural norms of an oppressive white society: hating white people, hating working class Black people, hating yourself.

She glanced at the photo of the boy one more time, then looked at Charity. "This won't happen again."

Charity stared at the floor.

"We won't let it happen again," Carmen repeated.

Charity knew better than to trust the lawyer's words. "You got a nice rug."

—⁂—

"Why are they doing this to you?" Alecia Hardwell pressed. "Get Bunny to put a stop to it."

"Bunny's behind it," Chris Hardwell replied. "She sent the woman."

"Then we need to leave."

"It's the same everywhere, Alecia." Hardwell paused. "You think it was better in Mississippi?"

Alecia thought about it. "I don't know. Maybe."

"It wasn't."

Alecia hugged her husband. "You're so good at what you do. Why won't they just let you do your job?"

Hardwell had little use for this conversation. "Politics, Alecia. It's always politics."

Alecia could not accept seeing her husband like this. Ever since they had met in college—he at Morehouse, she at Spellman—she believed in him. It wasn't just that he treated her, and now their kids, with the deepest devotion and respect. She truly believed in him as a man. He had integrity, gentleness, a genuine commitment to young people.

Maybe she was biased. She could admit that. She loved him, after all. But she was not the only one who saw these qualities in her husband. Everyone who knew Chris respected him. He was a gem. There were so few like him. She could not let him sink. For her family's sake, and for the community. "Chris, let's look for something else. It doesn't have to be in Mississippi. But we should do it now, before the kids start school."

Hardwell nodded. Knowing what he did, he could not in good conscience put his kids, Michela and Stevie, in Minnepious schools. Minnepious offered stark and unappealing choices: white-dominated schools or impoverished Black schools. Private school was not an option, either. It would cost a fortune and be inconsistent with his position in the district, not to mention his values.

Hardwell felt a frustration so deep he had no idea how to begin to address it, as an educator or a father. He had done what he could as principal to turn around Tubman Middle School. He had chased gangs from the building, installed metal detectors, removed the worst teachers, instilled a sense of pride and hope among the staff. But there was only so much one man could do, even with a team of dedicated professionals.

Despite each small improvement they made, the situation overwhelmed them. Mobility, family poverty, parents with bad school experiences, gang violence, lack of support from district headquarters—they all combined to sink the school. Even a great teacher could only reach two or three kids in a class of 35. The situation was impossible.

The district's obsession with test scores didn't help, either. Test scores had improved since Hardwell's arrival. But what did that really mean? At the current rate of improvement, the kids would still not be ready for high school. Most would drop out within a year or two.

It exhausted Hardwell to think about it. He had to find a better way, if only to save his own beloved children.

—⚮—

Carmen drove slowly by Afrocentric Success Academy. The ASA campus sparkled amid the blight of inner city north Minnepious. The building was massive and brand spanking new. Though now covered with snow, Carmen knew from photos on the school's website that the grounds would be immaculately manicured in spring, summer and fall.

The school's parking lot was full. Carmen kept driving, searching for a place to park. The streets had signs prohibiting parking between 7am and 5pm on school days. She circled the block, hoping to find a parking space on a side street. It took a while to find one. The closest space was nearly two blocks away. Clutching a folder, Carmen got out of her car and hurried through the cold wind to the grand entrance of the charter school.

Inside, the building was warm and cheery. Tall glass walls reflected shimmering sunlight into the foyer. The sunlight illuminated inspirational posters and banners:

"*I am somebody!*"

"*Respect.*"

"*Love community.*"

"*Do your best.*"

"*Work hard!*"

  "*Do the math.*"

"*Discipline = freedom!*"

A young woman with amazing braids approached Carmen. "Hello, can I help you?"

"Yes," Carmen smiled. "I was hoping to see Kweisi Providence."

"You'll have to check in at the office," the young woman explained.

"Where do you get your braids done?"

The young woman beamed. "I go to a small shop on the near south side, on Londale Avenue. There's a woman from Sierra Leone there who does braids."

"She does a really nice job."

"Thanks. Come on. I'll take you to the office."

Carmen followed the young woman through the large foyer to an office complex on the west side of the building. There were more inspirational posters and banners in the office bearing similar themes. The young woman left Carmen at a receptionist's desk.

"Can I help you?" an older woman asked.

Carmen looked around. There was something off about the place. *What was it?* The office was tranquil, almost like a morgue. But there was something else. There were no white people around. That wasn't what bugged her, though. She was used to that from growing up in Brooklyn.

Then it hit her. *There were no kids.* How could you run a school with no kids barging in and out of the office?

"Can I help you?" the receptionist repeated.

"Oh, sorry," Carmen replied. "I was hoping to meet Mr. Providence."

"Do you have an appointment?"

"I was just hoping to speak with him for a few minutes. It won't take long."

The receptionist stood up. "Just a minute."

She disappeared into an inner office suite. When she reappeared, a young man in a sharp suit accompanied her.

"Hi, I'm Shaka," he introduced himself.

Carmen shook hands. "Carmen."

"Melanie told me you want to see Kweisi. Are you a reporter?"

Carmen shook her head. "I'm a lawyer."

"Oh, I see..." Shaka exhaled. "Is there something specific you want to speak with Mr. Providence about?"

Carmen noted that he was now *Mr. Providence*, not Kweisi. "Yes, as a matter of fact, there is."

She reached into her folder and pulled out the photo of a beaten and bloodied Isaac. She handed it to Shaka.

He recoiled, handing the photo back to Carmen. "Mr. Providence is not available."

"When will he be available?"

"He's out of town."

"Well, I need to talk to him."

"I don't think that would be appropriate."

"This boy's mother deserves answers. She needs to know what happened to her son."

"You're a lawyer," Shaka countered. "You'll have to talk to our attorneys." He pointed to the door. "You need to leave now."

Carmen considered her options. Even if Providence was hiding somewhere in the executive suite, she would run into an ethical problem if the school district accused her of harassing non-lawyers. "No problem," she decided. "But tell your boss, he'll have to deal with me sooner or later."

Shaka pointed to the door again.

Carmen frowned and left the office. As she got to the front foyer of the school building, the young woman with the braids accosted her.

"How'd it go? Did you get to see Mr. Providence?"

Carmen shook her head.

"Aw, that's too bad. He's incredible." The young woman paused. "You want a tour of the school?"

"Definitely," Carmen agreed. "But we can skip the office."

—∞—

"Show five," Mrs. Beamon called out.

The children immediately raised their right arms and held their hands straight up, palms facing the teacher.

Unlike the other children, Lakeesha waved her arm back and forth to get the teacher's attention.

"Lakeesha?" Mrs. Beamon scolded. "Why you wavin' like that?"

"Mrs. Beamon," Lakeesha replied. "Why we gotta show five all the time?" She knew she was breaking two rules by waving her arm and asking a question.

"What you say?"

"Why we gotta do this? At my old school in Cheecago, we don't gotta do this."

"Well, why don't you go back to yo' old school in *Chee-ca-go* then?"

"My mama say it betta here."

"Yo' mama don't know it here. Now get in the corner and *take a break.*"

"What if I don't wanna *take a break?*"

"You don't got a choice. Now go in the corner and *take a break.*"

"Why I gotta *take a break?*"

"'Cause I tole you to!"

"Why I gotta be punish?"

"It ain't a punishment."

"If it ain't a punishment, why I gotta *take a break?*"

The other fifth graders giggled.

"Lakeesha," Mrs. Beamon seethed. "I'm goin' tell you one last time. Get yo' little black ass in the corner and *take a break.*"

"I don't feel I need a break. And since it ain't a punishment, I ain't goin' do it."

The fifth graders stared at Mrs. Beamon. She was steamed now for real.

Lakeesha eyed the teacher.

Mrs. Beamon stared back. She would have to break this child, for her own good. "Go to the *resolution room.*"

"Is *that* a punishment?"

Mrs. Beamon tried to stay calm. She would have to break this child soon. "No, Lakeesha, it is not a punishment. Now get out this classroom and get yo' ass to the *resolution room.*"

"If it ain't a punishment, I ain't doin' it."

Something snapped inside Mrs. Beamon. She grabbed Lakeesha by the hair and dragged the screaming child out of the classroom. She dragged Lakeesha all the way down the hallway to the resolution room.

"It ain't a punishment," Mrs. Beamon called out as she left the bawling child.

—⁂—

Carmen snuggled on her couch with Bob. It had been a long stressful day, and she was grateful for his company. Her tour of Afrocentric

Success Academy had unsettled her. She let Bob hold her tight. It felt good. She kissed him, a nice, long kiss. She pulled back, to keep control. "You wouldn't believe what I saw today."

"Try me," Bob replied, disappointed that Carmen had pulled away.

"It was all Black. And it was so sterile and organized."

"That's bad?" Bob slid closer to Carmen.

"There was something creepy about it. Militaristic almost. The kids all wear uniforms. They walk in straight lines. The kids are supposed to listen and be obedient. If they ask questions, they get punished *for their own good*. The school has the same lock step curriculum in every classroom. It's like a factory."

Bob did not say anything, which annoyed Carmen for some reason. She was not sure what she wanted him to say.

"All they care about is test results," she continued. "It's not like they care about *educating* children; they just want to *control* them."

"Aren't the kids from broken families?" Bob asked. "Don't they need discipline?"

Carmen pulled away, irritated. "That's just it. Everyone acts like there's something wrong with the kids, like they need to be fixed. They use some teaching methodology called *responsive learning*. The teachers love it. They treat the kids like Pavlov's dogs."

"That's not what I meant," Bob objected.

"But your comment assumes broken families and instability that supposedly calls for *discipline*."

"Am I off base?"

"Forget it. You wouldn't understand."

"What, because I'm white?"

"Why do you always have to go there? Does that define who you are? Is that how you see yourself: as a *white* person?"

Bob felt blindsided.

Carmen calmed down. "It's not only white people who make these assumptions about Black kids. You know, I didn't see a single white person the whole time I was at the school."

Bob was still stuck on Carmen's impression of him. "You didn't answer me. Are you saying I don't get it because I'm white?"

"Can you please drop it?"

Bob shifted away from Carmen. He wondered where they could go from here. If he left it this way, he was afraid she would never give him another chance. "Okay, Carmen, I'm white. I get that. But no, it doesn't define who I am." He paused. "You know, Carmen, I could probably help you check into some of the stuff going on with the schools. I can see certain things that maybe you don't, *because I'm white.*"

Carmen smiled. She was flattered that Bob was trying this hard. She knew he was out on a limb. If she rejected him now, he had no way back. She pulled him to her and kissed him. "So, *Mr. White Man*, tell me what you can see that I can't."

—⁓—

Ethan ambled into the kitchen. He looked like hell. "What's for breakfast?"

Eileen did not respond. She cradled her mug of hot coffee. She had stayed up until 2:30 last night.

"Did you hear me?" Ethan persisted. He stared at his mother.

"It's lunch time," Eileen replied. "What time did you get home last night?"

Ethan rubbed his eyes. "I don't know."

"Were you drinking?"

"No."

Eileen did not believe him. "Where were you?"

"*Are you stupid?* I told you I was going to Brenda's house."

"Were her parents there?"

Ethan did not respond. He opened the refrigerator and peered inside.

"Isn't she a little young for you?"

"She's a sophomore."

Ethan considered how big a fight he wanted. He closed the refrigerator. "There isn't anything to eat in this house."

"Go get a job and buy your own food."

"Where's Dad?"

"How should I know?"

"Last time I checked, you were married to him."

Eileen felt rage welling inside her chest. She gulped down the rest of her coffee. It scalded her tongue, mouth and throat. The rage subsided.

She got up and left the kitchen. She did not know if she could make it until August when Ethan left for college and she would have no more excuses for putting up with Joel.

—⚋—

When they got to the fancy office, Isaiah, Lakeesha and Isaac fidgeted and did not make eye contact with the lawyer.

Charity hovered nearby.

"So, how's school going?" Carmen asked Lakeesha after introducing herself to the kids.

"Okay," Lakeesha mumbled, uncharacteristically quiet. Her mama had warned her not to say too much.

"Just okay?"

Lakeesha nodded.

"Something bothering you?"

Lakeesha shook her head.

"How are your teachers?"

"I only got one."

"Is she nice?"

"Sometimes."

"Is she *not* nice sometimes?"

Lakeesha nodded.

Charity tensed.

"When she's not nice, what does she do?"

"Sometimes, 'Keesha exaggerates," Charity interrupted.

"I don't 'xaggerate," Lakeesha objected.

"It's okay," Carmen intervened. She needed specifics from the kids about how they were treated. "What does your teacher do when she's not nice."

"She pull my hair."

"'Keesha!" Charity scolded. "Don't be tellin' lies."

Lakeesha stared at her mama. "I'm tellin' the truth. She pull me by my hair. If you think I'm lyin', whyn't you go ask the teacher if she do that."

Charity glared at her daughter. If the lawyer found out Lakeesha was lying, she wouldn't believe anything any of them said. Then she'd drop them, and Isaac would never get help.

"Lakeesha?" Carmen prodded. "Why did your teacher pull your hair?"

Charity stared her daughter down.

The little girl kept her eyes fixed on the floor. "She did it 'cause I asked questions, and she got mad. But she say it weren't no punishment."

The words struck Carmen like lightning. She had to get to Kweisi Providence.

—⁘—

Chris Hardwell did not know where to begin his search. He could not talk to anyone. If word got out, he would have to make a decision in a hurry, under pressure. This was a complicated and difficult decision. It required time and a lot of thinking. Hardwell stared at his computer screen, trying to figure out what search terms to google. He had to narrow the search by geography. But even within an identified area, what exactly was he looking for?

If he considered only his career, that would simplify things, though the options still seemed paltry. What kind of school or school district would offer him meaningful opportunities to make an impact and advance his career? He had tried Black schools in Mississippi, and now in Minnepious. There was little difference between the two and little satisfaction in the work.

But career advancement was not Hardwell's main consideration. His children were. They would soon need to attend school. Their identities would be shaped by their school experiences.

Hardwell googled city after city. He looked at more than two dozen school and school district websites around the country. He looked across the South. He perused cities on the East Coast and in California. He skipped the Midwest.

What he found everywhere was an intolerable choice for Black parents: either opt for academic proficiency at the cost of social exclusion, or choose social acceptance with inferior academic and career prospects. Hardwell found a few Black schools that boasted superior academic performance. But when he compared their results to the top white schools, the claims did not stand up. The white schools were equally unattractive. They had white staffs and principals, with just a handful of Black students.

Hardwell had never before considered schools from this perspective. He had never looked at them as a parent of prospective students—his own precious children. He had always looked at how schools functioned from an administrative perspective, from a principal's perspective.

Hardwell pondered his dilemma. He wanted the best academically for his children. He wanted them to have a bright future. They deserved that. Maybe they would go to top colleges, like he and Alecia had, maybe not. But that was for them to decide, far in their future. Right now, more than anything, Hardwell wanted his children to be happy and confident. That was most important. But how happy and confident would they be if they did not feel respected and challenged academically?

The more he searched, the more frustrated he became. He could not find acceptable options. He began to resent a school system that failed to meet the needs of Black children. To make it worse, he was part of that system.

"Honey, come to bed," Alecia called from the bedroom. "It's getting late."

"I'll be there soon."

He did not want to involve his wife in the search yet. When he had found some acceptable options, he would share those with her, and they would make a decision together. At this point, he was having a hard time seeing how he would come up with any acceptable options.

Hardwell knew from experience that there were some messes in life so tangled and nasty, you just had to cut the Gordian knot. This felt like one of them. But if he could not find a suitable, nurturing, enriching elementary school for his beautiful Black children, he was not even sure what it would mean to *cut the Gordian knot*.

Hardwell thought about his dilemma. If the South, the East Coast, California and the Midwest did not work, then maybe he would just have to look elsewhere. Where, he did not know. But if that was the only way to save his precious children, so be it. On a whim, he typed the phrase *"international schools"* into the Google search bar. Then he added, *"in africa."*

—∞—

Bob drove Carmen to southwest Minnepious. He had insisted on chaperoning her to his 'hood. He said he was the best person to show her what he called the "white" Minnepious schools. After what she had seen and learned about the city's Black schools, Carmen found it hard to believe Bob's account of white schools in Minnepious comparable to the best suburban schools. The image of Bunny Washington in a north side housing project lecturing the host of *Black Power Positions* loomed in Carmen's mind. It did not leave room for the parallel "white" Minnepious school district that Bob described.

When they arrived in the neighborhood around Dewey Middle School, Carmen saw that the houses were nice, but not ostentatious. The Dewey school building itself, unlike the extravagant new ASA building in north Minnepious, was old and non-descript. At least on the outside, Carmen concluded, African-Americans were getting the better of separate but equal.

Carmen and Bob entered the Dewey school building. Unlike the sterile discipline of ASA, it was chaotic. Carmen figured any self-respecting Black parent would prefer the order and calm of ASA. Chalk up another win for African-Americans. Maybe Kweisi Providence was onto something, after all.

No greeter welcomed them, so Carmen and Bob walked in and looked for the school office. The building appeared to be about a hundred years old, built in the early twentieth century. Its institutional tiling and small windows screamed for an update. The bell rang, startling Carmen and Bob. The hallway flooded with rambunctious pre-teens and teens. Chaos reigned. Carmen stood aside as careening students, who wore no uniforms and appeared to have no regard for Carmen, Bob or any other adult in the building, flew by.

Kids milled about, jostling each other, shouting, teasing and carrying on as if they owned the place. How anyone could concentrate, much less learn, in such an environment was beyond Carmen. A tall boy brushed against Carmen as he tried to escape pursuers in the hallway. He did not say anything to her and continued racing away down the hallway.

"Hey, Joe! Slow down!" an adult called after the boy.

A sheepish middle aged white man approached Carmen and Bob. The man wore a casual black t-shirt and slightly baggy jeans. On his feet, he sported Converse All-Stars. "Sorry about that," the man said.

"No problem," Carmen replied, catching her breath.

A second bell rang. The chaos in the hallway subsided.

"Yo! Mikey!" the man in the Converse All-Stars yelled at a straggler.

The kid turned. "Whassup, Mr. C?"

"You get your science project done?"

"It's da bomb, Mr. C!"

The man in the Converse All-Stars grinned. "Get to class."

When the student had disappeared into a classroom, the man rolled his eyes at Carmen, as if sharing a private joke with her. He offered his hand. "I'm Fred Carver."

Carmen shook hands. "Carmen Braithwaite."

Carmen was still processing the scene in this supposedly model school. Then it hit her. In the chaos, she had missed it. All the kids in the hallway were white. Not one Black kid. Maybe an Asian or two. But she had not seen one Black kid.

The man turned to Bob and offered his hand. "Fred Carver."

"I'm Bob Levine."

"Nice to meet you both. What brings you to Dewey?"

Carmen and Bob looked at each other.

"Actually," Bob freelanced. "We're checking out schools for my cousins...they're moving here from Boston."

Carmen blanched. She could imagine what the lawyer's Office of Professional Responsibility would say about that misrepresentation, though technically it was Bob's misrepresentation, not hers.

"Wonderful!" Fred Carver responded. "Come with me. We'll find someone to take you around."

Carmen and Bob followed the man into an antiquated office. No one seemed to notice them.

Their host summoned a middle aged woman. "Janet, could you show Carmen and Bob around the school? Bob's relatives are moving to town and they're looking at schools."

"Sure, Fred."

Carmen glanced around the office. Then she saw the nameplate: "*Fred Carver, Principal.*"

"Thanks, Mr. Carver," Carmen said to the principal.

"Call me Fred," he mock chided her, then looked at Bob. "If your cousins are still seriously considering Eden or Lake after you see our school, give me a call. I'll talk them out of it."

Bob grinned. "Will do."

Janet ushered Carmen and Bob out of the office. She showed them around the school. They saw the library, the gym, the lunchroom, the computer labs, the music and art rooms, and science labs. Everywhere they went, Carmen and Bob felt welcomed by teachers and staff. The kids—all but seven of whom were white (Carmen kept count)—uniformly ignored them.

At the end of the tour, Carmen and Bob observed an eighth grade English class discussing Shakespeare's *The Tempest.*

Carmen whispered to Janet, "I noticed the chairs are set up in circles in all the classes. Why is that?"

"When teachers sit within the circle of students," Janet whispered back. "We see higher quality dialogue between teachers and students, and among the students themselves."

The teacher, who, like the principal, wore a black t-shirt, jeans and sneakers, queried his class, "What does Caliban represent to the civilized European?"

"I think you're taking too literal an approach," one of the boys corrected the teacher.

"Tell me more," the teacher urged.

"It just seems to me…" the boy began, then paused. "How much did Shakespeare really know about the Caribbean when he wrote the play?"

"He'd never been there," the teacher answered.

Another boy jumped in. "But he must have met sailors who had."

"Fair enough," the teacher agreed.

"Still," a girl with her hair dyed black volunteered. "Wasn't the character of Caliban really an archetype?"

A boy wearing a Boca Juniors Argentine soccer jersey frowned and said, "An archetype or a stereotype?"

The teacher picked up on the thread. "What would make you lean toward archetype, and what would suggest stereotype?"

The students thought about the question.

The boy in the Boca Juniors jersey broke the silence. "I'd say archetype if it isn't implying that Europeans are always superior to people from the Caribbean. Otherwise, stereotype for sure."

The other students nodded.

"Let's take that distinction up for homework," the teacher suggested.

The kids groaned.

Janet nodded toward the doorway. Carmen and Bob slipped out of the classroom.

When they exited the Dewey school building, the December sun glittered off the snow, dazzling them. Carmen grabbed Bob's arm to keep from slipping on a patch of ice. She felt dizzy and disoriented, as if re-entering the atmosphere from a brief foray into a parallel universe.

—⚮—

Chris Hardwell studied every word in the letter. His first reaction was that it had to be a practical joke. On closer inspection, he saw that the letter was genuine. It was on Minnepious Public Schools stationery and had been signed by Bunny Washington, Superintendent, though it had undoubtedly been written by Bunny's white alter ego, Eileen Jaeger.

It had to be in retaliation for the incident with that punk kid Jefferson and his big mouth mother. Maybe he shouldn't have taken it to Bunny. That probably provoked the letter. He read the letter again:

"Dear Mr. Hardwell,

It has come to our attention that you have violated district policy by addressing an African-American student at Tubman Middle School as a 'boy.' As you should know, we hold all our professional administrators to a high standard of excellence in Minnepious Public Schools. That includes an expectation that our principals treat all members of their school communities with respect.

Given the unfortunate vestiges of racial discrimination in our society, we as educators must form a wall of zero tolerance, and not allow racism to enter our schools. As you should know, the term 'boy' has an unfortunate connotation when applied to men (and young men) of African-American ancestry. Your use of that term in the context of a disciplinary hearing has exposed the school district to potential liability.

Accordingly, you are hereby notified that you have been placed on 60 days probation. You will be required to attend advanced sensitivity training from the district's outside provider, One World Training. You must attain a score of 90% or higher on the post-training assessment administered by One World Training. If you fail to achieve this score, you will be placed on permanent administrative leave and will be removed from your current position.

You may contact our Human Resources Department if you have any questions regarding what you are required to do to remain an employee of the district in good standing.

Sincerely,

Bunny Washington, Superintendent of Schools

Minnissippi

Carmen strolled into the cavernous Minnepious Conference Center. The place buzzed with energy. Colorful booths beckoned convention goers, all of whom wore badges with their names and designations. The badges highlighted participants' first names to encourage familiarity and networking. Yet despite the conviviality, this "25th Annual Eliminating the Gap Conference, Silver Jubilee Edition" promoted a serious objective.

According to the conference website, more than 3,500 educators from across the country had gathered in Minnepious for the sole purpose of eliminating the enduring learning gap between white children and children of color. Minnepious enjoyed the unprecedented honor of hosting this milestone event, which was more than three years in the planning and made Minnepious, at least for three days, the epicenter of all efforts to defeat this persistent nemesis.

Carmen entered the conference center with a different purpose. She was not a registered participant, but an interloper looking for a fight. She had Bunny Washington and Kweisi Providence in her sights. Within the hour, conference convener Washington would introduce keynote speaker Providence.

Even without an official "Hi, I'm CARMEN!" badge, Carmen found it easy to blend into the crowds in the vast conference center. She strolled across the main plaza, nodding to random people she encountered. They had no idea who she was or how they should address her as they craned to locate her missing badge. Carmen smiled, nodded and kept moving.

The first area she checked out featured mostly Latino, Somali and Hmong educators. Mexican-American, East African and Asian-American accents welcomed Carmen to their booths, all proclaiming "best practices" and cures for the "learning gap." These "recent immigrants" had their own physical space within the conference center, separated from African-Americans.

As she perused brochures and eavesdropped on conversations, Carmen heard educators characterize immigrant children as defective and dysfunctional in various ways. The educators spoke in hushed tones of brown immigrant children being tainted by some mysterious contagion when they arrived in America. It was as if a brain worm avoided white children and selectively preyed on brown immigrant children, eating its fill until it created a "gap" that had to be eliminated.

Disturbed, Carmen visited other areas of the conference center. She observed educators promoting various ideas for "eliminating the gap." Despite the conference's proclaimed focus on a unitary goal, Carmen found deep divisions among conference goers about how best to accomplish this goal.

Social service providers argued for a holistic approach that leveraged disparate resources to support children and families. For-profit companies and consultants claimed to "do more with less." Teachers unions defended the competence and good intentions of their members. Charter schools hailed their "proven success" and an ability to "beat the odds."

Some groups focused on improving schools, others on improving teachers. Some conference participants spoke of desirable "assets." Others spoke of dreaded "deficits." Some cited medical conditions: ADD, ADHD, fetal alcohol syndrome, cognitive dissonance, various psychoses, and other conditions Carmen had never heard of.

As Carmen listened to conference participants exchange ideas and debate their experiences, she realized that despite their differences, they all rallied around a set of core, unshakeable beliefs.

First, all conference participants appeared to share a belief that *children and parents were a problem.* Conference participants described children and parents in terms of *"challenges," "dysfunction," "poverty," "mobility," "pathologies," "criminality,"* and other attributes of the educationally and socially deficient, the unclean.

A second core belief was closely related to the first. To overcome the myriad problems posed by Black and brown children and families, conference participants uniformly summoned the word *"Community,"* as a sort of holy balm, a mystical elixir. People spoke of *"reaching out* to the Community," of *"legitimacy in* the Community," of being *"from* the Community," and of *"speaking for* the Community." Once invoked, the omnipotent *Community* apparently vouchsafed one's authenticity, validity and good intentions.

Carmen observed one last area of universal agreement. Despite their widely varying approaches to "eliminating the gap," all conference participants had seemingly agreed never to describe segregated schools that failed Black and brown children as *"segregated."* Not one brochure used the word. Nor did a single person utter it. It was as if the word "segregation" had been eliminated from the lexicon of urban educators and banned from the conference.

Carmen checked her watch. It was only ten thirty. She still had a half hour until Kweisi Providence's keynote speech. She spotted the charter schools wing of the conference and made a beeline for it.

This was by far the most visually striking and dynamic area at the conference. The charter school *"movement,"* as Carmen found its adherents preferred, leveraged cutting edge marketing techniques that spawned spiffy banners and glossy brochures. The marketing collateral featured stern brown leaders with inspirational messages and uniformed brown children marching in endless lines through pristine hallways. Proclaiming their commitment to transcendent results, charter school promoters from Harlem, Detroit, Oakland, Cleveland, New Orleans, South Central Los Angeles, East St. Louis, north Minnepious and anywhere else you could capture critical masses of brown children boasted of "untapped potential" and "opportunity" where others saw urban decay and educational toxicity.

Each charter school had *"Academy"* or *"Success"* or *"College"* or *"Preparatory"* or *"Prep"* or some other exalted, inspirational theme in its name. The brochures touted academic performance superior not merely to other urban public schools, but better than even the most exclusive private and suburban schools. Yet, as she had discovered when investigating Afrocentric Success Academy, Carmen found no support in the brochures for these claims, just more pictures of uniformed brown children with stern brown leaders exhorting them.

Carmen felt as if she were peering into a booming alternative economy, the buying and selling of futures in Black children. She knew from her online research that the charter school movement was backed by white venture fund bosses and other rich white conservatives, who saw charter schools as an interim step toward privatizing American education. *The Wall Street Journal* had run a series of articles touting unprecedented profit potential for *"first movers"* with the foresight to develop and exploit the *"education space."*

The charter school world that Carmen encountered at the conference seemed to invert Ralph Ellison's *Invisible Man*. Despite all their rich white backers, the charter schools' marketing collateral displayed only Black children and Black leaders. No white face dared show itself in charter school brochures.

As she took all this in, Carmen wondered what was going through the minds of conference participants. They moved about with such apparent purpose. They seemed to have serious work to do, presentations to make or to hear, people to meet, "best practices" to dispense. Yet beneath the frenetic activity, Carmen sensed futility, and despair.

Could conference participants really not see what she saw? Carmen wondered if all the educated, seemingly sophisticated and passionate people there really bought into this orgy of activity, self-importance and relentless self-promotion? Or were they just along for the ride because no other path beckoned? The more she observed, the more isolated Carmen felt.

As the 11:00 keynote address approached, a buzz swept across the conference center. Conference participants abandoned the booths and surged toward the main ballroom, ready to be entertained, enlightened, inspired. Carmen followed the crowd. She found a seat on the side of the main conference hall next to an earnest young white man whose "Vols 4 US" badge announced, *"Hi, I'm BRAD!"* It was a novelty to see a white person at the conference.

"Wow!" BRAD nudged Carmen as Bunny Washington entered the stage. "There she is! She's amazing! She spoke at our charter school in New Orleans a couple months ago. She's so inspiring!"

Carmen scanned the stage, looking for Kweisi Providence. The only person she saw other than Bunny Washington was a balding white man in a suit. The balding white man stuck out for the same reason BRAD did.

Bunny Washington approached the microphone and the crowd fell silent. The Minnepious superintendent beckoned to the balding white man, who joined her. "Welcome to Minnepious!" Bunny called out to the packed ballroom.

A smattering of cheers came from the audience.

"Welcome to Minnepious!" Bunny repeated, louder this time.

The crowd roared back.

"That's more like it!" Bunny smiled. "We hope you all have a good time while you're here. Mix it up a little, Minnepious-style. But don't you forget, people, we're here to do some serious work, too. We need you all to share your best practices so we can *eliminate the gap!*"

A roar rose from the crowd. BRAD and many others jumped to their feet, cheering.

Bunny raised her hands for calm.

BRAD sat back down. He turned to Carmen. "I told you, she's incredible!"

Before Carmen could respond, Bunny announced, "I know why you all are here...and it's not to see me."

The audience chuckled.

Someone yelled, "We love you, Bunny!"

"That must be one of my staff," Bunny joked. "On second thought, maybe not."

BRAD chuckled.

"Before I give you the man of the moment, I want to introduce to you the man for *every* moment." Bunny put her arm around the balding white man in the business suit. His balding head turned red. "If you don't know who this is, shame on you! This quiet, humble man can do more to save your children than anyone you'll ever meet... except maybe for our next speaker."

The balding man nodded vigorously at the "next speaker" comment.

"Who I am I so lucky to have my hands on right now?" Bunny asked the crowd.

"Warren Buffett!" someone shouted.

"Please!" BRAD groaned. "Everyone knows Buffett has a full head of hair. I'm going to work for Berkshire Hathaway when my two years at V4US are finished."

"No, he's not Warren Buffett," Bunny corrected.

BRAD nodded to no one in particular. *"Duh!"*

"This is Sam Irvine," Bunny continued. "He's the founder of Venture Parameters in Silicon Valley. And if you haven't heard of Sam and his company before, you soon will." Bunny nodded to emphasize the point. "I am so pleased to let you know that Sam has just announced a $100 million public-private partnership to support innovation in urban education!"

Bunny clapped. The crowd joined her. BRAD stood and whistled.

Bunny hugged the balding white man, who seemed both embarrassed and flattered by the attention. Then she waved Irvine off the stage and called out, "With Sam's support, we are well on our way to *eliminating the gap!"*

BRAD and the rest of the crowd rose, cheering and clapping. Carmen remained seated.

When he sat back down, BRAD asked, "Something wrong?"

Carmen ignored him.

BRAD looked searchingly at her chest. "Where's your badge?"

Carmen did not respond.

"You know," Brad admonished. "We need people like you to get off the sidelines." He paused, considering the best way to motivate, and not alienate, this dour woman. "Our kids need you. You can't imagine what it's like. People like you and me, we're so fortunate. I'm guessing you went to college. Well, I went to a college called Princeton. It's an Ivy League college. It's very hard to get into...in New Jersey...on the East Coast." BRAD paused again to give his credentials a chance to register. "At my charter school in New Orleans, you wouldn't believe what it's like. Most of my students are lucky to get dinner or take a shower..."

Before BRAD could say more, Bunny cut him off with her introduction of the featured speaker. He hoped his message had not fallen on deaf ears. Black middle class apathy toward urban education was a mystery to him. To be honest, it galled him, especially when so many idealistic white people from privileged backgrounds like his own were willing to commit a year or two of their lives, of their unique talents, to work with disadvantaged youth.

Bunny cleared her throat. The audience fell silent.

"We have all learned the hard way the challenges we face in trying to educate our urban young people," Bunny intoned from the stage. "Well, no one, and I do mean *no one*, has shown the way like our next speaker. He walks the talk in a way that brings shame to the rest of us. From his own humble roots in inner city Milwaukee to his sustained struggle for acceptance of his unconventional pedagogical methodologies to his indefatigable fundraising, lobbying and—let's be honest folks—*plain old begging!*"

Again the crowd rose to its feet. BRAD fell behind this time. Whether he was distracted by her own lack of enthusiasm, or disdainful of a cheer for begging, Carmen could not tell.

Bunny raised her hands again. The audience sat back down.

"C'mon, y'all. Ain't no shame puttin' your hand out for a good cause!"

Laughter rolled across the ballroom.

"If the politicians who control our purse strings would only put their own kids in our schools, we wouldn't be here today!"

Again the crowd rose and roared. Again, BRAD lagged behind.

"Sounds a little defeatist, huh?" Carmen gibed BRAD above the din of the crowd. "Not so inspiring?"

BRAD ignored her. The crowd sat back down.

"The most impressive thing about my dear friend Kweisi is he has succeeded on his own terms. He is building an empire of student achievement, success and excellence by refusing to bow to the naysayers. He refuses to accept that *our* children can't learn! He refuses to believe *our* children can't compete with the best and the brightest! I tell you, folks, this man is stubborn...*like a mule!*"

The crowd leaped to its feet screaming. BRAD hooted and whooped it up until his lungs felt like they would burst. He raised his fists and pumped the air.

Bunny motioned to the back of the stage. Suddenly, the chorus from Journey's 1980s rock anthem *"Don't Stop Believin'"* exploded over the ballroom sound system. Kweisi Providence burst into the ballroom, grooving to the beat. The crowd shrieked even louder, its collective hysteria raising the decibel level to rival a rock concert. Providence skipped across the front of the stage to the beat, high fiving hysterical educators. As the music faded, Providence skipped over to Bunny. The two hugged. The applause and cheering thundered.

After nearly a minute, Bunny gestured for the crowd to calm down. Reluctantly, people began to sit. BRAD was the last to sit. Bunny waited. The crowd hushed in anticipation.

"I am pleased to present to you," Bunny whispered into the microphone. "Mr. Kweisi Providence..." She paused.

The audience waited.

"...the most dangerous man in America!"

Again, the crowd leaped to its feet, screaming, clapping, cheering.

Carmen did not know how much more she could take. On the other hand, if she could get to Providence, it would be worth sitting through this madness.

"Sorry, y'all," Providence grinned as Bunny left the stage. "But twenty of Sam's hundred million is spoken for."

A hush fell over the crowd.

"Sam and I just agreed that his foundation is gonna finance a major expansion of Afrocentric Success Academy."

There was a smattering of polite applause.

"We're going national, y'all!" Providence shouted. "We're goin' need some partners, so let me know if you wanna franchise."

BRAD whipped a small notebook from his coat pocket and jotted a reminder to contact Kweisi Providence.

"Unless you join up with Afrocentric," Providence shrugged to the huge crowd. "Y'all just gonna have to fight over the crumbs."

—⚌—

For Eileen, the "25th Annual Eliminating the Gap" conference, Silver Jubilee Edition, had been a three year slog of preparation. Now, as Bunny worked the crowd near the stage, Eileen did what she did best—make Bunny look good. Eileen circulated, harvesting praise for the conference and, more important, courting potential supporters from other cities. With Bunny's front runner status an open secret, everyone at the conference wanted access to the presumptive incoming national Secretary of Education. And Eileen controlled that access. She offered some supplicants private audiences with Bunny. Others, she discreetly parried. No one with ambition in the field of public education could afford to ignore Eileen now. Every leader had a power broker. Eileen was Bunny's.

As she finished an impromptu meeting with the superintendent of Cincinnati schools, Eileen heard someone call her name. She glanced around. A mousy fifty year old man in a suit and bow tie approached. Eileen froze. *Oh, God!* It was charter school champion Moe Nuthin. And he had his arm around *Strib* education reporter Sue Wolfen. This was bad.

Like a stealthy tick, Nuthin crawled over your skin, looking for the ideal place to sink his little fangs and release anticoagulants so he could suck your blood. For some reason, Wolfen had a soft spot for Nuthin despite Eileen's repeated warnings that the man could not be trusted. Eileen suspected they were sleeping together.

Wolfen often quoted Nuthin in articles about school reform, referring to him as a "noted academic." *Noted academic, my ass!* The man was a hack. He had got his Ph.D. from an online university.

Pontificating endlessly about the evils of "the public school monopoly" and the supposed benefits of "competition," Nuthin acted as if the US education system were a business, which made sense since his Chair at the U's School of Education was endowed by the Gordy Lindt Foundation. Each year, Nuthin's "scholarly" articles touted astonishing new charter school achievements and innovations, none of which ever made a dent in the black-white achievement gap. But that never fazed Nuthin, Eileen noted wryly.

When his predictions unraveled, he would simply predict unprecedented success for the next year, which again never happened. Of course Nuthin had selective amnesia. Each year he claimed not to remember his failed predictions from the previous year. After twenty years of this, you'd think *The Strib* would catch on. But despite Eileen's best efforts to intervene, the tick was still attached to Wolfen, sucking her dry.

"Hi Moe," she greeted the tick. "Sue, nice to see you."

Wolfen nodded.

"Congratulations, Eileen," the tick grinned. "The conference is amazing!"

"Thank you."

"Have you seen the charter school wing?"

Eileen did not respond. She did not want to encourage the tick. She needed to get back to networking.

"It's incredible," the tick boasted. "This is our year. We've reached critical mass. And with Kweisi's keynote address, there's no stopping us now."

Wolfen wrote furiously in her notebook. Eileen felt like vomiting.

"We have so many programs that are a proven success," the tick continued. "And every one of those programs is scalable. Every one of them. They just need funding."

"*Really?*" Eileen interjected.

"Oh, yes," the tick nodded, ignoring her sardonic tone. "These programs are *guaranteed* to close the learning gap."

Wolfen wrote every utterance from the tick's mouth as if it were the Gospel. *They had to be sleeping together.*

"Never heard that before," Eileen needled.

"That's because you don't pay attention," the tick retorted. "And you're one to talk, Eileen. It's your *monopoly* that caused this mess in the first place!" The tick wrapped his arm tighter around Wolfen.

Eileen sighed and left them to their base pleasures. She had bigger fish to fry.

—∞—

Charity had a swagger. Even the fat ass landlord could see that. And he didn't like it.

"Bitch!" the landlord called out from the end of the hallway. "I'm coming for my extra rent payment."

"I don't gotta do that no more," Charity sneered. "I got a lawyer. She say she gonna sue your fat ass!"

The landlord started down the hallway toward Charity. She fumbled with her keys, trying to get the right one into the lock. The fat bastard moved faster than she thought he could. Charity panicked. She dropped the keys on the floor and scrambled to get them so she could unlock the door and get inside before he got to her.

—∞—

Kweisi Providence had finished his speech to thunderous applause. A long line of admirers and well-wishers now waited for the chance to meet and congratulate him. The rock star patiently received his admirers. He made deep eye contact, held hands, listened intently, promised to keep in touch. Carmen waited at the back of the congratulatory throng, studying her adversary. Providence was the consummate politician.

After fifteen minutes, Providence made eye contact with his handler from the Minnepious district. A dozen well-wishers still remained in line. The handler intervened to usher Providence away for his next engagement.

Carmen realized it was now or never. She pulled the photo of the bruised and battered Isaac from her folder, and held the photo in front of Providence. "You did this."

Providence stepped back. "Excuse me? Who are you?"

"This boy was beaten at your school."

"I didn't catch your name."

"Carmen Braithwaite. I represent this boy and his mother."

"You're a lawyer? You'll have to take this up with the district's legal department."

"I'm taking it up with you."

Providence's face hardened. "I told you to take it up with our lawyers." He pushed the photo back at Carmen.

Providence's handler brushed past Carmen, and hustled *"the most dangerous man in America"* from the ballroom.

—⁂—

Eileen could not imagine a better outcome to the conference. Bunny had met and hugged all the right people. Providence had done his thing. The local and trade press were happy. There had been no major incidents or untoward events. The conference had gone better than they had any right to expect.

Eileen wound through the crowded hallway. Conference participants made for the exits, congregating in small groups, making their evening plans. Out-of-towners would gather at pubs and restaurants strategically placed on the city's extensive downtown skyway system that connected buildings and provided a refuge from the harsh winter weather.

Eileen was looking forward to her own big plans for the evening. She and Kermit Casson had arranged for Bunny to host a VIP reception at the Minnepious Foundation. Eileen and Bunny had pared the list to 100 invitees, carefully selecting a cross-section of the nation's education elite. The crowd would be big enough to seem festive, but intimate enough to give everyone access to Bunny.

Eileen hurried. The reception started in less than an hour. She had to check on final preparations. In her haste, Eileen did not see the large black man before it was too late and she bumped into him. He was so tall, she could not see the man's face, just his torso. She tried to sidestep the large black man, but he also moved, blocking her path again. Under other circumstances, it might have felt like a comedy routine, but Eileen was in a hurry and in no mood for jokes.

"I got your letter," the man said. He had a strong Southern accent.

Eileen stepped back and looked up at the black man's face. He looked angry. She drew a blank. She glanced at the man's large chest, but he did not have a name badge. He looked vaguely familiar. *Who was he?*

The man towered over her. "You don't recognize me, do you?"

She did not. She was exhausted. With so many black people at the conference, and so many black men from the South, how could she be expected to recognize some random black man?

Then it hit her. The man was Chris Hardwell. He was not supposed to be there. He was not on the district's list of approved conference attendees. That explained the absence of a name badge. "I know who you are," Eileen sniffed.

"When I decide to leave the district," Hardwell scowled. "It'll be on my terms, not yours. You got that?"

"Don't push your luck," Eileen warned.

"Don't push yours. I won't go quietly."

"Mr. Hardwell," Eileen glared, her voice like steel. "This is neither the time nor the place. You have no idea who you're messing with. If you want trouble, I'll give you trouble like you've never seen."

She pushed past the large black man, then turned back and pointed her finger at him. "Don't you ever do that again."

—⁓—

Carmen was pissed. This was not how she had planned to spend her day. She had never been to jail before. She did not know the process and did not want to learn it. The closest she had come to the criminal justice system was a mandatory Criminal Law class during her first year of law school. About all she remembered from the class was how her professor revealed the depths of hypocrisy to which criminal courts could go. That had been entertaining. This was infuriating.

As she walked up and down the sidewalk, Carmen grew more and more frustrated. She had the address, but still she could not locate the jail building. The building with the jail's address had a modern glass façade and looked nothing like a jail.

The wind gusted. Large snowflakes pelted her face. There were few pedestrians dumb enough to be out in this weather.

Carmen stared at the building's immense glass foyer. Suddenly, she had an overwhelming sense of déjà vu. This building reflected the exact same exterior design sensibility she had seen at the Afrocentric Success Academy building. Carmen looked up. Chiseled in granite above its glass foyer, the building bore the Orwellian designation, *"Hennapious County Public Safety Building."* It had to be the jail.

The county jail and the ASA building had undoubtedly been designed by the same architect, built by the same contractor and paid for with the same public funds. It was the public sector equivalent of tract housing—standardized developments for impoverished Black people.

Carmen felt a deep rage. She was angry with Charity for drawing her to this place. She was angry with the government for building this obscene infrastructure of oppression (and making it look so banal, airy and bright). She was angry with Bunny Washington and Kweisi Providence for validating a racist system of segregation and oppression. And she was angry with herself for making decisions that had landed her in this snowy, windswept, urban tundra from hell.

Marshalling her anger, Carmen marched through the glass foyer and into the cavernous, glass encased lobby. A uniformed sheriff's deputy immediately intercepted her, directing her to a metal detector. Carmen's anger simmered as she complied with the instructions of the uniformed guards and proceeded through the metal detector.

Silent uniformed sentries, most of them white, stood at posts strategically located throughout the lobby. They wore grim expressions, discouraging interaction.

Everywhere else in the lobby, Carmen saw Black and brown people. There were a few Native Americans, some Latinos, and mostly African-Americans. Depressed people. Poor people. Desperate people. Carmen knew she had seen this pattern before. The buildings were the same. The lines of Black people obeying orders were the same. It was the other end of the urban factory, from uniformed Black children in charter schools to uniformed Black adults in the county jail.

Carmen spotted a line that snaked from a set of windows at the far end of the lobby. She walked over and asked the woman at the back of the line what the line was for. The woman looked weary and distracted. She stared at Carmen as if that were the dumbest question in the world.

"What you think? You got to pay yo' bail here." The woman sized Carmen up. "You best be sho' you really want him out, that 'fore you pay that bail. Whatever he do to get hisself in here, he goin' do it again." The woman paused. "Only next time, you ain't goin' look so good."

Carmen got behind the woman in line. She looked at the others ahead of her in line: Black and brown, all women. Carmen fit right in.

The women stood for a long time before they shuffled forward a few steps. Then they waited some more. Then they shuffled a few more steps, and waited. The line took forever.

Carmen promised herself this would be her last winter in Minnesoule. As soon as she got Charity out of jail, she would start applying for jobs elsewhere. She would take anything, anywhere. She had to get out of this place.

After forty-five minutes, Carmen made it to the window. She felt weary and disoriented.

The clerk at the counter called out, "Name?"

"Carmen Braithwaite."

The clerk typed the name into her computer system. "She's not here," the clerk pronounced. "You sure she was arrested in Minnepious?"

"Oh, sorry," Carmen smiled, realizing her mistake. "I thought you meant my name. I'm here for Charity Douglass."

The clerk rolled her eyes. She was tired of dealing with incompetent people.

"I like your braids," Carmen said to the clerk, trying the same tack that had worked at Afrocentric Success Academy.

The clerk stopped typing and glared at Carmen. "I don't know what you're up to. But if I was you, I'd think long and hard about who you hangin' out with."

Carmen froze, wishing the whole ordeal would end.

The clerk resumed typing. "Relationship to the accused?"

"I'm her lawyer."

Again the clerk stopped typing and looked up. "Honey, I'll put in anything you want. But just so you know, this is a county form. You give false information, you can be charged with a felony."

That was it. Carmen snapped. She sucked her teeth and stuck out her neck. "Are you always this rude?" she demanded. *Brooklyn was back in the house!*

Instantly, a uniformed security guard appeared. "You have to leave," the guard told Carmen. He placed his hand on Carmen's arm and began to remove her from in front of the window.

"Get your hand off me," Carmen said calmly but firmly.

The guard hesitated. A uniformed county sheriff's deputy appeared. He approached the security guard, ignoring Carmen.

"Is there a problem?"

"She's engaging in disorderly conduct," the guard replied. "I was removing her to secure public safety."

The deputy turned to Carmen. "Ma'am, if you do not leave this building quietly within the next thirty seconds, I will arrest you for disorderly conduct."

Carmen had used the discussion between the two men to reach into her purse. She held up her attorney registration card. "I'm an attorney. I just want to pay my client's bail without being harassed. Now if you don't mind, I'll pay the bail."

The deputy stepped back. He looked at the security guard and nodded. The security guard stepped back, his eyes fixed on Carmen.

The clerk smirked. "It's $250," she said, rolling her eyes. "Cash or cashier's check."

Carmen wanted to punch the clerk.

Charity had told Carmen to bring cash when she called from jail. Carmen counted $250 from her purse and gave it to the clerk. The clerk gave Carmen a receipt.

"How long until she's released?" Carmen asked.

"She'll get out after they process her. You can wait over there." The clerk indicated an area of the lobby crowded with the same people who had been waiting in line ahead of Carmen.

"Thank you," Carmen replied. *And fuck you too. I hope it's worth it, whatever they pay you.*

Carmen waited another hour before Charity appeared with a large group of Black and brown men. Charity was the only woman in the group. The men greeted their wives, girlfriends, mothers and "business associates." Based on their nonchalance, this was a familiar routine.

Carmen stood with her arms crossed. Charity did not make eye contact.

"You know I don't need this," Carmen lit into her client as they left the building together.

Charity did not respond. She was tired. She braced herself against the blustery winter weather.

"Are you listening to me? I don't need this shit."

Charity stopped. The two women faced each other.

"You cussin' me out?"

"You don't deserve it?"

"Why don't you tell me what I deserve, since you all high and mighty like that."

"You think I *have* to do this? You think I need to take your shit? It's bad enough I've got to fight *them*," Carmen said, gesturing toward the jail building. "I shouldn't have to fight you, too."

"Oh, you too good for me, bitch? You afraid maybe one day you goin' end up like me?"

Carmen was so angry she wanted to cry, but she could not give Charity the pleasure of seeing that. "We're done."

Charity knew she was getting to the hoity-toity little bitch. "Only difference 'tween you and me, is I know the deal. I don't act like I'm somethin' I ain't."

"I didn't bail you out to take abuse from you. And I sure as hell didn't take your kids' case thinking I'd have to bail you out of jail." Carmen paused, deciding how far she wanted to go. "When I agreed to represent your kids, it was because I believed in *you*, Charity. And you let me down."

"Well, you and Bill Cosby could kiss my mothafuckin' ass."

Carmen turned to walk away, but Charity blocked her path. Carmen put her arm out to keep Charity from blocking her way again.

Charity slapped Carmen's hand away. "Get off me, bitch!" she shouted. "Get yo' fuckin' hands off me!"

Carmen was shocked. She did not know how to get away from this woman without creating more of a scene.

"You ain't better than me," Charity hissed.

"I never said I was."

"You think 'cause you got money to pay yo' rent, that make you better than me?"

"You need to calm down."

The snow fell heavier as the two women stood on the sidewalk. Charity did not have a coat. Still, neither woman noticed the snow.

The few pedestrians in the area hurried around the two Black women, eager to stay clear of their feud.

Charity was getting more and more wound up. "You don't gotta fuck yo' landlord just so yo' kids don't gotta sleep in a shelter where someone goin' fuck with them."

"What?"

"How you think I got in jail, bitch?"

"The charge sheet says aggravated assault."

"You believe the police?"

"I didn't say I believed them. I said that's what the charge sheet says."

"How many times I gotta fuck the landlord?"

"What?"

"You heard me, bitch. You don't gotta spread yo' legs 'cause you can't pay yo' rent. So don't go tellin' me you goin' help me out. How you goin' help me? You goin' pay my rent? You goin' fuck my landlord? Bitch, you don't know shit!" Charity paused, shivering.

"Yeah, I hit that fat mothafucka nice and good. So fuckin' what?"

"I didn't know…"

"You didn't wanna know."

The two women stood in silence, the snow coating their hair and clothes.

Shivering, Charity muttered, "I told that fat motherfucka I wouldn't do it no more. I told him I got me a lawyer and we goin' sue his fat ass. That's when he jumped me. So I got him good. In the balls."

The two women stood facing each other in the snow. It was getting colder.

"I'm sorry," Carmen murmured.

The snow whirled around the women.

"Yeah," Charity shivered. "Me too."

Chapter 6

Carmen knew what she had to do. She had the facts. The Minnepious school district was operating two school systems—one for Black and brown children, the other for whites. The two school systems were separate and unequal. There was no doubt about that. Now Carmen needed law to fit the facts and make her case.

She went online to find out what the law had to say about segregated schools. She started with *Brown v. Board of Education*, the Supreme Court decision from 1954. Carmen read the entire ruling. It was short and to the point. The key part of the Supreme Court's ruling was:

"We conclude that, in the field of public education, the doctrine of 'separate but equal' has no place. Separate educational facilities are inherently unequal."

Carmen considered the evidence of segregation in Minnepious. She had seen "separate educational facilities" with her own eyes. There was no doubt which schools in Minnepious were for which race. There had not been a single white student at Afrocentric Success Academy. And there had been only a couple Black students at John Dewey Middle School. Less than five miles separated the schools, so there was no question the students could have attended either school if their parents wanted them to *and* the school district allowed them to.

So why was one school all Black and the other virtually all white?

Carmen reflected on the facilities. Afrocentric Success Academy's fancy new building was *far* better than Dewey's old building. ASA's modern, airy building would have cost $10 million or more to build. The physical space at ASA was much cheerier than the gloomy classrooms with small windows at Dewey. Everything looked better at ASA – *on the surface.*

But what had Carmen found inside, *in the classrooms?*

At ASA, children wore uniforms, were drilled to stay in line, submit to authority, not ask questions, accept punishment as "not punishment," prepare for tests, and be physically and emotionally abused. At Dewey, children were encouraged to express themselves in a variety of ways, were treated as equals by adults, were pushed to evaluate their assumptions and think critically, and were free to challenge authority.

What were the student outcomes at these schools?

Carmen reviewed the data. The children at Dewey *far* outperformed the children at ASA on standardized tests. More important, virtually all the children at Dewey went to competitive four year colleges, including some of the top colleges in the nation. By contrast, most graduates of ASA did not pursue any higher education. Of the few who did, they generally enrolled in community colleges or technical programs. And according to the research Carmen could find, almost none of the ASA students who enrolled in college was able to graduate. Most dropped out within a year, presumably unprepared for the freedom of expression and critical thinking that Dewey inculcated and colleges expected.

So what did this tell Carmen about the Supreme Court's ruling in *Brown* that "separate educational facilities are inherently unequal?" For a ruling over a half century old, it sure did stand up well to the test of time.

Carmen thought about why the Supreme Court's decision in *Brown* was still relevant a half century later. *Separate* was *inherently unequal* not because of unequal school facilities, or even unequal student outcomes. Separate was unequal because of the social stigma it inflicted, the message that one group of children was superior, and the other inferior. *Segregation inculcated a sickness of the mind that caused the society itself to decompose.*

That was what Carmen had witnessed at ASA and Dewey. Despite their facilities, the schools conveyed a clear, unmistakable message that some children were more equal than others. And what made it particularly creepy was that the society made a massive and very expensive effort to make the inferior school look *superficially* superior.

But even so, no one was fooled. Everyone—adults and children alike—knew which school was designed to train society's future leaders, and which was designed to inculcate obedience to those leaders.

Even the names of the schools screamed their segregative intent. By naming his charter school "*Afrocentric* Success Academy," Kweisi Providence might as well have announced, "*Black students only.*" Providence was well aware that no upper middle class white parent would voluntarily *choose* to put her child in a school called "*Afrocentric* Success Academy." Carmen knew this. The Minnepious school district knew it. White parents knew it. And as the Supreme Court had intimated, Black children knew it on some level, too. They knew whites wouldn't send their kids to this school because the society considered it inferior.

Carmen re-read the entire Supreme Court decision in *Brown*. She found that the Court described exactly what she had seen in today's Minnepious schools:

"*...the policy of separating the races is usually interpreted as denoting the inferiority of the negro group. A sense of inferiority affects the motivation of a child to learn. Segregation...therefore, has a tendency to [retard] the educational and mental development of negro children...*"

Carmen thought about it. *A tendency?* Carmen had seen herself what segregation did to Black children. Segregation had more than a *tendency* to inculcate a sense of inferiority in Black children. It was *guaranteed* to do just that. That was the whole point of segregation.

For the rest of the day, and the next, Carmen immersed herself in legal research. What she found did not encourage or surprise her, though her research unearthed one stunning fact. It turned out the *Brown* decision in 1954 was the *only* time in history that the United States Supreme Court had found a large scale constitutional violation but nonetheless refused to order a remedy. The Court ruled the following year in *Brown II* that even though segregation killed the hearts and minds of young Black children, *de*segregation need not be immediate, but could be implemented "*with all deliberate speed,*" which the white power structure interpreted to mean *never*.

Carmen could not grasp why the Supreme Court would back away in *Brown II* from its clear, courageous ruling the year before in the first *Brown* decision. Legal commentators claimed the Court's loss of intestinal fortitude in 1955 had been caused by a reasonable fear that white resistance to school desegregation would erode the very legitimacy of the Court. This struck Carmen as a racist cop-out since the phrase "all deliberate speed" *invited* and encouraged that resistance.

Indeed, from the very day the Supreme Court ruled that separate could not be equal in public education, whites resisted the ruling and courts found myriad reasons not to implement it. It took nearly two decades of litigation after the original Supreme Court decision in *Brown* for court-enforced school desegregation to be implemented across the country. And even then, widespread white opposition to desegregation continued.

By the 1970s, in the face of relentless legal pressure applied by the NAACP in school desegregation lawsuits around the country, federal courts finally began enforcing desegregation orders. For one brief decade—from 1970 to 1980—Black and white students in school districts across the country were finally allowed to go to school together en masse. That decade of desegregation proved short-lived, however.

By 1981, the newly elected Reagan administration reversed course and instructed the federal Departments of Justice and Education to oppose all school desegregation. In response, courts across the country stopped issuing desegregation orders and began dismantling school desegregation. The movement to *reverse* desegregation and *re*segregate the nation's schools picked up steam in the eighties and nineties, rolling unabated through the present, embraced equally by both major political parties. Politicians of all hues decried "forced busing." They called for "local control" and claimed desegregation was a failed "experiment" that no one wanted.

Politically appointed federal judges eagerly validated this trend. Judges became heroes to their upper middle class friends, families and neighbors as they ruled in favor of white plaintiffs challenging school desegregation. Carmen was amazed at the intellectual dishonesty of the judges who dismantled desegregation. Despite decades of proven racial discrimination and school segregation targeting Black children, the courts began to rule that *white* children were the victims of *reverse discrimination* if they had to ride buses to attend school with Black children.

The courts had no problem with white children being forced to take long bus rides across vast suburbs or in rural areas, as long as those children attended school with other white children. But if a bus transported one white child to sit next to Black children, then busing suddenly violated the holy Constitution that had designated Black people as three-fifths of a person. Unlike the violation of the Constitutional rights of *millions* of Black children caused by segregated schools, the supposed violation of *one* white child's right not to be forced to attend school with Black children trumped the rights of all Black children and *had to be remedied immediately* to ensure that no other white child would ever suffer this irreparable harm.

The hypocrisy of the legal system took Carmen's breath away. A nation of laws, as the United States loved to portray itself, looked like anything but. There was one standard for the dominant racial and political majority and another altogether for the disfavored minority. This clear double standard made Carmen nervous about her ability to put together a successful lawsuit. She considered whether there were gaps in her legal analysis. She knew any case she might bring would be subject to intense scrutiny. Was she missing something important?

As she looked at all she had uncovered, Carmen did indeed find a key gap. She understood that segregation harmed Black children. She had seen plenty of evidence of that. But she had no research on the impact of *de*segregation on Black children. She needed to understand what the evidence showed about this.

Carmen plunged into this research. She looked for studies and scholarly papers exploring the correlation between school desegregation and student achievement. To her surprise, she found little research devoted to this important subject, particularly compared to the voluminous studies trying to claim that segregated schools *might potentially* work despite their actual dismal results.

After hours of research, Carmen finally found a few studies showing the impact of desegregation on Black student achievement and life outcomes. What those studies demonstrated stunned her. They showed a clear, irrefutable link between school desegregation and improved educational and life outcomes for Black students.

The studies revealed that the only decade during which the learning gap between whites and Blacks had ever decreased nationally occurred from 1970 to 1980—the only decade of widespread desegregation. This narrowing of the learning gap occurred not because whites did worse (white test scores actually improved during this lone decade of desegregation), but because Black students did so much better that they gained on whites for the first time ever.

No wonder whites would do anything stop school desegregation!

As she did this research, Carmen realized she had stumbled onto something far bigger than just a violation of Charity's kids' legal rights. She had uncovered a massive, open conspiracy by politicians and the legal system to keep the schools segregated and inculcate a sense of inferiority among Black children. School segregation was not just an anachronistic remnant of the racist past. It was alive and well in the present. And if no one did anything to challenge it, school segregation would remain, as George Wallace had proclaimed, America's cancer *forever*.

Carmen knew she had to do something radical. She had to challenge not just the treatment of Charity's children in their schools, but the system of school segregation itself. She would pursue legal action not only on behalf of Charity's children, but on behalf of *all* children harmed by this duplicitous, illegal system of oppression. How to do this, she was not sure. She needed a legal framework that could withstand the scrutiny of judges dedicated to protecting the status quo of segregation and white supremacy. That would not be easy.

Carmen kept researching, looking for a legal theory that offered a new way to attack an old problem.

—◊◊—

Bunny accosted her daughter. "What is wrong with you? I just saw your school choice for Melissa."

Bea was taken aback. "What did you expect me to do?"

Bunny could not believe her daughter was this stupid. "How could you put your own daughter in there?"

"It's only kindergarten," Bea protested.

Bunny was incredulous. "*Only* kindergarten?" She wanted to shake some sense into her daughter. "Don't you know they can undo in one year all the advantages you've given Melissa?"

Bea was infuriated. She knew the school district better than her mother, even if her mother was superintendent. As a teacher, Bea had a more reliable view from the ground up than her mother had at the top. She felt like crying, she was so frustrated. "Mama, I have looked at every single school..." her voice trailed off. She did not know what else to say.

Bunny stared at her daughter, unable to believe it had come to this.

Bea looked away. She could not withstand her mother's withering glare. "What do you want me to do, Mama? You want me to send her to one of those elementary schools in southwest Minnepious? Haven't you seen what that's done to Brent?"

Bunny did not respond.

Bea wept.

Still, her mother did not relent.

"I can't do that to my daughter," Bea sobbed. "I can't do it..."

"But *Afrocentric*," Bunny shuddered. "How could you be so stupid?"

Bea wiped her tears away. She realized there was no point trying to reason with her mother. "I don't want to talk about it," she said, her voice icy. "You wouldn't understand."

—◊◊◊—

Carmen pulled to the curb in front of Charity's apartment building on the north side and sat in her car for a moment. It was December. No one was crazy enough to hang around outside in the winter cold. Still, three police cruisers drove by within a two minute period. Each slowed and crawled by Carmen's parked car. The white cops eyeballed her. Annoyed, Carmen waved to the third cop as he inched past. He stared back.

Carmen got out of her car and carried a small bouquet of flowers. Against her better judgment, Carmen had lent Charity $1,400 to cover the security deposit and first month's rent for this apartment. The loan depleted Carmen's meager savings, and even though Charity promised to repay the money, Carmen had already written it off.

Carmen pressed the buzzer to Charity's apartment. Charity buzzed her in, and Carmen pushed through the heavy security door. The carpet in the building was old and worn. The hallway needed paint. But at least Charity would no longer have to fend off a rapist landlord.

Carmen had tried to convince Charity to press sexual assault charges against her previous landlord, but Charity just laughed. She told Carmen to get real. Carmen then quietly negotiated a $1,000 settlement payment from the landlord and an agreement to drop the criminal assault charges against Charity. As part of the deal, the landlord demanded Charity move out immediately.

Finding an affordable apartment for Charity on short notice had not been easy. The city's rental market had tightened after the collapse of the housing market. Thousands of families fled their foreclosed homes for rental units. One of the partners in Carmen's firm, Tim Pound, had profited nicely from this trend, buying up foreclosed homes for pennies on the dollar and converting them to rental units.

Fortunately, Pound owned an apartment building in north Minnepious with a two bedroom unit available. Normally, Charity's arrest for assault would have disqualified her from rental housing, but Pound agreed to rent the unit to Charity as a favor to Carmen. The $1,000 settlement payment from Charity's old landlord would cover her second month's rent and a little extra. Carmen took no attorney's fee for negotiating the settlement. Today was Carmen's first time seeing the apartment.

Charity opened the door.

Carmen handed the flowers to Charity as she entered the apartment.

"These are for you. You got something to put them in? They need water."

Charity looked at the flowers. No one had ever given her flowers before. "What you want from me?"

"It's just a house warming gift. That's all."

"House warming? What the hell's that? Don't nobody just give you shit, don't want somethin' back."

Carmen considered how to get through to Charity. "Okay, I want something."

"Um-hmm," Charity nodded. "I knew it. What you want?"

Carmen sat on the living room couch. She sank deep. A spring bit into her back. "I want you to be a hero."

"A *hero*? First, you give me a *house warming* gift. Now say you want me to be a *hero*. You playin' me?" Charity paused, trying to figure out what the lawyer was up to. "I already told you I'll pay you back the money."

"This isn't about the money. I really want you to be a hero. Seriously."

Charity listened, skeptical.

"I want to file a case against the schools for mistreating your children."

"We already agreed on that." Charity knew the lawyer was up to no good. "You tryin' to back out on me now?"

Carmen shook her head. "Nope. I'm going to file the case."

"Well like I said, we already agreed on that. And that don't make me no hero."

"To your children, it will." Carmen paused. "But I want you to be an even bigger hero."

"Um-hmm," Charity nodded. "I knew you was playin' me. What you want from me?"

"I want your permission to file the case as a class action."

"What you mean *class action*?"

"I want to file the case on behalf of *all* children in schools like the ones Isaiah, Lakeesha and Isaac are in."

"I don't get you."

"I want to file a case against segregated schools."

"We don't got no segregated schools. 'Less you didn't hear, that got outlawed a long time ago." Charity enjoyed lecturing a lawyer about the law.

"Supposedly," Carmen corrected.

"What you mean *supposedly*? Someone playin' a trick?"

"You could say that."

Charity thought about it. She didn't know what Carmen was getting at, but the lawyer seemed to really need something from her. There might be something in it for her if she just played along for a while. "So what you need from me exactly?"

"I just need you to let me file the case on behalf of your children and all other children in segregated schools."

Charity considered the request. She still did not get what Carmen needed from her, but she knew the lawyer needed something. She liked the feeling of having power over a lawyer. On the other hand, she was pretty sure there was a catch or she was getting screwed somehow. Nobody did nothing for nothing. If there was one thing life had taught her, it was that. "If I say yes, what do I get?"

"You get to do the right thing, and be a hero."

"All right, Miss Carmen, I ain't stupid. First, you make that fat man pay me $1,000. Then you get me this apartment. Then you give me the security deposit and first month rent. Now you bring me flowers and tell me you want me to be a hero." Charity eyed the lawyer. "What you really want from me, girl?"

The conversation was not going well. Carmen decided to come clean. "Look, Charity. Here's the deal. I want to help you and your kids. I think what the schools are doing to them is wrong. But it's going to be a big fight, and if I take on that fight, I want to take on the whole damn system. I want to make them stop what they're doing to *all* the kids, not just your kids."

Charity knew there had to be more to the story. But still, even though she didn't understand exactly what a class action was, she decided to roll with it for a while and see what happened. She figured she could learn along the way. She was good at that. Then, depending on how things went, she could always ask for more later. "All right. You could do the class action."

—⚋—

Carmen had to line up one more duck before she could proceed. She needed Bob's father. She had not talked with Bob about it, which was probably a mistake. But she did not want him in the middle of it. And she did not want his father to feel like she was pressuring him through Bob.

"You wanted to see me?" Mr. Levine inquired at Carmen's office doorway.

"Yes. If you have a minute."

Mr. Levine came into her office and sat down. He leaned back and folded his hands behind his head. "If this is about Bob, I don't think I should get involved."

"I'm sorry, I don't follow..."

Levine leaned forward. He was amazed that his dilettante son had captured the fancy of such an attractive and highly educated woman. "I have to be honest with you. Bob...is a different sort of person. He and I often don't see eye to eye. If he's causing you problems, I'm probably not the best person to get involved."

"Problems? I don't think he's causing problems. Unless there's something I don't know..."

Levine relaxed. "If this isn't about my son, what did you want to see me about?"

"I need your professional opinion."

"Sure. About what?"

"I want to file a new case."

"Great. You need form pleadings? You want me to take a look at what you've drafted? What do you need?"

"It's not that kind of case."

Levine considered his son's girlfriend. Her inscrutability was part of her appeal. But for a lawyer as busy as he, time was money. He needed her to stop beating around the bush and get to the point. "What kind of case is it?"

"A school desegregation case."

"School *desegregation*? As in *Brown v. Board of Education*?"

Carmen nodded.

"School desegregation is dead," Levine stated.

"I know. I've been visiting Minnepious schools. Bob took me to your nephew's middle school. The schools are completely segregated."

"That's a different kind of segregation."

"Really?"

"Yes, really. I practiced some civil rights law in the seventies. People litigated school desegregation cases all over the country back then. We even had a case here in Minnepious. But those cases all involved *intentional, de jure* segregation."

"And today?" Carmen prodded. "What would you call a school district in which 26 of its 32 elementary schools have over 90 percent children of color, and five of the remaining six elementary schools are over 90% white?"

Levine was stunned not just by the statistics, but at how Carmen rattled them off. He had underestimated her. "I'd call that segregated. Where'd you get those numbers?"

"From the state Department of Education website. They're all there. You just have to spend some time finding the right links. They don't make it easy."

"Those statistics do look bad. I'll give you that. But without evidence of *intent*, you've got no case. Federal courts require *intentional* segregation."

Carmen was ready for this objection. "The school board is elected by a 70 percent white majority. The board and superintendent use census data when they set the school attendance boundaries. They know exactly who lives where, by race and income."

Levine thought about it. "So it's not by chance when the Black kids all end up at certain schools and the white kids at other schools."

"It can't be. The school district switched from magnet schools and open attendance areas to neighborhood schools."

"Which locks you into your neighborhood school," Levine observed.

"Your *segregated* neighborhood school," Carmen added.

Levine thought some more. "You know, my sister loves the new neighborhood schools."

"I'm sure she does. I visited her son's middle school. It's got the same student demographics as the top suburban schools, like Eden, and a curriculum comparable to the best private schools. Bob and I sat in on a class where they dissected Shakespeare's *The Tempest*."

Levine listened intently.

"But look at the other side," Carmen continued. "Flip the mirror and look at the segregated *Black* schools. They're a disaster. Over 60 percent of the kids fail to graduate. Those who do make it through high school will be lucky to flip burgers with the *Bantu* education they receive."

"Bantu education?"

"It's what Black South Africans called the segregated schools under apartheid."

"I know the term. I just haven't heard it in thirty years."

Carmen could tell Mr. Levine was still skeptical. "Don't be fooled by the passage of time. We're dealing with the same segregation that has been around for decades. You asked about *intent* to segregate? Would your sister send her son to a school called *Afrocentric* Success Academy?"

Levine laughed.

"I didn't think so. So let's not pretend the district lacks intent to segregate the schools."

Levine admired Carmen's determination and preparedness. But he still felt she was being naïve. She was ignoring certain political realities.

"You haven't talked about the superintendent," he said. "She's…"

"Black?"

Levine nodded. "In the seventies, the school board was run by white people. The superintendent was white. It was easy to prove unlawful intent to discriminate."

"But you think having a Black superintendent makes it harder."

Levine raised his eyebrows. "Don't you?"

"Maybe that's why they put her there," Carmen replied.

"Do you really want to try to prove that?"

"What? That the white political majority hired a Black person to be the face of a discriminatory, illegally segregated school system?"

"Let's face it," Levine said. "It does not make your case easier to have a Black person in charge of the schools. Legally or politically. That's just a fact."

"I'll deal with it."

Levine was not persuaded, but he saw no reason to belabor the point. There was another problem with Carmen's legal theory. It was as if Carmen had emerged from a time warp with a case from the past that today's courts would never accept. "I take it you're aware that all cases over the past thirty years have gone *against* school desegregation?"

"Actually," Carmen countered. "I researched that. *Federal* courts have abandoned school desegregation. You can't win a school desegregation case today in federal court. But state courts are a different story."

Levine was intrigued. "I didn't know that."

Carmen kept going. "Under most state constitutions, including Minnesoule, all children are guaranteed an adequate education. It's a fundamental right. That's not the same under the federal constitution."

"So your argument is that a segregated education is not an *adequate* education and therefore violates the state constitution?"

"Exactly."

Levine thought about it. "It's an interesting theory. Has it been tested anywhere?"

"Connecticut."

"And what happened?"

"The plaintiffs won on liability. They're still litigating the remedy...ten years later."

Levine shook his head. "Just like *Brown*. The court finds a mass violation of fundamental civil rights, but refuses to order a remedy. Courts fear resistance from the political branches. They think it will erode their authority."

"They also fear white backlash," Carmen added.

"True. These days, you might face a pretty severe *black* backlash, too."

"I've thought about that," Carmen replied. "I'm prepared for it."

"You sure about that?" Levine considered whether it would be appropriate, then figured he should say it now rather than leave it for later. "They'll criticize you for dating my son."

This was the least of Carmen's concerns. "Mr. Levine…"

"Jamie."

"Jamie. This is bigger than who I may or may not be dating."

"You're missing my point, Carmen. When you start digging up old skeletons, people will attack you with everything they can. They could care less if it has anything to do with the merits of your case."

"I understand. And I really appreciate your advice." Carmen paused. "But I was actually hoping for something more."

Levine waited, intrigued.

Carmen summoned her courage. She had no idea how Mr. Levine would react. "I was hoping you'd agree to be my co-counsel on a school desegregation case against the City of Minnepious and State of Minnesoule under the state constitution. An adequacy case."

Levine was floored. It had been over two decades since he'd even *thought* about civil rights cases, much less litigated them. He was also flattered. Perhaps Carmen had only come to him because of her relationship with his son. But he preferred to think she had also come to him because she saw something in *him*.

At this point in his career, he liked to think of himself as an eminent lawyer. But with each passing year, he also had a gnawing fear that he was becoming just another doddering old man, holding on, hoping to remain relevant in a legal profession and larger society that had long since passed him by. "Why me?" Levine couldn't help asking.

"I need someone more senior on the pleadings. Someone with *gravitas*, who can give me good advice, help me avoid mistakes. You're the only senior lawyer in the firm who talks to me." Carmen paused. "I haven't told Bob…in case you say no."

"I'll do it," Levine decided. "Do you have a plaintiff?"

Carmen smiled. "Do I have a plaintiff!" *If only I can keep her out of jail.*

Levine grinned. "Should I be scared?"

"No. Bunny Washington should be scared."

—◆—

Eileen sat very still. She had been sitting this way, watching Bunny read the 37 page legal document, for nearly an hour. Bunny remained silent as she pored over the document. Finally, the superintendent read the last page and looked up. She shoved the legal document back at Eileen.

"Is this someone's idea of a joke?"

"I don't think so," Eileen replied. "They seem serious, based on the cover letter." The one page cover letter said the law firm would file the case on Wednesday if the district did not schedule a settlement meeting by then. Today was Tuesday.

Bunny frowned. *"Braithwaite,"* she muttered. "That's the girl who was at Pleasant Village with Onyekachukwu."

"I don't know much about her," Eileen admitted. "From what I could find out, she went to Harvard Law School, and she's only been in Minnepious…"

"Who is the other lawyer, James Levine?" Bunny demanded, cutting her off. "Why's he doing this? Is she *fucking* him?"

Eileen quickly shut the door to Bunny's office, afraid someone might hear. "Bunny?"

"I want to know *everything* about her. And I mean everything! You got that?"

Eileen had never seen Bunny this worked up before. Ever. What had so gotten under Bunny's skin? Eileen knew better than to ask. "I'll use Vinny," Eileen offered. A retired cop's relationships would come in handy.

Bunny glared at Eileen. "Use every resource we have." She pointed at the legal document in Eileen's hand. "If I hear another word about this, *ever*, if I have to deal with it in any way, if I ever have to see that lawyer again, you have failed. Is that clear enough for you?"

Eileen got up, legal document in hand, and got out of Bunny's office as fast as she could without appearing rude. She did not understand Bunny's reaction to the lawsuit. The district got sued all the time. They dealt with obnoxious lawyers all the time. Bunny never even paid attention.

Maybe it was the pressure of the upcoming decision by the President-elect. If that was it, Eileen could reassure Bunny. She had good news. Bunny had no reason to worry. Eileen had heard that morning from Munson, the head of the Presidential transition team. Bunny was a shoo-in. It was a done deal. Next month, the President-elect would announce he had selected Bunny to be national Secretary of Education.

—ᴗ—

After Eileen left, Bunny sat in her office a long time. She ignored phone calls. She had Alain cancel her morning meetings. All she could think about was that one statement in the legal complaint. She had read it over and over again until she memorized every word.

Who had written it? Was it that vicious, stupid little bitch? Or was it a white man ignorant of what loose words could do to a reputation painstakingly built over an entire career? In her heart, Bunny knew it had to be that little bitch.

Bunny took a deep breath, trying to calm herself, but the words danced across her mind.

She closed her eyes, but the words seared her brain.

She imagined what others would say. She thought of what her grandmother, who had followed her north from Mississippi, would say.

Bunny tried to think positive thoughts, but those hateful words from the legal document remained, like a watermark across the back of her mind:

"Coordinating closely with MPS school board members, who were elected by a white majority electorate, Superintendent Bunny Washington personally directed and approved the division of the school district into two separate and unequal segregated school systems: a high performing sub-district for white students and a failing sub-district intended to inculcate inferiority in children of color, particularly African-Americans."

Bunny saw prisms and felt a migraine coming on. She put on her winter coat, and turned off her office lights. She took three Extra Strength Tylenols. She did not feel up to driving herself home, but she did not want Vinny to drive her home either. She wanted him to stay focused on helping Eileen. Time was of the essence. They had less than 24 hours to dig up dirt on Braithwaite.

Bunny was sure Carmen Braithwaite would collapse under scrutiny. They would bury her. And they would bury that statement in her vile legal complaint with her. They would make a quiet settlement before anything could be filed in court. These scandalous allegations could never see the light of day.

—⚉—

Bob and Carmen lay together in bed. Carmen hoped she would not regret having let Bob progress from the couch to the bed. They were still fully dressed, but the bed was suggestive, to say the least.

They had not slept together, and Bob wasn't pushing it. In any case, she would not sleep with him. Yet. What the future held, she could not say.

"What do you think they'll do?" Bob asked. He was trying to keep his mind off Carmen's incredible body, but it was not easy. His hand caressed Carmen's back and slid along her ribs to the side of her breast.

Carmen removed Bob's hand. "Is this a good idea?"

"Maybe not," Bob admitted. He rolled away from Carmen until he reached the far edge of the bed. "How about if I stay here?"

"Better," Carmen giggled. "Now, what were you asking?"

"What do you think they'll do tomorrow? About the case."

"I don't know. They probably deal with stuff like this all the time."

"My dad doesn't think so. He thinks you've stirred a hornet's nest."

"Maybe."

"He thinks black people and white people are locked in a dance, with all the steps choreographed."

"He may be right."

"He says you're trying to teach people new dance steps."

"Actually, they're old dance steps. But nobody remembers them."

"My dad does."

"Why is that?" Carmen asked.

"To be honest, I'm not really sure."

"I think I know."

Bob raised his eyebrows, just like his father.

"He doesn't like where we are now. He knows there's a better way."

"You're talking about *my* dad?" Bob teased, then grew serious. "He thinks they'll go after you. That they'll find a way to hurt you."

Carmen shook her head. "I don't think so."

"My dad's sure of it. He says he's seen it before, in the sixties and seventies. He says nothing's changed now, except they've got more black people to do their dirty work for them. He says black leaders don't even have to be told what to do any more. They just know. They've basically been paid off. My dad thinks people like the superintendent will do anything to protect what they have."

Carmen rolled across to Bob. She put her arms around him and gave him a long kiss. His kissing, which was good to start with, kept improving. His hands began roving again. "All right, mister," she said. "That's it. I've got a big day tomorrow, and you've got other ideas."

"Can I stay if I behave?" Bob pleaded.

"No."

Carmen removed Bob's hands and eased him off the bed. "If you stayed, I wouldn't want you to behave. And I'm not ready for that."

With a groan, Bob rolled away. He consoled himself with the silver lining in Carmen's rejection. She had at least admitted she wanted more intimacy. Bob was sure Carmen would be worth the wait.

—⚉—

Eileen introduced herself to James Levine. She knew from his *Linked In* profile and photo to call him by his nickname Jamie. Vinny and his team had compiled a dossier of extensive background research on Levine and Carmen Braithwaite. Bunny had nothing to worry about.

Eileen ignored Braithwaite and introduced the district's General Counsel, Ezekiel Hendricks III, to Levine.

"This is Carmen Braithwaite," Levine interjected, introducing Carmen.

When all had shaken hands, the four negotiators sat at the conference table. The view of the western suburbs from this 32nd floor conference room was stunning. The dark wood of the conference table and cabinets lining the walls reinforced an atmosphere conducive to deal making and negotiations of great import. Each seat at the table had a notepad and pen bearing the legend, *"Flint, Hardy and Zoellig."* Glasses and chilled bottles of mineral water stood ready to quench negotiators' thirst.

"I'd like to speak first, if that's okay," Eileen said to Levine. She was prepared to take charge and put this distraction to rest.

"By all means," Levine agreed.

"Perfect," Eileen smiled, or grimaced. It was difficult, even for her, to tell the difference. She made direct eye contact with Levine and held his gaze. "Zeke and I want you to know we have the full backing of the superintendent and school board to be here today. We also have full settlement authority, subject to board approval."

Levine nodded. "Okay."

"I also have to tell you your complaint has caused hard feelings, especially with our superintendent."

Levine did not react. Nor did Carmen.

"We feel strongly as a district that we are part of and accountable to the community. We believe in building win-win relationships. And where we've been remiss in not building relationships, such as with your law firm, we're always open to correcting those oversights. Jamie, if I may call you that, I personally want to assure you that the district is always looking to develop new relationships that will benefit our stakeholders."

Levine raised his eyebrows.

The roundabout doublespeak annoyed Carmen.

"We believe," Eileen continued. "That there are ways to deal with… *disagreements*…that can potentially be productive. At the same time, we also feel that other ways are always…*counterproductive.* And I have to tell you, Jamie, your lawsuit falls squarely into the latter category." Eileen paused.

Levine and Carmen listened, but did not react.

"Here's what we propose. First, we would ask that you not file your complaint while we work out a mutually acceptable settlement."

Levine looked at Carmen. "Depending on the terms," Levine responded. "We could consider that."

"Excellent," Eileen confirmed. She kept her focus on Levine. She had not once looked at Carmen. "It's always a pleasure to deal with reasonable people." She paused, ready to get to the meat of the proposal.

"Here's what we have in mind. We will conduct an internal investigation into the circumstances surrounding the Douglass child's injuries. If we find any wrongdoing on the part of our employees, we will subject them to discipline in accordance with our collective bargaining agreement. We will also consider paying nominal cash compensation to the family, although you should be aware that we're under austerity constraints, and our budget is extremely tight." Eileen paused.

"Would you like us to respond?" Levine asked.

"Not yet, if you don't mind. There's more to our proposal."

"Okay."

"For the Douglass girl, and the older boy, we can certainly look at alternative placements if the mother's convinced their current programs are not a good fit. I must say, though, their programs employ only best practices. The programs have been thoroughly evaluated and highly rated. They're in high demand from families that fit the Douglass family's demographic profile." Eileen paused.

For the first time, she looked Carmen. "We often find that less educated parents do not comprehend the full social and academic benefits of our programs."

"Anything else we should know before we respond?" Levine interjected.

Eileen returned her laser focus to Levine. "Yes, I'm glad you asked. There is. While we are not in a position to pay attorney's fees as part of a formal settlement, we can look at other ways to compensate your firm. We're currently in the process of evaluating the district's relationships with outside law firms. As you may know, we rely on outside counsel to handle numerous legal matters for the district. We're currently giving most of that work to Dickie & Pittney.

"This year, our budget for outside legal fees was $3.4 million. It's projected to increase by twenty percent next year. We're thinking of spreading some of that legal work around. While we can't make any guarantees, Zeke has assured me he would look favorably on your firm's qualifications to do legal work for us next year if we can find a mutually acceptable resolution to this matter."

Levine looked at the district's general counsel. The black man nodded. "Anything else?" Levine asked.

Eileen looked surprised. "I should think we've put together a rather comprehensive proposal given the *unconventional* and unfounded nature of your allegations."

"I just wanted to be sure before we respond," Levine explained. "Now, I'll turn it over to Carmen." He looked hard at Eileen. "Carmen will speak for us. This is *her* case."

Carmen was caught by surprise.

Eileen frowned and held Levine's gaze. She was getting tired of dealing with stupid men. "Very well," she said, turning to the petulant black child lawyer. "I'm listening."

Carmen quickly gathered her thoughts. She was not sure whether to address the sour white woman who had done all the talking for the district, or the silent Black lawyer, who carried the General Counsel title. She decided to put the sour little white woman in her place first. "You seem to have misread the complaint," Carmen began. "While we certainly intend to obtain redress for the Douglass children, this case has been drafted as a class action because it's about more than one family."

Eileen maintained her smile-grimace, but her eyes betrayed disdain. She was beginning to understand Bunny's reaction to this self-righteous little ass of a lawyer. Eileen looked forward to slapping Braithwaite down.

"I did not hear one thing in your proposal about the core of our complaint," Carmen continued. "Which is that you have segregated your schools by race and class. I assume your failure to address that in your proposal was intentional."

Eileen looked at Levine. She had to ascertain if he approved of this insolence. If so, they were done.

Levine suppressed a smile. Carmen was on fire, and he was loving every moment of it. He raised his eyebrows at Eileen.

"Miss Braithwaite," Eileen sneered. "I suggest you save your *faux* indignation for court. If you thought the district would take seriously your spurious allegations of racial segregation, you are naïve indeed."

Eileen glared at Levine, addressing him next. "Frankly, Mr. Levine, I'd have thought you'd provide better guidance to your inexperienced associate." She maintained her piercing gaze at Levine. "Apparently you and your firm aren't what you once were." She stood up and looked at her attorney, who also stood up.

Carmen watched the Black lawyer-lapdog follow his master. Not once during the meeting had Ezekiel Hendricks III made eye contact with her. He left all the talking to this shriveled up evil white elf of a woman. The man reminded her of Supreme Court Justice Clarence Thomas, who never spoke—trained to be seen, but not heard.

Hendricks tossed a magazine onto the conference table. It was an old *Minnesoule Lawyer*. The cover story, splashed across the front of the magazine, screamed, *"Flint, Hardy and Zoellig: White Dinosaurs?"* Carmen stared at the cover. From the date, she could see it had come out during her third year of law school, when she was desperate to find a job.

"Haven't you seen this before?" Hendricks accosted Carmen. "It explains why you were hired."

"Get out of here," Levine ordered. "We're done."

"Oh no, we're not," Eileen replied. "We're just getting started."

"You threatening us?"

"We don't make threats," Eileen warned. She glanced at the magazine on the table. "That's child's play compared to what you'll see from us."

—∞—

Carmen and Levine remained in the conference room after the school district representatives had gone. Levine shut the door. He and Carmen said nothing for a long time.

Finally, Carmen said, "It's no big deal."

Levine shook his head. "No, it's not right."

Carmen looked away. "It's not like I didn't know on some level…"

Levine waited for Carmen to look at him. "I told you before that I was the first Jew in the firm. Remember?"

Carmen did not respond.

"I implied that it was somehow comparable to your situation as the firm's first black lawyer. Well, it's not. This is a racist place. There's no getting around that."

"I told you, it's okay," Carmen replied. "I should have known about the article." She sighed. "When I got the job offer from the firm, I was relieved. I didn't care about anything other than having a job. I didn't care about the firm. I didn't even know where Minnepious was. I just needed a job. I was graduating from law school with student loans to pay." She paused. "I went to Harvard Law. And I didn't have a job offer…" She held Mr. Levine's gaze.

"All these firms are racist," she frowned. "That school district is racist. Don't worry about me. If I couldn't handle it, I wouldn't be here."

"I believe that," Levine replied, then grinned. "Perk up, Carmen. You just turned down a couple million dollars in fees for the firm!"

Carmen laughed. She glanced at the cover of the magazine on the table. "I guess the white dinosaurs hired the wrong Black woman."

Levine also laughed. "I got to tell you, Carmen. The way they tried to bribe us reminded me an awful lot of the seventies. After we file the complaint, there's someone I want you to talk to. She's an old client. She never had much formal education, but she may be the smartest person I've ever met. You'll like her."

—∞—

Reverend Hal threw the newspaper onto Kweisi Providence's desk. "What the fuck is this?"

Providence didn't say shit. He just sat there. Reverend Hal stared him down.

"Kweisi, I known you when yo' name was still Theodore. So don't go thinkin' you goin' take this kind a money, and not do nothin' for me."

Providence looked at the headline on the cover page of the local Black newspaper, *The Minnepious Word*: *"Afrocentric Success!"* The headline was not the problem. The huge color photo of Providence was. It showed him standing next to financier Sam Irvine, holding an oversized cardboard check for $20 million.

"Twenty million dollars?" Reverend Hal spat. "What you goin' do with that kind a money?"

"It's not for me," Providence objected. "It's for our charter school network."

"*Puh-lease*, Negro. Don't you play that *it's not for me* bullshit. Who you think you talkin' to, *Theodore!*"

"I ain't goin' argue with you, Hal. What you want?"

"Now we talkin.' I want a piece, man. I want somethin' for me, too."

"You know I can't do that. Too many people lookin', man. The dude gave us the money put a accountant in my office. We can't spend nothin' she don't approve."

Reverend Hal shook his head. "Fuck that, man. You betta figure it out. 'Cause I ain't goin' away."

—⁓—

Carmen and Bob jostled through the crowd toward the escalator inside the Wal-mart Wal-rena, home of Minnesoule's perennially underachieving NBA team, the Cyber Hounds. As she walked, Carmen looked around at the eager throng. She was surprised that people got so dressed up for a basketball game. Considering the NBA had a reputation for being a "Black" league, she was also surprised at how few Black people were in the crowd, though this was Minnepious.

Bob grabbed her hand. "C'mon. We're gonna miss the tipoff!"

Carmen and Bob rode the escalator to the Stadium level. Then they took another escalator to the Sky level. Carmen had never been to the arena or seen a professional basketball game before. Bob had sprung for the tickets to celebrate the filing of her big case earlier that afternoon. When they entered the Sky level, Carmen briefly felt vertigo. She followed Bob up and up until they were four rows from the roof of the arena. Bob's DJ income had limited them to nosebleed seats.

Carmen would have to take on faith that the African-American and Eastern European men in shorts and jerseys on the court far below were tall. From where she sat, the players looked like midgets. Strobe lights and house music pumped across the arena. A mascot in a dog suit shot packaged t-shirts through a tube into the crowd. People scrambled to get the t-shirts, which all landed at least twenty rows below where Carmen and Bob were seated.

"Sorry about the seats," Bob said, holding Carmen's hand. He kissed her.

Carmen felt self-conscious. Other than the players far below, she was one of the few Black people in the arena. She kept the kiss quick. "Don't worry about it," she assured Bob. "This is fun!"

Bob grinned. The boy was obviously in love.

Carmen tried to follow the action on the court, but it was hard to see the features of the players. It was like watching pieces move on a chessboard with a tiny ball flying among them. Carmen noticed that the man in the seat next to her had binoculars. That was foresight. She mostly watched the game on the large video scoreboard screen, which was easier than straining to see the players on the court far below.

"My dad told me they tried to buy you off today," Bob said during a break in the "action," if you could call it that.

"I don't know. I think they were just testing us. They didn't seem to have a clue what the case is about."

"My dad said their offer could have been worth a couple million dollars to the firm. And you would've got credit for bringing it in."

Carmen shrugged. "That's not what the case is about."

Bob looked at her. "What is it about?"

"I told you before. It's about school desegregation."

Bob raised his eyebrows. "But you know the school district won't agree to busing."

"I didn't say the case is about *busing*. Kids already take buses to school. They take buses to segregated schools. The case says they should desegregate the schools."

"Carmen, I know what the case says. I'm just asking if you've thought through what the case can really deliver. I mean, realistically."

"Are you a DJ or a lawyer?" Carmen shot back, then regretted it.

Chastened, Bob released Carmen's hand and pretended to watch the midgets on the court below.

Carmen was too irritated to apologize, though she felt bad about attacking Bob. His assumptions about what was possible annoyed her. They betrayed his white perspective. The more she thought about it, the worse she felt about Bob.

Since the game was unwatchable from their nosebleed seats, and she did not want to talk to Bob, Carmen scanned the crowd. She traced the outline of the court with her eyes, looking for celebrities. Bob had told her the courtside seats went for $400 apiece. It was hard to tell who they were, but Carmen spotted one Black couple sitting courtside. The man looked familiar. She tried to place him. Was he an R&B singer? She wasn't sure. Maybe an actor? He was too far away. She couldn't make out his features.

At a break in the action, Carmen borrowed the binoculars from the man next to her. Through the binoculars, she tried to locate the Black couple courtside. After a moment, she found the Black woman. The woman was in her twenties or early thirties and extremely attractive. She might be a model or actor, but Carmen could not place her. Carmen panned left with the binoculars to get a close up view of the man next to the attractive young woman. When she caught a full view of his face, she recognized him instantly: Kweisi Providence.

Carmen returned the binoculars and glanced at Bob, who was still pouting. She looked at the tiny Black players running up and down the court tossing around the tiny ball. She sat back in her chair, surrounded by screaming white people. It was going to be a long game.

—⁂—

The next day, blowback hit.

First, a small headline on the third page of the *Strib* Metro section noted: *"Woman from Chicago claims school discrimination."*

Carmen read the article. It mentioned nothing about the lawsuit's main allegations of racial segregation. Instead, the writer, Sue Wolfen, quoted superintendent Bunny Washington denigrating the case as a *"baseless"* complaint from a *"disgruntled parent with a history of mental and legal problems."*

Wolfen also quoted *"unnamed sources"* saying the complaint had been filed by a *"junior lawyer"* in a firm that *"was investigated recently for allegedly discriminatory hiring practices."* At the end of the article, Wolfen quoted the district's general counsel, Ezekiel Hendricks III: *"We have retained outside counsel and will soon be filing a motion to dismiss this frivolous lawsuit. We expect the motion to be granted, and we intend to pursue sanctions against the attorney who filed this case so we can recover the precious public funds that are being squandered to defend against this baseless lawsuit."*

Carmen figured she better talk to Mr. Levine. She had not anticipated such a one-sided account in the newspaper. She considered calling the reporter to complain, but she doubted that would help.

Her office phone rang. She picked it up. "This is Carmen Braithwaite."

"I'm Kermit Casson," an unfamiliar voice greeted Carmen. "Calling from the Minnepious Foundation."

"Oh," Carmen replied. She had no idea who this person was.

"I just want you to know that as a Black man, I am personally offended by your lawsuit."

What? Carmen's mind spun. She considered hanging up.

"If I were you, I'd drop this lawsuit," the caller warned. "You're messing with the wrong people."

Carmen could think of no suitable response.

"You got that?"

Carmen hung up.

Her cell phone rang. Maybe it was Bob. The Cyber Hounds basketball game had been a blowout and they left early. She had not invited Bob to her place after the game. It was not over between them, but there was definitely a frost. After the creepy call from Kermit Casson, whoever he was, she could use someone to talk to, though. "Bob?"

"Bitch!" a voice assaulted her. "You fuck with Bunny, you fuck with all of us. I know where you live, bitch. Drop the case."

Carmen hung up. She checked the number on her display. It was blocked.

Minnissippi

Chapter 7

Charity went to the community center hoping to get a lead on a job. When she told the receptionist her name, two guys she didn't know walked up to her. One of the guys was kind of good looking. The other was funny looking.

"You go, girl!" the good looking one said to Charity.

She stared at him like he was crazy.

"Yeah, girl, you go!" the funny looking sidekick repeated.

"This sista's the real deal!" the good looking one shouted so everyone in the community center reception area could hear.

"The real deal!" his echo repeated.

This was crazy! Charity was not used to being praised, and certainly not by people she didn't know. Nobody ever noticed her, unless they were trying to get some, or get her money. Since she never had much money, it was men trying to get some that noticed her. But these guys were different. They were acting like she was a big deal, and they didn't seem to be coming onto her. Charity wondered if they were gay.

"This sista's a hero!" the good looking one called out to the staff of the community center.

The staff ignored him.

"That's right!" the funny looking one parroted. "You could call her a *she-ro!*"

Charity had *never* been called a hero, or *she-ro*, before by anyone. Carmen had told her she would be a hero, but that was just the lawyer trying to play her.

"She's suin' the school district for segregation!"

"Seg-re-ga-tion!"

"Hey, Rufus, keep it down," the receptionist at the front desk called out to the good looking guy. "Unlike you and Andrew, we got work to do."

"I got you, sista Latifa!" Rufus responded. "You got important work to do while Africa is burning."

"Yeah, Africa is burning," Andrew repeated.

"And the Black man is doin' the freak!" Rufus sang.

"Hey," Andrew grabbed Rufus. "I heard that before. Where'd you get that?"

"It's from a song, man. A calypso song."

"That's cool."

"Sista," Rufus introduced himself to Charity. "I'm Rufus. This is my comrade Andrew."

"You all faggots?" she whispered.

"Come again, sista?"

"You all fags?" Charity repeated. "You know, like Rupaul or somethin'? I seen him on Oafrey once."

Rufus and Andrew looked at each other and laughed.

"Naw!" Andrew shouted. "We ain't gay!"

Latifa glared at them. "Good to know. Now, if you all don't mind?"

"Sorry," Rufus waved to the receptionist. "We'll be quiet." He turned back to Charity. "Sista, we're socialists. We're with the Socialist Workers Party."

Charity was pretty sure they were homos. "You Black Russians?"

"Naw, Russia ain't socialist no more. We're the real deal. Pan-African socialists. We'll back you all the way, sista. You gonna need our help if you wanna win your case."

"I already got me a lawyer."

"We're not lawyers," Rufus clarified. "We're *activists*. We can help your lawyer win the case. This is a case you got to win in the streets."

"In...the...streets," Andrew repeated.

Charity did not know what to make of these two gay Black Russians.

—∞—

Bunny sank her teeth into the best fried chicken north of the Mason-Dixon line. No one made fried chicken like Aretha. At least no one else in Minnepious did. Down South was another thing altogether. But she wasn't down South. Hadn't lived there in more than thirty years. So Aretha's fried chicken was as good as it got for Bunny. The collard greens were something, too. And Bunny always saved room for the sweet potato pie. That pie was as good as anything Bunny could remember from down South.

She glanced at Kweisi. He ate like a white woman. All he had on his plate was a side of mac and cheese, with one biscuit and no gravy. Bunny had heard he worked out every day, too. Hang out with all those rich white people and their habits will rub off on you.

When she finished her fried chicken and greens, Bunny pushed the empty dishes to the side and waited for her pie to arrive. Kweisi was not having dessert.

So far, she and Kweisi had eaten in silence. Bunny had called this meeting on neutral turf, in the heart of north Minnepious. *Aretha's Soul Food Palace* was an institution.

"You know why I called you," she said before her pie arrived.

"I got an idea," Providence replied.

"I need to know what you know."

"I never heard about any of this before the lawsuit."

"Never?"

Providence shook his head. "Never."

"That's not what I hear."

Providence did not respond.

"I hear that lawyer was snooping around ASA, and got a tour. I hear she got to you at the conference, too."

"I don't know about any tour of ASA. At the conference, she pushed some picture at me. I told her to get out my face. That's it."

"What do you know about the Douglass woman?"

Again, Providence shook his head.

"Her kids?"

"They started school last month. That's about it."

Bunny knew Providence was holding back. "Kweisi, we've known each other a long time. I've known your parents a long time. This mess happened in your schools."

"They're your schools, too," Providence countered. "We're chartered under the district."

"Funny you should say that. You've been pulling in a lot of greens lately."

"What's your point, Bunny?"

"Some things are important to me. Other things are important to you. If you want what's important to you, I suggest you help me with what's important to me."

Providence considered whether it was possible, or even desirable, for this meeting to have a good outcome. He felt little need to humor Bunny. He was well established now. On the other hand, he had no desire to appear ungrateful for what Bunny had done to help him get started. She had sponsored his initial charter school application, guided him through the politics, helped him recruit teachers, and put the required policies in place. But that was all in the past.

"Bunny, I appreciate what you've done for me. I would never do anything to cause you trouble…"

"But?"

"We're moving in different directions now."

"Really?" Bunny seethed. "You think so?"

Providence shrugged. "Bunny, right now, you need me more than I need you." That was the truth. No two ways about it. He had a new sponsor now, with deeper pockets and bigger dreams. White people sized dreams.

Bunny's sweet potato pie arrived. The timing could not have been better. Bunny immersed herself in the pie. She ate slowly, trying to focus on the intense warm sweetness. The pie was as good as ever. When she finished, bitterness returned.

"Kweisi, I know you're on a roll. Maybe you're feeling big and all. Good for you. You should enjoy it while you can. But you need to remember something. I've been around a lot longer than you. Things go up and they go down. People go up…and they go down.

"But there's one thing that never changes, Kweisi. We can only do what white people let us do. White people let me run these schools in Minnepious. They let me do it so long as I don't mess with *their* schools." Bunny looked hard at Providence. "So I let you run a few of our schools, Kweisi. That doesn't mean I *need* you." Bunny paused.

"Don't you ever forget that, Kweisi. 'Cause you ain't really *all a that*. The only reason you got any opportunity at all is because white people ain't really payin' attention. You might be the flavor of the month today, but if you mess with anything white people care about, they'll kick you to the curb so fast yo' mama won't know what hit you." Bunny held Providence's gaze.

"Kweisi, you should think long and hard before you cross me. I got a long memory. And I'll be here a lot longer than you think."

Providence tuned Bunny out. She was a dinosaur, stuck in the past. All Providence could focus on now was how to end the meeting with a minimum of fuss.

"How many schools you think you goin' set up in the *suburbs*, Kweisi?"

Providence did not respond.

Bunny laughed. "How many white children you goin' enroll in your *Afrocentric* Success Academy *network*?"

Providence was growing irritated. "Bunny, I didn't come here to argue with you. But let's be honest. Let's call a spade a spade. You runnin' a school system that's failin' our children. You *do* need me."

Bunny cackled. "I don't need you, Kweisi. I *created* you. You know who needs you? That rich white man giving you all the money—he's the one who needs you. He needs you so he can pretend white folk haven't abandoned us. *All* them white folk need you, so they can pretend they ain't doin' to us what they doin' to us. Whyn't you think about that."

Providence felt a burning pit in his stomach. It was this sort of stale thinking that held Black people back. It was time to pass the torch to a new generation before Bunny and her like burned down the whole damn house with their bitterness.

"Bunny, we need to move on. I'm already movin' on. You need to deal with *today*, not what you think white people did to you in the past. My schools are the future. They may not be perfect, but they a whole lot better than that mess you runnin'. We're making progress, Bunny. Real progress. You need to deal with that."

Providence stared at Bunny. She stared back.

"That's right. You need to deal with it, Bunny. 'Cause if my students don't get those test scores, the state gonna shut *you* down. Just like they did in Detroit and New Orleans. Hell, you should know. You been down to New Orleans. State turned the whole damn district into charter schools." Providence paused. "You think the State of Minnesoule goin' keep givin' you all that money to run failin' schools?

"By my reckonin', you on the clock, Bunny. Sooner or later, they goin' say, *'Bunny can't do it. Get us someone who can.'* And you know who they goin' turn to?" Providence paused. "You lookin' at him."

He sat back, put his arms behind his head, and grinned. "I don't need to put you out of business, Bunny. We could coexist. I could be your best friend. Shoot, I give you a story to sell. I give you Black children *passin'* tests. Who else goin' give you that? Without me, Bunny, you in some serious trouble."

Bunny realized Kweisi was too far gone to reason with. The publicity, the money, it had all gone to his head. The best she could hope for was some dirt to use against Braithwaite. "Kweisi, if it makes you feel better, I'll say I need you. Right now, I need you to tell me what happened to the Douglass kids."

Providence decided he would never again meet with Bunny. She had nothing left to offer him. Even though the Douglass lawsuit was her problem, not his, he would throw her a bone, just to let her save face, so he could end this meeting.

"Okay, Bunny, here's what I can tell you. The daughter got a mouth on her. She's crossin' all the teachers in the Hornets program. They discipline her, but nothin' out the ordinary. Nothin' to get worked up about.

"The older boy, he's in our Alternatives program. Seems he mighta got hurt when he was on some slavery re-enactment field trip. But it wasn't nothin' serious. Kids were just role playin' runaway slaves. The Douglass boy fell and got scraped up a little. Like I said, nothin' serious. Never heard nothin' 'bout it from his mama. And the boy got a record from Chicago anyway. In and out of juvie. He'll be locked up here, too, before you know it."

Bunny nodded. This was the sort of detail she needed. "What about the younger boy?"

"Look, Bunny, you got to understand, those kids just arrived from Chicago. They was only in school here a month. We gave 'em the MBSA pre-assessments and they all failed. By a lot. Bunny, they was well below Minnesoule state standards. We knew they was goin' fail the state tests, so we pulled 'em out on the test days. No harm in that."

Bunny nodded. She really didn't want to hear more. What Providence chose to do to protect his reputation was his business, as long as it didn't affect her.

"So the oldest boy, he didn't care none. We told him he ain't goin' be marked absent and he left the building without a fuss. The girl, she complained, but they say she complains 'bout everything. They put her in the resolution room for the day. Gave her some fashion magazines or something and she calmed down right quick.

"The youngest boy, he was the problem. Seems he don't like change. Got some kind a learnin' disability." Providence paused, reflecting on the situation. "Never got him diagnosed. Probably should have."

Bunny nodded.

"Anyway, the boy wouldn't leave the classroom. So they had to get him out. They say he's a big boy. Took a little bit, but they got him out the classroom and down to isolation. Got him restrained. Nothin' out the ordinary. Followed district policy on everything. Used the standard restraints—arms and legs in straps. Kept him face down to prevent choking. Like I said, everything consistent with district policy.

"Well, I guess the kid got scraped on the way down to iso. Nothin' serious. Just some cuts and bruises. They kinda looked bad, though, 'cause they was on his face."

Bunny figured there was more to the incident than Kweisi was letting on, but she had other ways of finding out. She glimpsed a waitress carrying a piece of sweet potato pie to a nearby table. She considered ordering another piece to go.

Providence stood up. "Bunny, you takin' this whole thing way too serious. You need to offer that ghetto mama some cash. She goin' snap it up and the whole thing goes away."

"We already tried that." *You fucking moron.* "Kweisi, you of all people should know, money can't buy everything."

Providence flashed his twenty million dollar smile. "You'd be surprised, Bunny."

—⚹—

Jamie Levine was shocked when Carmen told him about the hate call. "Jesus! If you get another call like that, we'll contact the police, just to be safe."

Carmen had never considered contacting the police a way to be safe. She had no sense of how real the threat was. Still, she appreciated Mr. Levine's concern.

"Look, Carmen. This will all blow over. Nothing's going to happen on the case for quite a while. The court schedule plays out over a long time, and everything will calm down.

"It'll work something like this. The school district will take a few weeks to plan their legal strategy. Then they'll probably file a motion to dismiss. We get 21 days to respond. They get another week for their reply brief. The judge will take a few months to issue a decision. Believe me, things will calm down once the litigation process takes its course."

There was a knock on Levine's office door. A paralegal entered, carrying a pleading. "This was just served," she said.

Levine and Carmen reviewed the pleading together. It was from Dickie & Pittney, the outside law firm representing the school district. It was entitled, *"Notice of Motion to Dismiss the Complaint and Compel Sanctions."* The document claimed that the school desegregation lawsuit was frivolous and should be dismissed without a trial. It also requested that the plaintiffs' lawyers be fined for wasting scarce public resources.

Concerned, Carmen looked to Mr. Levine.

"Don't worry about it, Carmen. It's bullshit."

Despite his reassuring words, Levine was worried. In more than three decades practicing law in Minnesoule, Levine had never seen such a fast and hostile response to a lawsuit. This might happen in New York or California. But in the small, collegial Minnesoule legal fraternity, this sort of aggressive response to a lawsuit was just not done. It seemed Carmen's desegregation lawsuit had touched a nerve.

Levine's office phone rang. "This is Jamie Levine."

He listened. "Just a minute." Levine muted the phone.

"It's Sue Wolfen from the *Strib*," he told Carmen. "I'm going to put her on speaker phone."

Carmen nodded.

Levine unmuted the phone. "Sue, I have you on speaker phone. Carmen Braithwaite is with me. Carmen's the lead lawyer on the case."

"Oh, excellent," Wolfen responded. "I have a few questions for both of you."

"Shoot away," Levine encouraged. He winked at Carmen. It was not often that one of his cases made the papers.

"I've been talking to people in the community about your case," Wolfen started. "And I'm hearing some things I'd like to get your comments on."

"Sure," Levine agreed.

"I'll get right to the point. People in the black community say they've never heard of either one of you, and they don't support your lawsuit."

Levine looked at Carmen and mouthed silently, *"What bullshit!"*

"Who are these people?" Carmen asked the reporter.

"I'm afraid I can't share that. The people I talked to said they were concerned about reprisals."

"Reprisals?" Levine blurted. "Reprisals from whom?"

He and Carmen waited for a response, but the reporter did not respond.

"Right," Levine said sardonically into the speaker phone. "We're going to retaliate against anyone who opposes us." He rolled his eyes for Carmen's benefit.

There was a long pause before Wolfen's next question.

"People say you have some kind of vendetta against Bunny Washington. They say Ms. Braithwaite threatened to file this lawsuit if the district did not give your firm legal work."

"What?" Levine exploded. "That is utter crap! Where are you getting this information?"

"I'd rather not say."

"I'll bet," Levine snorted. "This so-called interview is over."

"Just one more question, if you don't mind. How do you respond to those who say you're living in the past, that you want to refight yesterday's lost battles?"

Carmen looked at Mr. Levine. She pointed to herself, indicating she wanted to take this question. He nodded.

"I say yesterday's battles were never lost," Carmen said into the speaker phone. "And they never ended. School desegregation was never given a full chance precisely because it started to work. Everybody benefited from it, except maybe for steadfast racists. The children in desegregated schools benefited, that's for sure…"

"That's not what I hear," Wolfen interrupted. "A lot of blacks told me they were abused in majority-white schools."

"Were they district employees?" Carmen asked.

"I don't see how that's relevant."

"Well, I'm guessing they were professionals."

"That's true," Wolfen acknowledged.

"Which means their education in desegregated schools gave them the skills and self-awareness to articulate their grievances to you."

"They were very clear about the harm done to them by busing," Wolfen agreed.

"That's not what they told you," Carmen corrected. "They didn't say they were abused by busing. They told you they were abused by white people in majority-white schools. Isn't that right?"

Wolfen did not respond.

"Here's what I understand you to be saying. A number of highly educated Black professionals, who are currently gainfully employed, expressed in very articulate terms their grievances against white people who abused them when they went to desegregated schools." Carmen paused.

"That sound about right?"

"Could be," Wolfen acknowledged.

"While I do not for a moment excuse or condone the racist abuse those successful Black professionals may have suffered in desegregated schools, I would note that at least they have the ability to articulate their grievances."

Wolfen remained silent.

Carmen was feeling it. "Let's compare that to the Black children stuck in hyper-segregated schools in Minnepious. Most of them will never graduate from high school. 90 percent will never graduate from college. 99 percent will never become a professional.

"So what happens to them? A few might find work as menial laborers or entry level service employees. Most will end up relying on social services. They'll probably be victimized in a number of ways. Maybe they'll get enmeshed in the criminal justice system.

"But I'll guarantee you this. Pretty much all of them will be angry. Or depressed. And worst of all, since they won't have received an adequate education, they'll be incapable of diagnosing, much less articulating, the true nature of their grievances."

Carmen was on a roll. She no longer cared if Wolfen was listening, much less transcribing her words. "Children in segregated schools may be surrounded by Black classmates, teachers and administrators. I'll give you that. But they still do in fact suffer racist abuse just as profound, if not more so, as any abuse suffered by Black children in desegregated schools. Why do I say that? Because the white power structure in this country set up a separate and unequal school system that is predictably and reliably destroying Black children." Carmen paused.

"So Ms. Wolfen, you can quote me on this. Segregated schools are not a symbol of Black empowerment or self-sufficiency, as they're so often portrayed in the media. They're in fact nothing more than a brand of inadequacy and inferiority seared into the minds of Black children. Even if they lack the education and skills to articulate their grievances, those Black children in segregated schools know darn well that this society has abandoned them.

"And the real shame," Carmen concluded. "Is that those with the skills and opportunity to talk to you of their own grievances refuse to acknowledge the far greater harm done to the vast majority of Black children in segregated schools." Carmen paused.

"Does that help clarify things for you, Ms. Wolfen?"

"You have a very interesting perspective, Ms. Braithwaite," the reporter responded in a tight voice. "Thank you for your time."

Wolfen hung up.

Levine laughed. "That was magnificent, Carmen! Pardon my French, but *fuck them!* I don't care if she publishes a word of it. That was magnificent."

—⁂—

Alain eavesdropped on the confrontation in Bunny's office. Even though confrontations happened in there all the time, they never ceased to amuse him. Lately, it had been a veritable cornucopia of conflict. *The desegregation lawsuit was bringing out all the crazies!*

Alain stood outside Bunny's door with Sue Wolfen, who needed some quotes for her story on the lawsuit. Alain cracked the door open so they could see what was going on inside. They peered into a room full of angry white parents accosting the black superintendent.

Alain shut the door again. "They're complaining about attendance areas in the southwest schools," he explained. "They want more spaces reserved for kids who live in the neighborhood. It's our fastest growing attendance area."

"Aren't they guaranteed seats in those schools under the neighborhood schools plan?"

Alain eyeballed Wolfen. "Honey, that's *supposed* to be the deal. But right now we still have some Somalis and Latinos in those schools. The parents who live in the local attendance area want the Latinos and Somalis out, so they can have smaller class sizes."

Wolfen frowned. "Why don't they just shift the Somalis and Latinos to other schools?"

Alain smiled. He loved stirring the pot, which was not difficult given all the dishonesty and manipulation around him. He conspiratorially pinched the reporter's arm. "Aren't you the clever one!"

The confrontation in Bunny's office appeared to be escalating, so Alain decided to intervene. He knocked on the door and opened it wide enough that he and Wolfen were visible to those in the office.

Bunny nodded at Alain and Wolfen. "We'll take care of it," she assured the angry parents. "But you have to understand, until this lawsuit is dismissed, we have to be careful about how we do these things."

The apparent leader of the parents, a blond woman in her late thirties, remained impassive. "Bunny," she warned. "This won't go away. If you don't take care of it soon, we're going to start losing parents to the suburbs and to private schools."

Bunny nodded. "I understand. Believe me, we'll take care of it. I just need to do it in a way that doesn't draw the wrong kind of attention." Bunny glanced again at Wolfen in the doorway. "Now, I'm sorry to cut this short, but I have another meeting I have to take."

"So we have your word, Bunny?" the blond woman pressed. "You'll guarantee us at least fifty more slots for southwest residents, and you'll get our class sizes down."

"You have my word."

The parents filed out of the office satisfied that their children, and their neighbors' children, had secured coveted slots in southwest Minnepious' neighborhood schools.

Eileen was relieved at the outcome of the meeting. She was keenly aware of the fine line she walked between placating the white parents, on the one hand, and making sure they did not unnecessarily offend her black boss, on the other. Bunny's promise at the end of the meeting would go a long way toward alleviating pressure from the district's key white supporters.

And this was no small accomplishment. By accommodating the parents' demand for more seats in southwest area schools, Minnepious was achieving something few other urban districts in the nation could even dream of. Minnepious had not only staunched white flight, but was actually reversing it. Of Eileen's many professional accomplishments, this was undoubtedly her finest.

Alain ushered Wolfen into Bunny's office, then withdrew.

Eileen saw the parents out and assured them she would stay on top of Bunny to make sure the superintendent kept her commitment.

When the parents had gone, Eileen returned to the meeting with Wolfen. "I told them we'll follow up with them next week," Eileen reported to Bunny.

Bunny frowned. "They need to calm down, 'Leen. We'll do what they want. But we need time. Tell them to quiet down. It can't look like we're transferring 250 Somalis and Latinos out of their schools just to placate a bunch of angry white parents."

Eileen nodded. She knew Bunny was right. "Why don't we announce we're adjusting attendance areas," she suggested. "We could say it's in response to changing birth rates."

Bunny thought about it. "That'll work," she decided. "With so many Black kids leaving for charter schools, we've got plenty of space on the north side for Latinos and Somalis."

"You should reach out to Abdul at the Somali Youth Center," Eileen advised. "So he can explain it to their elders."

Bunny frowned. "They won't like it."

"I could talk with Patricio at Centro Justicia," Eileen offered. "He might get worked up when he finds out we've transferred more than a hundred Latino kids out of his territory to the north side."

Bunny shook her head. "I wouldn't bother. Patricio's got other priorities. By the time he finds out what's happening, the kids'll already be in other schools. If he complains, we'll contribute some money to one of his after school soccer programs or something."

"That'll work," Eileen agreed.

Bunny looked at Wolfen. "This is all off the record."

Wolfen motioned as if zipping her lips. "But I do need some quotes from you for tomorrow's piece about the lawsuit."

—⁓—

Carmen stared at the newspaper headline. It was the top story on the front page of *The Strib*. Ordinarily, a young lawyer would be thrilled to have her case plastered across the front page of the major local paper, but not with this headline: ***Black leaders and parents disavow school lawsuit.***

A sub-heading beneath the main headline clarified: "*Suit allegedly sparked by firm's attempt to pressure district for legal work.*"

Carmen read the article. It was an old fashioned hatchet job. The article, written by education reporter Sue Wolfen, stated:

"In a remarkable show of unity, the city's black leaders made clear today that they do not support the controversial discrimination case against the Minnepious school district filed by a black family from Chicago. Minnepious NAACP branch President Lyle Cousins proclaimed, 'Nobody's ever heard of this family or their lawyer. We love our schools in Minnepious. We don't know where these people get off slandering our superintendent, who is nationally recognized for her visionary leadership.'

"The complaint makes lurid, unfounded allegations about racial segregation in Minnepious schools even though Superintendent Bunny Washington has been recognized as one of the most innovative and effective black educators in the nation. Black parents expressed bafflement at the lawsuit's allegations. 'I don't know where that lawyer gets off attacking our schools,' black parent Fran Jefferson observed. Ms. Jefferson, whose grandfather was the first black school board member in Minnepious, currently has three children in schools that the lawsuit describes as 'segregated.' 'I love my children's schools,' Ms. Jefferson stated. 'We don't need no lawyer telling us our children need to sit next to white children.'

"The host of popular radio show Black Power Positions, Lily Onyekachukwu agreed that the most important consideration for black

parents is having black teachers and principals. 'My son loves his school. He feels safe there. He's treated with respect by people who understand our culture. I would never let some lawyer force me to put my baby on a school bus and send him to some school in the suburbs where white people could abuse him.'

"When confronted with universal black hostility to her lawsuit, attorney Carmen Braithwaite became defensive and suggested that black parents are ignorant victims of a grand white conspiracy. Blaming an amorphous and sinister 'white power structure' for setting up the schools, Braithwaite surprisingly alleged that 'black children suffer racist abuse in schools with black teachers and administrators.'

"'This kind of irresponsible, hurtful talk does more to harm our community than anything Bull Connor ever could have done,' NAACP President Cousins noted. 'It fuels self-hatred. We really have to come together as a community and support our leaders and our schools.' Cousins was one of the few black leaders willing to speak on the record. When approached for comment by this reporter, most black leaders declined to talk about the lawsuit, saying they feared retribution.

"Flint, Hardy and Zoellig, the law firm behind the case, is no stranger to racial controversy. Two years ago, Minnesoule Lawyer published an expose of the firm's allegedly discriminatory hiring practices. When informed that the lawsuit was engendering fear of retaliation, James Levine, one of the firm's senior partners and attorney of record on the case, warned, 'We're going to retaliate against anyone who opposes us.'

"Investigative reporting has unearthed another shocking revelation at the core of the lawsuit. According to a confidential high level source within the school district, who also fears retaliation by Flint, Hardy and Zoellig if her name is used, the firm's lawyers requested a meeting with the school district during which they threatened to sue if the district did not steer unrelated legal work to the firm.

"'We agreed to investigate the Douglass family's concerns,' the senior district employee explained. 'We even offered the family cash compensation. But the Douglass' lawyers didn't seem interested in that. They wanted a lot more, and they got very worked up when the district refused to steer millions

of dollars in legal work to their law firm.

"'It would violate state law to give lawyers legal work as a quid pro quo for not filing a legal case. We told them we could only consider hiring their firm as part of our regular RFP process. But the lawyers became very agitated. They said we didn't understand. Frankly, I felt extremely uncomfortable with the direction of the meeting, so we walked out. The next day, the law firm filed this discrimination case against the district.'"

As Carmen finished the article, her door opened. Mr. Levine and the President of the firm, Elmer Liechtenstein, walked in. Liechtenstein was holding a copy of the newspaper article. "Carmen," Liechtenstein said. "We need to talk."

—※—

"Okay," Bunny smiled, putting down the newspaper article. "You can keep your job."

"That's all you have to say?" Eileen mock pouted. "How about, *'Eileen, you're amazing.'* Or *'Eileen, I don't know what I would ever do without you.'*"

"'Leen, don't' push your luck. This is what we do. If it were easy, you and I wouldn't be where we are."

Eileen was floored. Bunny rarely offered praise. And this was more than just praise. The highest compliment one could ever hope to receive from any leader was to be recognized as sharing positive traits with that leader—being accepted into the leader's club, so to speak. Bunny had just acknowledged that she and Eileen shared an ability to handle the greatest challenges in urban education. Eileen savored the moment.

"You know I'm with you, Bunny," Eileen pledged. "I'll do whatever it takes."

—※—

Charity waited for Carmen at the front door to the community center.

When she arrived, Carmen hurried inside to escape the frigid December weather.

Charity led Carmen into a small meeting room. They had ten minutes before the big meeting that Carmen did not know about.

"How's the new apartment?" Carmen asked.

"It's alright," Charity responded, careful not to appear too grateful. She was eager to change the subject. "Why you wanna see me?"

Carmen would have preferred more small talk before diving in, but Charity seemed preoccupied with something. Carmen tried to formulate the best way to start. There was no easy way.

This meeting with Charity had not been Carmen's idea. She did not want to raise the subject of settlement now, but Elmer Liechtenstein had insisted. He told her she had an ethical duty to communicate all settlement offers to her client. And Liechtenstein, who was not even attorney of record in Charity's case, had just received a formal written settlement offer from the school district. The offer was addressed to Liechtenstein and Charity, but not to Mr. Levine or Carmen. *Wasn't that a breach of some ethical duty by the district's lawyers?* Carmen wondered what other dirty tricks the school district had up its sleeve.

Still, she had no choice under the ethical rules but to present the settlement offer to Charity. So her task now was to find a way to make the district's settlement offer unacceptable to her client, the very person for whom it was designed to be irresistible. "Charity…"

"What you want?" Charity interrupted, eager to get Carmen to the next meeting, the one Carmen didn't know about.

"The school district thinks you're a sell-out," Carmen blurted, hoping the attorney-client privilege would keep these words forever private.

"Sell out?!" Charity repeated. "Who they callin' a sell-out, mothafuckers!"

Carmen raised her hands in solidarity over this outrage. Obviously, she had chosen the right words. "I told 'em to stick it up they ass," Carmen agreed, adopting an unfamiliar vernacular and hoping it didn't sound too contrived.

It did.

Charity looked hard at Carmen. "You playin' me?"

Carmen laughed. "No. I'm just stressed out."

If there was one thing Charity could understand, it was a stressed out sister. "Sista, you could relax. I got your back."

Carmen realized she still had not met her ethical obligation to share the details of the settlement offer with Charity. The school district had a finely honed understanding of poor people's interests, which meant Carmen still had a high hill to climb to get Charity to reject the district's settlement offer. Carmen thought about her options. She could either share the number and then go to work undermining the offer, or she could first try to poison Charity against *anything* the district might offer, including even a big cash settlement. She was leaning toward the latter approach since she had already started on that path. The size of the cash offer loomed as a major problem, though.

Carmen had one other lingering doubt. She wanted to ignore it, but she could not. Was it right for a Harvard-educated lawyer to advise an impoverished client to reject a substantial cash settlement offer when their likelihood of prevailing in the case if they did not settle was small? And even if they did win the case, any cash compensation the court awarded to Charity would likely be a lot less than the district's current settlement offer. No matter how much Carmen wanted to proceed with the case, no matter how much she wanted to show Bunny Washington she could not be intimidated or beaten, Carmen could not shake the thought that it was wrong for her to put her own interests ahead of her client's interests.

"Carmen," Charity prodded. "What's wrong with you?"

Carmen knew she had to leave the decision to Charity. She would not substitute her own judgment for the client's. "Charity, the school district is offering you fifty thousand dollars to drop the case."

"Fifty thousand dollars!" Charity repeated, stunned.

Just then the door to the room burst open and two men came in, laughing.

"What you got, sista!" Rufus exclaimed, delighted to find Charity and the bold young lawyer who was taking on the system.

He offered his hand to Carmen. "You must be the astonishing Carmen Braithwaite!"

"I don't know about *astonishing*…" Carmen reached to shake hands with this strange man.

"I thank you, sista, for what you've done," Rufus pledged and kissed Carmen's hand. "The community is eternally in your debt."

Carmen was stunned.

Charity was even more shocked. *Maybe Rufus wasn't gay, after all.* Then Charity remembered that Rupaul kissed Oafrey the same way on television.

Carmen pulled her hand away. "Who are you?"

"My fault, sista. I thought sista Charity would have told you by now. I'm Rufus. This is Andrew. We're down with the cause, sista, 'cause desegregation is the real deal."

Carmen did not know what to make of Rufus, but she liked what he had to say about desegregation. She looked at Charity. "You know these guys?"

Rufus answered for her. "Does she know us? She's our hero! She's takin' on the heart of the capitalist beast! Just like you, sista!"

Rufus sat down at the little conference table in the meeting room. Andrew sat next to him.

Carmen looked at Charity, who shrugged. Carmen sat next to her client.

"Here's the deal," Rufus explained. "We called a community meeting for today. It starts in less than ten minutes. People are already coming in. They're angry about the schools abusing Black folk all these years. Andrew and I been doing some legwork explaining to folk that the root cause of their problems with the schools is segregation.

"We've been telling them that if white folk had kids in our schools, too, none of this mess would be tolerated. And let me tell you, sista, people are down with that. They want to do something to support sista Charity and the bold sista from out East who came here to go after the Toms been selling us out all these years."

Carmen tried to process all that Rufus was saying, but he just kept going. He talked fast.

"I know you're focused on the legal case," Rufus continued. "But sista, you need to understand this kind of battle has to be won on the streets, too. The courts are controlled by capitalist stooges put there to protect the interests of the bourgeoisie." He paused to catch his breath, then continued.

"I'm not saying drop the court case. We need that. It gives our people a rallying point. See, Black folk always want to believe the system's gonna save 'em. Of course, the people got to learn to save themselves. But that's a process. That is the struggle. What I'm saying now is your court case cannot succeed without a grass roots movement behind it."

Carmen was intrigued, though she was not about to agree in front of Charity that the court case had little chance of success. Especially not with Charity still considering the district's $50,000 cash settlement offer.

Sensing an opening, Rufus was relentless. "You can't let Bunny Washington and her *chumchas* define this case through the mainstream capitalist media."

"*Chumchas?*" Carmen repeated.

"Sounds cool, huh? I learned it from a brother in India. It's all the suck-ups shuckin' and jivin' for their capitalist masters."

This fellow might be crazy, but he had Carmen's attention.

"Bunny Washington and all her *chumchas* are already discrediting you and your case. They say you're a greedy, unethical shakedown artist, playing the race card for your own financial benefit. We all know who really plays that way. That's why they're comfortable throwing it at you."

Rufus had obviously read the article in *The Strib*.

"But we can't let that happen," Rufus continued. "We got working people coming here today to plan a big protest at the next school board meeting. We'll teach those skanks a lesson. *Black parents disavow school lawsuit*, my ass! C'mon, y'all. Let's go see the people."

Rufus stood up. Andrew also stood up.

Carmen looked at Charity. *Pretty hard to take the district's cash offer if you could be a hero to the people instead.*

"Sounds good to me," Carmen agreed and stood up.

Charity thought about it for a second. $50,000 was a lot of money. But she could always talk to Carmen about that later.

"What do you think?" Eileen asked the superintendent.

Bunny thought about the situation. "How many people can they turn out, realistically?"

Eileen shrugged. "It's Rufus and Andrew…I don't know…twenty, maybe thirty."

"Then let's not worry about it," Bunny decided. "I think we can even make it work for us. Tell Wolfen these guys are with the Socialist Workers Party."

Eileen smiled. "For all we know, Carmen Braithwaite could be a socialist, too."

Bunny nodded. "I like that. Her father's originally from Trinidad. There are a lot of leftist-socialist political parties in the Caribbean. Go online and see what the leftist party in Trinidad is called."

"Anything else we should do?"

"The more I think about it, the more I like it. Contact Adrian Jefferson and tell him we need him to travel here from Arizona."

"He's pretty old," Eileen pointed out.

"That's all right. We'll pay for his trip. Anyway, he owes me. I gave his granddaughter a job. Tell him we need him. He'll jump at the chance to be relevant again."

❖

Chapter 8

"They're leading us to slaughter!" a white girl named Amelia screamed.

"Shut up!" Rufus shouted back. Amelia screamed like this at every protest. Maybe he shouldn't have broken up with her the way he did.

Carmen raised her hands. "We all need to stick together," she pleaded with the huge crowd.

The parents and activists turned to her. It was well over a hundred people.

Carmen had no idea what she should do or say to manage such a massive group. "We don't know what we're going to face in there. But we have to stick together, no matter what."

The parents and activists crowded closer.

Carmen spotted Bob at the edge of the crowd. She had not expected him to be there. They hadn't talked since the basketball game. His father must have told him about the protest. She nodded at Bob. He grinned, but stayed at the edge of the crowd.

Rufus seized the moment. "Brothers and sisters! Sister Carmen is right. We must stay united!"

The crowd turned to Rufus, whose chest swelled as his voice boomed. He commanded the group's attention. Carmen knew she should do something, but was not sure what. She trusted Rufus, to a point. But Rufus lacked common sense.

"We're here to protest against this racist education system!" Rufus proclaimed, his finger stabbing the air. "We gonna go in there and throw all those Uncle Toms out on their behinds!"

"On their behinds, brother!" Rufus' sidekick Andrew shouted.

The crowd cheered.

Carmen grew nervous. She preferred a calm, orderly march into district headquarters. But Rufus had maneuvered himself into a position of leadership, and she did not want to be perceived by the crowd as standing in the way of justice. Other than a couple student protests she had attended at Harvard, Carmen had no experience with anything like this. *How bad could it be if she let Rufus roll with it for a while?*

Rufus got out front and waved people toward the district administration building. The group began to move, slowly at first, in fits and bursts. Parents grabbed their children, children grabbed their siblings, activists grabbed their signs. The mass of diverse personalities, ethnicities, languages, ages and interests began to move as one toward the imposing brick edifice.

Carmen spotted Charity and her three children.

Charity seemed intoxicated by the huge crowd. The idea that she was a "hero" seemed to be growing on her.

"They're leading us to slaughter!" Amelia screamed again. "They're leading us to slaughter!"

No one paid attention.

The group surged forward.

"I got the back!" Andrew shouted to Rufus and peeled off to the side. He flung open the main door to district headquarters and stood aside, holding the door as the throng passed through.

Rufus and Carmen led the way into the dingy hallway toward the school board meeting room. Carmen glanced back at the throng entering the building. She saw old, young, men, women, African-Americans, Latinos, Asians, Somalis, people in American clothes, people in traditional dress from their native countries, headscarves, light colored skin, brown skin, dark skin, mothers, fathers, grandmothers, grandfathers, teenagers, pre-teens, kindergartners, toddlers, and even babies carried by parents, grandparents and siblings.

Carmen had never seen anything like it. She was pretty sure the school board would have never seen anything like it, either. In her research, Carmen read articles in which Minnepious school board members railed against the district's multiethnic, multilingual student population as some sort of insurmountable handicap. They said Black and brown parents didn't care about their children's education and were not "involved," whatever that was supposed to mean. Carmen felt a surge of anger that the people who had come to this protest, whose passion for their children's education was so obvious, could be treated with such contempt by politicians purporting to represent their interests.

Rufus stopped suddenly. He turned and raised his arms to halt the crowd. Those closest struggled to stop as people behind bumped into them. The hallway filled with protesters. Rufus waited with his arms raised until the last stragglers caught up.

When everyone had stopped, Rufus lowered one arm and left the other raised. He clenched his fingers into a fist. Everyone watched, riveted, as Rufus called out slowly at first, then with greater force, "Hey hey, ho ho, segregation has got to go! Hey hey, ho ho, segregation has got to go!"

The crowd stood transfixed.

Again, Rufus repeated the refrain, "Hey hey, ho ho, segregation has got to go!"

Those closest to Rufus picked up the chant: *"Hey hey, ho ho, segregation has got to go!"*

Surprising herself, Carmen joined in. *"Hey hey, ho ho, segregation has got to go!"*

The chant thundered through the hallway. It was as if voices previously silenced now rose as one to shake off their oppressors.

Carmen spotted Bob shouting, *"Hey hey, ho ho, segregation has got to go!"*

She glimpsed Charity pumping her fist, shouting, *"Hey hey, ho ho, segregation has got to go!"*

Rufus turned, his fist pumping to the beat, and marched toward the closed doors of the school board meeting room. The chant continued as the people marched.

"Hey hey, ho ho, segregation has got to go! Hey hey, ho ho, segregation has got to go! Hey hey, ho ho, segregation has got to go!"

Carmen and Rufus flung open the doors to the school board meeting room. Inside, Bunny sat on high alert. Elevated on a dais next to the seven Minnepious school board members, the superintendent bore her sternest schoolmarm glare. The few members of the petitioning public in attendance sat below.

Although there were enough chairs in the room for at least a hundred members of the public, the seats were less than a quarter full. And most of those contained high ranking district staff. A handful of white, middle-class parents with grievances to raise before the board also sat near the district staff in the public gallery. The school board meeting was their forum of last resort.

The clamor in the hallway seized the attention of everyone in the school board meeting room, rendering them hyper-alert. As the door opened and chanting echoed into the room from the hallway, Bunny and all seven board members gripped the dais. They stared, mouths agape, with a mixture of fascination, fear, revulsion and anger.

The protesters stood poised in the open doorway. The cable access television camera crews swiveled to train their cameras on the protesters. Chanting from the hallway pulsated into the meeting room.

"Hey hey, ho ho, segregation has got to go! Hey hey, ho ho, segregation has got to go! Hey hey, ho ho, segregation has got to go!"

Rufus raised his hand to silence the crowd. The chanting faded, then stopped. For a moment, it seemed as if time itself had stopped. Carmen and Rufus took in the scene, sizing up the board, the superintendent and the empty seats. The meeting room was completely still, completely silent. It was like the perfect calm before a tornado, everything in suspended animation.

Carmen suddenly felt a malevolent glare. She turned and spotted the source. Not ten feet from her, standing at the podium before the school board, was the angriest senior citizen she had ever seen. Gray hair betrayed the man's age, though he bore a young man's fury, all directed at her.

The old man said nothing. He just glared at Carmen. His cheeks quivered. His nostrils flared. He wielded the microphone at the podium as if it were a weapon.

Bunny Washington ignored the protesters in the open doorway, and called to the angry old man, "Mr. Jefferson, please continue with your remarks."

Maintaining his baleful glare at the protesters massed in the doorway, Mr. Jefferson opened his mouth to speak.

Before he could get a word out, Rufus shouted, "Hey hey, ho ho, segregation has got to go!"

Instantly, the protesters picked up the chant: *"Hey hey, ho ho, segregation has got to go! Hey hey, ho ho, segregation has got to go! Hey hey, ho ho, segregation has got to go!"*

Then, still chanting, Rufus led the crowd forward. Protesters surged into the school board meeting room. Like a dam bursting, the people flooded the room, washing over and around Mr. Jefferson and the few white middle-class parents, who sat like boulders, staring at the black and brown hordes invading this hallowed sanctum of democracy.

Mothers led children by the hand. Activists guided the timid. Protesters seated themselves wherever they could. As the room filled up, people searched for places to sit. Throughout, the protesters kept up their chant.

"Hey hey, ho ho, segregation has got to go! Hey hey, ho ho, segregation has got to go! Hey hey, ho ho, segregation has got to go!"

The chant thundered across the meeting room until every seat was filled.

"Hey hey, ho ho, segregation has got to go! Hey hey, ho ho, segregation has got to go! Hey hey, ho ho, segregation has got to go!"

Yet even with all the seats filled, people continued to stream into the room and chant.

"Hey hey, ho ho, segregation has got to go! Hey hey, ho ho, segregation has got to go! Hey hey, ho ho, segregation has got to go!"

People stood behind and between the chairs, wherever they could find space. After more than five minutes, people still poured into the room, filling the gaps between chairs. Those seated and those standing kept up the chant.

"Hey hey, ho ho, segregation has got to go! Hey hey, ho ho, segregation has got

to go! Hey hey, ho ho, segregation has got to go!"

Carmen watched Bob guide a group of Latino mothers and children to an unfilled corner of the meeting room. She felt a surge of affection.

Charity and her children sat in seats of honor at the front reserved for them by Rufus. Charity did not know all these protesters from Adam, but they acted like she was a hero for real. When Rufus showed Charity the seats he had saved for her and her kids, Charity found herself wiping away tears. Nobody had ever done anything like this for her before.

Lakeesha stared at the people marching and singing about segregation. She saw her mama's tears. Her mama never cried. Lakeesha knew these were tears of joy. She had never known such pride before. She cried, too.

Isaiah tried to stay cool at first, but he found himself chanting and pumping his fist in the air along with the others. It felt good, especially when Rufus patted him on the shoulder and told him, "You're gonna help lead our people one day, brother!" After that, Isaiah shouted as loud as he could.

Isaac mostly just took in the scene. He was astonished that so many people could march and chant together. He saw his mama smiling, then crying, then smiling again. He saw his sister smiling. Even his brother was smiling. He looked at the big shots sitting up high above everyone frowning. They looked small and weak compared to the people marching and shouting.

Isaac started to laugh. He could not remember the last time he had laughed. He laughed from deep inside. He laughed and he laughed and he laughed.

When the last protester had settled into a space in the room, Rufus held up his arms to quiet the crowd. Then, in a moment that forever endeared him to Carmen, Rufus nodded in her direction, giving her the floor.

Everyone in the room looked to her.

Though trained as a lawyer, Carmen found that her voice failed her. She tried to clear her throat, but a lump blocked it. She could not swallow.

Bunny spotted Carmen's weakness and pounced. "You need to sit down!"

The superintendent's tone shook Carmen. "We have some questions for you and the board," Carmen replied, her voice cracking.

"You will have to wait your turn, Ms. Braithwaite. Mr. Adrian Jefferson has traveled all the way from Arizona to address the board. Mr. Jefferson was our first African-American board member in Minnepious. He has something to say that you and your friends need to hear."

Carmen hesitated, unsure what to do.

Rufus jumped forward. "Adrian Jefferson is a sell-out. He's an Uncle Tom dug up by the school district to try to silence the people!"

The protesters cheered.

School Board Chairwoman Julie Harmer pounded her gavel on the dais and shouted, "Silence! I demand silence!"

In response, Rufus and Andrew instigated another round of chanting.

"Hey hey, ho ho, segregation has got to go! Hey hey, ho ho, segregation has got to go! Hey hey, ho ho, segregation has got to go!"

When Rufus raised his arms to stop the chant, the protesters cheered.

Carmen felt her voice returning. She gestured toward the protesters. "These people have interrupted their busy lives to come here and ask you some questions. I think they deserve to be heard."

"Are you deaf?" Board member Reverend Hal Ballman shouted at Carmen from the dais. "Did you not hear the woman? Mr. Jefferson done flown hisself all the way down from Arizona to teach you people a history lesson!"

"Who you think you're talking to, boss?" Rufus shouted back. "Only one 'round here needs a history lesson is you!"

The crowd cheered again, further enraging Reverend Hal. He stood up, towering over the protesters from the elevated dais. The good reverend was used to being the one to rile up a crowd. He pointed at Rufus. "Boy, you and all yo' Samolians and Mexicans need to get up on outta here!"

Relishing the conflict, Rufus stepped forward, challenging Ballman's manhood. "Look at your ignorant self! You think you ain't African? You think you're better than our Somali brothers and sisters because you sittin' up there like the white man's dog?"

"*Oh no, he didn't!*" Andrew screamed.

The room exploded with laughter.

"You're supposed to be a role model, dog!" Rufus taunted. "If you're gonna sit up there on that school board and claim to know something about education, you should learn to use proper grammar!"

The crowd again exploded in laughter.

Isaiah laughed the loudest. He had never seen Black men like Rufus and Andrew, who stood so tall and confident against power.

Further enraged, Reverend Hal considered leaping down from the dais to attack Rufus. The boy was younger than he was, but Reverend Hal could handle himself. He had been in a scrape or two in his younger days, before he found the Lord. He was pretty sure he could take the socialist punk with the big mouth.

Bunny reached across to restrain the reverend. Reverend Hal shook her off. He didn't need no mama protecting him. Reluctantly, he sat down, his eyes still fixed on Rufus.

The cable access cameras captured every moment of the confrontation. This was unexpectedly sensational, unscripted reality TV drama.

Reverend Hal took personal umbrage at the behavior of young Black males like Rufus. Yes, they were angry. *So was he!* But unlike these ignorant youngsters, Reverend Hal had learned to channel his anger into constructive pursuits. He could not abide the rude exhibitionism of young Black men, who disrespected their elders and wore their pants around their ankles.

Reverend Hal tried to calm himself, but he felt bile rise in his throat. He stood again, pointing at Rufus, and shouted, "Them Mexicans and Samolians you got there don't even speak no English. No wonder they singin' about *segregation.* They don't even know what the word means!"

Adrian Jefferson took this as an invitation to jump into the fray. "You see, that's what I'm talking about." The old man trained his severe gaze on Rufus and Carmen. "You young people don't know the damage you're doing. Those people up there," he said, gesturing toward the board members on the dais. "Are not your enemies. They're your allies. You need them. Without them, you're nothing. You'll be torn to pieces."

Rufus started up the chant again: *"Hey hey, ho ho, segregation has got to go! Hey hey, ho ho, segregation has got to go! Hey hey, ho ho, segregation has got to go!"*

Again, Board Chair Harmer pounded her gavel on the dais and demanded silence. Again, to no avail.

After a full minute of chanting, Rufus shouted over the crowd, "The people united can never be divided! The people united can never be divided!"

The protesters responded with this new chant: *"The people united can never be divided! The people united can never be divided!"*

The chant was deafening. Adrian Jefferson covered his ears.

Rufus raised his hands and the chant died down. The old man glared one last time at the protesters and stalked away from the podium.

The crowd cheered.

Rufus turned to Carmen. "What do you think, sister?"

Carmen looked at the superintendent and the board. "I think it's time the people got some answers."

—⁓—

Dinner with Bunny and Julie Harmer after the school board meeting had been brutal. The two women took turns pummeling Eileen over her failure to head off the protest. *Talk about pathetic scapegoating.* Bunny conveniently forgot that she had agreed to let the protest proceed.

And what was Eileen supposed to have done anyway? How could she have known it would go so badly? She was tired of everyone blaming her for their own mistakes and inadequacies.

When she got home, Eileen found her husband Joel in a drunken stupor, as usual. She stood right in front of him, but Joel did not acknowledge her. Nursing a glass of Drambuie, he stared at an episode of *South Park*. The image on the television screen appeared to be of a child entering Hillary Clinton's vagina.

Eileen felt a surge of rage. She would normally have gone straight to bed to avoid a confrontation, but this time she decided to give her husband a taste of his own medicine. The night before, she had been forced to deal with yet another of their teenage son's transgressions.

"Not that you would care, Joel," she spat. "But Ethan was out wilding with his friends last night!"

She stared at her husband, waiting for a response, *any* response. He ignored her. "He's your son, too, Joel!"

Her husband sucked on an ice cube, then sipped his Drambuie. A commercial interrupted *South Park*, so he switched to another show, a terrorist drama. With his eyes glued to the screen, he said, "Look, it's Chocolate Jesus' favorite show."

Eileen ignored her husband's sardonic reference to the President-elect. "You're not listening, Joel," she seethed. "The police brought Ethan home. He was drunk." She paused. "Remind you of anyone?"

"What a cocksucker," Joel mumbled.

It was unclear whether he was referring to their son, the President-elect, or the villain on the television screen.

"Fucking dirty traitor..."

—⚏—

Carmen was astonished and delighted when the cable access video feed of the school board protest became a local television sensation. Minnesoule winters are long and cold, which leaves a lot of time for watching television. With precious few shows affirming their humanity, Black viewers in Minnepious usually watched whatever stupid, insulting or violent fare they could find to take their minds off the grind of daily living. By contrast, the cable access video of the school board meeting turned out to be an unexpected, and exceptionally affirming, treat for Black viewers.

According to the Nielsen ratings published online, the school board protest video outperformed all television shows and sports events on the major networks and cable channels in the Minnepious market. It was the ultimate unscripted, unanticipated, reality show smash hit. Realizing they had a hit on their hands, the cable access channel's programming staff exploited the school board protest video to the hilt. They ran the protest video continuously for a week, pre-empting the usual medley of city council committee meetings, community talk shows and neighborhood cultural events. Over Lily Onyekachukwu's strenuous objections, the school board protest video even pre-empted her popular *Black Power Positions* show.

Carmen could not say for sure what drew channel surfers by the thousands to the protest video. Maybe it was the chanting. Or the faces of irate, impotent school board members. It could have been the diversity of the protesters—a vision of what true empowerment might look like. But there could be no doubt: captured in HD splendor, the video mesmerized viewers. The Nielsen ratings proved it.

For days after the protest, random people stopped Carmen on the street to tell her they had seen her on TV. People gleefully congratulated her, saying Minnepious had never before seen an uprising like this. It was as if the city's beaten down Black citizens had received a jolt of adrenaline, an infusion of hope.

Sue Wolfen did not share this enthusiasm. She had missed the school board meeting because of a conflict with her daughter's figure skating practice. She heard about the protest the next day from her editor, who had seen the cable access video on television. He instructed her to watch it, which she did the next evening. After calling Eileen to get the lowdown, Wolfen wrote a small piece that appeared on page 13 of *The Strib* Metro section. Claiming the protesters were *"20-30 disgruntled activists, who seemed more pre-occupied with the socialist organizers' offer of free food than with education policy,"* Wolfen wrote:

"Despite remarkable restraint shown by Minnepious school board members

and superintendent Bunny Washington, the professional anarchists who crashed the school board meeting threatened violent retaliation against those who disagreed with their radical socialist agenda and demands. The protest appeared to be yet another tactic concocted by the Flint, Hardy and Zoellig law firm to pressure the school board to cave in to the firm's unreasonable and unethical demands."

Local conservative columnist Kathy Kreitzner wrote a companion commentary piece that appeared next to Wolfen's article. Kreitzner's piece stated:

"The protesters stormed the school board meeting like Nazi brown shirts. Hell bent on destroying democratic institutions and democracy itself, the obviously uneducated mob was led by Socialist Worker Party operatives and a carpetbagging, East coast firebrand radical socialist lawyer..."

By 8am the morning after the protest, Carmen's phone was ringing off the hook. Callers said they had seen the protest on cable television and wanted to know when the next one would be. Many callers apologized for missing the protest. A few scolded Carmen for not having coordinated with them. Carmen had no idea who these callers were. She took down names and numbers. She promised to include them in the next protest.

By 10am, Carmen was exhausted. The calls invigorated her, but they also wore her out. People had all kinds of advice about what she should do or not do, and what should happen next. They were adamant that they should be included or be allowed to take charge. It was impossible to know what motivated each caller or to reconcile their deeply held, divergent views.

Carmen was also tired from last night. She had stayed out late with Bob after the protest. She had not made a specific decision to give Bob another chance, but when he suggested after the protest that they have dinner, she could not say no. She needed to decompress with someone safe. Bob's enthusiasm, both for the protest and for her, made him safe, at least for one night. It was a nice night, too. They ate. They talked. They kissed goodnight.

A phone call shook Carmen from her thoughts of Bob.

"Sister Carmen!"

"Hey, Rufus," Carmen responded. "Congratulations. That was quite an event."

"You don't know, sister. It's big! People are coming out the woodwork. Everyone wants a piece of this."

"I know. They're calling me, too."

"Be sure to get names and phone numbers."

"I'm getting them."

"Sister, we need a plan. We haven't seen a people's movement like this in Minnepious since the millworkers' strike of 1913."

Carmen had no idea what Rufus was talking about. "I agree. We need a plan."

"I've already started assembling our steering committee."

"Let's not get ahead of ourselves, Rufus."

"Sister, you don't understand. We need to move fast. This is our Arab Spring! We need to strip off Bunny Washington's *hijab* of pseudo-Black nationalism. We need to expose these capitalist cronies for what they are—rank sell-outs."

Carmen wanted to slow Rufus down, if only so she could think. "Hold on a minute."

But Rufus was on a roll. "The next school board meeting is in two weeks. We need to set up an executive committee, a media committee, and a social media committee. We'll also need a fundraising committee, an outreach committee, a young workers committee…"

Young workers committee? "Rufus, stop. I'm not agreeing to any of this."

There was a long pause. "Well that's all right," Rufus decided. "We can work with that. See, Carmen, you're a licensed attorney. You need *plausible deniability*." He paused again. "That way, when the power structure counterattacks, you can't be formally tied to our organizing. They'll try to get you to stop the protests. But you can say it's not in your power to stop us. You can say it's a people's movement resisting capitalist oppression…or racist oppression, if you like that better."

Carmen sighed. She realized that no matter what she said, Rufus was already off and running. He had hijacked the protests. As long as he did not try to hijack the lawsuit, she could live with his exuberance. In a way, it made life simpler.

—⁓—

This was a disaster. Eileen could not deny it. But as with all disasters in urban public education, Eileen knew it would blow over. She hoped Bunny was past the blame game, but it did not look good. For the first time in her career, Eileen could not get to the superintendent. Alain would not let Eileen into Bunny's office, no matter what she said. Claiming he had strict orders from Bunny, Alain forced Eileen to stay in the waiting area. He pretended to be apologetic and empathize with her plight, but Eileen knew the gay bastard was loving every minute of it.

She paced and fretted. She wondered if she were being blamed for the whole fiasco. Eileen knew how Bunny could hold a grudge. She just hoped Bunny wasn't foolish enough to try to throw her under the bus. If Bunny tried to lay this all on her, Eileen would fight back. Her career was on the line. She would not take the fall for Bunny. She had already sacrificed too much, lost too much.

Eileen paced outside Bunny's office for more than an hour. She wondered if Ethan had made it to school. When she had awakened him before she left for work, he was hung over. She wondered what time he would get home in the evening, and what condition he would be in. She cursed her husband. Without Joel's support, she could not discipline, much less control, their wayward son.

—⁓—

Elmer Liechtenstein summoned Jamie Levine and Carmen Braithwaite to his office. He had no interest in sitting in a young associate's office this time, particularly when the associate was causing so much trouble. The conversation would be serious this time. Everyone needed to know their place. Liechtenstein was pissed, in an understated, Minnepious kind of way.

Liechtenstein rued the day he had allowed the firm's executive committee to pressure him into hiring a minority to improve the firm's public image. This woman was doing more harm to the firm's image than a hundred articles accusing the firm of racist hiring practices. Liechtenstein had already fielded half a dozen calls from major corporate clients demanding to know how the firm had gotten mixed up with the Socialist Workers Party. Long time clients wanted to know when the firm would issue a press statement disavowing Braithwaite and her school board protest.

The clients expected the firm to get rid of Carmen as soon as possible. Liechtenstein understood this. He was already working on it. He had scheduled a meeting with Human Resources for later in the day, and he had a good handle on the approach he would take. Braithwaite's billable hours were far below the firm's minimum expectations. These things just had to be handled the right way, one step at a time. He had no intention of making a bad situation worse by being hasty. Under no circumstances would he give Braithwaite any hook to use against him, especially given her demonstrated willingness to play the race card.

Braithwaite walked into his office with Levine, an unholy duo if ever there was one. "What in the world are you doing?" Liechtenstein demanded, glaring at Carmen.

"Excuse me?" Carmen responded, surprised at the accusatory tone. "What is this about?"

Her insouciance further enraged Liechtenstein. "I may not have gone to *Harvard*, young lady, but I'm not stupid."

Carmen was baffled at the man's anger. She had no idea what he expected her to say, or do.

Levine stepped into the breach. "Elmer, calm down. Let's deal with this as adults."

"I'm calm!" Liechtenstein snapped. He did not need a Jew telling him to calm down.

"Is this about last night?" Levine asked.

"What do you think? Have you seen the paper? It was one thing to file your ill-conceived, half-baked excuse of a lawsuit. I mean, school *desegregation*? *Really?* Have you two been living under a rock?"

Levine suppressed a grin. "Carmen presented the district's offer to Ms. Douglass, as you instructed, Elmer. The client didn't want the cash. I believe that makes her a woman of principle."

Carmen gagged and pretended to cough.

"From what I hear," Liechtenstein spat. "She's more a woman of the night."

Carmen knew enough to stay out of this fight. She realized that whatever was going on between the two men had little to do with her.

Levine stared at Liechtenstein. "Elmer, don't do this. It's beneath you. You once had principles yourself, Elmer."

"Principles, my ass! Don't patronize me, Jamie. Your client was charged last week with assaulting her landlord! Poor fellow had to go under the knife." Liechtenstein winced. "Required testicular surgery."

Carmen pretended to sneeze this time to cover her giggle.

Liechtenstein glared at her. "It's not funny, young lady. Apparently, they had to remove one."

Carmen looked away and bit her hand, but another giggle escaped.

Levine intervened. "Let's get back on track. Elmer, what do you want?"

"I don't pretend to know how you two could have got mixed up with the Socialist Workers Party. It's unseemly, if I do say so myself. Under no circumstances can you use any of this law firm's resources to support anti-democratic and potentially unlawful activities."

"Elmer," Levine chided. "I hope you're not insinuating that the firm intends to impede parents and citizens from exercising their constitutional right to petition the school board."

Liechtenstein felt dizzy. His grip on the meeting was slipping away. He was not a man of violence, but he wanted to punch Levine, preferably in the nose. "Jamie, I'm not going to be out-lawyered by you. You can twist my words any way you want. But last time I checked, I'm still President of this firm. That means I have a duty to safeguard the financial health of this firm. It's a sacred trust, Jamie. And I intend to hand this firm over to the next generation of partners in a financial condition at least as strong as when I took over." Liechtenstein caught his breath. "Jamie, you may relish the role of noble loser in your foolish lawsuit, but a noble loser is still a *loser*."

Liechtenstein glared at Carmen. "And as for you, young lady, I don't know what your future plans are, but I suspect they don't include staying here very long."

Carmen did not respond.

"You may think just because you went to Harvard, you can get away with using people. Well I'm here to tell you, this firm has been an institution in this community for over fifty years. That longevity means something. It means we value relationships.

"They evidently don't teach you that at Harvard. Your behavior has already hurt some of our most important relationships. Those relationships pay your salary, by the way. Now some of our clients are asking tough questions, and I need to be able to answer them."

"I can think of no one better able to answer those tough questions," Levine needled.

Liechtenstein glared at Levine. "I will not let you two damage this firm any further."

He turned back to Carmen. "You may think you can waltz off to New York and leave us holding the bag, young lady. But I'm telling you right now, I will not allow you to get away with it."

"That's enough, Elmer," Levine intervened. "Carmen is zealously advocating for her clients. That's all."

Liechtenstein calmed down. He had got what he needed to say off his chest.

"What's your bottom line, Elmer?"

Liechtenstein relaxed. Doing deals came naturally to him. That was how he had secured his position as President of the firm. "We're already locked into the lawsuit," he mused. "We can't very well back out of it. And it would be unethical to force the client to take a settlement she's truly opposed to, though I would expect you to encourage her to reconsider at every opportunity."

Carmen and Levine did not react.

"You're going to lose your case," Liechtenstein stated. "We all know that. It's unwinnable. It'll most likely be dismissed on the pleadings." He paused, getting to the core of the deal. "But there can be no more publicity." He paused again to emphasize his next point, which was really his entire point. "And *no more protests*. That's not negotiable."

Having remained silent throughout Liechtenstein's tirade, Carmen felt an urge to have some fun. She knew her days with the firm were numbered anyway. So, borrowing from *The Book of Rufus*, she replied, "I understand your frustration, Mr. Liechtenstein. I really do. Unfortunately, there's nothing I can do to stop the protests. You see, I'm not leading them. And I can't very well ask parents not to attend school board meetings. As Mr. Levine said, we can't ask citizens to give up their constitutional rights. That might look like the firm was engaged in some kind of conspiracy to violate people's civil rights."

Liechtenstein's neck turned pink, then red, then purple. His veins bulged out. He clenched his jaw and held his breath. Carmen wondered how long the president of the firm could contain his rage, and what the effort would do to his health.

—∞—

There turned out to be more truth in what Carmen said to Liechtenstein than she knew. Fueled by Rufus, Andrew and a growing cast of volunteers, the protest campaign took on a life of its own. The next school board meeting was two weeks away, but already dozens of parents, activists and parasites had jumped on and hijacked the protest bandwagon.

Carmen attended the first meeting of the protest "steering committee," which consisted of Rufus, Andrew and a bunch of their friends. The white girl Amelia, who had screamed about Rufus leading everyone to slaughter at the first protest, now snuggled with him. Evidently, they were back together.

Most of the steering committee's discussion was about who was sleeping with whom, and who was looking for new romantic partners. Carmen realized some things were universal. Bring together a bunch of passionate, idealistic young men and women, and their passions would get the better of them. She left the meeting early. Her absence did nothing to derail the rapidly growing protest "movement," however, which took on a life of its own.

There was no consensus among the newly minted protest committees about what to do or say, so everyone went their own way, plugging their own importance and their pet themes to whomever would listen. To Carmen's chagrin, the word "segregation" disappeared from the newly self-appointed activists' lexicon. The most prominent themes pushed were:

The school district is racist!

We want more Black teachers.

Schools use tracking to sideline poor students.

The district is arrogant and lacks accountability.

Holding themselves out as "spokespeople," the usual suspects, and many Carmen had never heard of before, crawled out of every crevice in the city and pontificated to the local media about the protesters' grievances and demands. These Black "leaders" were all on the payroll of government agencies, charitable foundations, designated community organizations or other officially sanctioned arms of the Minnepious power structure. Carmen noted that they were also all men, and all in their late forties or older. Some acted like ants eagerly sucking the sweet nectar of publicity. Others were more like wasps. Either way, they appeared everywhere, sucking and stinging, doing what they always did when racial controversy beckoned.

The media poured fuel on the fire, breathlessly amplifying each complaint. The cacophony drowned out any coherent message, including the one message that had dominated the first school board meeting—that Black and brown people did not want segregated schools.

As she watched the circus unfold, Carmen realized with satisfaction that Elmer Liechtenstein could not accuse her of leading the protest movement. Still, she refused to be sidelined altogether. She worked out of sight from the mainstream media, which in any case had no interest in broadcasting a black socialist attorney's radical views on the harm caused by school segregation.

She spent hours reviewing school achievement data and reports to find evidence for her case. The documents proved the Minnepious district had intentionally gerrymandered school attendance boundaries to coincide with well-known patterns of residential segregation. Carmen prepared summaries of what she found.

Unlike traditional legal advocacy, however, her summaries were intended not for the courtroom, but for the people. The summaries were simple, clear and provocative. Carmen added graphics and catchy headings to the data, so her summaries could be understood by regular people. One of her favorite headings was *"Segregated Schools Fail All Children!"*

To avoid being accused by Liechtenstein of using law firm resources to support the protest movement, Carmen steered clear of the firm's photocopiers. She took her summaries out of the office on a jump drive to a FedEx Office store with a young Black employee who gave her instant feedback on the huge signs and posters she printed. The employee's favorite poster showed images of stunted children to compare Black student performance in segregated versus desegregated schools.

SEGREGATION SHRINKS STUDENT ACHIEVEMENT FOR BLACK STUDENTS!

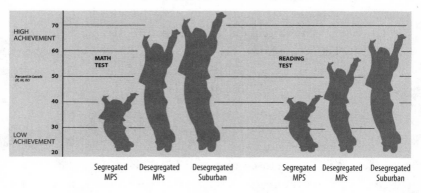

For the first time in her brief legal career, Carmen felt good about what she was doing. She was connecting with real people in real ways. She was using her analytical and communication skills to make an impact. She could see herself doing more of this.

—⁂—

The dinner invitation did not come as a complete surprise. Still, Carmen did not feel ready for it. Mr. Levine swore Bob had not put him up to it, but Carmen was not convinced. Why else would he invite Carmen to a Levine family gathering?

Carmen's relationship with Bob, if you could call it that, was still in limbo. She had not had much time to think about Bob lately. The school case consumed her every waking moment. What she wanted from Bob at this point, she did not know. Though she had little interest in meeting Bob's family, she did not see how she could decline an invitation from his father. So as she pulled up to Mr. Levine's house in southwest Minnepious, Carmen braced herself for the family "once over."

"You must be Carmen!" Mrs. Levine greeted her at the door with a hug. "I'm Leslie! Come in! Everyone's dying to meet you!"

Mrs. Levine was thin and stylishly dressed. Carmen followed her into the house. The entire Levine clan was in the family living room. Carmen realized she had been set up.

Bob sat there grinning like an idiot. At least he was smart enough not to try to hold her hand or otherwise claim possession of her affection. He got up and introduced Carmen to his *extended* family. There were more than thirty Levines jammed into the living room, all dressed up. There were uncles and aunts, cousins and nieces and nephews.

Carmen had never imagined there could be a Jewish family this large in Minnepious. She was more than a little flattered that they had all gathered just to meet her. Then she found out the dinner had nothing to do with her. The Levine family gathered every second Sunday for dinner. It was a family tradition.

Bob handed Carmen a glass of wine and they joined a group of younger adults. Bob's cousins and their spouses welcomed Carmen warmly, making her feel at home. After a few minutes, the men disappeared to watch basketball or hockey or whatever sport was on television. The children also soon disappeared to play in the basement.

Bob left with the other men, but returned periodically to check on Carmen. This both annoyed and charmed Carmen. She did not like the implication that she needed Bob's help to handle his female relatives. But she did enjoy his attention.

By their second glass of wine, the women loosened up. They slid closer together conspiratorially, ready to dish.

Bob's cousin Ruth clinked her wine glass against Carmen's. "Isn't this Cab amazing? It's so fruity and chocolaty!"

Cab? Carmen smiled.

Bob's other cousin Sarah butted in. She touched Carmen's arm. "Ruth's such a snob. I'll take a decent Merlot any day. Don't you agree, Carmen?"

Carmen knew better than to get in the middle of a fight between cousins over wine varietals. "Actually, I prefer rum."

Ruth and Sarah glanced at each other.

"Oh, of course," Ruth replied. "You're from the Islands."

"Brooklyn, actually."

"Do you and Bob have any plans to visit the Islands?" Sarah asked.

Carmen ignored the question.

"Oh, I love it!" Ruth squealed. "Just imagine. They'll elope to St. Thomas!"

"I would hope our family will be invited," Sarah mused.

Carmen's head was swimming.

Ruth winked at Carmen. "Is Bob also into rum?"

All the women leaned forward, looking at Carmen.

"Carmen, do tell. What *is* Bob into?"

The women giggled.

"If anyone would know, Carmen, it would be you."

Carmen frowned. "Bob's not much of a drinker."

The women fell silent.

Carmen glanced toward the basement door, wishing Bob would reappear to rescue her from this silliness.

Ruth broke the silence. "So Carmen, tell us about your discrimination lawsuit. *Everyone's* talking about it."

The women all leaned forward again, eager for any rumor-worthy morsels they could glean.

Carmen smiled, guarded.

Sarah touched Carmen's arm. "How did you get Uncle Jamie to do it?"

Carmen leaned away. "I just asked him."

"Really?"

"Uncle Bob doesn't seem like the type," Ruth concurred.

"It just doesn't make sense," Sarah observed. "Uncle Jamie knows so many people."

The women nodded.

Carmen did not get their point.

"I don't think he really cares," Ruth sniffed. "I mean, it's not like Bob and Carmen are going to have kids any time soon."

"Excuse me?" Carmen interjected. "First, you have me eloping. Now you're talking children. Bob and I are just good friends."

Sarah grinned. "Friends with benefits?"

Carmen looked toward the basement door again. *Where was Bob?*

"Oh, leave Carmen alone," Ruth scolded the other women. "She doesn't have kids. How can you expect her to understand what's at stake in the schools?"

"I think I understand," Carmen replied. "And your Uncle Jamie definitely understands. He's a smart man."

Ruth and Sarah exchanged knowing glances.

Where the hell was Bob?

"Uncle Jamie is impetuous," Ruth said. "He lacks self-control. He does things because he feels like it, without considering the consequences. He's basically an overgrown teenager."

"Aunt Leslie always has to clean up his messes," Sarah agreed.

"She won't be able to clean this one up," Ruth snorted.

The other women nodded or shook their heads.

Sarah looked at Carmen. "Do you know what your case is doing?"

"I think so."

"Really?"

"Why don't you tell me," Carmen replied, miffed.

"It's alienating a lot of good people."

"Don't take this the wrong way, Carmen," Ruth joined in. "But if you lose *us*, you've lost everyone. We're the *most* committed to Minnepious schools. All my children are there."

"Let me guess," Carmen said. "They go to school in southwest Minnepious?"

Ruth frowned. "Duh?" She rolled her eyes. "Where else would they go?"

Bob's cousin Susan spoke up for the first time. "Everyone is not as committed to Minnepious as we are, Carmen. My best friend's pulling her kids out. She says everyone she knows is thinking about it now. These are *very involved* parents, Carmen. Your lawsuit's undoing a lot of good work."

"When you vilify good people," Ruth sniffed. "You lose the very people you need."

Sarah nodded. "Exactly. You lose the people who will carry your water. People of good conscience will find it harder now to justify keeping their kids in Minnepious." She paused, considering the implications. "If people like us take their kids to Eden or Lake, our city schools will look like...Detroit..."

"Or Oakland," Ruth volunteered.

"Or me," Carmen rejoined.

Ruth's jaw dropped. "Oh my God, Carmen. You shouldn't take it *personally*."

Bob emerged from the basement with Ruth's three children in tow. He had a huge grin. "Wow, you ladies are intense! Are we eating soon?"

Carmen looked away.

The Jewish women frowned. Bob's infatuation with this black lawyer was a bit much.

"Yo, Joey," Bob summoned his nine-year-old nephew. "Show us your moves!"

Ruth's son Joey grinned and stepped forward. He looked at his mother and hesitated. She looked like she smelled a fart.

"C'mon, Joey," Bob urged. "Show Carmen how you can dance."

Bob started his human beatbox routine. Joey felt the beat. The boy began to sway, then broke out krumping, his body jerking in synch to the beat. Joey flipped onto his back. His body surged into a spasm of rhythm, as if Bob's beatbox had taken over the nine-year-old's central nervous system.

Joey's krumping to Bob's beatbox broke the tension. The Jewish women clapped to the beat. The men, hearing the commotion, tore themselves away from the television and returned to the living room. Before Carmen knew it, she was surrounded by a beatboxing, krumping, stepping Jewish family.

Carmen remained aloof. She withdrew to a safe space in her mind. It was the only way she could get through the rest of the evening.

—∽—

The second school board protest far surpassed the first in one crucial way. It leveraged the internet. Rufus set up a live internet stream of the cable access feed. This transformed a purely local event into a national sensation, at least for long suffering Black Minnepioutans, who shared the video link with out of town friends and family, who in turn shared it with their friends and families.

Within hours, the video of the second school board protest became a hit on YouTube and Facebook. As the "Likes," tags and number of views climbed into the thousands, then tens of thousands, the second Minnepious school board protest brought either acclaim or notoriety, depending on your perspective. Everyone had an opinion: pro or con. You were either with the protesters on social media, or against them. There was no middle ground.

—∽—

Bunny did not care much for social media. She did not operate her own Twitter account or Facebook page. The superintendent's tweets and web posts were ghostwritten for her by the district's public relations staff. Bunny never looked at the tweets and posts that went out in her name. Nor did she particularly care what they said, as long as nothing came back to haunt her in the real world—the world reported in the mainstream press. That turned out to be a mistake.

The second school board protest derailed Bunny not because of its real world vehemence, which she had anticipated, but because it brought the online world into her real world with a vengeance. Bunny's masterful control of public relations was undermined by her inability to grasp the cumulative impact of thousands of young adults typing ungrammatical nonsense with their thumbs. The tweets, texts and posts caused real damage in Bunny's real world. She watched in horror as the online and real worlds collided.

Hostile tweets and blog posts piled up, cluttering social media sites. Before long, the hostile tweets, blog posts and online commentary migrated to the online edition of *The Strib*, their wrath directed at Bunny:

"Bunny Washington is incompetent…"

"Bunny Washington should be fired…"

"This shows what happens when government puts skin color ahead of competence…"

"Bunny Washington should be ashamed…"

"Bunny Washington is a sell-out…"

Before Bunny or anyone around her knew what had happened, the Minnepious school district and its illustrious superintendent became synonymous online with racial controversy and failing schools. Bunny knew she had to act fast to limit the damage. She just hoped it was not already too late.

❖

Chapter 9

Charity received the phone call offering her a job out of the blue. At first, she thought the call was a joke. A job offer from a suburban school district could not be real. Someone was messing with her. They were probably trying to get her back for all the newspaper and radio interviews she was doing.

Charity was beginning to consider herself something of an expert on schools and desegregation. All week, she had done newspaper and radio interviews about her case and the protests. She used simple words when she talked to the media about complicated ideas, just like Carmen told her to. But really, this stuff wasn't so complicated. Desegregation was pretty straightforward to Charity. Kids shouldn't be separated by their skin color. Period. And anyway, talking straight and simple came natural to Charity. She did that every day. She didn't know any other way. This was baby stuff. It was fun.

Charity did interviews with so many people she couldn't remember them all. Her best interview was with the *African-American Word*. They had a photographer take a picture of her, too. It was the first time her picture got in a newspaper. She looked pretty good in the picture.

The *Word's* reporter was a trip, too. Homeboy was the nephew of the newspaper's owner. He had the nerve to tell her should be ashamed for making Bunny Washington look bad. So Charity went off on the boy. She told him he should be ashamed to support Bunny Washington's policies of educational genocide. She said no

Black leader should be allowed to sacrifice 50,000 Black children for one fancy job. They didn't put that statement in the article. But they got in another good one Charity said: *"'I believe in desegregation,' plaintiff Charity Douglass stated. 'Because if you ask any child, they'll tell you it's not right to make kids to go to certain schools because of their skin color.'"*

Carmen told her the quote was awesome. But when Charity showed the article to her kids, they didn't care about her quote. All they cared about was how she looked in the picture. Lakeesha told her to get her hair done next time before she did an interview.

In all the excitement about the case and the school board protests, Charity had forgotten about the school district's $50,000 settlement offer. Now, this phone call with an unexpected job offer brought her need for money back to the forefront. Her kids could not eat quotes in the newspaper. And even if she was becoming famous, a hero who could not feed her kids or pay her rent was not much of a mama.

"Yes, this is Ms. Douglass," Charity confirmed to the caller. She liked referring to herself as *Ms. Douglass* now. It sounded better than Charity.

The caller sounded like a white woman. She told Charity that the Eden-Updike Consolidated School District wanted to hire her as a community liaison for minority parents. Charity did not know what to do, so she gave the caller Carmen's number and told her to "call my lawyer."

Ten minutes later, Carmen called Charity.

"Charity," Carmen said, all excited. "A woman from the HR department at the Eden-Updike schools just called me. She said she talked to you. They want to hire you to help Black parents deal with the schools out there, in the suburbs."

"Ain't those white schools?"

Carmen laughed. "Eden's are. But Updike has Black kids going there from north Minnepious under open enrollment. The woman said there's a lot of affordable housing in Updike, too. Black families are moving there. They also have a lot of Latinos now."

Charity thought about her situation. All her previous jobs involved physical work. She didn't have to think in those jobs. This job sounded different. Charity was not sure she was ready for it. Things were going good with the lawsuit and the protests, too. If she got tired of the case and protests, she could always take the $50,000 settlement from the Minnepious school district. She didn't want to jinx everything by taking some job in the suburbs and disappoint her kids. "I don't know," she hedged. "I got some other things going."

"What kinds of things?" Carmen asked gently. She knew the prospect of change, even positive change, would be threatening to Charity.

"I'm workin' on some things."

"Charity, there's more."

"What's that?"

"The school district is offering your kids spots in their schools. They have some really good schools."

Charity's head started to hurt. "Why they doin' that?"

"They want you fully committed to their district. They want you to be able to talk to other parents as a peer. You know, parent to parent. If your kids are there, people will relate to you better, trust you more."

The words sounded right, but it all sounded too good to be true. There was something fishy going on. "How much they gonna pay me?"

"The starting salary, not including benefits, is fifty thousand dollars."

There it is! Charity knew the whole thing smelled fishy. "*Fifty thousand dollars?* They just pull that number out they ass?"

Carmen did not want to go there. She had had the same thought when she heard the salary. But on the other hand, Charity needed a job, and her kids needed better schools. This could be a life changing opportunity for them. "Does it really matter?"

"The school district's playin' a trick."

"Maybe so. But that's their problem, not ours."

"So I gotta drop the lawsuit if I take the job?"

"No," Carmen assured her client. "You don't. It's not like that. We don't have to drop the case if you take the job." Carmen paused. "Remember, when you said we could do the case as a *class action*? That was a big decision. It means we're doing our case for *all* the kids in Minnepious, not just yours. Even if your kids go to Updike schools, we'll continue with the case. Nothing changes."

There was a long silence. Charity turned the situation around and around in her mind. "I guess that makes you pretty smart, huh?"

Carmen smiled to herself. Charity was about as sparing with praise as a Harvard Law professor. "Maybe I learned something from you."

"Maybe you did," Charity agreed. She was still not sure what she should do. She generally did not have to make big decisions like this. "So I get the fifty thousand, and we can still do the case?"

"That's right. And your kids get to go to good schools."

"Fifty thousand? No tricks?"

"The fifty thousand's a salary. You got to work for it."

"Girlfriend, I been workin' all my life."

—⁓—

Chris Hardwell thanked the caller again and put his cell phone down on the table. He glanced at his son and daughter playing in the backyard. The snow sparkled. The sun shone bright. The children looked happy.

Still, the place was foul.

Hardwell thanked God that his children were young. They would not remember Minnepious within a couple years.

This phone call would change their lives. Hardwell had just accepted the Middle School Principal position at an international school in Uganda. It would be an adventure. He wasn't sure what to expect. But he and Alecia would show the kids a new reality, an African reality.

Hardwell thought about all he had experienced in his two years in Minnepious. He did not believe in regrets. You learned from your mistakes. But moving to Minnepious had been a monumental mistake, one that had to be corrected before the harm to the children was irreversible.

Alecia joined him in the kitchen. She also looked out the window at the kids playing in the snow.

Hardwell put his arms around his wife. "I just got the call."

Alecia looked at her husband. "Uganda?"

She held her breath.

Hardwell nodded. "I got the job."

Alecia pulled her husband tight. She buried her face in his chest and held him. Tears poured down her cheeks. Her body melted into her husband's. After two years of unrelenting pressure, she could relax. They were leaving this godforsaken place.

Hardwell held his wife. Her body pressed against his. Her tears dampened his chest. Tears rolled down his cheeks as well. They would make love that night as they hadn't in years. It was not just his children he was saving, but his marriage, and his self-respect.

Before he left, though, Hardwell had to take care of one piece of unfinished business.

—⁂—

This was the call Bunny had been waiting for her whole life. It was not unexpected, but for a Black woman of Bunny's generation, you could never truly expect a call like this, either. That would only invite disappointment.

"Yes, this is Bunny."

The caller was Dan Munson, head of the President-elect's transition team.

"Bunny, we just want to touch base with you about the timing of our announcement, and your availability to travel to Washington."

"That won't be a problem."

"The announcement will be on the morning of Inauguration Day. The President-elect wants to announce the appointment then to emphasize his commitment to education. He truly believes education is the key to social mobility. His own personal journey embodies that."

"Of course."

"We'll need you travel to DC at the end of the week to prepare for the announcement. Can you do that?"

"Of course. Just let me know when I should get my ticket." Bunny pinched herself. She couldn't believe this was really happening.

"The President-elect will call you personally by Wednesday, latest."

"Okay."

"There's just one outstanding item of due diligence."

Bunny frowned. "Really? I filled out all the forms last month. We completed the FBI background interview. I didn't think there was anything else."

"It's something that just came up."

Bunny did not respond. She held her breath, wishing Munson's last words would go away.

"The desegregation lawsuit that was filed against the district," Munson continued. "Who's behind it, and what kind of support does it have?"

Bunny exhaled. This she knew she could handle. "Oh, it's nothing. A junior lawyer from out of town is using a family from Chicago to try to shake down the district. I can send you some newspaper articles that put it all in perspective. Our outside counsel says we have a slam dunk legal case. He expects the judge to dismiss the case in a few weeks."

"Our lawyers came to the same conclusion when they read the complaint," Munson agreed. "We've already read the articles online."

"Of course," Bunny purred.

"It's not the lawsuit *in and of itself* we're concerned about."

"Oh?"

Bunny's chest tightened.

"It's the protests. They don't look good." Munson paused. "Do they have legs? Or have we seen the last of them?"

"We've seen the last of them."

"Good. The President-elect doesn't like drama." Munson paused. "Those protests look like drama."

"You can tell him not to worry," Bunny promised. "There won't be any more drama."

"I'll let him know."

"Thank you."

As soon as the call ended, Bunny summoned Eileen. It was time to stop the protests. No matter what it took. No more drama.

—m—

"Does your client like her new job?" Bunny asked.

Carmen bristled. She had agreed to this meeting only at Mr. Levine's insistence. *"You have to go hear what she has to say,"* he had told Carmen when she informed him of the superintendent's call.

"Don't you think she's a little *street* for a job in the *Eden*-Updike district?" Bunny snickered. "She's not called 'Charity' for nothing."

This was pointless. Carmen stood up to leave.

"We're not finished. Sit down. I have some things to say to you."

Carmen considered what she would say to Mr. Levine if she left now, then reluctantly sat. If the superintendent crossed the line again, she would leave.

Bunny stared at the young lawyer. "In case you're wondering, no, I'm not happy. You've caused a lot of damage. Not just to me. To a lot of people."

Carmen felt like she had heard this speech before. "Maybe you should look in the mirror."

"You think you have all the answers, don't you," Bunny seethed. "Yes, it's easy to tear people down. You're good at that. But can you actually *build* something? You went to Harvard. You're expected to be a leader one day. You should try trading places with me."

"No thanks."

"Aren't you special," Bunny scoffed. "When you're young, everything's black and white."

"Or maybe Black, white, *Somali and Latino*. Isn't that how you see things?"

Braithwaite's self-righteousness was like fingernails on chalkboard to Bunny. The superintendent realized she might not be able to talk sense into the young lawyer, after all. She recalibrated her objectives for the meeting. She decided to make sure of one thing; Braithwaite would leave her office diminished.

"Do you have any idea why I invited you here?"

"I have some idea."

"It's not why you think."

"Oh?"

"I'm not worried about your lawsuit. That will be dismissed soon. Or it will be a nuisance inherited by my successor. Either way, I'll be Secretary of Education, and your lawsuit will go nowhere."

Carmen sighed. "Is that why you brought me here? To give me your expert legal opinion?"

"No, that's not why. And I didn't call you to talk about the protests, either." Bunny paused. "There won't be another protest. We've already taken care of that."

Carmen did not react, though she wondered what Bunny was talking about.

"I called you here because I need to tell you some things. For your personal benefit. I don't usually do this, but I think you have potential."

Carmen sucked her teeth.

"You're young," Bunny continued, ignoring the provocation. "You have a lot to learn. I'm going to help you."

Carmen regretted having agreed to this meeting.

"You seem to think you have some unique handle on the truth," Bunny continued. "You think you see things the rest of us can't…"

"Or don't want to see," Carmen corrected.

Bunny smiled. "Sure. That's fine. As I said, you think you have all the answers. Well, let's see how your assumptions hold up."

Carmen held the superintendent's gaze.

Bunny smiled. "In the seventies," she said, waxing nostalgic. "Before you were born, your daddy was walking along some road, hitching a ride past sugar plantations on his little island."

Carmen stared at the superintendent in disbelief. *What the hell was she talking about?*

Bunny winked. "I know about Trinidad. I went there for Carnival one year with my girlfriends from college. I know about those little… what do they call them? Maxi Taxis? With the calypso music blaring."

It occurred to Carmen that the superintendent had lost her mind.

"You think I don't know about you, Carmen *Braithwaite*? I know your daddy came to this country to escape his impoverished little island."

Again, Carmen considered walking out of the superintendent's office, but she had to hear where this bizarre, wretched woman was going. "It's not *impoverished*," Carmen corrected. "Trinidad has oil."

Bunny smiled. "Whatever." She knew she had the uppity child. "Your daddy came here to get a college education. He came here as part of a deal."

Carmen was sure the old hag had lost her mind.

Bunny savored the moment, drew it out. "Your daddy needed affirmative action to get into Georgetown."

Carmen frowned. "What does that have to do with anything?"

"No Black man could get into Georgetown in the 1960s. But when your daddy applied and got in a decade later, in the seventies, do you think he got in because he was smarter than all those Black men who got rejected in the sixties?"

Carmen did not answer.

"Your daddy got into Georgetown because of affirmative action."

"Okay, so what? And you got your Ph.D. from the University of Minnesoule through affirmative action. Big deal."

"That's right," Bunny agreed. "Affirmative action helped us all back then. There was no other way." She paused. "But do you think white people just gave away all those seats at Georgetown and the University of Minnesoule and Harvard and all those other white universities for nothing?"

"No," Carmen replied. "They didn't. They gave up those seats because people pushed them. Protesters forced those doors open. White people let us in because they were afraid of what would happen if they didn't."

"Well said," Bunny agreed. "Kudos to you, young lady. You've studied African-American history. White people let us in because we pressured them."

"That's right."

Bunny appraised Carmen. "But what were the terms of the actual deal to let us in?"

"What do you mean *terms*? There was no actual deal."

"Oh, there was a deal," Bunny corrected. "You better believe there was a deal. White people don't give up *anything*, except in a deal. The Civil Rights Act was a deal. The Voting Rights Act was a deal. Even the Emancipation Proclamation was a deal. That's what white people do. They do *deals*."

"I don't need you to tell me that," Carmen frowned. "Just ask Native Americans."

"Yes! Yes!" exclaimed Bunny. "That's right. We're talking about deals with the Devil. That's exactly what affirmative action was: *a deal with the Devil*."

"You think just because affirmative action helped me," Carmen mocked. "I've done a deal with the Devil? Is that what you think?"

Bunny chuckled to herself. This was one of those moments in life too good to hope for. She had the self-righteous little lawyer right where she wanted her. From here on, it would be all fun. "Young lady, you and your generation are so lost. You think you have the freedom to walk away from the Devil." Bunny laughed.

"My generation *won* affirmative action through struggle," she continued. "You weren't even born when we took to the streets in the late sixties and early seventies." She paused. "Do you have *any* idea what the struggle was like? White people didn't say, *'Go ahead, take away all these college seats, take away all this opportunity from our children.'* White people fought tooth and nail to keep us out."

"Just like they fought to keep the schools segregated."

"Exactly. I'm glad you made that connection, because white people made the connection, too. White people wanted their pound of flesh. Before they let your father into Georgetown and let me into the U, they demanded something in return."

"I've read *Faust*," Carmen retorted. "I know all about the proverbial deal with the Devil, and I can assure you, my father would never have stooped so low."

"Ah, the myth of the noble West Indian radical."

"My father *was* a radical."

"Well, good for him. White people made some mistakes back then. Maybe he was one of those mistakes. They did let in some radicals from the Islands like your daddy. They also let in some unqualified ghetto kids…" Bunny paused. "But really, if you ask me, I don't think it was a mistake. I think it was all calculated. Even the whites who were supposed to be our allies in the civil rights movement were actually working against us from the inside. They were shrewd.

"Take the Jews. They went from being outsiders fighting for civil rights to the ultimate insiders. And just look at them now. Jews control almost everything in this country." She paused. "When I first came to Minnepious, there was actually a Jewish ghetto on the north side. Can you believe that?" Bunny laughed. "Today, no Jew would be caught dead on the north side."

Carmen could not fathom the purpose of Bunny's anti-Semitic rant. Listening to Bunny was like peering into a damaged building after a massive earthquake. You could only imagine that at one time there had been a sense of order and logic in there.

"Believe me," Bunny continued. "Jews think things through. They always end up on the side of whoever has power and money. Think about it. Jews financed slave ships. Then they switched to our side for the civil rights movement. Now that's what they would call *chutzpah*!"

Carmen regretted not having walked out earlier.

"Back in the day," Bunny continued. "They called a spade a spade. So I still call a Jew a Jew. If it makes you feel better, I'll call them whites. That's what they are."

Carmen considered the possibility that Bunny was suffering from dementia.

"When ghetto brothas and sistas were admitted to white universities under affirmative action in the seventies, they started carrying on like fools. That's when we knew we were in trouble. The white power structure had us where they wanted. They'd supposedly given us 'uppity Negroes,' a chance. And we were proving ourselves unworthy."

Carmen understood the superintendent had been holding this speech in for a long time. Like listeria-tainted meat, it had to come out. Carmen just didn't want to be in the line of fire.

"Back then," Bunny kept going. "We had free love, the antiwar movement, the poor people's movement, *you dig?*" Bunny smiled, reminiscing. "You may think I'm old and out of touch, but back in the day, I was part of something you can only dream of, young lady. Back then, we actually had white cops shooting at white students over Black issues. Imagine that!"

Carmen could not imagine it. Not in the America she knew.

"We had white cops protecting Black children so they could go to school with white kids. Back then, that was what folk wanted. I know. I was there." Again, Bunny paused, reminiscing. "But that didn't last. Everything fell apart. White people fought back. They weren't just angry about desegregation, though that was the heart of it. Affirmative action got caught up in all that drama, too. We were in a fight for our future as a people.

"Folk argued about what we should do. Some said we should fight for everything, even if we lost it all. Others said we should take what we could at the time, cut our losses, live to fight another day. They said we should keep affirmative action and let desegregation go. They said affirmative action was less threatening to white people than desegregation.

"But as it turned out, even that wouldn't be enough to satisfy white people. They just couldn't stomach the idea of Black folk rising, even a little. We had to convince them we wouldn't rock their boat. So we agreed to tighten college admissions criteria. We agreed to keep out the radicals and the ghetto brothas and sistas." Bunny paused and did not speak for a long time.

Carmen waited.

"We thought that would be our deal with the Devil. But the Devil always wants more. He wants your soul. And the Devil, he don't take you at your word. You got to sign in blood. No, white people weren't satisfied with tightening up affirmative action. They wanted more. They wanted what W.E.B DuBois called *The Souls of Black Folk*." Bunny paused, and looked away. "There was only one thing we could give up to appease that Devil and keep affirmative action…"

Carmen felt her stomach tighten.

"No one really understood at the time what we were giving up." Bunny hesitated, as if debating herself. "It just sort of happened. When the admissions criteria for affirmative action tightened, universities stopped admitting kids from the inner city. That opened up more slots for the rest of us. We were grateful for the opportunity. After some time, we took those seats for granted. They were ours. We started having babies. We wanted those seats to be there for them, too." Bunny stopped again. This was not coming out the way she wanted it to.

"It's not like we planned it that way," she muttered. "It just sort of happened."

Carmen remained silent.

"We had good jobs. We could live where we wanted…well, maybe not *anywhere*. But it's not like we wanted to live near crackers anyway. Our kids were in good public schools, or private schools." Bunny looked hard at Carmen. "You attack us for putting other people's children, but not our own kids, in segregated inner city schools."

Carmen did not react.

"Well, if you were a parent, you'd do the same."

Carmen had heard enough. "The difference is I don't say it's okay to force *other people's children* into segregated schools. That's a big difference."

"You have a bad habit of thinking you're smarter than the rest of us," Bunny sniffed. "You blame us for doing things that are in our own children's interests. And you pretend you haven't personally benefited from our decisions."

Carmen did not see the connection.

"You don't know what I'm talking about, do you? Don't underestimate me, Carmen Braithwaite. Things do not happen by accident. They happen for a reason. Just ask your client."

Carmen got up to leave.

"It was them or us," Bunny hissed. "You're one of *us*. You got into Harvard because your daddy and the rest of us made a deal."

"That was *your* deal," Carmen shot back. "Not mine."

"Maybe you don't like it. But we made that deal for you. *Your father* made it for you. You benefited from our agreement not to fight segregation."

Carmen stared at the superintendent. "You're sick."

Bunny laughed. "Yes, little girl, I am. We're all sick. You got into Harvard because we agreed to let them re-segregate the schools. We agreed to look the other way and let them crush all those ghetto Negroes, just so long as our own kids had a future."

Carmen turned to leave.

"Don't you ever forget," Bunny called after her. *"We took the deal so Herman Braithwaite's daughter could go to Harvard."*

Carmen turned back. "My father would never have agreed to that. You're making this up now to justify how you and your kind have sold us out."

"Maybe I am making it up now," Bunny sighed. "But the truth is still the truth. Who had the skills to lead the fight against segregation?"

"Thurgood Marshall."

"He didn't do it alone."

"Obviously."

"It took a lot of other brave Black lawyers, ministers and leaders working together. When affirmative action was tightened up, who had those skills?"

Carmen did not respond.

"I'll tell you who did. Those same lawyers and ministers and leaders. They had the skills. But they had to make a choice. Fight segregation and risk losing the war. Or take what they could. By walking away from desegregation, we gained white support for affirmative action. Just so long as we restricted affirmative action to reliable middle class Negroes, who saw their own self-interest in joining with whites to keep ignorant Negroes down and out."

Carmen shuddered. "A real win-win..."

"Oh, it was ugly," Bunny agreed. "But you know I'm telling the truth. Everyone with the skills to challenge segregation was silenced. That was the deal."

Carmen shook her head. "Your fairytale may make you feel better about yourself, Ms. Washington. But *everyone* makes decisions. Take responsibility for yours."

"Oh, I have," Bunny smiled. "And unlike you, I'm comfortable with *my* decisions."

"The more I see of you," Carmen replied. "The more comfortable I am with my decisions."

Bunny considered the implications. "That would make you a dangerous Negro."

"You got one part right. I'm dangerous."

"I hope you know what this country does to dangerous Negroes..."

Carmen laughed for the first time. "The same thing they try do to *all* Negroes."

—◊◊◊—

When Braithwaite was gone, Bunny considered her options. She had to isolate Braithwaite and run her out of town. Fast. There was no other way.

—◊◊◊—

Alone in her apartment, Carmen tried to concentrate, but Bunny's words kept haunting her. She had a sense that she had failed to see the obvious. Worse, she feared she was part of the problem herself. Did her own success somehow validate segregation? If so, was it part of a conspiratorial grand bargain between the Black middle class and their erstwhile slave masters? The thought sickened her.

Carmen reflected on her college days and her law school experience. She thought of her Black classmates. On the surface, they acted as if they were the Chosen Ones, as if they had made it to the top of society. But if you scratched below that veneer of self-confidence, you found defensiveness. If you suggested the Black middle class had some special responsibility to lift the impoverished Black masses, Carmen's classmates offered bromides about personal responsibility, opportunity, leadership and "job creators." Some rejected outright the notion that they bore any responsibility to help their Black brethren. Others were not so sure, but still did nothing.

Was this refusal to take responsibility, this refusal to deal with a racist society that oppressed most Black people, an attempt by the guilty to deny their role in a conspiracy that all grasped on some level? Carmen's Black peers in college and law school mostly tried to skirt the question of whether they, as educated Black people, had a special duty to give something back to the oppressed Black masses. Yet the question was always there, unanswered, perhaps in the background, but always there. The question could not be avoided.

Why?

Because on some level all knew that their individual good fortune was tied to the ongoing oppression of the masses. Carmen was sure of that. She was sure her peers knew that some sort of deal had been made on their behalf. What the deal was they might not know and did not *want* to know. With a willful ignorance of the specifics, they could then take solace in the deal having been made decades before by their parents' generation.

Carmen struggled with this. She could not accept that the complete absence of Black middle class support for desegregated schools today was simply the byproduct of an old conspiracy from the 1970s. That let her generation off the hook. It pretended that every Black beneficiary of affirmative action today had no choice but to continue the conspiracy. Carmen knew this was false. Her Black middle class peers made important choices every day. And Carmen had seen today's Black middle class consistently choose *not* to speak out against segregation, in effect continuing their parents' deal with the Devil. What did that say about the nature of the Black middle class, those with the skills and ability to stop the madness?

Carmen turned it around and around in her mind. The more she looked at it, the less she liked what she saw. She wished she were wrong. But however she turned it, she saw the same thing. It was more than Bunny had admitted. Much more.

Carmen could accept Bunny's point that the Black middle class wanted to eliminate competitors for the few crumbs the white power structure allowed Negroes to fight over. But she also saw that the perpetuation of a disenfranchised, uneducated, ignorant Black *underclass* gave the Black middle class something it sorely needed: an ongoing bargaining chip to hold whites to their ugly deal from the 1970s. Carmen could not escape the conclusion that the Black middle class *needed* to keep the Black masses oppressed and excluded from opportunity. The Black middle class oversaw and cultivated this ongoing exclusion not just for the benefit of whites, but for their own benefit as well.

Why?

Because the presence of a potentially volatile Black underclass served as a constant reminder to whites that they needed the Black middle class to control and subdue the Black masses. Black middle class beneficiaries of affirmative action—all the little Bunnies out there—now coveted jobs overseeing the continued exclusion of the Black masses. *The Black middle class had in effect become poverty pimps.* They lived off the misery of their brothers and sisters. They had an *incentive* to keep the Black masses in bondage, the rage of the masses a necessary, constant reminder to whites that they needed their Black middle class partners.

Carmen shuddered at the thought, but could not escape its logic. If the threat of Black rage were to subside, the Black bourgeoisie would lose its importance and status. So even as they took jobs as educators, prison wardens, government administrators and ministers, the Black middle class stoked resentment and rage daily, prodding their less fortunate Black brothers and sisters to express resistance to white oppression in self-defeating ways.

Carmen considered her own situation. What choices was she making? On the one hand, she craved the moral clarity of an all-out fight against segregation and white supremacy. On the other, she liked being a lawyer—not just the status, but being able to use her professional skills to help others, maybe even do her small part opposing racial oppression.

But if her lawyer's skills had been purchased as part of a grand bargain to preserve segregation and white supremacy, then what should Carmen do? By buying into the system, and the power and privilege she obtained as a lawyer in that system, was Carmen validating the oppression of the Black majority?

The complexity and implications of the situation made Carmen's head spin. She did not want to think about it. She hated Bunny for polluting her mind, for making her feel like part of the problem. Carmen wished she had never heard of Bunny and her nasty deal with the Devil. But she had.

Carmen tried to reframe the problem. It was a device she had learned at Harvard Law School. If you did not like a projected outcome, change your frame of reference. If she accepted that the Black middle class, of which she was undeniably a part, had sold out the masses, what did that mean? A number of questions entered her mind.

Had affirmative action been the basis of a grand bargain with the Devil?

Had America's rising Black middle class been complicit in the re-segregation of the Black masses?

Were segregated schools for the masses the price of opportunity for a privileged few?

Was the Black middle class conspiring with whites to oppress the Black masses?

These questions burned in Carmen's mind. She needed answers.

The most obvious way for her to find answers was to use her legal training. She opened the browser on her computer. Her first step was to research the legal definition of "conspiracy." What was required under the law to prove a conspiracy to violate the constitutional rights of the Black masses? Could the evidence provided by Bunny Washington help Carmen prove school segregation was the result of an illegal conspiracy?

Carmen dug into the research. In *Black's* online law dictionary, she learned that a conspiracy is:

"an agreement by two or more persons to commit an unlawful act, coupled with an intent to achieve the agreement's objective, and [often] action or conduct that

furthers the agreement; a combination for an unlawful purpose."

Another website, lectlaw.com, identified four requirements for proving a conspiracy:

First: That two or more persons, in some way or manner, came to a mutual understanding to try to accomplish a common and unlawful plan.

Carmen knew she could meet the first requirement. The unlawful plan was to reinstitute segregated public schools for the Black masses in exchange for a limited number of seats in elite colleges for children of the Black middle class.

Second: That the person willfully became a member of such conspiracy."

This was an interesting question. Carmen could accept that many Black middle class parents whose children benefited from affirmative action were unaware of the existence of the conspiracy. Like herself, they were unaware that a deal had been struck in the seventies. Carmen realized she would have to come back to this requirement after getting more information.

Third: That one of the conspirators during the existence of the conspiracy knowingly committed at least one overt act in furtherance of the conspiracy.

This one was easy. The filing of Carmen's lawsuit and the school board protests had already elicited numerous overt acts. Every time Bunny Washington and her Black supporters took action to defend segregated schools, they were, by the superintendent's own admission, engaging in yet another overt act in furtherance of the conspiracy.

Fourth: That such 'overt act' was knowingly committed at or about the time alleged in an effort to carry out or accomplish some object of the conspiracy.

Again, this one seemed tricky to Carmen. Every one of the hundreds of thousands, if not millions, of middle class African-Americans who had benefited from affirmative action since the 1970s could not have known that their failure to object to segregated inner city schools for the Black masses was part of a conspiracy. But what if they did not know about the conspiracy because they did not *want* to know about it?

Carmen kept reading. The website's next line sealed the deal:

A person may become a member of a conspiracy without knowing all of the details of the unlawful scheme, and without knowing who all of the other members are. So, if a person has an understanding of the unlawful nature of a plan and knowingly and willfully joins in that plan on one occasion, that is sufficient to convict him for conspiracy even though he did not participate before, and even though he played only a minor part.

Carmen stared at the screen. The irrefutable proof of a hideous conspiracy stared back at her. Every middle class Black person who remained silent in the face of the harm done to the Black masses by segregated schools played a minor part in the conspiracy and was, according to the law, guilty.

—⁓—

"Look, Carmen," Jamie Levine acknowledged. "It's a creative legal theory, no doubt."

"They'll never see it coming."

"I agree with that. But I think there's a bigger question."

Carmen could tell Mr. Levine was missing the point. "It's about pressure," she explained. "Leverage. This new legal theory labels Bunny Washington an Uncle Tom. It makes her a co-conspirator in a conspiracy to segregate the schools and violate the constitutional rights of Black children."

"It makes pretty much all Black middle class people co-conspirators," Levine pointed out.

"True."

"My question is whether it's necessary or even advisable to do that. For two reasons. First, you unnecessarily complicate the legal proceedings and force the judge to enter new legal territory when we already have a sound legal theory and strong evidence to back it up. In my experience, it's always a bad idea to ask courts to go into new legal territory when you don't have to. They assume you're doing it because your case is weak." Levine paused. "But the bigger problem is you unnecessarily create thousands of new adversaries by putting this new legal theory out there. Every middle class black person is suddenly by implication a defendant, rather than a potential ally."

Carmen frowned. "But they're not potential allies. They're a big part of the problem."

"That may be," Levine replied. "I would agree it's definitely not helpful when black people like Bunny Washington front for segregated schools."

"Right."

"But we've got to keep our eyes on the prize, Carmen. Are black sell-outs really the main problem? I don't think so."

"Don't underestimate them."

"Don't underestimate *yourself*, Carmen. You're getting off track. You can prosecute this case. You can win it. But you have to stay focused on who your real adversaries are."

Carmen listened.

"Your real adversaries are the people in the power structure of this society who make damn sure the schools are segregated and stay that way."

Carmen nodded.

"People like Bunny Washington work for *them*, not the other way around. They're business leaders, political leaders, power brokers. They decide what the rest of us are allowed to do. They put judges on the bench. They give school administrators like Bunny Washington their marching orders." Levine paused.

"That's the beauty of our lawsuit. We're suing the state because the state has the constitutional obligation to provide all children an adequate education. The Minnepious school district may be like a dog biting children, but that dog is owned and controlled by the state. If we want to stop the dog from biting, we've got to hold the owner accountable. Otherwise, even if you put the dog down, the owner will just get another, meaner one."

Carmen grinned at the image of Bunny Washington as a rabid dog.

"Let's go after the real power," Levine urged. "Let's not get sidetracked by biting dogs."

"I agree," Carmen said.

"By the way, the biting dog analogy isn't mine," Levine confessed.

"I got it from the wisest person I know. I told you this before, but now I'm going to insist. You've got to meet Miss Bea."

—⟋⟍—

"Order anything you want," Eileen offered. "I'm paying."

"You mean the district is paying," Rufus corrected.

"Yes, the district is paying," Eileen agreed. She was not familiar with the menu at Aretha's. She did not care for soul food, but Bunny had told her to let Rufus pick the place. "We can afford it."

"I don't know," Rufus shrugged. "I got a big appetite." He ordered the chicken-fried steak, a side order of onion rings and a large piece of pecan pie.

Eileen ordered only a side salad.

The black waitress frowned.

"You should consider the chicken fried steak," Rufus advised Eileen. "You look like you could use a couple pounds on your hips."

The waitress grinned, pen poised to add to Eileen's order.

Eileen gritted her teeth. She ignored the comment and the waitress' grin. "I'll stick with the salad."

The waitress gave Eileen a withering look. Eileen could not be sure if the dirty look was because Eileen was white, because she was having lunch with a black man, because she was thin, or because she refused to order soul food.

The food came right away. Eileen's salad was iceberg lettuce and shredded carrot with an unripe cherry tomato. The waitress gave her a choice of two packaged dressings, like the ones you might get at Taco Bell: Italian or French. She took the Italian and set it aside so the waitress would leave.

Eileen looked at Rufus, prepared to start their conversation, but he would not make eye contact. The man looked famished. He tucked into his banquet of fried food. Eileen picked at her naked salad.

Rufus looked up from his plate and offered Eileen some of his onion rings. She declined. Shrugging, he finished them off, then belched.

Eileen ordered a cup of coffee while Rufus ate his pie. He seemed to be enjoying the pie, savoring each bite and chewing slowly. Eileen looked for an opening to talk, but every time she tried to say something, Rufus raised his hand to stop her, pointing to his unfinished food.

When he had finished his pie, Rufus pushed back from the table, his belly distended. He had not actually been hungry, but he had no intention of allowing this stooge from the school district talk to him without watching him eat. He nodded to indicate she could talk.

"Rufus..." Eileen began at last.

"Just a minute," Rufus interrupted. He waived his hand to the waitress. She came over to the table. Rufus pointed to Eileen's largely uneaten salad and empty cup of coffee. "She's still hungry, Sheila. Bring her two pieces of pecan pie."

"No, I'm okay," Eileen protested.

Rufus held up his hand, instructing Eileen to stop, so she did. "You can pack the pie to go, Sheila," he said, winking at Eileen.

Oh! Eileen realized the ploy and winked back.

"Rufus," Eileen began again when the waitress left. "May I call you Rufus?"

Rufus shook his head. "I'd prefer you call me Mr. *Tolstoy.*"

Eileen was not sure if he was serious. "Mr. Tolstoy..."

Rufus smirked.

Eileen was getting annoyed. "You may think this is a game..."

"Not really, sister."

Eileen was taken aback. No black man had ever called her "sister" before. Again, she wondered if he was mocking her.

The packaged pecan pie arrived with the bill. Eileen took the bill and pushed the pie across the table to Rufus. He pushed it back. Eileen gave him an inquiring look, as if he had forgotten his devilish scheme to use her as a foil to get more pie to go.

"I told you," Rufus said. "You're looking skinny. You need to put on some weight. I thought you could use the calories."

A slow rage bubbled in Eileen's empty stomach. She resisted the urge to respond with a cutting remark, knowing what was on the line for the district, for Bunny, for herself. "I asked you to lunch to talk about how the district might partner with you."

Rufus' eyes widened. "You want to partner with the Socialist Workers Party? Excellent!"

"We were thinking more of a partnership with you *personally*."

"Are you trying to get personal with me?" Rufus looked at Eileen's left hand. "You have a wedding ring…"

"Mr. Tolstoy…er, look…" Eileen fumed. "This is a serious proposal."

"How much we talking about?"

Eileen paused. She could not tell if this was another put on. "I can't give you a number right now. It would have to be under a legitimate consulting agreement."

Rufus nodded. "Of course."

Eileen saw her opening. "It would be a substantial amount."

"Like a million?"

Eileen blanched. She hoped he wasn't serious. "No. More like ten or twenty thousand."

Rufus patted his belly. "You saw how I eat. That wouldn't last more than a couple weeks. What would I do then?"

Eileen was growing disoriented. She could not tell if the man was negotiating with her in a roundabout way, or mocking her. There was only one way to find out. "I could make a phone call."

"Let's do it," Rufus encouraged.

Eileen smiled. She had her prey. Every man had his price. She got out her cell phone. As soon as she pressed the talk button, Rufus snatched the phone from her and hit the speaker button.

"'Leen?" the familiar voice answered. "Did he go for it?"

"Bunny!" Rufus shouted so everyone in the soul food restaurant could hear. "It's Rufus!"

There was shocked silence on the other end of the phone.

"Thanks for lunch, Bunny! It was fabulous! You can never go wrong at Aretha's!"

Eileen reached for the phone to try to get it back, but Rufus pulled it away.

The waitress giggled. The other restaurant patrons watched the commotion.

Eileen tried to remain calm, so as not to make an even bigger scene.

"I'm sending some pie home for you with your *chumcha*. You might have to share it with her, though. She's looking sickly. You should feed her better."

Laughter rolled across Aretha's. On the north side, it wasn't often folk got to see a fancy white woman cut to size. Lately, though, with the school board protests and all, north Minnepioutans were beginning to feel anything was possible.

"See you at the next school board meeting, Bunny!" Rufus called out.

The cell phone line went dead.

—⚍—

Charity got off the bus in the suburbs and looked around. She spotted the Updike High School building, where the Eden-Updike school district headquarters were located. As soon as she saw the school building, she had a sinking feeling. She knew she'd made a mistake accepting the job.

She considered staying at the bus stop and waiting for the next bus back to downtown Minnepious. From there, she could catch another bus home. She shivered. It was cold. It might be a long wait for the next bus back to downtown. She decided to give the job a try, at least for one day. If it didn't work out, she could always take the $50,000 settlement from Minnepious.

Charity pulled her coat tight and walked through the wind to the school building. She held her breath as she entered the school. She found the office and walked in. It was full of white people looking important and busy. Again, Charity realized she should never have agreed to take the job. It was a setup. She turned to leave.

"Ms. Douglass?" a voice called out.

Charity froze. A white woman was standing in the middle of the busy office waving to her. The woman walked up to her.

"I'm Diana Ellison. We're so excited to have you join us!"

Charity did not know what to say. It was too late to leave. She followed the woman to a large room inside the office. People went in and out. Charity filled out a bunch of forms. She wasn't sure what some of the forms were asking for, but she did her best. Then she followed the woman out of the office and into the school hallway.

"I want to introduce you to our other community outreach specialists," the woman told Charity. "They're coming out of a meeting in five minutes. We'll catch them here."

A loud bell rang. Suddenly, doors burst open and students poured into the hallway. Charity could not believe how loud it was! Kids moved everywhere, jumping on each other, fist bumping, calling out. It was crazy. About half the kids were white. The other half were Black and Latino and Asian. They were normal looking kids. Charity nodded to a couple of the Black kids who passed her and they nodded back. After five minutes, the bell rang again and the hallway emptied.

Charity relaxed. It wasn't so bad. She looked at the white woman, Diana, who was waving to a group of adults at the other end of the hallway. They saw Diana and started walking toward her. There were two white men, a white woman, a Latino man and an Asian woman. Diana introduced Charity to the group.

"Hey, I'm Ramon," the Latino man said and shook Charity's hand. "Great to meet you."

"I'm Lynne," the white woman said.

"Joe," one of the white men said.

"Janet," the Asian woman said.

"Frank."

"These guys will show you the community outreach office," Diana told Charity. "They'll give you a sense of what we do, what we expect."

"What we expect?" Ramon joked. "To have some fun! That's what we expect."

Janet rolled her eyes. "Come on," she said to Charity. "You'll like it here."

Charity looked at Diana, who nodded. "You're in good hands."

—m—

Eileen had never done this before. She had never even considered it. She did not feel good about it, but she saw no other way. "Vinny," she said to the school district's director of security. "We need help with a sticky situation."

Vinny nodded. He knew how to deal with almost every sticky situation Minnepioutans could get themselves into. He could see Eileen was under a lot of stress. "Not a problem. Consider it taken care of."

—⁂—

Bunny took no chances. She got the word out that no further protests would be tolerated. In close collaboration with County Attorney Nancy Grandishar, Bunny had her staff prepare an official notice unlike any they had ever put out before. She instructed her team to disseminate the notice, printed on flyers and posters, everywhere poor people might be found in Minnepious.

The school district plastered the notice all over Minnepious' low income neighborhoods. The notice covered community bulletin boards. It showed up in barber shops, restaurants and places of worship. It greeted visitors to every school building on the north and near south sides. It traveled home in the backpacks of every student from low income schools. It appeared on the front door of all local and county government offices where poor people congregated.

The notice stated:

"OFFICIAL NOTICE: Until further notice, all meetings of the Minnepious School Board will take place on alternate Thursday afternoons at 3pm. Any person wishing to attend a meeting must submit his or her name in advance to an authorized police community liaison officer and submit to a background check.

"No recording device of any kind, including cell phones, will be allowed in the meeting room. Anyone attempting to smuggle a recording device into the meeting room will be subject to arrest and the recording device will be confiscated. There will be no further broadcasts of school board meetings on cable television. These rules will ensure the calm,

orderly proceeding of school board business.

"*BE FURTHER ADVISED, IT IS A FELONY IN THE STATE OF MINNESOULE TO INTERFERE WITH GOVERNMENT FUNCTIONS, PUNISHABLE BY A FINE UP TO $10,000 AND A MINIMUM FIVE YEARS IN PRISON. Minnepious police officers will strictly enforce this law at all school board meetings.*"

—◦—

Andrew wore Skullcandy ear buds and listened to Elton John's *Daniel* as he crossed the street in downtown Minnepious on his way to work. He never saw or heard the cops before they grabbed him and threw him down in the middle of the crosswalk. His head cracked against the pavement. An ear bud lodged deep inside his ear. A boot kicked his ribs and rolled him over onto his stomach. A knee pressed into his back, pinning him to the ground. The cops pulled his arms back hard and cuffed him. The cuffs bit into his wrists.

"What did I do?" Andrew yelled, as the cops dragged him to their squad car.

"Loitering," one of the officers replied.

"With intent to commit a felony," the other added.

—◦—

It surprised Eileen how much she enjoyed making this call. She did not generally think of herself as a vengeful person, but he had it coming. "Rufus," Eileen said when he answered. "You can call me *Ma'am*."

Rufus did not say a word until the end of the call. He had already talked with Andrew, who had called him from the back of a police squad car. The cops were holding Andrew in the car. They had not yet taken him in for booking. They were awaiting instructions from someone they would not identify.

Rufus knew they were stuck. Andrew had child support payments for his three kids. If the arrest was recorded, Andrew would lose his job as a janitor at Minnepious Technical College. He would lose his apartment. He would probably lose visitation with his kids, too, if his ex-wife got pissed because he stopped paying child support.

"Okay," was the first word Rufus said, at the end of the call.

"Okay, *Ma'am*," Eileen corrected, indulging her base desires for once. He had it coming.

"Fuck you," Rufus replied and hung up.

—⁊⁊—

Charity couldn't wait to tell her kids about her first day on the new job. She had met a lot of people. She couldn't remember most of their names, but everyone seemed to know her. They made her feel like she belonged, like they weren't better than she was. At the end of the day, Diana had talked to Charity about when Isaiah, Lakeesha and Isaac could visit schools in Updike. Charity was sure the kids would like the schools in Updike a lot better than their shitty schools in Minnepious. There were more Black kids than she had expected, and even the white people seemed okay.

The school board protests were fun, and it was cool to have people say she was a hero and all. But Charity liked the feeling of having a job. And she was even more excited for her kids to go to good schools that actually wanted them. She could get used to this.

—⁊⁊—

"You don't need to explain," Carmen said into her phone.

"Look, sister," Rufus tried again. "It's only temporary. We just need to take care of some things."

"Really, Rufus, you don't need to explain. You guys drove the protests. If you can't do it now, I understand. I'm okay with that. I've got the lawsuit."

"Sorry to let you down, Carmen."

"You're not letting me down, Rufus. It's a long struggle. Do what you need to do. You got to live to fight another day. I'll be there when you're ready."

"Thanks, sister," Rufus said. "I know you're down for the cause."

After she hung up, Carmen sat back in her chair and closed her eyes. The *"people's movement,"* such as it was, had arisen out of nothing and was now dissipating back into nothing.

Carmen knew the protests could not be sustained anyway once their novelty wore off. And of course the power structure knew that as well. In a way, Carmen was relieved not to have to deal with the protests any more.

She considered the bigger picture. The legal case would proceed, unless the judge dismissed it. If he did dismiss the case, she would appeal. That would take at least a year. But the case would be out of the public eye during the appeal process, which meant the district would continue operating segregated schools. Business as usual.

The real question for Carmen was how long was she willing to stay in Minnepious? She knew she had outworn her welcome at the law firm, not that they had given her much of a welcome in the first place. Charity now had a job, and her kids would soon switch to better, desegregated schools. Carmen had no friends in Minnepious. She saw no reason to stay.

That left Bob. Carmen wasn't sure what she wanted to do about him. She felt like she hadn't really given him a chance. But, on the other hand, the distaste from the Levine family gathering still lingered. Maybe it was unfair to lump Bob in with his family, but his family's behavior tarnished him in her mind. She didn't feel good about that. Maybe she should be more open-minded. But in her heart, Carmen knew she could not give Bob a fair chance any more, especially with how she felt about his family and his hometown.

So that decided it. She would find a job elsewhere. She would look for something in New York. She might not find something right away. And whatever she eventually found might not be her dream job. But it was better to deal with reality now than wait for the decay and rot of this place to consume her.

—m—

The front page headline in the next morning's *Strib* proclaimed: ***"School Board Protests Called Off."***

The sub-heading read: *"Blacks to work out differences with district."*

Carmen did not bother reading the article.

—⁓—

The call she had waited a lifetime to receive came on Wednesday. But it was Munson, not the President-elect. Bunny's heart sank. She knew what it meant that the President-elect himself had not called.

Munson apologized profusely for the President-elect not making this call. He said the President-elect was busy with final arrangements for the historic Inauguration. He said the entire transition process was turning out to be far more complicated than any of them had anticipated. He complimented Bunny for ending the school board protest drama.

Bunny listened politely, bracing for the bad news, waiting for the other shoe to drop. She had heard these sorts of lame excuses from white people her whole career. She did not know which disappointed her more: that she was not getting the appointment of a lifetime, or that the President-elect was too gutless to do her the courtesy of calling to give her the bad news himself. It did not bode well for his future success as a leader, Bunny reflected.

Then Munson gave Bunny the shock of her life. He told her the President-elect had decided to appoint her Secretary of Education, after all.

It took a while for Bunny to process this information. Her brain had so conditioned itself to bad news that this unbelievably *good* news just sat there, knocking on her skull, trying to get in. Munson droned on, but Bunny could not react, afraid that if she did, the dream would burst.

The appointment would be announced the morning of the Presidential Inauguration in Washington, DC. Bunny would be the President-elect's first official cabinet appointment to demonstrate his personal commitment to education reform. "Go ahead and buy your ticket," Munson said, closing the call. "Welcome aboard, Madame Secretary."

When the call ended, Bunny nearly fainted.

She called her daughter Bea. They shared tears of relief and joy through the phone. After the call, Bunny thought of her dear departed mother and her father. They would have been so proud. Then she thought of her grandmother, who was still alive. What her grandmother would say, Bunny could only guess. Before she left for Washington, Bunny would give her grandmother the news in person. She savored that prospect. She had waited too many years to miss that chance.

—⁜—

Principal Chris Hardwell's request for a meeting came as a surprise. Carmen did not know Hardwell. She could not fathom why he wanted to meet with her. But he had insisted on a meeting at her office as soon as possible. He said he had information she needed for her case.

Now that he was in her office, Hardwell seemed like the last person Carmen would expect to be a whistleblower. He was a large man, and dour. He was not old, but he moved and spoke slowly, with a Southern accent. He wore a suit that seemed out of style.

Hardwell looked hard at Carmen. "You can't tell anyone you got this from me."

"I understand."

"You were at a school board meeting a few weeks ago where there was a presentation about student performance, broken out by different ethnic groups. Do you remember that?"

"I remember it."

"The district's head of statistics, a guy named Loofa, made the presentation. The superintendent put him up to it so she could embarrass Reverend Ballman at the board meeting."

"You mean where they showed that Somalis are doing better than African-American students."

"Right," Hardwell replied. "They fudged the numbers."

"Okay."

"There was a trend they didn't report. Third generation Somalis."

"*Third* generation Somalis?"

"Kids whose parents were born here, not in Africa."

"Somalis have been here that long?"

"Quite a few have been here long enough to become grandparents. We've got more than a hundred third generation Somalis in our schools."

Carmen did not see the significance of this information. "Okay, so what? An urban school district cooking data is hardly a surprise."

Hardwell frowned. "Remember how Somali students outscored African-American students on the state tests?"

Carmen nodded. She knew all the reported test data by heart.

"Well, the test scores of third generation Somali kids are indistinguishable from the scores of other native born African-American students."

Carmen took a moment to absorb this information. "So what you're saying is the school district is hiding data that shows they turn all Black children, no matter where the families come from, into failing African-Americans?"

"That's one way of putting it."

"Okay, that sounds bad," Carmen agreed. "But it doesn't exactly prove my case. I hope you have more than that."

"Bear with me. What I just told you shows that Bunny Washington is personally involved in the district's fraudulent use of student achievement data."

"Agreed. What else do you have?"

"Test score fraud."

"I'm listening."

"You've heard that Afrocentric Success Academy does as well as the top performing suburbs, like Eden, on the state tests?"

Carmen frowned. "I've heard it. *Everyone's* heard it. All you have to do is pick up the newspaper, or listen to Black radio. Providence is a miracle worker." She paused. "It's bullshit."

"Yes, it is," Hardwell agreed. "I have the proof."

Carmen waited. Now this was interesting.

"They systematically remove students before the tests."

This rang a bell with Carmen. She had noticed a disparity between the number of students enrolled and the number of students taking the tests. She had never grasped its significance, however, until now. "Are you saying they remove the ones they think won't pass?"

"Exactly. They're scientific about it. They give the kids practice tests every week for months leading up to the real tests. They *know* who will pass, and who won't."

Then it hit her. "That's what happened to my client's kids. They took the kids out of class. The kids didn't know why. It must have been about the tests."

"If they weren't going to pass the tests, they'd be pulled out."

Carmen thought about what Hardwell was saying. "My client's kids *couldn't* have passed the tests. They just arrived from Chicago." She paused. "But how can ASA get away with it? If it's systematic cheating, wouldn't the state catch them?"

Hardwell frowned. "This isn't the kind of cheating that ever gets exposed. Providence isn't stupid. They don't feed answers to students, or change answers after the fact. That would be stupid. No, Providence covers his tracks. If they questioned him, he'd say his student population is mobile, with unreliable attendance."

"And he knows nobody will ask him anyway," Carmen predicted. "Right?"

"You got it."

"Because it's a great story. Segregated schools so successful they beat the suburbs!"

Hardwell nodded. "Except they don't. It's pure fiction."

"A mere inconvenience," Carmen added. "But why let the truth get in the way of a great story. Separate but equal...the ultimate American fantasy."

Hardwell liked this young attorney.

"What evidence do you have?" Carmen asked. "No offense, but I need more than your suspicions."

"My wife goes to Zumba with the woman in charge of testing at Afrocentric Academy."

"*Zumba?*"

"You'd be surprised what people tell each other while they're exercising."

Carmen laughed. She could imagine how this would look in court. She hoped the judge's wife—if he were married—did Zumba or some other similar workout. Then the judge might understand.

Hardwell also grinned, for the first time. "It's not like my wife goes to Zumba to get dirt on Afrocentric Success Academy. An assistant principal at another school in the district told me about ASA, and I told my wife. She was scandalized. She asked her friend at Zumba, and the woman didn't deny it. She actually said she was proud of it. Felt they were just beating a racist system stacked against them."

"So why'd you come to me?"

"You're not the only one who sees what's going on."

"What do you mean?"

"The schools…segregation…corruption." Hardwell sighed. "I have young kids…"

Carmen nodded.

Hardwell thought about how much he wanted to tell Carmen. "We also have a common enemy."

"I don't have enemies," Carmen rejoined.

"I read your lawsuit," Hardwell said. "You and I both know what Bunny Washington is up to."

"It's nothing personal," Carmen objected.

Hardwell smiled. "Oh, I think it's personal."

—∞—

When Hardwell left, Carmen was not sure what to do. She could go to Mr. Levine, but her last interaction had not unfolded the way she expected. She was not sure how he would react to this new information.

Systematic cheating on state tests was more likely to cause a scandal than help Carmen prove a desegregation case. In her research, Carmen had come across dozens of major school districts around the country ensnared in cheating scandals or committing fraud on standardized tests. The scandals sometimes led to criminal prosecutions of teachers or administrators. But Carmen had never seen them result in compensation or legal recourse for the children defrauded of an adequate education.

Carmen decided not to take this new information to Mr. Levine, at least not right away. Instead, she called the Office of the Superintendent of Minnepious Public Schools. "This is Carmen Braithwaite," she explained to the receptionist. "I'm a lawyer, and I need to speak with Bunny Washington. It's urgent."

After a pause, the receptionist put her through.

"Hello, Ms. Braithwaite," a male voice answered. "This is Alain Fried. I'm Superintendent Washington's executive assistant. How can I help you?"

"I need to speak with the superintendent," Carmen replied. "It's urgent."

"Oh, I'm sure it is," Alain purred. "I'm sure it is. Unfortunately, honey, the superintendent is out of the office. She's not reachable."

Carmen did not feel comfortable saying more to an office assistant. What she had to say was for Bunny Washington's ears only. "Please tell her I called. It's important that she call me back right away."

"Oh, I surely will tell her," Alain promised. "I surely will." Then he disconnected the line and shivered at the deliciousness of it all.

—∞—

Carmen's went to Mr. Levine's office and told him everything Hardwell had told her. Then she told him about her attempt to reach Bunny.

Levine grasped the significance of the information right away. "Here's what I think. Before you do anything, talk to Miss Bea. She's seen it all before. She'll have good advice."

Carmen did not understand Mr. Levine's fascination with Miss Bea. She could not imagine how some ancient client of his from the 1970s could help her sort out what to do now. But out of respect for Mr. Levine, and perhaps because she still had not decided what to do about Hardwell's bombshell, Carmen agreed to the meeting. She had no idea what she was in for.

Minnissippi

Chapter 10

Carmen peered into the dim living room. It took a while for her eyes to adjust to the gloom. The window shades were lowered. The lighting was faint. It was as though the room awaited a funeral.

"Where you from, honey?" a quavering voice queried from a big chair in the corner of the room.

"You mean originally?" Carmen asked.

"You ain't from here."

"How do you know, ma'am?"

"It's how you carry yourself."

Miss Bea chuckled softly. "Gives you away."

Carmen shook her head. "I'm sorry?"

"Ain't no need to apologize, child. We all used to carry ourselves that way. Least for a little while. In the fifties and sixties. First time since slavery we thought maybe we just might be free."

Carmen wanted to hear more. She had a feeling it was a story never told, a story erased from the collective consciousness of Black people.

"Sit down, child," Miss Bea instructed. "This goin' take a while."

Carmen sat on the old sofa across from Miss Bea's oversized easy chair. The springs in the sofa were shot and Carmen sank down as if she were a child in a sling. Miss Bea looked so old and frail, and Carmen felt far, far away from her, unable to help if anything went wrong.

"I been waitin' a long time for you, child," Miss Bea smiled. "Don't nobody come see me no more."

Carmen frowned. She pondered the universal isolation of old people in America. Those deemed irrelevant to the fast-moving world of youth, vigor and money. Unlike in Trinidad, where young and old shared the same houses, the same food, even the same soca music, here the old withered away out of view, their stories lost, their pleas silenced, their wisdom unappreciated by those most in need of guidance.

"See, my grandma," Miss Bea continued. "She told me what it was like after slavery. People was free. Course they wasn't really free. Didn't have no education. Didn't have no money. Didn't have none of the things that make freedom real."

"I think I understand," Carmen whispered. "I *need* to understand."

Miss Bea smiled. "You understand more than you think. That's why you here now." Miss Bea paused. "I'm guessin' you heard talk 'bout house Negroes and field Negroes, that sort of thing."

Carmen did not respond.

"See, after slavery, all that madness went away for a while. Not all the way away. But for a time, we was all just free, after a fashion. Can you imagine that?"

"I think so."

"Well, you know what happened? After a time, them house Negroes, they got back in with the old slave masters. They never took to freedom, them house Negroes. See, they thought life was pretty good with that old slave master. Least that's what they told themselves. You ask me, I think that's what they knew. And it's hard to go against what you know. Know what I mean, child?"

"I think so," Carmen began. "But there's something I'm not too clear about."

"Go ahead," Miss Bea encouraged. "You could ask me."

Carmen hesitated. "Ma'am..."

"Call me Miss Bea."

"Miss Bea, if you just got freedom from someone who's been raping and murdering you and your people, why would you ever go back to him?"

Miss Bea smiled. "See, I knew you wasn't from here. That's why you ask that question."

"I'm sorry, I don't follow..."

"I'm goin' tell you some things don't no one want to hear. You understand?"

"I think so."

"That's why you here. I'm goin' tell you things don't nobody want to hear because they bring too much pain. You ask why a woman would go back to live with her rapist. Why would you go back to serve the people that destroyed your family, raped your mama, sold away your brothers and sisters?"

Carmen shuddered. "I don't know."

"Seem crazy, huh? But house Negroes, they don't even ask that question. It's just what they know. It's what life is. You born, you get beat, you grow up, you get beat some more, you pray, your mama get raped, you keep quiet, you get beat some more, you get raped, you keep quiet, you get beat, you pray, you get beat, your brother get killed, you pray some more."

Carmen winced.

"What you think slavery was about, child?"

"I never really gave it much thought," Carmen admitted.

"That's because you ain't one of us."

Carmen frowned. "We had slavery, too. In the Caribbean, slavery was harsher than here. Average life expectancy was *seven years* for slaves from the day they arrived."

"What you all do about it?" Miss Bea asked.

"What do you mean?"

"Some of y'all kicked that slave master out."

"I guess."

"I know you did. See, when I was a young child, my daddy took me on a trip to Haiti. We went on a church mission to save them nappy-haired, backward Negroes." Miss Bea paused. "When we got there, you know what my daddy said?"

Carmen shook her head.

"He said, *'Take a good look at them dirty Negroes, child. That's what happen if you leave Negroes to they own selves. They be lookin' all ignorant, like Africans. You need to thank God you ain't like them.'* That's what my daddy told me when we got to Haiti."

Carmen looked away, embarrassed.

"That's what my daddy saw. You know what *I* saw in Haiti?" Miss Bea's eyes bored into Carmen. "I saw people who was proud. I saw people standin' straight, no white man around. They done kicked the white man out, and they damn sure know they done it themselves. And they ain't never goin' let him come back, neither.

"I'd never seen Negroes like that before. To this day, I've only seen one American Negro proud like that. *Malcolm X*. He's the *only* one. In his heart, he be from Haiti.

"My daddy took me back home after a week. Whenever I act up after that, he used to say he goin' send me back to Haiti. He thought that's the worst thing you could do to a Negro. Send her back to Haiti. But me, I didn't see it that way. Ever since I was a little girl, I want to be free like the Africans in Haiti. I want to live proud and free, no white man 'round tellin' me what to do, tellin' me what I could be.

"When I grew up and left home, I tried to find out more 'bout Haiti. It was like lookin' for hidden treasure. Didn't nobody know nothin' 'bout it. They all act like I was the crazy one. But I couldn't get the idea out my mind that Africans in Haiti was free. I kept askin' people, tryin' to figure out how I could learn more. I read books 'bout Haiti, but I figured out right quick that most of them books was written by white men, and they was full a lies. Then one day in the library, I found what I was lookin' for.

"I found a old newspaper article from the 1850s 'bout a escaped slave. That Negro got hisself all the way to Indiana. He weren't a slave no more. He was free. Least the law say he was free. But that crazy Negro, he want to be free for real. So he didn't stop in Indiana. He kept right on walkin'. He done walk hisself all the way to Boston! Now if you think a Negro goin' walk a thousand miles to stop in Boston, child, you don't know Boston."

Carmen smiled. "I know Boston."

"Why you think that escaped slave walked all the way from Indiana to Boston?"

Carmen could not imagine why. "I don't know. He had family there?"

Miss Bea smiled. "Child, his family was still on master's plantation. That man walked all that way to Boston so he could catch a ship to Haiti. That man want to be free *for real.*" Miss Bea paused again, letting the impact sink in.

Carmen felt a mixture of pride and anger. Tears welled up in her eyes. "Why you?"

"Now you gettin' there, child," Miss Bea encouraged. "You askin' why I could see it, but my daddy couldn't."

Carmen nodded.

"I was just a child. My daddy was grown up. He thought he already knew everything there was to know 'bout Negroes. Most important thing, he knew a Negro's place. So when he went to Haiti and seen all them dirt poor dark Negroes with no white master in charge, he just knew they had to be savages. First time in his life, my daddy feel bigger than another man. You shoulda seen my daddy's chest push out. Daddy was proud to be American."

Carmen cringed.

"Me? I was just a little girl. I listened to my daddy. I seen his chest puff out. But I saw it different. I didn't see what my daddy seen. When I looked 'round, I didn't see no white man making my daddy lick his boots. I didn't see no white man lookin' at my mama like he own her. I just see beautiful brown people lookin' like me. And Lord, the way those Africans in Haiti done carry themselves! I ain't never seen nothin' like it. They was free, no doubt. They wasn't Negroes. They was Africans." Miss Bea paused. "Difference between my daddy and me was he couldn't see what was right in front of his face. Me? I didn't know better. I just look at what's there."

"This can only happen when you're young," Carmen mused.

Miss Bea reached out and held Carmen's hand. "They thought they could domesticate us," the old woman whispered.

"Excuse me?"

"The Europeans. They tried to domesticate us. Like cows, or pigs, or dogs. They still tryin', truth be told."

Carmen shuddered.

"Oh, yes. Lord knows, they tried. But they never could do it. 'Cause you can't domesticate people." Miss Bea paused. "You ever see a cow give birth?"

Carmen shook her head.

"The mama cow give birth to a baby cow. That little cow goin' grow up to be just like her mama. Don't matter what you do, that little cow goin' grow up and sit there waitin' to be fed and milked. You ain't never goin' find no *wild cow* no matter how hard you look. But people's different. We all born wild. Every human child born the same way—wild. Ain't no two ways about it. Don't no child come into this world wantin' to be a slave. Not a one. You could mark my words on that."

"True," agreed Carmen.

"You can't domesticate people like you do a cow or a pig or a dog."

"True."

"So if you wanna make a person into a slave, you gotta make her think she was *born to be a slave*. And if you wanna do that, you gotta get to that child right early, when she's little."

"Yes."

"And you best off usin' her parents to do it for you. So the European abused those parents. They whupped 'em. They raped 'em. Then, like all parents, thinkin' they know what's best for their children, Negroes go and tell their children, *'Got to be careful, child. Watch out for the white man. 'Cause as long as he around, you ain't never goin' be free.'*

"And those little children, they believe it. 'Cause no little child want to believe their parents lyin' to them. If mama say it, it gotta be true."

Carmen saw the logic. Disparate experiences were congealing into something powerful, and troubling, in her mind. "So you tell your daughter," Carmen observed. "You may not be white, but at least you're not…Haitian."

"You could always find a Haitian," Miss Bea confirmed. "Someone always nastier and lower than you, 'specially if you in the master's house."

"You're saying after slavery, anyone who could get back into the master's house did?"

"It wasn't that simple, child. Never was. After slavery, we was feelin' heady. We was feelin' like a new world's out there for us. We didn't know what was out there, so we dipped a toe. Want to get a idea what freedom feel like. Hard to just plunge in after all them years in bondage. Course a few giddy Negroes did just that. Then we saw what happen to a giddy Negro. The white man hang that Negro from a tree. The white man ain't goin' let Negroes just walk on out to freedom without a fight.

"Child, the Europeans convinced themselves back then that we was already domesticated. They figure only a wild, heady Negro lose his mind want freedom. So we all begin to understand that in America, Negro freedom got to have limits. Long as you stay in yo' place, don't cause no trouble, you goin' be all right. Moment you raise a hackle, they goin' raise you by yo' neck."

"But people did fight back," Carmen pointed out. "Why take that risk?"

"You right, child. After some time, Negroes start feelin' their oats. A wind start blowin' in the fifties and sixties. That wind blow all over. Startin' in Africa. Africans was fightin' back. All over Africa. Gave us the idea of freedom, too. The Russians helped. Gave money and guns to Africans. But Africans was fightin' for their own freedom.

"Negroes here start askin' why Africans in Africa could be free, but Africans in America can't? Next thing you know, we was marchin', too. Took to the streets, we did. And you know what? Even house Negroes came to join us in the streets. Dr. King and all them preachers told 'em to.

"First time we could see what real freedom might look like. Sisters was wearin' their hair natural. Brothers in *dashikis*. People talkin' 'bout Black Power. Malcolm, he showed the way. He done talk to us like we was already free. And he done talk to the European like we don't have no fear no more. Only time in my life, I start to feel like a Haitian. I was proud, child. I was proud of my people.

"The Europeans in this country got scared, too. They know for sure we ain't domesticated then. Somethin' goin' wrong with all their plans for us. They thought the Devil hisself got hold of us. They came after us hard, they did. 'Specially when we went for their schools.

"They done segregate those schools so our children would never be free. Europeans knew what they was doin', sure 'nough. The same people set up all them factories and took over countries all over the world made damn sure they goin' keep our children out their schools. They knew what they was doin' all right. Separate but equal? There weren't nothin' equal 'bout it, and that was the whole point of it.

"When the Supreme Court said they can't do it no more, we was dancin' in our hearts. But they never meant it. Not after they give it a thought. Then, we had to take to the streets. We emptied the big house. Even them house Negroes joined the rest of us already in the streets! Wasn't no one left in the big house. That gave 'em pause, sure 'nough."

Carmen shook her head. "Look how times have changed. Today, all the Black leaders, like Bunny Washington, say a Black kid shouldn't have to sit next to a white kid to learn."

"Who you callin' a leader?" Miss Bea scolded. "Bunny sure ain't no leader. She *paid* by Europeans to say that nonsense. I'll tell you this, child. Back in the day, didn't none of us want to sit next to a white child. They could be right nasty. But we sure ain't never goin' let 'em tell us we ain't good enough to sit next to their children!

"That was the biggest fight of all. We knew it back then. If their children sit next to our children, they can't hold us back no more. You see, a teacher can't only teach the white kids but don't teach the Negroes if they all in the same classroom. Don't get me wrong. They goin' try all kinds a tricky ways to hold us back. But when our children's in the same classroom with theirs, they can't stop us no more. And they knew it, too. So they done go against their own Supreme Court! They say they goin' fight us instead."

Carmen was beginning to see the big picture and she didn't like it. Some realizations are so brutal you want to get them out of your head, but you can't.

"Europeans ain't goin' give up what they got without a fight," Miss Bea warned.

"But they have given up a lot," Carmen pointed out. "We have made progress."

"Yes, we have, child. We made a lotta progress from a lotta struggle. We got the right to vote. Lotta struggle to get that. We got to sit wherever we want on a bus. That was a lotta struggle, too. We got to eat any place we want and drink from their water fountains. More struggle. But there was always only one real struggle. That was for the one thing they can't never let us get and keep. 'Cause if they do, they can't never keep us down no more."

Carmen listened, not sure where Miss Bea was going.

Miss Bea smiled. "What if you got a nice dress you could wear to church every Sunday. Everyone goin' see that dress. They all goin' covet that dress. But you got it, and they don't. You with me?"

Carmen nodded.

"But see, that ain't really your dress, now, is it?"

Carmen frowned.

"Did you make it? Of course you didn't. That old Negro tailor made it 'cause sure 'nough that man could sew! Did you earn the money to buy it? What you think? Your husband done give you that money. No, child, you didn't make that dress, and you didn't earn the money to buy it. So how come you carryin' on 'bout that dress, like it make *you* special somehow?

"You carryin' on *because* you didn't make it, *because* you didn't earn it! You *need* every lady in town starin' at you, dreamin' 'bout one day gettin' them a dress like yo' dress. Otherwise, you ain't got nothin'. 'Cause if you can't make nothin', and you don't earn nothin', then you ain't got nothin'...So how you look now?"

Carmen grinned. "Not good."

"Not good? Child, you ain't *white* if you ain't got somethin' everyone want. So sure 'nough, you goin' carry on like you got somethin' *everyone* want. Problem is, that fancy dress you got, what you say everyone want...that dress ain't lookin' so good if folk just take a close look. That old dress seen better days. That old dress lookin' like a rat hide if folk look close enough. So you better keep folk away. Don't let no one take a close look." Miss Bea paused. "Now you see it, child?"

"You're saying the only way Europeans, as you call them, can stay *white*," Carmen concluded. "Is if they don't let us get too close."

Miss Bea smiled. "That's right. If you ain't really better than me, you ain't goin' let me get close." Miss Bea paused. "And they know it. Only way they get away with it is we do the dirty work for 'em."

Carmen felt uneasy. Was Miss Bea blaming the victim? Was she saying the real problem was not white people, but Black people? "Ma'am...Miss Bea...I have to ask you something."

"You go right ahead."

"You say white people need Black people."

"That's right, honey. They can't exist without us. Can't be white without a Negro."

"See, ma'am...Miss Bea...I don't disagree with you. But I don't think you can just say white people need us to do all the dirty work. They do plenty of it themselves."

"Well you can and you can't."

"I don't follow."

"The hangman's noose be real, no doubt about that. I lost a lotta folk. You need to know that. But wasn't white people what killed 'em. It was people."

"It *was* white people," Carmen insisted. "You can't let them off the hook."

"They was murderers, all right. But they was still just people. Don't tell me they's white. I was there. Saw 'em myself. Their skin's pinky-peachy. But their blood's African, just like you and me. Maybe that's what they tryin' to lynch."

Carmen frowned. "I have to disagree. Whiteness is more than just an idea. It's had real and terrible consequences in the real world, for a long time."

"I been in this world a sight longer than you, child," Miss Bea scolded gently. "I seen a lot of what these people capable of."

Carmen held her ground. "Still..."

"Child, they capable of killin' off the Indians. They enslaved us, lynched us, raped us… abused us every which way they could. They done chase after every brown people on God's green earth. They try to kill off every wild livin' thing bigger than a rat. You think I don't know what the people you call *white* could do?"

Carmen was stunned at the breadth of the old woman's perspective.

"But you know the worst thing them pasty old devils done?"

Carmen shook her head.

"They done try to kill our children's minds. Europeans know the only way they could stay *white* is if our children accept that they better than us. 'Cause if our children ever look at that pasty old white thing, and say, *'You ain't white. You just a pasty, murderin', rapin', nasty ole man who need to be stopped!'* What you think goin' happen?"

"That will never happen," Carmen muttered.

Miss Bea cackled. "Never goin' happen? Child, it already *did* happen! What you think we was doin' in the sixties and seventies? Malcom got us goin'. He told that pasty old man the truth. Ain't no Negro before or since ever say it like Malcolm. But he wasn't the only one. There was always two sides to it. On one side, Malcolm told the white man the truth to his face. On the other side, Thurgood and the NAACP was pushin' hard for desegregation."

Carmen was confused again. "But didn't Malcolm call the NAACP and people fighting segregation *Uncle Toms*?"

"Yes, he did. But child, you need to look beneath the surface. They was all really workin' together, like two sides of the same coin. Maybe they say some nasty things 'bout each other. But don't you forget, back then we was all in it together. We all knew the deal. You can't get desegregation if you afraid to tell the truth 'bout how the white man keepin' you down. Segregation's always built on lies. *Separate but equal,* the biggest lie of all!

"See, Thurgood and the NAACP went after white schools 'cause we had to show them pasty things we wasn't scared no more. What's braver than sendin' your own child into the lion's den? You know we love our children. We'll do anything to protect our children. Only way we could ever protect our children from that white devil was to let our children see for their own selves that the white devil ain't but a thing."

Carmen saw it. "The only way was to desegregate the schools."

"Child, how you goin' overcome your fear of the dark if you always keepin' the lights on? You gotta turn off the lights and learn for your own self that you goin' be all right. Only way you goin' learn for your own self you just as good as some white girl, you gotta go on into her school and sit next to her. The moment that white girl know you ain't afraid, she ain't white no more. She could *pretend* to be white. But if nobody don't believe it, she just pretendin'."

"I get it. So what went wrong?"

"Soon as our children got into white schools, a box come off our children's heads. Negro children start to see the world for what it is. They see white folk was just pasty fools."

Carmen nodded.

"But them pasty fools fought back. They got to put the box back on our children's heads. They went to court. They called out the police. They brought out mobs. It was like post-Reconstruction all over again. We wasn't sure what they was goin' do, how far they was goin' take it. But yet and still, we was gettin' our children a education. We had that old white devil by the throat. And he knew it, too." Miss Bea paused, remembering the pivotal moment of the civil rights struggle. "That old devil was fightin' for his life. He couldn't control us no more. We was lookin' to Africa. Sisters was wearin' their hair natural. Brothers was holdin' up a fist. Black Power was real."

"What went wrong?" Carmen asked again.

"What went wrong?" Miss Bea took a deep breath. "Some a them Negroes, they couldn't take it no more."

"Couldn't take what?"

"Couldn't take bein' regular Negroes, like the rest of us." Miss Bea paused. "See, you can't be a house Negro without a house."

"Was the new house affirmative action?" Carmen asked. "That's what Bunny Washington told me. She said the Black middle class did a deal to save affirmative action for themselves. She said they agreed to abandon desegregation."

Miss Bea chuckled from somewhere deep inside. "And you believed her?"

Carmen did not respond, embarrassed at the intensity of Miss Bea's reaction.

Miss Bea laughed again. "You think them house Negroes had the brains to *negotiate*? You think they had the guts?" Miss Bea laughed again, for a long time. "They was scared they goin' lose their importance is all."

Carmen did not grasp Miss Bea's point.

"Let me explain somethin' to you, child. You could only negotiate if you got somethin' to negotiate with."

"You mean leverage."

"Call it what you want. House Negroes didn't have nothin' to offer their master, 'cept to put a brown face on their master's designs. Only thing a house Negro got to offer is to help the master keep the rest of us down."

"But what about the demand for desegregation?" Carmen pressed. "That's a serious demand. Didn't Thurgood and other middle class Black people make that demand? Didn't they lead that movement?"

"Yes, they did," Miss Bea agreed. "But what happened when the schools started to get desegregated?"

"The learning gap began to close across the country for the first time ever," Carmen said. "I know that for a fact. I researched it."

"That's right," Miss Bea smiled. "And *white* folk took to the streets this time."

Carmen nodded.

"They had to keep us out their schools. You know why?"

"It made it harder to keep us down."

Miss Bea shook her head. "No, child. It made it *impossible*."

Carmen nodded.

"If little Black children go to the same nursery school as white children, and after that they go to the same elementary school as those same white children, and then the same middle school, and the same high school, those little Black children will be on their way to freedom. No way to stop 'em." Miss Bea paused. *"You see, child, yo' classmate can't never be yo' master."*

Carmen thought about this. "It wouldn't matter even if your parents thought *they* were inferior," she agreed. "You'll still see yourself as equal."

Miss Bea smiled. "It never was really 'bout learnin'," she whispered.

Carmen leaned forward.

"Desegregation was *always* 'bout sittin' next to those white children...so they ain't *white* no more."

Carmen absorbed this. It turned the Black bourgeoisie's "conventional wisdom" on its head.

"See," Miss Bea continued. "If you sit next to 'em, you goin' get educated. But you also goin' *know* they ain't no better than you. Separate can't never be equal 'cause Black children in segregated schools, they *know* you sayin' there's somethin' wrong with *them*. That's why they ain't allowed to sit next to white children."

"What's wrong with me?" Carmen mused. *"Why am I not good enough to sit next to a white child?"*

Miss Bea nodded. "That's right. Our children could never get that question out their minds."

"But today, no one talks about it," Carmen observed. "All everyone focuses on is the learning gap."

"Who done focus on the learnin' gap?"

"I don't follow."

"You just said *they* focus on the learnin' gap. Who you talkin' 'bout?"

"Educators, I guess."

"Which ones?"

Then it dawned on Carmen. *"Black* educators."

"That's right, child. White educators don't give no importance to the learnin' gap. You know why not?"

"It's not their concern..."

Miss Bea laughed. "Oh no, child. It's their concern, all right. Remember what happened in the 70s, when that ole learnin' gap start to come down?"

"White people took to the streets," Carmen replied.

"That's right. But today, white people ain't worried no more. Why not?"

The answer hit Carmen so hard she almost lost her breath. "Because Bunny Washington and all those Black educators monitor it for them."

Miss Bea beamed. "Now you startin' to understand, child! See, Bunny and all them didn't make no deal with the white man to walk away from desegregation. The white man never goin' make no *deal* with us on desegregation. The white man goin' fight to the death to protect segregation. The white man goin' let Bunny run them segregated schools just so long as she keep a close eye on the learnin' gap…"

"And make sure it never closes," Carmen interjected.

"Exactly, child. Exactly. *That* was the deal Bunny and all them made."

"I have to ask you something."

"You go right ahead."

"Why do they all defend Bunny? Don't they care about the children?"

Miss Bea smiled. "It's a old dog and a old trick."

Carmen waited.

"You see, child, none a this ain't new. It started way back when some Black folk got all uppity. But that was way back. You see, when Negroes started gettin' uppity, that old white man got him a big dog. And he train that big dog to bite Negroes, 'specially children.

"*'You go bite 'em hard!'* that old white man tell his dog, and he give the dog treats for bitin' hard."

Carmen frowned.

"See, but after a while, Black folk tell everyone, *'Watch out! That dog comin'. Get out the way! That dog workin' for the white man. He bite hard!'*"

Carmen smiled. "So people figured out to avoid the dog."

"Only a damn fool goin' let his child get bit by that dog."

"So what does that have to do with everyone getting behind Bunny?"

"Mercy, child, have patience. Can't a old woman tell a story in her own time?"

Carmen grinned. "Sorry."

Miss Bee feigned exasperation. "Ain't no need to apologize neither." Miss Bea paused, remembering where she was. "You see, everyone know 'bout that white man's dog, and they all know to keep their children away from that dog. So the white man need a new plan. You with me?"

"I think so."

"Good. 'Cause that old white man got to doin' some thinkin'. He need a plan. First thing he try, he take that old dog to the barbershop and get him a nice shampoo and haircut. Then he brush that old dog and get him a new collar and leash. Doggone it if he don't make that mean old nasty dog look like a nice, sweet new dog!

"And sure 'nough, that old white man put on his Sunday best, and he walk his new lookin' dog down the street, showin' him off. That old white man be struttin' and smilin' and whistlin' and carryin' on like he got hisself a brand new dog.

"Next thing you know, word spread. Everyone runnin' out to see the old white man with the new lookin' dog. 'Fore you know it, the street full a folk starin' at that old white man and that new lookin' dog. Everyone crowd 'round. And don't you know it, that old white man done tip his cap and apologize for what he done all them years siccin' that old nasty mean dog on us. You never hear a sweeter apology! Folk was dumbstruck. Like Jesus hisself done descend from Heaven."

Carmen waited for the other shoe to drop.

"*'C'mon over here and pet my dog,'* that old white man smile to a little Negro child. *'He won't hurt you.'*

"What you think happen next?" Miss Bea asked Carmen.

Carmen frowned. "I don't like stories with bad endings."

"You think that old dog changed just 'cause he got hisself a shampoo and haircut?"

"Does a leopard change his spots?" Carmen responded.

"Oh, you gettin' all African on me now," Bea teased. "You know, I can't lie. They was nervous. They know that old dog can't be trusted. All they gotta do is look at the scars on their arms and legs. That old dog sure could bite. Far as they could tell, that dog still got teeth. But sure 'nough, after some time, one fancy dressed Negro push his daughter toward that old white man and that old dog.

"'Go on,' he tell his little girl. 'That dog ain't the same one. Mister a changed man, alright. He got hisself a new dog.'

"Now that little girl, she was scared. She done heard all them stories 'bout that old white man and his dog. She don't wanna go nowhere near that dog. She could see that dog's yellow eyes, and she could see that dog's sharp teeth. She know that dog's dangerous.

"But her daddy push her. 'Go on, girl,' he say. And he push her right up to that dog's mouth. Lord strike me down if that old dog don't bite that girl hard as before."

Carmen shook her head.

Bea paused. "Oh, c'mon now, child. Don't tell me you wasn't hopin' for a different ending? Somewhere inside a you, you was hopin' that old white man and his dog done change. You don't want that little girl to get bit."

"What happened next?" Carmen asked. "The white man and his dog haven't exactly gone away."

"Funny you should say that," Bea replied. "'Cause truth be told, that old white man did go away. After all a that, he couldn't show his face no more, now could he? So that old white man disappear for a while. But he leave his dog behind. And that old dog keep snarlin' and bitin' anybody he can."

"The white man's gone, and he just his dog left behind?" Carmen challenged. "That couldn't last long."

"You right about that," Bea agreed. "It didn't last. Folk got organized. A whole lotta people got together and decided they goin' put that old bitin' dog down. Young folk and old got together. They went lookin' for that dog in the street. When they find that dog, you ain't never goin' believe what they saw."

Carmen waited.

"God strike me down if this ain't so, but they found a *Negro* walkin' that dog! Imagine that! A Negro done tame that dog!"

Carmen was lost.

"Sure 'nough, the pastor's wife was holdin' that dog's leash. And she was lookin' fine, too. She was wearin' a new hat, and a new dress, and shiny new shoes. From a catalog, no less."

Carmen frowned.

"Word got out, and everyone, I mean everyone, had to see this! More folk come out now than when that old white man wear his Sunday best and had that dog all cleaned up.

"'Fore you know it, the street's full. Then the pastor's wife blow a whistle, and doggone it if that dog don't stand up on his two hind feet and start beggin' from the pastor's wife! And we all thought old dogs can't learn new tricks. Then the pastor's wife blow that whistle again, and doggone it if that old dog don't roll over for the pastor's wife!

"Folk was so excited. They crowd all 'round. They ain't never seen nothin' like it. Folk crowd in real close. So the pastor's cousins and some of their friends step in and push folk back, just to keep control. They was wearin' new suits, too. From the same catalog. They was lookin' fine, too, like nothin' that town never seen before. And best of all, ain't no white man nowhere to be seen.

"Just then, a little girl step forward. *'Can I pet your dog?'* she ask the pastor's wife.

"*'He's not my dog,'* the pastor's wife say to the little girl. *'He's your dog, now, too.'*

"Just then, somebody shout, *'That dog look a whole lot like the old white man's dog! Better watch out!'*

"The pastor's cousins and their friends, they don't like the sound of that. They done go after that man who shout.

"The pastor's wife smile. *'He okay,'* she tell everyone. She pet the dog. *'We done train him good. He our dog now.'*

"The little girl look at her daddy. She don't know what to do. Her daddy look at the pastor's wife. The pastor's wife say, *'She'll be okay.'*

"*'You could pet the dog,'* the little girl's daddy say."

Carmen shuddered.

Miss Bea paused.

Carmen waited.

"Now you know why they still with Bunny."

"They all scolded the little girl's father when the dog bit her," Carmen finished the story.

"*Why she put her face so close to that dog's teeth!*" Miss Bea scowled.

"I see it," Carmen nodded. "It's not just Bunny Washington, right? Kweisi Providence, he's been grooming a mighty fine dog, a *miracle dog*. He's got Black kids in his segregated charter schools scoring above statewide averages on math and reading. At least that's what the state says."

"That's a mighty fine dog!" Miss Bea agreed.

Carmen shook her head. "And those same kids who score high on math and reading are forty points below the state average on science tests."

"That dog need more training!" Miss Bea barked. "Only so many hours in the day to teach to tests. Take every wakin' minute to get those children ready to pass math and readin'. Ain't no time for science."

"It means the kids can't really think," Carmen observed.

"That's the whole point," Miss Bea agreed, her voice weakening. "If you want white supremacy, Kweisi Providence is your man. That's why all them rich white folk pay him so good and call him a miracle worker. They drop millions into his beggin' cup."

"They sure do."

Miss Bea closed her eyes for a moment.

Carmen reached out and held her bony hand. Miss Bea's grip loosened.

"Are you okay?" Carmen asked, concerned.

Miss Bea opened her eyes and smiled. "Just a little tired, child, that's all." She held Carmen's gaze. "Them rich white folk don't *never* put their own precious children in the miracle worker's schools. They don't never say, *'Here, Mr. Miracle Worker, take mine.'*"

Carmen smiled. "That won't ever happen."

"Child, you know that. Kweisi Providence is the white man's best friend. He done train our precious children to be slaves. That's why he makin' all that money. He doin' the Devil's work, just like Bunny. He makin' segregation look pretty."

"I'm beginning to think," Carmen said. "That if you're Black, you have to be mentally defective or fundamentally dishonest to cooperate with this system."

Miss Bea closed her eyes again and kept them closed as she spoke. "That's why most Black folk *don't* cooperate. Problem is, they don't know how to do it right. They play the fool, go to jail, disrespect their own selves 'cause they know the system's rigged. Most Black folk know they ain't got no chance if they play by the white man's rules." Miss Bea paused. Her breathing sounded labored. "Only a few a them house Negroes, like Providence and Bunny, goin' make it anyhow. And then again, only long as they keep the rest of us down."

"Miss Bea, why don't you take a rest," Carmen suggested.

Miss Bea opened her eyes. "You know the difference between those poor Haitians I saw when I was a child, and a Negro like Kweisi Providence?"

"Haitians know they defeated the white man," Carmen answered. "Providence knows he works for him."

Miss Bea smiled. "Child, I been waitin' forty years for your visit." She closed her eyes. "I been waitin' since before you was born."

Chapter 11

Carmen sat at her small kitchen table and looked at her computer screen. She was still processing the *experience* of being with Miss Bea. There was so much to think about. She had to figure out what to do next.

An official notice from the court appeared in her email inbox. She clicked on the file, and the document opened on her screen. It was the judge's decision on the school district's motion to dismiss her case. Carmen was confused. The decision was premature; it should not have been issued yet. The briefs had been submitted on an expedited schedule, but the lawyers had not yet been given an opportunity to present oral arguments in open court. This meant the judge had issued his decision on the written pleadings alone, a significant departure from the usual court procedures.

Figuring it would be bad, Carmen forced herself to read the judge's decision. The very first words were a shock:

"It is undeniable that the Minnepious Public Schools are segregated by race and class."

Carmen's heart raced. Could this really be? She read on.

"Of the district's 32 elementary and middle schools, 26 are identifiably segregated. The following elementary and middle schools in Minnepious have over 95% children of color and over 90% children eligible for free or reduced price lunch (the federally accepted measure of poverty in schools): Douglass, Dubois, Jefferson, King, Lincoln, Malcolm X, Mandela, Success Academy, Tubman, Urban Academy. The following elementary and middle schools in Minnepious have fewer than 10% children of color and children eligible for free or reduced price lunch: Dewey, Eleanor Roosevelt, Ericson, Lindgren, Shakespeare, Spielberg.

"To say that Minnepious Public Schools operates as two separate school districts is, in the view of this court, undeniable."

Carmen stopped reading. In her wildest dreams, she had never imaged the judge would adopt her recommended findings! She read on, holding her breath.

"The plaintiffs urge this court to stop there, and find that such segregation is in and of itself a violation of their constitutional rights. This court disagrees."

Carmen exhaled. There it was. But how could it be? She read on, grimly.

"As the Supreme Court has long held, 'naturally occurring,' de facto segregation is beyond the reach of our legal system. In the case before us, as undeniable as the existence of segregation is this court's finding that such segregation is not imposed on unwilling victims, but is the naturally occurring byproduct of choices freely made by parents, students, and most important, by people of color themselves."

Carmen resisted the urge to delete the opinion and send it to her trash bin. She read on.

"The Superintendent of Minnepious Public Schools is an African-American. The CEOs of virtually all charter schools within the city are people of color. The most successful educator of African-American children, Kweisi Providence, is an African-American. These and other eminently qualified educators and community leaders have affirmed in sworn affidavits submitted to this court that people of color do not want, and will not accept, the paternalistic racism of those who claim African-American students can only learn if they sit next to white students.

"This court agrees. The courts cannot allow themselves to be used by activists with political agendas, who want to impose unproven, experimental remedies on African-Americans and other children of color. This court must defer to the proven expertise of educators of color, who are best positioned to determine what is right for their children. The age of grand social engineering schemes, such as forced busing, is over. In the jurisprudence of this state, the doctrine of desegregation has no place.

"If plaintiffs are unhappy with their schools, they should do what other families have long done: pick themselves up by their bootstraps and sort out

their grievances with their teachers and principals. Or, if they prefer, they can leave the Minnepious district altogether. This court notes that the plaintiffs in this case have in fact already done just that. They have left the Minnepious school district and enrolled in suburban schools of their choosing. For all of the reasons stated herein, this case is hereby DISMISSED."

—⚍—

On her way to the airport, Bunny stopped to see her grandmother. In the dim lighting, her grandmother appeared to be in a deep sleep. Her grandmother looked gaunt, exhausted. Still, Bunny had to admit the woman looked good. If only Bunny had inherited the FOXO genes that kept her grandmother's mind and body so sharp into her nineties.

Bunny had another reason for being glad her grandmother's mind was still sharp. She wanted to share the big news before she left for DC. She had waited a long time for this. Bunny wanted to share the news of her professional achievement not to receive her grandmother's praise, but to gloat. And now, her grandmother would not stir, depriving Bunny of this precious triumph.

"Grandma," Bunny whispered to the inert body on the bed. "I made it." She considered shaking her grandmother to wake her up.

"I'm going to meet the President, Grandma. We have a Black President, Grandma, and he's making me Secretary of Education. Did you hear that? *Secretary of Education!*"

A sharp, bony hand suddenly shot from the bed and clamped above Bunny's fleshy elbow. The grip shocked Bunny. She tried to wriggle free of the viselike grip, but she could not release herself. The harder she tried to wriggle free, the more the bony hand clamped down on her elbow. Bunny realized she was trapped.

"Let go!" Bunny cried. "You're hurting me, Grandma! Let go!"

Miss Bea did not respond, and she did not loosen her grip on her granddaughter.

—⚍—

Carmen knew better than to call Sue Wolfen. She needed to find someone else, someone with the courage to expose the truth. She researched all the other *Strib* reporters on the internet, reviewing their articles to see which of them might have the guts to write this story. It was a sorry bunch.

The Strib reporters all appeared to act as mouthpieces for those in power, repeating the party line verbatim. They peddled half-truths, quarter-truths and outright lies that could not withstand minimal journalistic scrutiny. But of course, there was no scrutiny. What passed for journalism in Minnepious looked to Carmen like an incestuous ritual—beat reporters in bed with their influential patrons, beholden not to truth but to power. Was there no pride among these so-called journalists? Where was the vaunted Fourth Estate to hold those in power accountable and make democracy work?

As she scanned articles looking for just one journalist with integrity on *The Strib* staff, Carmen began to lose hope. She needed to find someone local. If she went to an out of town newspaper, how much interest would they have in a story about school corruption in Minnesoule?

Then she got her breakthrough. A writer named Jeremiah Hicks covered the local business community. His articles criticized local CEOs who laid off thousands of local workers while they accumulated artificially depressed stock options. The articles were hard hitting.

Then, for some reason, they stopped. Carmen kept searching, but she could not find any recent business articles by Hicks. Maybe he had been run out of town. She checked *The Strib* website's listing of reporters. Hicks was still there. His new beat was Families and Children. Either Hicks had a recently discovered passion for domestic life, or *The Strib* assignment editors had dumped him there to protect the newspaper's corporate patrons. Carmen knew which was more likely.

She rang Hicks' number. *Did she ever have a family and children's story for him!*

—⁓—

The headline on the front page of a special edition of the *African-American Word* said it all: ***"FOREIGN LAWYER COLLUDES WITH WHITE MEDIA TO DEVOUR BUNNY!"*** It was the biggest headline in the *Word* since the headline proclaiming the election of the nation's first Black President.

Referring to Carmen as *"of Somalian and West Indian descent,"* the newspaper article, written by someone named Gary Smalling, claimed that the lawyer, *"who came to Minnesoule with an agenda to take down our proud Black leaders,"* had played a hoax on *The Strib* in order to embarrass *"our Bunny"* on the eve of her ascension to the nation's top education position. *"This is the sort of crab in the barrel behavior that will forever destroy us,"* the *Word* reporter lamented. *"Is Braithwaite's self-esteem so low she must tear down the best among us? She has no idea the damage she has done."*

Later in the article, the reporter wrote:

"The real tragedy here is not the destruction of yet another great Black leader, but the tarnished reputation of our Black children. After so much hard work our children have put into preparing for and passing the state's racially biased tests, this lawyer makes slanderous accusations that the test results were somehow not valid.

"We expect this type of sordid stereotyping from white racists, but when it comes from a lawyer who claims to be Black, it harkens back to days of old, when Black turncoats were secretly collaborating with the enemy. Ms. Braithwaite might as well have exhumed J. Edgar Hoover and his COINTELPRO program."

Carmen skimmed the rest of the article. She saw quotes from Reverend Hal Ballman, Kermit Casson and others savaging her as an embarrassment to the race and a secret operative of a white racist conspiracy to destroy Black progress. Bunny Washington and Kweisi Providence were conspicuously silent. They evidently had nothing to say about the disclosures implicating them in educational testing fraud.

Carmen's cell phone rang. "Hello?"

"You did the right thing," Chris Hardwell said. *"African."*

Carmen smiled. "Thanks, Chris. You did, too. Good luck in Uganda."

—⟋⟋—

Minnissippi

From the moment Wolfen tipped her off to the impending smear, Bunny had ducked all calls and gone into hiding. This call she could not avoid, however. The 202 area code flashing on her cell phone was a giveaway. She had to take it.

It was not the call Bunny had been waiting for her entire career. It was the call a survivor of Jim Crow tried to stay one step ahead of throughout her life. But you never could really beat Jim Crow. Like the Grim Reaper, he always caught up with you.

"Bunny?"

"Yes?" she answered.

"This is Dan Munson."

"Uh-huh."

There was a long pause.

"I take it you know why I'm calling."

Bunny did not respond.

"The President-elect has decided to move in a different direction."

Bunny remained silent.

"Are you there?"

After a long pause. "I'm here."

"I know this must be hard."

"Mr. Munson?"

"Yes?"

"Have you ever had the police sic a dog on you?"

"Excuse me?"

"Do you know what it's like to see your daddy beaten by white men?"

"I'm sorry, Ms. Washington. I don't follow…"

"Mr. Munson, those things are hard."

Munson did not respond.

"Mr. Munson, you work for a Black man, right?"

"Ms. Washington?" Munson stammered, unsure what he should say.

Bunny waited, drawing it out. "Oh, I know you think you're all a that and a bag o' chips…"

Again, Munson did not respond. He knew the call would be difficult, but this was ridiculous.

"Well, you ain't all a that."

"Ma'am?"

"All right," Bunny said after a long pause. "Just tell me what you want me to do."

Munson hesitated, unsure how this woman would react to what he had to say.

"The President-elect needs you to withdraw from consideration…" Munson hesitated again, wondering if there was an easy way to say this. "And issue a public apology."

"That all?" *You want me to get down on my hands and knees and bark like a dog, too?*

Munson felt a wave of relief. "Yes, ma'am."

Well you could tell him to suck my dick.

"Okay."

———

Eileen felt a slow rage building. She had believed in Bunny. She had committed her entire career to urban public education. It had been a monumental mistake. Eileen was now exposed as a fool, ignoring all the warnings, all the obvious signs. She had known all along that the charter school "movement" was a fraud, dressing up pseudo-public schools as some kind of reform. Charter schools were dumping grounds for children society did not want. If they were truly innovative and effective, why had charter schools never caught on in the suburbs, where public schools delivered what parents and children needed and expected?

Eileen made the arrangements for the press conference that would end Bunny's career. There was no way to perfume this pig. Bunny was finished, which meant Eileen was finished. What irritated Eileen most was that despite the warning signs, she had never seen it coming. How could she have been so blind to the risks? Was it arrogance? Was it hubris? Did she suffer, like *Othello's* Desdemona, from some tragic character flaw?

For a white woman to cast her lot with blacks was, in and of itself, folly. Eileen knew that to her dying day, she would never be able to explain it. Not to her friends or her extended family. Not even to her daughter. There were some places you just could not go.

Isaiah was not sure what to say. No grown up had ever asked him what he liked. It had to be a trap. He waited, hoping the question would go away. "I don't know," he mumbled after a while.

Mr. Johnson, the school counselor, nodded. "That's all right, Isaiah. You don't have to decide today. Why don't we register you for Computer Science, and you can see how you like it."

Isaiah shrugged. "Okay."

Mr. Johnson looked over the class selection form. "So here's what we've got you down for. We've got Language Arts, Math, and Science. Those are all required. You said you'd like to try World Geography. If you don't like that after a few days, we can switch you into American History. You've got Physical Education, which I know you'll enjoy. And we have you down for Computer Science. Again, let's see how you like it. We can always change that one to Wood Shop. You okay with these?"

Isaiah felt overwhelmed. It was a lot of new stuff to remember. And it would take some time to get used to grownups asking you what you wanted. He wasn't sure how to handle the questions to stay out of trouble. "I don't know, Mr. Johnson. Could I think about it? I could let you know tomorrow."

The guidance counselor put a hand on Isaiah's shoulder. "Let's just try it out for a day, Isaiah. See how it goes."

Isaiah thought about it.

"I'll tell you what," Mr. Johnson suggested. "How about I come see you last period? That'll be World Geography. You can tell me then."

"You got tests tomorrow?"

"I don't get you."

"You know," Isaiah said. "If you got tests, you could just tell me. I don't have to come those days."

The guidance counselor tried to figure out what Isaiah was getting at. "We don't do a lot of tests, Isaiah. If you're concerned about tests, you can come talk to me. We'll figure it out together."

Isaiah looked Mr. Johnson in the eye for the first time.

The guidance counselor held Isaiah's gaze.

Isaiah looked back at the floor. "Okay."

—⁓—

Lakeesha sized up Ms. Antonin. She wasn't fooled by the teacher being nice. Mrs. Beamon started out nice, too. They all started out that way for a little while. But Lakeesha knew that was fake. They all turned nasty before too long.

"Why you make us read out loud?" Lakeesha asked, interrupting a white girl who was reading to the class.

"Lakeesha," Ms. Antonin replied. "Let Mimi finish. Then we'll talk about why we read to each other."

"But I aksed you first," Lakeesha objected. "Why you let her read first?"

The white girl stared at Lakeesha. Lakeesha stared back.

Ms. Antonin looked at the white girl. Lakeesha knew they were up to something.

"What do you think, Mimi?" Ms. Antonin asked. "Since Lakeesha is new, could we give her a chance first?"

The white girl shrugged. "I'm okay with that."

Ms. Antonin turned to Lakeesha. "Sounds like we're a go."

Lakeesha didn't know what that meant.

"The only thing I would request, Lakeesha," the teacher said. "Is in the future, if someone else is reading, please let them finish."

Lakeesha was embarrassed to be scolded like this in front of the class. She wanted to say something mean to the teacher. And for sure she would do something mean later to get that white girl back. That would be easy. The white girl looked weak.

The white girl leaned over to show Lakeesha where she had left off reading. Lakeesha looked at the page. The words were longer and harder than she was used to. Lakeesha put the book down and thought about how to get out of this mess.

"How about we read it together," the white girl whispered.

Lakeesha almost jumped, she was so surprised. She looked hard at the white girl to see if the girl was teasing her, or if it was a trick. The white girl didn't react. Lakeesha looked back at the page again. The words looked really hard. "Okay," she whispered back to the white girl.

"Ms. Antonin?" the white girl said to the teacher. "Lakeesha and I want to read it together."

The teacher nodded. "I think that's a great idea."

—⁂—

Isaac wasn't sure what time lunch started. He was already hungry, though. He wondered if this school would have good food. He didn't know where he was supposed to go at lunch time. The school was big, and he didn't know anyone. The teacher was talking, but Isaac couldn't follow what she was saying. He was getting awful hungry.

The bell rang, and the other kids all jumped up and ran out of the class. Isaac moved slower. He got left behind.

"Isaac?"

At first he didn't realize someone was calling him.

"Isaac?"

Then he realized.

Isaac looked toward the door to the classroom. A Black man stood there, blocking the doorway. Isaac knew the man was there to take him away. The man was big. And he had that mean look like they always did when they came for him.

Isaac looked around to see if there was another way out of the classroom, but the Black man was standing there in front of the door, blocking his way out. Isaac wondered what kind of bad place that Black man would take him to.

"Isaac," the man said. "I'm Mr. Leonard."

Isaac stared back.

"I was wondering if you wanted to have lunch with me in the cafeteria."

Isaac still did not react. It sounded like the kind of trick grown ups could use on you.

The man smiled. "Your mama told me you'd let me know if our school food is any good."

Isaac frowned. He didn't understand why the man was talking this way. It didn't sound like a trick.

"She told me you really know food. She said she thinks you'll be a chef one day."

Isaac looked away to hide his grin. Then he got up and followed Mr. Leonard to the cafeteria.

—∞—

Eileen took the morning of the Presidential Inauguration off. It was the least she could do for herself after the trauma of the past few days. She could not face the prospect of seeing anyone at work, especially today. She hadn't gone into the office since the scandal broke.

When Bunny announced that she was withdrawing from consideration as a candidate for national Secretary of Education to focus on her job as superintendent, the Minnepious school board formally reprimanded her for "inadequate oversight" of charter schools. Bunny was supposed to take a one week unpaid leave, starting today. But knowing Bunny, she might be in the office. Eileen wasn't taking any chance of seeing her, not today.

Eileen turned on the television. She found the C-SPAN coverage of the President-elect's press conference in Washington, DC. The President-elect was about to announce his selection of Boston Public Schools CEO Art Donought to be Secretary of Education.

Out of curiosity, Eileen had read up on Donought when she heard he was the choice. Unlike Bunny, Donought was not well known in national education circles. According to profiles Eileen read online, Donought was a former professional badminton player, who had dominated the Australian badminton circuit for a decade after his graduation from Harvard College.

Donought returned to the States fitter than when he left and with a truly global perspective. He worked in various consulting and corporate management roles around the country for fifteen years. Then, spotting an opportunity, Donought rebranded himself as an education reformer.

According to a piece in *Education Week*, Donought's timing could not have been better. With the help of his former Harvard roommate, who had become a Boston City Council member, Donought landed a position in the Accountability Office of the Boston Public Schools. Within two years, Donought had unearthed massive fraud in the district, including a scheme by the district's transportation department to fence unused student public transportation passes. Donought orchestrated a sting in which Boston Public Schools employees were caught at MTA turnstiles trying to sell student passes to tourists. The ensuing scandal brought down the schools' black superintendent at the time, Aurelio Horace. The publicity and acclaim for the dogged, incorruptible, Irish "white knight" Donought sparked an artfully funded "Draft Donought" campaign that delivered him the superintendency.

Eileen had to admit, Donought's résumé was impressive. He boasted a number of signature achievements as superintendent in Boston. He crushed the teachers' union over performance-based pay. He reduced teacher salaries through unilateral imposition of an "accountability" contract with unachievable bonus milestones. He garnered overwhelming support from Boston's white community and business leaders by spearheading the district's return to neighborhood schools after its "disastrous experiment" with desegregation.

A profile in *Men's Health* noted that Donought had met the President-elect at an education conference in Chicago two years ago. The two men bonded instantly over their shared love of sports and their Harvard experiences. They made it a point to get together every few months to exchange ideas about education and play badminton, though neither was quite as nimble as in his younger days.

As the press conference began, Eileen watched the President-elect stride up to the podium. She closed her eyes for a moment and imagined Bunny standing at his side, rather than Donought. She could envision herself standing just off camera, advising Bunny and doing all the important but unseen things that made a leader great.

"It is with great pleasure," the President-elect announced. "That I present to you a dear friend and true visionary, Art Donought, to be this nation's next Secretary of Education."

The press contingent applauded.

"Art is that rare blend of strong mind and soft heart," the President-elect continued. "He loves children. He really does. And he hates the shackles we adults put them in."

Donought stared at the ground, circumspect despite the high praise. Eileen admired his modesty.

"What we need in our schools today is tough love," the President-elect observed. "Love, yes. But also tough. I have already discussed with Art our administration's priorities. He and I have agreed that in our first 100 days in office, we will implement a new competition among the states for federal education dollars. We're calling our initiative the *Race for the Race*. By making government leaner and meaner, we will be able to save money and repurpose it in innovative ways, so we can stop rewarding failure. That will allow us to commit $10 billion to our *Race for the Race* competition.

"We are confident that the *Race for the Race* will remind all educators across our great nation that we can no longer afford, as my predecessor aptly said, 'the soft bigotry of low expectations.' We are no longer competing only among ourselves. We are now in a global race for the race. This global education race will require us to tighten our belts. Failure is no longer an option. With Art's able leadership, I am confident that we will be able to expand the number of charter schools around the nation, make our teachers more accountable, and reduce the influence of those invested in the status quo who would stand in the way of accountability and educational excellence."

Eileen wiped a tear from her eye. She so believed in the President-elect. His vision, his skills of oratory, his commitment to children and true change. She thought again of what might have been…it was an opportunity lost forever.

"Given his international and private sector experience," the President-elect continued. "I can imagine no one better qualified than Art to make this happen. He is truly a leader whose time has come. Art has a demonstrated track record of success. He delivered on the promise of reform in Boston.

"I look forward to working with Art over the next four years to better educate our children across our great nation and prepare them so they can be employable workers in the future. Let us never forget, the children are our future. Our economy depends on them." The President-elect paused. "Unfortunately, I cannot stay to take your questions. I have a busy day *and evening* ahead of me. My wife has already warned me not to be late."

The press chuckled. The President-elect was in his honeymoon period with them, if not with his wife. The President-elect embraced Donought. The White House press corps cameras captured the moment for a nation eager to know what it would mean to have a black President.

"Thank you," the President-elect waved. "And may God bless America."

—⚏—

At a press conference hosted by billionaire Mayor Francis Blumboo in New York City's swanky Manhattan Club, Kweisi Providence and venture capitalist Sam Irvine announced a major new expansion of the Afrocentric Success Academy charter school network. Introducing the newest member of his executive team, Providence proclaimed, "We are pleased to introduce to New York City one of the most distinguished and effective education reformers in the country. Our new Senior Vice President of Outreach to the Greater African Diaspora has a proven track record of building consensus and bringing communities together. His initial focus will be on outreach to New York's large West Indian and African communities. He will coordinate their support for our model of proven academic success.

"It is with great pleasure that I present to you Afrocentric Success Academy's Senior Vice President of Outreach to the Greater African Diaspora, the Reverend Hal Ballman."

Reverend Hal stepped forward to a smattering of applause from the "grassroots" community supporters the non-profit Sam Irvine Foundation had hired for the press conference. The applause was more muted and less enthusiastic than it might have been. It was cold outside on this January morning, and the "grassroots" supporters, most of whom had been recruited from the Malcolm X Community Center Shelter, were hungry and annoyed. They had not yet received their promised box lunches or the $20 stipends for attending this event. And now they had to stand around and listen to bullshit from a hustler and some hick preacher from the South, or wherever Minnepious was.

"Reverend Ballman brings a trove of experience from his public service on the Minnepious School Board," Providence continued. "Where he developed a legendary reputation for his ability to build strong bridges to the city's Somali community, the largest East African immigrant community in the nation."

The two educators embraced, and Reverend Hal stepped up to the microphone.

"Thank you, Kweisi," Reverend Hal intoned. "I am humbled and honored to be part of this important milestone." Reverend Hal opened his prepared statement that had been written by Sam Irvine's communications team.

"School choice is the civil rights issue of our day," Reverend Hal read. "The public school monopoly must yield to healthy competition in which the successful thrive and the unsuccessful are defunded. We are at a crossroads in American education in which we must bring *all* children into the mainstream of American society. My focus will be to engage the broader African diaspora, so they can come to know the unique benefits of American freedom."

Reverend Hal took a deep breath. The next sentence would be the toughest of his long and distinguished career. He focused on the $275,000 salary Kweisi had promised him. It was a lot of dough. *Two...*

hundred...seventy...five...hundred...thousand...dollars. Reverend Hal took another deep breath and forced himself to read the last sentence of the prepared statement. "I hope to replicate the extraordinary success we had in Minnepious building partnerships between African-Americans and...*Samolians.*"

The press representatives gave each other funny looks at Reverend Ballman's pronunciation of the last word.

"We won't be taking any questions," Kweisi Providence hastily added, shooing Ballman away from the microphone.

—⚡—

The front page of the next day's *New York Times* proclaimed in a banner headline: ***"New Venture-backed Charter School Network Brings Proven Success, Hope to New York Blacks"***.

There was no mention of the academic testing scandal in *The Times* story.

—⚡—

One week later, a headline on page 3 of *The New York Times* Business section noted: ***"Charter School Leader Tipped to Lead Venture-backed Afrocentric Learning Pride."***

The Times story stated:

"CEO Kweisi Providence of the acclaimed Afrocentric Success Academy charter school network announced today that he has been tasked with heading up a new for-profit venture backed by financier Sam Irvine. With an initial capital commitment of $50 million in startup financing, Afrocentric Learning Pride will develop and market a targeted educational curriculum that has been proven to work in high poverty schools.

"Sam Irvine released a statement announcing the hiring of Amy Donought as Afrocentric Learning Pride's Vice President of Marketing. In the statement, Ms. Donought expressed optimism about the company's prospects. 'I am so proud to follow in my father's footsteps in the education space. Afrocentric has already signed up 23 state boards of education to fast track our proposed curriculum for high poverty schools receiving federal Title I grants. We also

anticipate that we will be an ideal candidate for grants under the federal government's upcoming Race for the Race program.'

"In an unrelated development, Afrocentric Success Academy today announced the firing of Reverend Hal Ballman, ASA's Vice President of Outreach to the Greater African Diaspora. The firing took place in response to a YouTube video that surfaced earlier this week in which Reverend Ballman can be seen standing on a raised platform shouting, 'Boy, you and all your Samolians (sic) and Mexicans need to get up on out of here!'

"In announcing this personnel decision, Afrocentric CEO Providence explained, 'Our charter school network has a zero tolerance policy for intolerance.'"

—⁓—

Carmen turned on her television to watch the Presidential Inauguration. If nothing else, the images would distract her from the disappointing dismissal of her school case. There was, after all, a bigger victory to celebrate—*wasn't there?*—the election of the nation's first Black President.

Carmen watched the Black man on the television screen smile as he shook hands with a white man in a robe and prepared to take the oath of office. The robed white man—the nation's highest judge—believed fervently in "separate but equal."

The television camera zoomed in on an old Bible on a stand. "The President-elect has chosen Abraham Lincoln's Bible for the swearing in ceremony," the deep voice of network anchor Bob Schmokit intoned solemnly.

The voice of his co-anchor Lisa Krahnked added, "It would be hard to imagine a more appropriate choice than the Bible of the man who freed the slaves."

"Indeed," Schmokit murmured.

The television screen cut from the tall thin Black man with his hand on the Great White Father's Bible to a shot of the soon to be First Lady. "Oh," Krahnked gasped. "Look at the First Lady-elect. It's eerie, isn't it? She so closely resembles Jackie O."

"And like her husband, she's a graduate of Harvard Law School. What a role model."

Carmen stared at the soon to be First Lady. Most articles about her swooned over her great sacrifice, cataloging all she was giving up to become First Lady. The media noted that she was sacrificing her career, her independence, and even her close relationship with her mother—all for husband and country. But Carmen did not see a whole lot of sacrifice. Homegirl was sitting up there looking all fly in her Versace dress and pearls and expensive shoes. Still, no matter how many times the white media tried to say she looked like Jackie O, the new First Lady and fellow Harvard alum still looked to Carmen like *a big woman with a big butt and big legs that no amount of accessorizing could make little and skinny and white.*

Carmen stopped herself. It was catty, uncalled for, to think that way. She looked at herself in the mirror. She wore pajamas with no makeup. No white news anchor would compare her to Jackie O.

Her phone rang. It was Bob. Carmen couldn't decide whether to answer. The phone kept ringing. She turned down the ringer volume.

The television cameras panned the massive crowd. The Inauguration was the biggest crowd to descend on the national capital since the 1963 civil rights March on Washington. The cameras zeroed in on African-Americans. They showed Black men and women in their sixties and seventies braving the chill. The cameras showed young Black men and women. They showed Black children perched on their parents' shoulders.

Carmen's phone started buzzing. She had left the buzzer on. It was Bob again.

—⚹—

Bunny sank into the sofa next to her grandson. Her daughter Bea's eyes were glued to the television screen, absorbing the spectacle. Bunny watched her grandchildren. She could not bring herself to look at the incoming President.

—⚹—

She bit her lip and tried to think of something else, anything else. She had been beaten so many times over the years, she knew the pattern by heart. She clenched her stomach, tightening the muscles. She knew this was where he would hit her next. He always hit her there. Over and over again. Until she retched and everything emptied from her stomach. He always hit her in the stomach because he knew it left marks no one else could see.

"Bitch!" he ranted in a drunken rage. "Bitch, you think I don't know you? Huh? Bitch!"

She tensed for the blow.

Whack!

She gasped and slumped over. The pain ripped through her abdomen. She tried to hold back the tears. That would only egg him on. She told herself, as she always did, that she was putting up with this for the sake of her children. Once Ethan graduated, she would leave the bastard.

Joel pushed her upright, exposing her stomach again.

Whack!

Eileen gasped and fell over. Tears rolled down her cheeks onto the carpet, where they were absorbed and no one could see them.

—⁓—

"With us is Michael Hamilton, the first African-American mayor of a major American city," Bob Schmokit said to his national television audience. The camera panned back to show the ancient Mayor Hamilton seated next to the two young white anchors, Bob Schmokit and Lisa Krahnked.

"Mayor Hamilton, what a day this is!" Schmokit said. "Isn't it remarkable how far we've come. Today we describe you as the first *African-American* mayor of a major city. Back when you were elected, you would've been known as a Negro."

"That's right, Bob," Mayor Hamilton nodded. "That's what they'd call me on a good day."

Schmokit and Krahnked chuckled.

"We're so glad to have you here on this historic day, Mayor Hamilton," Schmokit said.

"And we understand today is a big day for another reason, Mr. Mayor," Krahnked observed. "You're ninety-four years young today! You don't look a day over eighty."

"I feel like a teenager today," the mayor smiled. "I never thought this day would arrive in my lifetime."

"Mayor, I don't think it's a stretch to say our new President-elect would not be here if not for the sacrifice and courage of leaders like you. Tell us why you never thought this day would arrive and what it means to African-Americans."

"Well..." the mayor began, then looked away, choking up. "I don't think I can put it into words just now."

"Thank you, Mayor Hamilton," Schmokit said, patting the old man's arm. "And God bless you."

The television panned back as Mayor Hamilton left the set and Krahnked wiped tears from her eyes. Her blonde hair did not move as she wiped away the tears.

Schmokit patted Krahnked on the shoulder.

"This is such a meaningful moment for everyone in our country," he noted. "It shows how far we've come in realizing Dr. King's dream. I wonder what Dr. King would say if he were here today."

"I think he'd say we've joined him on the mountain top," Krahnked sniffled.

"Indeed," Schmokit agreed. "What an extraordinary moment for our country,"

"For the world, really."

—∾—

Eileen applied her make up slowly. First the moisturizer, then after the moisturizer had seeped into her skin, the foundation. She was proud of her clear complexion, especially at her age. Today's gala celebration was not what they had all hoped for, of course. It was not a coronation of Bunny, local hero. But then again, there was a bigger picture: the

Inauguration of the first black President of the United States. Eileen knew it was a momentous occasion. What it would mean for her, and for her children, she was not sure.

She reached for her blush and eye shadow. The pain shot through her abdomen again. She collapsed to her knees by the toilet, retching, stomach acid and lunch exploding through her lips, filling the toilet bowl. She retched again and again until her stomach emptied and the muscles cramped. At least the bastard hadn't seen it. She flushed the toilet and watched the vomit swirl around the bowl before it slid into the sewer.

Eileen lifted her silk camisole and touched the angry red welts on her beautiful skin. Then she stood up, rinsed her mouth, wiped her face and re-applied her moisturizer and foundation. The blush and eye shadow completed the picture. She studied herself in the bathroom mirror. She was beautiful. She slipped into a black dress that set off her creamy complexion, and treated herself to her classiest glossy faux pearl necklace, which nestled against her dainty cleavage. She paused to check her appearance again in the bathroom mirror. She looked beautiful. She was ready for the party.

—⁓—

Lisa Krahnked cooed, "Just look at that family! What a vision to behold!" The camera panned the VIP dais. The young black President-elect was smiling at his wife and two girls. He locked eyes with his wife and mouthed, "I love you."

Krahnked's muffled crying provided background audio. "I'm sorry," she whispered. "I cry at weddings, too."

The First Lady-to-be did not respond to her husband. She maintained her stern expression, a suitable demeanor for such a momentous and portentous occasion. The soon-to-be President turned back to the white man in the robe, whose grim colorless lips were moving. The robed white man's steely gray eyes bore into the black man.

"The nation's Chief Justice is about to administer the oath of office," Schmokit intoned.

"After that, the new President will give his much anticipated acceptance speech," Krahnked added.

"Our advance copy of the speech suggests it'll be up there with Lincoln and FDR," Schmokit predicted.

"And *Kennedy*," Krahnked gushed. "By all accounts, this will be a speech for the ages."

—∞—

Though she was sitting with her daughter Bea and her grandchildren, Bunny felt alone. She sipped a glass of wine as the others stared at the television set, riveted. It had been a long painful road, considering what might have been. But she would never stop walking that road, barefoot if necessary.

Bunny put down her wine glass and gave her grandson a hug. She hoped he would one day appreciate all she had done for him.

—∞—

Carmen watched the incoming President place his left hand on Lincoln's Bible and raise his right hand to take the Oath of Office. She closed her eyes. She could not watch this Black man swear fealty to the Great White Father. With her eyes closed, a voice whispered in Carmen's ear:

"Why yes, missuh massah. Of course, missuh massah. I'll do whatever you say, missuh massah. I'll take care of yo' chillens, missuh massah. I promise to keep all duh li'l nigglets away from yo' precious li'l white chillens.

"I's sorry to aks such a thing, missuh massah, suh. But would it be okay if juss my two li'l angels could sit in the cornuh of yo' chillens' school, missuh massah, suh? Deys duh ones sittin' ovah dey, missuh massah suh."

Jarred by the voice in her head, Carmen opened her eyes for a moment and glanced at the image on the television screen. The President-elect smiled at his two daughters standing by his side. Carmen closed her eyes again. The voice returned:

"Just dohs two, suh. Jus dem. We sho' nuff won't let none a dem other dirty nigglets in tho,' missuh massah, suh. Jus' my two li'l ones, suh. Dats all I's aksin, suh. Jus' my li'l uns. Dey won't botha yo' precious li'l white chilluns none, doh. I's

can promise you dat, missuh massah, suh. Dey knows dey Negroes, suh. Dey knows dey place, massah, suh."

Carmen could not get the voice out of her head. She opened her eyes and forced herself to watch the President's speech.

The new President spoke of Dr. King, of justice, of people coming together, of an America so exceptional it could do *anything* (except desegregate its schools). He spoke of a new dawn for American civilization.

The television interspersed the inspirational words of the nation's first Black President with images of Black Americans waving flags, tears streaming down their cheeks. Carmen stared at the television screen. She saw in the patriotism and emotion of African-Americans a fervent hope that the election of this Black man would somehow bring *acceptance* from their white oppressors, from Europeans.

Carmen realized that until all Black people saw themselves as Africans, and no longer saw the European as *white*, they would never be free.

For the first time in her life, Carmen felt African.

She was free.

—∞—

Carmen turned off the television and picked up her phone. She dialed Jamie Levine.

"Carmen?"

"Hi, Mr. Levine. Did you see the decision?"

"I saw it," Mr. Levine replied. "Aren't you watching the Inauguration?"

"No, I'm bored with it. What did you think of the judge's decision?"

"Pretty gutless, if you ask me. The judge was stupid and arrogant. He ruled against us, but the idiot adopted our proposed statement of facts. *He actually agreed with us that the schools are segregated!* We'll use that against him on appeal. Hoist the bastard with his own petard. I'm sure we'll get the decision reversed."

"Good. I'll prepare the notice of appeal tomorrow morning. I'll get started on the appeal brief right away, too."

"There's no hurry, Carmen. We have sixty days to file our notice of appeal."

"No," Carmen replied. "There's a hurry. This appeal is forty years overdue."

—⁓—

Next Carmen called Rufus. "You watching the Inauguration?"

"Hell no!" Rufus gagged. "Have you lost your mind?"

Carmen laughed. "I tried. Couldn't do it."

"Didn't think I'd hear from you any time soon, sister."

"I'm not that easy to shake."

"Well, all right, sister. What you need?"

"More plaintiffs. I want to file another case. A companion case with more allegations and some new legal theories."

"You go, girl!"

"And I want to organize a protest."

Rufus hesitated. "I don't know…It could be kind of hard to get it going again."

"Not at the school board," Carmen clarified.

"Huh?"

"At the court house."

"Come again?"

"The judge just dismissed our case," Carmen explained. "In his decision, he said Black folk want segregated schools. I just want to let the judges know what we really think about segregated schools."

"Sista," Rufus laughed. *"You da man!"*

—⁓—

Carmen's last call was the easiest, and in its own way, the hardest. She waited, as the phone rang.

"Carmen?" The familiar voice was excited and relieved.

"You got plans?" she asked.

"Nothing I can't change."

"Then get your sorry ass over here."

◆ ◆ ◆

This book is dedicated to the love of my life J-M

About the Author

J Shulman is a human rights lawyer, filmmaker, writer, activist and professor, who has lived in the United States, Africa, the Caribbean and India. As a human rights attorney, the author has litigated against systems of oppression, such as racial segregation of schools, job discrimination, and police abuse. Along with Jeanne-Marie Almonor, J Shulman wrote and directed the critically acclaimed, award winning human rights movie JUSTICE, which was nominated for an Image Award by the NAACP. J Shulman and Ms. Almonor received the Emancipation Filmmaker's Award at the Juneteenth Film Festival in Dallas, Texas. The author received an A.B. in English from Harvard College and a J.D. from Harvard Law School. J Shulman has written numerous fiction and non-fiction books, including three books on negotiation, *On African Liberation*, and a children's fantasy novel entitled, *The Lama, the Snow Leopard, and the Thunder Dragon.*